Fugitive Shoes

Fugitive Shoes

Erin O'Rourke

Five Star • Waterville, Maine

First Edition
First Printing: April 2006

Published in 2006 in conjunction with Tekno Books.

Set in 11 pt. Plantin by Elena Picard.

Printed in the United States on permanent paper.

Library of Congress Cataloging-in-Publication Data

O'Rourke, Erin, 1972–
    Fugitive shoes / Erin O'Rourke.—1st ed.
        p. cm.
    ISBN 1-59414-444-3 (hc : alk. paper)
    1. Immigrants—Violence against—Mexican–American
Border Region—Fiction. 2. Women rock musicians—
Mexican–American Border Region—Fiction. 3. Vigilantes—
Mexican–American Border Region—Fiction. 4. Smuggling—
Mexican–American Border Region—Fiction. 5. Border
patrols—Mexican–American Border Region—Fiction.
I. Title.
PS3615.R585F84 2006
    813'.6—dc22   2005033730

To Travis,
who knows where
all the bodies are buried,
but has conveniently forgotten
where we put the shovels.

"It's hard to be free,
but when it works,
it sure is worth it."
—Janis Joplin

Chapter One

She watched the man bleed to death in the desert sand, surrounded by a thousand shoes.

His head had opened up, and the image that came to her was of those plastic eggs she had hidden in the grass for Jazmyn to find on Easter mornings of years past, the kind you could pull apart and fill with jellybeans—except this was a skull and it wasn't supposed to separate in such a manner. And those red globs weren't jellybeans. The impact had tossed him in such a way that his head had come to rest on an open-toed, patent leather pump.

Size four, Sally thought. *I could never fit into that thing.*

Countless shoes lay scattered on that patch of desert ground as if a strange storm had vanished suddenly and deposited them there. High-topped basketball wonders were heaped among delicate slip-ons and the random biker boot. Clogs were popular, as were skimmers of a dozen colors. The most distant shoes had fallen up to fifty feet away. Against the sage and chaparral they looked as out of place as those probes on the empty face of Mars. Spiked heels were stabbed into the hard earth. One immaculate wingtip was perched upon a cactus frond as if on display for passing desert shoppers.

Shoppers? Coyotes don't buy oxfords.

Was that humor? Sally realized her mind was firing warning shots: *Look out! Reality ahead.*

But for the moment, reality was suspended. The scene was too unreal. She wasn't actually standing on this simmering blacktop. The truck behind her wasn't really lying on its side and leaking steam from its engine. The shoes were images from a dream, and that man in the dirt was not draining his life through a fissure in his head.

From somewhere near the truck a voice said, "Nowhere."

Sally tried to turn away from the sight before her, but she no longer had control of her body. The man had dusky skin, as rich as the soil on which he was sprawled, and a thicket of black mustache—a thicket that glistened with pellets of blood. A dented canteen was slung around his neck.

Sally heard herself speak: "What did you say?"

"Nowhere," Dawn-Marie repeated. "That's where he came from. Right out of it. That must be a real place because I swear to God he wasn't in sight one second and the next he was."

Dawn spoke the truth. Sally had been driving. She hadn't seen a thing until the thing was all there was to see.

"Nowhere must be an extra-dimensional world," Dawn went on, "and skaters and deer and joggers are just waiting to step through a magic door and run right out in front of you . . ."

"Stop it." This voice belonged to Anne, and as usual, she spoke each word as if she'd first inspected it and stamped her approval on it. She'd been sitting in the backseat—the truck was an extended cab—when the man had run out of the desert with his raggedy clothes and his empty canteen whipping like a wild pendulum around his neck. "There's no such thing, you know that, no such place.

Don't start falling apart on us, Dawn, not now."

If anyone's falling apart, it's me, Sally thought. Resting near the man's head was a lidless box containing a pair of embroidered satin mules that retailed for thirty-nine dollars a pair. Sally had sold some just like them only yesterday. The shoes had pancake heels, with sequins on the toes. She wrested her eyes from the man's face and focused instead on his shoes. He wore nondescript nylon lace-ups, a mutt variety of shoe without apparent lineage or worth. That pair of mules he was dying beside probably could have fed him for a month.

"They're coming," Anne said. "Sal? Do you hear me?"

Never before had it required more effort to turn her head. In the time it took to look over at her friends—her oldest friends, friends entwined like ivy in the trellis of her soul—she thought about a great many things, the most absurd of which was the fact that it was seven a.m. and she hadn't fed her fish all day, and she was sure to have a floater in the aquarium when she finally made it home. If she ever made it home.

Anne held up two phones. She waved the cellular. "I have no service this far out." Then she displayed the satellite phone which she always carried, because Anne was like that: connected. "But I could call the moon with this thing, if there were anyone up there who would answer." She lowered both instruments and blinked rapidly, as if to ambush the coming tears. "They're sending an ambulance from Tucson. Help is—"

Sally shook her head. "Don't say it."

"Don't say what?"

"Help isn't on the way." She folded her arms across her chest, chilled despite the heat waves that coiled up from the blacktop. "Help is what happens before it's too late."

9

Overhead came the cry of a carrion bird.

Sally didn't look up, just stood there and formed one-third of a human triangle, hoping this shape would be enough to sustain her in whatever hard days came next. There had been a time when that triangle had been a square, and the world had made geometric sense and black crows didn't circle a sea of shoes, waiting for a meal.

Dawn bent down and retrieved a wooden-soled clog. She studied it, then said, "There's some shade over here on this side of the truck. You guys want to sit down?"

Sally was amazed that her feet responded when she sent them a signal. Though Anne glided to the truck with her usual poise, Sally felt like a refugee, stumbling toward the prospect of solace. Funny that a few hours ago her biggest concern was paying the lease on the shop. She sank down in the shadow of the overturned flatbed, Dawn-Marie started jabbering about the heat, and the birds gathered and flew in menacing spirals.

Sally closed her eyes.

"What I'm saying is that the old rent is twenty years out of date. Understand?"

Standing there on the sidewalk in front of the bakery, her arms laden with streamers and colored bunting, Sally Jasper studied this man called Horace Shine and thought what a peculiar name that was for a man who shined so infrequently. Horace Frown would have been more appropriate. His head was round and bald, save for a ghostly ring of white hair around its circumference, which made his skull look like a planetoid rising up from the clouds. He was five and a half feet tall and Sally could stare him in the eye, which she did. "Horace, I've been paying that amount for seven years now."

"Seven years, eleven months, and three weeks. The lease is up for renewal in six days."

"You're talking about an increase of two hundred dollars a month."

"Hey, look, I gotta eat, all right?"

"And I don't?"

"I have a family, Ms. Jasper." He laid a slight emphasis on the *Ms.*, as if to remind her that—unlike him—Sally wasn't married and did not have a family to support, which of course wasn't true at all because she had Jazmyn. At least as much as anyone could have Jazmyn.

"I don't like doing this," Horace said, "but that's just the way it is. Six days. New lease. End of story. Now good evening to you."

"Yeah, see ya around." She watched him walk away with the evening sun stretching his shadow out behind him like a long black piece of elastic that Sally hoped would snap and pop him in the ass.

She smirked at that, and then the bells sounded: seven big brassy strokes from the steeple of the Fresh Waters Lutheran Church, resounding throughout the town square, into the residential streets, and out like a dirge into the desert beyond.

Seven o'clock already? Where had the day gone?

In twelve hours Sally would be standing on the side of an empty highway while a stranger she'd hit with a moving truck lay dying in the dirt at her feet. But it wasn't this accident that started everything. It was Horace Shine telling her that she'd be evicted in six days if she didn't come up with an extra two hundred bucks.

In a past life, Horace was a Philistine tax collector.

That made her feel better. She wasn't sure if she believed in reincarnation or not, but she was certain that in a

11

previous existence she'd been the bejeweled queen of an ancient nation of fabulous wealth, because now karma was getting its revenge. Could she scrape together that much extra cash every month? Walking the last block to the shop—and making it a matter of principle not to look at the trendy Foot Tracker that was crushing her under its franchise-supported heel—she made a mental list of all the necessities, all the things that were must-haves. They numbered only two. One, a new guitar for Jaz. Most high school sophomores pined for chic clothes, MP3 players, and class rings; most did, anyway. And two, a bottle of bubble bath, with two uninterrupted hours to enjoy it.

Sally reached her shop as the sun began its final descent. Eight years ago Dawn-Marie had painted those letters on the window: *SALLY'S SOLE MATES.* The paint was faded, but only slightly, and the service was the best in town, not the impersonal kind you'd get down the street at Foot Tracker. Fastened to the door was the same handbill that appeared on nearly every business and municipal building in town.

SET YOUR SPIRIT FREE!

CITY-WIDE CELEBRATION

TWO FULL DAYS!

MEMORIAL DAY, MAY 26

& TUESDAY, MAY 27

LIVE MUSIC, PRIZES, GAMES

FRESH WATERS CITY PARK

DON'T MISS THE FUN!

Sally groaned. Today was Saturday the twenty-fourth,

which gave her only two days until she was supposed to have the dunking booth set up at the park. Why had she volunteered for that task? She couldn't remember. She had too much to do. Her shop had been closed for an hour, and yet here she was, about to hang patriotic-colored streamers from the store's façade when she should have been at home to make dinner for Jaz. She balanced her burden in one arm and raked the key into the lock.

"Miss Sally?"

Halfway through the door, she turned around.

Jeffrey Longbranch, age fourteen, sat astride his battered bicycle.

"Hello, Jeff."

"Hi."

"How are the new cleats holding up?"

Jeffrey grinned and looked away. "They're great, thanks." Jeffrey loved baseball but his family couldn't afford new cleats for the upcoming summer league. Sally had given him a pair on credit. Jeffrey was paying her back three dollars a week, and this was one more reason that Sole Mates was barely making ends meet while Foot Tracker ran circles around her, so to speak.

"Something I can do for you, Jeff? Or did you come by to help me put up these banners? I've never been the most graceful woman on a ladder."

"I would, Miss Sally, I really would, but I've got practice. I'm on my way right now."

"No problem. The team needs you more than I do. Coach Sutter says he's never seen anyone your age more at ease in the batter's box."

Jeffrey gave her an aw-shucks look and shoved his thick black glasses up his nose.

Past life? Buddy Holly.

He held out a shoebox. "I brought something for you."

Sally raised her eyebrows. It was the very box that had contained his cleats, with its bright orange lid now held shut with electrician's tape. "What, you're returning the shoes? Not speedy enough for you?"

"No, the shoes are tight." *Tight* meaning *cool* in modern parlance, Sally supposed. "Just wanted to bring you something, sort of pay you back for what you did. You're generous, and most people aren't."

"Oh, well . . ." Maybe there was hope for kids these days, after all. Sally set the tangle of ribbons and bunting inside the door and accepted the package. "I appreciate it, Jeff, you are truly a young gentleman, but it's not really necessary."

"Yeah, it is." He looked serious, the look he probably wore when staring at an opposing pitcher, his world narrowed down to only that which mattered. "Some things are necessary. This is one of them."

"Well, I don't know what to say. Thank you."

"You're welcome." In one perfect motion he put his feet to the pedals and glided down the street. He didn't look back.

Sally watched him disappear around the corner. One reason she'd given him the cleats was because he'd have otherwise gone without. But the second reason was that she felt sorry for him; Jeffrey was diabetic, and Sally had once seen him in the throes of a seizure so violent that even months later she sometimes dreamed of it. Any kid who had to live with such an unfair disease deserved a new pair of shoes every now and then.

She examined the box. Almost weightless, the box might have been empty. What could be inside? Nothing very heavy, that was for sure. Feathers that Jeff had picked up

14

from his father's chicken coop? A piece of paper on which he'd rendered a personal picture of his gratitude? Sally gave the box a shake, but nothing rattled inside.

Curious.

The first star appeared in the darkening sky.

Or maybe it wasn't a star, but a planet. Sally didn't know for sure. Anne's husband was an astronomer and could have told her in an instant, but to Sally it was star light, star bright, first star she saw tonight. So she took the chance to cast up her wish. She was a wisher from way back, and never missed a chance to toss a penny into a well or blow out all the candles on the cake in a single breath. Tonight she didn't ask for Jazmyn to grow into a confident woman or for sales to pick up so she could pay the rent. The thought she pushed toward heaven was this: *Let Jeffrey put the rich kids to shame with his bat, because whoever said nice guys finish last has to be wrong as least once.*

With this little prayer wafting skyward, Sally carried her box inside.

Darkness happened.

To Dawn-Marie Johnson, that's how it always went: darkness, not there one minute, smothering her the next. She avoided the window so as not to have to stare into the gloom, for fear that it would swallow her.

"Great show tonight, Dawn," Rudy said, apron slung over his shoulder. "You really had 'em rolling on that thing about zebras and Democrats."

"Rolling's how I want them, Rudy. The rollier, the better."

"You got any more?"

"Any more what?"

"Material, you know. Jokes." He stood there with both

hands on the door's metal push-bar, the exit sign glowing above his head. He and Dawn both worked the eleven-to-seven shift, his kitchen duties ending just as her evening stage routine drew to a close. "Say one more so I can tell the wife."

"What? You asking for a freebie?"

Rudy smiled. Apparently he was indeed asking for exactly that.

Dawn sighed dramatically and wondered how a woman with an English degree had ended up tending bar in her hometown and how this same unintentional bartender had found the nerve to try a bit of stand-up on Saturday nights. "You know I'm a sucker for short men with greasy aprons on their shoulders." She tossed her limp blond hair out of her face and plucked out the first thing that came to mind. "Okay, so this pirate walks into a bar."

Rudy straightened up, his smile clinging in anticipation to his lips.

Dawn knew she had him. Regardless of what she said next, no matter how agile or inept her delivery turned out to be, he would laugh, simply because he was prepping himself to laugh. Did people always do that, predetermine an outcome by fixing it in their brains? For a moment Dawn hovered on the cusp of epiphany, but then the revelation skated out of reach. She refocused on Rudy's face. "A pirate walks into a bar. He has a peg leg, a parrot on his shoulder, and a steering wheel on the crotch of his pants."

Rudy nodded gleefully. A steering wheel on his crotch. What a hoot.

"And the barkeep says—"

Something crashed.

Dawn turned toward the sound. So did Rudy. A second later came the squall of electric feedback and someone mut-

16

tering apologies into the mike. Out in the taproom a local band was setting up for the dinner show. They called themselves Spur Nation and were a potpourri of Hopi and white college kids trying to edge their way into the country-western scene. The city was holding a music festival on Tuesday as part of its Memorial Day gala, and Spur Nation was sadly one of the better acts on the lineup. "Sorry about that, folks," the lead singer said. "I think we just lost an amplifier."

"You break it, you buy it," a heckler fired back.

"Probably for the best," said another.

General chortles ensued.

Rudy said, "Looks like you left the crowd in a rowdy mood."

"Troglodytes, every one of them. Five hundred years ago those were the kind of people that never missed a public witch-burning."

"You handled them easily enough."

"Sugar, I'm a pro, that's what I get paid to do. Or, now that I mention it, I'm an amateur, and what Buddy pays me out of petty cash is hardly enough to keep me in nail polish and rocky road ice cream. Damn, my life sucks, doesn't it?"

"Yeah, this town's no good for you. You should be in Vegas."

"Nah, then Wayne Newton would always be pestering me for my autograph."

Out in the taproom, Spur Nation launched into a cover of "Ring of Fire" that was at least dimly recognizable as the original hit by Johnny Cash.

"I gotta get going," Rudy said, pushing the door open a few inches and revealing a vertical band of darkness.

"Me too, as soon as my ride gets here. See you Monday. We can do it all over again and pretend we're secretly wealthy and just slumming here for kicks."

"No, I'm not going anywhere until you finish. The joke. The pirate in the bar."

Dawn blinked twice before remembering. "Oh. Right." Where was her mind at lately? Why couldn't she concentrate? She'd told Rudy her life sucked, but that wasn't true. She had Anne and Sally, the pitons that kept her fastened to the cliffs and safe from falling. And she certainly had her goofy but lovable hubby, Alex, and their twin sons, Coy and Caleb, aka Poncho and Lefty. And she couldn't forget Jaz, who was her daughter as much as she was Sally's and Anne's. So what was so sucky about that? "Nothing."

"Huh?"

Dawn waved it away. "Just flipping out for a moment, sorry. Now where was I?"

Rudy feigned exasperation. "This pirate walks into a bar . . ."

"Right, of course. How could I forget? So this pirate, he's got a wooden leg, a parrot perched on his shoulder, and a steering wheel fastened to the crotch of his pants."

Rudy nodded.

"And the bartender says to him, 'Hey, you have a steering wheel on your pants.' And the pirate says"—Dawn scrunched up her face and affected her best Blackbeard accent—" 'Arrr, I know. It's driving me nuts.' "

For a moment, Rudy didn't move. His face was locked. Then it hit him.

"Driving me nuts!" he exclaimed. "Yeah, I get it. Hell, that's a good one, driving me nuts." He laughed. "I'll see you around, Dawn." He stepped out into the hot night, still chuckling.

"Not if I see you first," Dawn said softly.

At least she didn't have to wait long for her ride. At quarter till eight, the back door opened and Sally was standing there, munching on a D'Anjou pear.

Sally swallowed her bite and said, "You're being kidnapped."

"Am I? God, I hope they don't expect Alex to pay a ransom. He wouldn't hawk his table saw to save his own life, much less mine."

"Come on. I need your help for a couple of hours. Or do you have to be home right away?"

"Help doing what?"

"Is that a yes or a no?"

"To you, it's always yes. Where are we going?"

"Tucson."

"For?"

"Shoes. A truckload of them. I called the distributor and said not to bother delivering. I can save a hundred and twenty bucks by picking them up myself."

"So you're picking them up now? At this hour?"

"They're sitting on a loading dock. It's either tonight, or I let the local hoodlums open up their own shoe store." She offered her arm. "Is it really okay?"

Dawn took a tentative step beyond the door, then another. She put her hand on Sally's elbow. "I'll call Alex along the way and let him know. I'm sure it's fine. Lex is a sucker for hard-up cases like you."

"So you two didn't have any big Saturday night plans I'm interrupting?"

"Have you forgotten who you're talking to?"

"Glad to know I'm not the only one of us who's never had a social life."

Dawn allowed Sally to guide her to the car. The high-necked security lamp helped a little, but beyond the perimeter of its light lay nothing but impenetrable shadow. Born with a deficiency of rods in her eyes, Dawn suffered from extreme nyctalopia. In her comedy act, she made fun of herself by intentionally confusing that word with nymphomania, and the mix of sex and night-blindness jokes usually had them clutching their guts in merriment.

"So," she said to distract herself from the sack the night had thrown over her head, "why do you need the extra hundred and whatever dollars?"

"Hundred and twenty. Because the ends are getting farther apart, and if I can't make them meet, I'm going to lose the store and the better part of the last eight years of my life as a working adult."

Dawn winced. "Oh." She reached out, groped, and found the handle of the passenger's door. "I guess this is serious business then."

"Serious enough that I don't want to do it alone."

"Hey, Sal?"

"Yeah?"

"You want me to drive so you can concentrate on being serious?"

Sally poked her in the ribs. "Things aren't quite that desperate yet. Now get in."

Dawn-Marie did as instructed. When the dome light came on, the visible world returned and she felt instantly relieved. But as soon as both of them shut their doors and the light went out, it was back to being a cave-dweller before some wise person invented fire. "Really, dear, I can drive fine at night. Just between you and me, I've been taking correspondence courses in echolocation."

Sally started the engine. "I'm not giving you the keys till I see your diploma."

"Don't hold your breath," Dawn said, and somehow seriousness crept in when she wasn't looking, and they rode for miles in silence.

Anne Kobayashi froze as her house shook.

The walls rattled. Anne held very still. She sat before her vanity mirror at eight-thirty on a Saturday evening, brushing her long hair. In the mirror, her arm was poised above her head, brush unmoving.

The trembling in the walls took on a steady beat.

No earthquake. But music with too much bass.

"Trevor," Anne sighed. Hadn't she told him about his stereo? She resumed her brushing. Arizona was close enough to California to worry about the occasional earth tremor, but this particular shockwave was musically induced.

The music didn't bother her unless she was trying to study. She was a year away from a doctorate—which was a feat that sounded so outlandishly unlikely that thinking about it always caught her by surprise. She was getting her Ph.D.? You mean her, the kid we all used to make fun of because her eyes were slanted?

Your mama may be white as snow, but your dad's a Jap from head to toe.

There were other rhymes, one of them sung to the tune of "Yankee Doodle," and though Anne had galvanized much of her heart over the years, there were still certain parts . . .

Boom-boom-boom—

She put down her brush and went upstairs. They still came easily, those stairs, even though her personal odometer had just clocked to the number thirty-six. Like earning a doctoral degree, the age of thirty-six was difficult to comprehend. Vividly she recalled competing in elementary

21

school track meets and having slumber parties with her friends, the four of them indivisible, connected to one another as intimately as paper dolls. Could decades have passed since then? Dawn-Marie was always making wisecracks about her own battles with aging, but so far Anne had exercised and yogaed herself into a form she thought moderately pleasing when she stood before the big mirrors in the gym and compared herself to all the coeds. Not that Barry ever mentioned her body anymore, but that was another story.

She didn't rap on Trevor's door. One did not snap fingers in the percussion section of an orchestra and expect to be heard. She opened the door.

Her son, Trevor Kobayashi-Greene, thirteen years old, was applying white powder to his face. His eyebrows were festooned with chrome rings, his hair spiked two inches high and tipped with midnight-blue frost.

Bracing herself for battle, Anne dialed her voice up a notch and said, "Could you please turn that down?"

Trevor spun around, saw her, and made a face that bordered on disgust. "Aw, Mom, do you have to interrupt me like this?" He sprang from his chair and killed the noise with a touch.

Silence dropped like a net, ensnaring them. The room was decorated in what Dawn had once referred to as Fart Deco: mucus-green drapes, posters of vampiric rock singers, dangling black crepe and monuments of unidentifiable insignia. Fart Deco, Dawn said, meaning this décor really stinks.

Trevor threw up his hands. He wore fingerless gloves. "So now what?"

Anne didn't know where to begin. The face paint? The tattoo he'd tried to conceal from her but she knew was there anyway? The violent lyrics of his music? She was in no mood for a tussle, not with her son, not tonight, because she'd been planning on surprising Barry with lasagna, just like she used to do before they'd grown complacent in their marriage, but he'd called and told her not to bother, as he wouldn't be home until the wee hours. Again. So let Trevor play the rebel one more day. What would it hurt? "Just promise me one thing," she said.

Trevor drew back. "What?" Though not as severely angled as his mother's, his eyes were nonetheless Asian, and the mascara made them look especially exotic, which she knew was his intention. "You're still letting me go out tonight, right?"

"One thing."

"Yeah?"

"You won't be seen anywhere near Dublin Blake. Your father says the police are watching him closely. I don't want you involved in whatever he's doing."

Trevor shrugged. "Whatever."

"I'm serious."

"Yeah, okay. Dub's not so great, anyway."

"And this get-together you're going to tonight. It's not a—"

"Rave party?" Trevor turned away and began filling his baggy pockets with loose change, breath mints, his miniature cell phone. "I'll be fine, Mom." By presenting her with a view of his back, he was announcing that he was dropping his end of the conversation.

Many things occurred to Anne in the few seconds she observed him. She realized that even good mothers, even devout mothers, must face detours such as these on the road to rearing good children. She realized that she loved Trevor just as much as she always had, even though he sometimes accused her of favoring Jazmyn. And she realized that Trevor had lied to her. He would see Dublin Blake tonight, and party with him, and to hell with grown-ups and the world.

"Goodnight, Mother," Trevor said, still not turning around.

She let a few more seconds pass, but she failed to find anything more to say. "Come home safely." She shut the door quietly.

The doorbell rang.

The sound startled her. She made her way downstairs, careful to keep her concerns about Trevor placed in an orderly array in her mind, never to let emotion intrude to the point of distraction—

The door opened before she reached it.

"Trick or treat," Dawn said. She and Sally let themselves in.

"Hey," Anne said in way of greeting. She walked by them and headed into the kitchen. She went directly to the double-doored, brushed-aluminum refrigerator and pulled out a bottle of water. She poured herself a glass, screwed the lid back on, and returned it to its former position inside the fridge.

"Something wrong?" Sally asked.

Anne took several deep swallows and studied her friends over the rim of her glass. Sally had playful brown hair that seemed to get shorter every year, and a face that wasn't so much beautiful as it was cute; it was a face that Anne knew as comprehensively as she knew her own. Dawn-Marie was five-ten, built like a volleyball player but not half as coordinated. In school she'd taken abuse for her gangly limbs. But how many times had those arms encircled Anne and made embracing like a little miracle?

24

"It's just the books," Anne said. "My dissertation. Yuck."

Dawn nodded as if she understood, then helped herself to a banana. "Ah, hell, Annie, what can you do about it? Forge ahead, you know. Stay the course and all that crap."

But Sally was looking at her like she knew better. Which she did. But apparently she wasn't going to press the issue. "How are you for a road trip?" Sally quickly related a story of higher rents and shoes to pick up, and would Anne want to get away from her studies for awhile and come along?

The answer was yes. "Barry called an hour ago. Said he was staying over again. One of the meteor showers or something like that. Prime viewing conditions. In other words, SOS." That stood for same old story. Except it wasn't a story, it was the truth. Barry was the director of the Maxon Array, the new stellar listening post thirty miles from Fresh Waters. He divided his hours between Maxon and Kitt Peak National Observatory up in the Quinlan Mountains. "And Trevor won't be home until midnight, so I guess . . ."

"It's a date," Dawn said, and flipped her banana peel through the air. By mad luck it landed in the waste bin. "Don't you have any real food in this house? By that I mean cookies."

Anne didn't reply, just fetched her purse and checked to make sure she had both phones and that their batteries were charged. She also carried a slender set of binoculars, because Barry was a fiend for meteor showers and his love of spying them had over the years rubbed off on her. She then printed a note for her son. She was not a woman given to premonitions. She was, now that she considered it, the most grounded person she knew, the lightning rod for her friends' erratic discharges. But tonight the sameness of her life was affecting her reason. Her routine was this: she typed away on her dissertation, Barry phoned and said he'd be out all night studying nebulae or quasars or something, and Trevor put on makeup and strategically avoided her.

"Sally?" she said.

"Hmmm?"

"Can we drive with the windows down?"

Sally held her gaze. "Sure."

Sally had borrowed a truck. The cab had two bench seats. Anne climbed into the back, then leaned forward with her arms resting on the seat in front of her, so that she was flanked by her friends and thus defended from whatever the evening might bring.

Chapter Two

They drove through the wasteland.

Sally's window was open to the night air, her elbow sticking out, probably a prime target for mosquitoes but at the moment she didn't care. She drove through the tunnel which the headlights opened in the darkness, the barrens of the Sonora Desert encroaching from either side of the highway; fingers of sand grasped the blacktop, as if one day to lay claim to it. The city of Fresh Waters stood on the edge of the Papago Indian Reservation, an hour southwest of Tucson. The land in between consisted of scrub brush, beavertail cacti, and scorpions. And a town called Maxon.

Maxon was an official dark-sky community. Municipal law prohibited outdoor lighting beyond the barest minimum. Streetlamps were heavily shielded so as not to cast their illumination toward the stars and pollute the firmament for all the amateur and professional astronomers who lived and worked in the area. The bulbs in porch lights were night-vision red.

Sally passed the Maxon exit sign doing seventy. Though the town lay only a hundred yards off the highway, it was as invisible as a submarine under the sea. Barry Greene, Anne's husband—it had caused a knockdown row in the Greene family when Anne kept her maiden name—spent a lot of time in Maxon, as he coordinated the array of satellite dishes that aimed upwards every second of every day, searching for something they'd evidently yet to find.

From the backseat, Anne pointed through the windshield. "See the moon?"

"No," Dawn said automatically.

But Sally did. The moon was only half there, like a blinking eye.

"That's not really the moon at all," Anne said. "That's the moon of one-point-three seconds ago. Everything we see up there, it's all part of the past."

"And this is why?" Dawn asked.

"Because the distances are so great, and light only travels so fast. We're never actually beholding the real thing. The stars we're looking at right now are not the stars at all. They're how the stars were thousands of years ago. Get it? Whenever we look up, we're not really seeing how things are, but how things used to be."

"Weird," Dawn said. "Why does that make me feel lonely?"

They left the cloaked town of Maxon behind.

A mile later Dawn had apparently forgotten the weirdness of outer space. "What's this?" She held up a shoebox she'd found. She hadn't been able to see it, but she bumped into it when she shifted on the seat.

Sally looked over briefly. In the backsplash of light from the dashboard, Dawn wore an eerie green aura, and so did the shoebox with its taped-down lid. "Jeffrey Longbranch gave it to me. Sort of a thank-you, I guess, for letting him have his baseball cleats on credit."

"Feels empty."

"Maybe it is. I haven't had time to look. Go ahead and open it if you want."

"Nah." Dawn put the box aside. "One of my rules is never to open anyone else's gift unless you think it's something you might like to have for yourself."

Sally smiled. For some reason Dawn's remark reminded her of that day with the bucket. She must have been— what?—twelve years old? She'd found a bird in an old dented pail. A barn swallow. The nest inside the bucket was very tidy, a wonder for young eyes. Sally had run off to fetch the others, because nothing was really a wonder until all four of them saw it at once and named it so. Anne the smart one. Dawn the tall and funny one. Sally their leader without knowing why. And Tatyana . . .

"You want to know a second rule?" Dawn asked.

"Sure."

"Never let a man touch you when you're wearing a girdle. You may have to explain yourself."

Tucson appeared like an apparition, its glitter masking the ancient light of the stars.

The shoes were gone.

Sally had little trouble finding the distributor's warehouse, as she'd lived in this city for four years as an undergrad at the University of Arizona, and had driven here countless times since. Tucson was the place to come when you were from a bump in the road like Fresh Waters and needed to breathe a little city air. In her college days, she and the girls had flirted with cowboys at the dance halls and dated a few, and in Dawn's case even married one. The wedding had been held here in Tucson, and Sally had ducked adroitly when the bouquet came flying her way. Through the years she'd come to know the city streets, so it wasn't for lack of speed that they arrived and found no shoes. She got them there in timely fashion, pulled up to the big loading bays where the semi-trucks usually parked, and found neither semi-truck nor pile of shoeboxes. The entire lot was abandoned, the big metal doors screwed down tightly, the bugs swarming around the orange lightbulbs in wire mesh cages. But no one to be seen.

"Maybe we're at the wrong place," Dawn suggested after they'd circled the building twice. "Me, I'm always showing up where I don't belong, and where I'm supposed to be is usually at least a good mile in the opposite direction. Sometimes two."

"I was told specifically bay number four. My shoe order should be on two wooden pallets, and that includes the sixteen pairs of burnout-velvet Mary Janes that I ordered for the women at the theater for an upcoming play. The men were going to leave the pallets on the concrete ramp outside bay four. That would be right there. Where there is definitely no pallet waiting."

"Yeah, even I can see we're pallet-deficient. So what now?"

"Call someone," Anne said. "You have a contact number, I assume?"

Sally shifted the truck into park and let it idle. So much for a joyride with the gals. Now she had an actual problem, which was exactly what she'd been trying to avoid in the first place. It was ten o'clock at night, her order of shoes was trapped inside the building or possibly stolen, and she hadn't been on a date since October. And this was May.

Maybe it wasn't really the shoes that were bothering her. Maybe it wasn't Horace Frown and his rising rent.

"Sal?" Anne touched her arm. "Is there a building manager with whom you can speak? Perhaps they can send someone to open the door."

What had Jaz said to her the other night? *Most people*

ain't even realized they're alive.

Not the kind of grammar you want to display to visiting dignitaries, but Jazmyn's rootsy wisdom was sometimes accidentally profound. Not bad for a kid barely old enough to drive. Jaz had never known her mother, so maybe her perceptive powers were due in part to her trio of surrogates. Nurture rather than nature. On certain nights, Sally still prayed that Tatyana would look down upon what they'd done with her daughter and approve. Sometimes it was such a struggle.

"Houston here, calling Captain Jasper," Dawn said, speaking through her hand like a mini-megaphone. "Captain Jasper, we seem to have lost contact. Do you read?"

After a moment Sally emerged from her reverie. "Copy that, Houston." She turned on the dome light and reached for her purse, but Anne was, as usual, one step ahead of her. Sally accepted the slim cell phone and spent the next twenty minutes getting the runaround from a variety of sources. Apparently one set of keys was at the bar, as this was Saturday night and that's where people went, where there was sawdust on the floor and butts in painted-on jeans. Someone else with the authority to open the warehouse was on his way to Flagstaff with his family for the weekend, and the head custodian was nowhere to be found. Sally got his number from the brother of the guy at the bar, but his phone just rang and rang, and who the hell didn't have voice-mail these days?

She turned off the phone and pinched the bridge of her nose.

"We could always practice a little breaking and entering," Dawn offered.

"This was supposed to be easy," Sally said.

"That's what they always say."

"And fun. It was supposed to be that, too. I don't get to see you guys as often as I used to. How is this so far on the fun scale?"

"Well, if we're using my scale, it's a few pounds light, because that's how I prefer to lie to myself. My scale always reads light. I'm still stuck in the denial stage of weight loss."

Anne asked, "Is there anyone else you can call?"

They sat for awhile and watched the bugs dancing at the light.

"Jaz and I made a bet," Dawn said.

Sally unscrewed the cap of her water bottle and drank deeply. The water was warm.

"You know the battle of the bands they're having during the Memorial Day festival?" Dawn pantomimed a guitar and plucked a few soundless notes. "I'd really love to see Jaz do her thing in public. She's so damn good, right? And she only plays in the garage. Her friend Dakota has a band—I forget what they call themselves but it's something dumb—and he plays the drums. At least he did before he broke his arm. Boy could make those drums sound like a herd of kicking mules."

"A barren," Anne said.

"Huh?"

"A group of mules is a barren, not a herd."

"You don't say."

"Or a span."

"A span of mules? Is that true?"

"Have I ever once lied to you since we were nine years old?"

"No, you haven't, but a span? Who comes up with these things?"

"Span isn't so odd. A group of pheasants is called a nide."

"Good God, woman. How can you possibly stand

learning such things?" Dawn shook her head, un
conceive of such a person. "Anyway, of course Dal
invited Jaz to join the band about ten thousand tin
cause she's great, everybody knows that, but we're a
of what a loner she is."

"She does enjoy her solitude," Anne agreed.

"Too much so," Sally said. "I worry about he

Dawn tossed up a hand. "Join the club, sister
really no big deal. She's a nonconformist like I
Anyway, the other day I bet her that I could hur
back door at night and climb up into Coy an
treehouse in less than fifteen seconds."

Sally looked over at her. A few june bugs had
the cab. "You did what?"

"I made a bet. I told Jaz I could step off the l
go across the yard, and climb up into the treeh
teen seconds or less."

"At night."

"Well, yes, that's the rub, isn't it? At any r
the wager, then Jazmyn has to play in Dakota's
name notwithstanding."

"And if you lose?"

"I have no intention of losing."

"Pretend for a moment."

"Okay, pretending that I might lose, which
will not, then I've agreed to do all of her la
next three months."

"I always make her do her own laundry,"

"As do I," Anne added.

Dawn struck a contemplative pose. "Funn
a girl who limits her wardrobe to miniskirts
can have clothing spread out over three d
holds."

33

"You won't be able to see a thing," Sally reminded her. "If Caleb leaves a toy lying in the yard, you'll trip and break your neck. And you're doing this in fifteen seconds? How are you ever going to manage to win this bet?"

"Hell, I don't know. I'll think of something."

They sat there talking, waiting for a telephone call. Their old rhythm returned, so that their thoughts folded into themselves, their body language, their unspoken pasts—all of it swirling around them so that they got caught up in its wind and the hours were blown away unnoticed.

"Can you believe it's almost one in the morning?" someone finally said. Their voices, much as their minds, had become indistinguishable.

"How long are we going to wait for the key?"

"I'm starved. I'm thinking—"

"Pancakes."

"There are husbands to call first."

"Barry will still be at the observatory, ogling pulsars."

"And Alex will be snoring with the TV on."

"So pancakes first, then call."

"Deal."

At the all-night restaurant they laughed, swam in coffee, and talked about that time Dawn got caught shopping when eight Pez dispensers came tumbling out of her skirt. Remember when we got drunk at Kenny Scarlo's keg party and Dawn puked all over Kenny's cousin? Remember that field trip to the Grand Canyon, the one where Anne was approached by those tourists from Tokyo who talked her leg off until she screamed at them that she couldn't speak a word of Japanese? Remember when Amy's sports bra broke during that junior-varsity basketball game but she was too embarrassed to call for a timeout? Remember that night we all sat around talking

about what it was like to let a boy feel us up for the first time?

At some point the darkness in the east was serrated by an orange horizon, and one of them looked out the window and realized it was daybreak.

The telephone rang.

A custodian with one arm unlocked the warehouse door at five-thirty a.m. on Sunday morning. He didn't help the women load the truck, only stood on the dock and smoked and stole furtive glances at Anne's butt, which Dawn had once pronounced *The Ass That Launched a Thousand Levi's*. They stacked the boxes on the flatbed and tied them down with stretchy cords the man provided. They covered the completed bundle with a big green tarpaulin and affixed the tarp's grommets to the truck's steel bed. When they drove away forty-five minutes later, the man hoisted his hand in a wave, the other arm nothing but an empty sleeve that tossed like a windsock in the breeze.

They drove out of the city and into the desert.

Dawn-Marie tried to stay awake.

She hadn't stayed up all night since the twins were babies. But here she was, riding shotgun without enough caffeine in her blood and too much sagebrush out the window. Even if her inadequate eyes had been able to see anything beyond the window, she was sure the scenery offered nothing to pique her usually rampant imagination. She knew without being able to see it that the juniper was nice, as were all the pretty colored rocks, at least they were if you hadn't been raised in these parts. Otherwise the sandy landscape was monotonous, even tedious. There were days when Dawn wanted a fresh countryside so desperately that she had to bite a knuckle to keep from telling Alex they were moving. How many people lived their lives that way, biting knuckles in lieu of taking a chance?

She felt herself nodding toward the window. She forced her eyes open, sat up straight.

Sally was driving with both hands on the wheel and a vacant look on her face.

Was something wrong these days with good ol' Sal? Dawn had been sensing it for awhile now. Maybe it was that man thing again. Sally had never married. Dated, yes. Even been engaged; Lord, but what a fiasco that had been. But she'd never taken the leap. And she was only four years away from the big four-oh, so there was your explanation for her recent doldrums. Sally invested so much of her strength into raising Jazmyn, as if she felt some unpayable debt to the girl's mother, that she had little energy left for that crazy little thing called lust. Or even, perish the thought, love.

They whipped past a tumbleweed and set it spinning in their wake.

Dawn peeked at the speedometer, noted in that dim way of people only half awake that they were doing nearly eighty. Hopefully Sally was more alert than Dawn herself. And Anne? She was no longer leaning forward with her arms propped on the seat in front of her, but sitting back and being very still. She'd just gotten off the horn with Barry, who apparently had returned from Maxon and was climbing into bed. Their boy Trevor—the poster child for the term *wayward son*—had made it home and was asleep in his room. Dawn knew that, back at her own *casa,* Alex was snoozing with no intention of getting the boys up and ready for church. Lex was a backslider but too lovable to be mad at for long. He'd no doubt fix the boys big plates of waffles for breakfast and then crank up his 'seventies rock on the garage turntable and spend the day fixing his '71 Camaro, quotation marks around the word fixing.

Dawn felt herself slipping again. She knew she'd better do something to maintain consciousness, because one of their oldest rules was that no one could sleep unless they could all sleep; if one was up all night with the flu, if one was giving birth at three in the morning, if one was cramming for mid-terms, then it was the old Musketeer motto for the lot of them. So to stay awake she cleared her throat and said, "Do you want to know a hundred and one reasons why a cucumber is better than a man?"

"Is that all?" Sally asked. Her voice was flat. "I would have guessed higher."

"How about reason number eleven?" Dawn paused for effect. "A cucumber won't mind hiding in the refrigerator when your mother comes over."

No one said anything.

"Damn, tough crowd. Let's see, reason forty-two. Cucumbers don't tell you they liked you better with long hair."

At this, at least, Sally showed the hint of a smile. Sally's locks had gotten cropped upon attaining the earth-shaking epoch of three decades. For the last half-dozen years, her hair had curled playfully at a respectable shoulder length, rather than cascading midway down her back like it used to. Dawn found it amazing that twenty years had passed since they'd all had bangs teased high on their heads and petrified by layers of mega-hold hairspray. Dawn had been the first to surrender her tresses to the hair gods. Anne was the last hold-out, her inky black hair still streaming down her back like a river at night.

"Reason nine. Cucumbers are easy to pick up."

The sun rose higher behind the truck. The morning

came alive. With the coming of the light, Dawn saw stubborn wildflowers clinging to the powdery soil. She recognized the creamy ghost flowers and vibrant yellow beeplants. Fresh sunshine glittered off distant silicate rocks, making it seem as if jewels were to be found out there amongst the worthless scrub brush.

"Reason twenty-two. The average cucumber is at least six inches long."

A man appeared in the middle of the road.

Later that's how Dawn would explain it to the police, that this man—zap!—materialized on the highway as if by teleportation, and there was no way an expert driver could have avoided him, much less an ordinary driver running on sleep fumes. Dawn was picking her brain for the funniest cucumber joke she knew, simultaneously thinking that she really needed to pee, and then the man sprinted across the road.

"Sally!" Anne yelled.

Dawn slapped her palms against the dashboard just in time. Sally went rigid and hit the brakes with both feet, her back arcing, her head rising toward the roof of the cab.

Dawn's seatbelt locked. Her body traveled forward with the inertia of the truck, but her shoulder harness wouldn't let her move. The sudden pressure vised her ribcage painfully. At the same time, the sound began, a squall like a pterodactyl might have made in a distant age, the peal of hot rubber on pavement.

The man turned, looked right at them. He seemed surprised. Maybe he'd been running in a daze, running from whom or running toward what, God only knew, and blinking from his stupor he was shocked to see a truck six feet away from him and closing.

Dawn screamed.

She wasn't a woman prone to fear. She didn't fret about the possibility of being mugged or having a heart attack or losing her house to an electrical fire. First of all, mama didn't raise no sissy, and secondly, Dawn had learned from Tatyana an incalculable courage. But she cried out now, the sound torn from her lungs by the certainty that they were going to hit this man, and hit him hard.

Six feet became five became four became three—

Sally almost saved them. What she did was rather amazing, Dawn would later tell the officers of the Arizona Highway Patrol. The truck was veering to the left, tires smoking. Instead of panicking and fighting the wheel, Sally let off the brake completely and turned straight into the direction of the vehicle's momentum. At once the strain on the shuddering rear end was relieved—Dawn felt the shift in her bones—and the front bumper missed the man by half a foot.

But now the truck was sliding sideways.

The back tires whipped around and Dawn's door struck the man so violently that his skull shattered the glass in the passenger's window and his body caved in the steel.

She saw him up close in that small fraction of time. He looked right at her. His deep Hispanic eyes were beautiful and terrified. He wore a dirty ballcap that read *CHEVY CRUISIN'*.

The noise was the worst. Though the sound of a half-ton pickup smashing into a human body was solid and jarring, like the crack of a bat, there was a softness about it that was sickening, like punching a mound of ground beef.

That was the last detail she remembered.

She shut her eyes after that. Shut her eyes and prayed. Her mental message wasn't much in the way of anything holy, just a simple *Please, God,* but she meant it, she clung to it, and then her stomach lurched the way it did on roller-coasters and she realized they had left the ground.

The truck flipped.

For two counts of Dawn's heart, they were airborne.

The top of the pickup crashed against the blacktop.

Glass shards blew out like shrapnel. The tarp snapped loose. Shoeboxes of every hue blossomed into the air. Engine dying, the truck rolled onto its side, jettisoning more boxes, higher and farther than before. Their lids came off in mid-flight, so that they birthed high-tops and flip-flops and pumps. The shoes left the boxes like outlandish birds breaking free of their eggs as they hurtled through space.

The truck leaned on its side, almost tipped over again, then rocked back and was still.

Shoes rained.

They thudded the highway and the desert floor in rapid succession. Dust rose up from the small dents they carved in the ground. The lids of the boxes wafted down after them, their motion erratic, like thrown playing cards. A tall, leather woman's boot with a two-inch sole landed upright in the middle of the road.

When the last of the shoes settled, there was only silence.

Dawn swallowed a single, painful breath, then another. Strapped into the passenger's side of the bench seat, she now found herself at the highest point in the vehicle; Sally was at the bottom, with nothing to see from her window but pavement. Dawn tried to speak but she hadn't the air.

Bits of gummy safety glass tinkled from her window.

"Tell me that you're both okay," Sally blurted. She still clasped the wheel with both hands. She appeared unhurt, pinned to the seat by her shoulder harness, but she didn't turn her head or otherwise move. "Annie? Dawn?"

"I think I'm fine," Anne said. Her voice was like the notes of a poorly played flute.

"Dawn?" Finally Sally's paralysis broke and she looked up at where Dawn was snared in her seatbelt. "Dawn-Marie, don't you do this to me. You have to be okay, got it? Now please say something."

Dawn wanted to be herself. She wanted to respond to her friend's obvious fright with a disarming joke, maybe cucumber reason number sixty-seven, but she couldn't for all the Elvises in Vegas remember what number sixty-seven was. The sensation of hanging weightless like this made her think of space flight. She wouldn't have been surprised to see the jagged stars of glass floating in zero-g around her head.

"Dawn!"

"Shhh," she finally managed. "I don't think . . . anything's broken."

A hiss from the motor preceded a gout of vapor that spurted from the mangled hood.

"Jesus, we hit him," Anne said. "Sally, we hit that man."

"I know." Sally fumbled with her seatbelt latch. The normally facile task of pushing the release button was compounded by the trembling of her fingers and the fact that she was positioned on her side, her body weight tightening the belt. "Can you guys get out? Can you get yourselves loose? We've got to . . . got to see if he's all right."

That was the only action Dawn could comprehend. Sally knew best. Sally always knew best. Just get out. Just get free of this space-shuttle harness and into the open, upright world, and the rest would take care of itself. Concentrating on every new breath, Dawn worked to liberate herself, careful not to do it too quickly and go crashing down on top of Sally. And then something occurred to her. "What was he running from?"

"What?" Sally had shrugged out of her shoulder strap. "What are you talking about?"

"That man," Dawn said. "I saw his face, Sal. I saw his eyes. And he was running from something. I'm sure of it. Someone was chasing him."

Chapter Three

"I have no cell service this far out," Anne said, though to her own ears the words sounded as if they were coming from someone else's mouth. She lifted her other phone— the satellite version—and gave it a shake, in case anyone needed reminding that she possessed it and that they would never be without assistance. "But I could call the moon with this thing, if there were anyone up there who would answer."

She looked to Dawn for some kind of response, but Dawn's eyes were fixed to the man on the side of the road. His trousers were simple cotton and hand-stitched. His T-shirt was stained dark with dirt, dried sweat, and now blood. Dawn covered her mouth with her hand.

At the sight of her friend in such distress, Anne felt a sudden advance of tears. She fought against them. When they were kids, Anne had always been the last to cry, even when the other three were weeping oceans over one sad thing or another: a dead puppy, a jerk boyfriend. She remembered specifically the last time she'd lost control; that hour was the most indelible of any in her mind. But sixteen years had passed since the funeral, a regular drought of tears; even here in the Sonora it rained more frequently. "They're sending an ambulance from Tucson. Help is—"

Sally interrupted her. But whatever she said, it sounded far away, like someone calling from the far side of a mesa.

Dawn invited them to sit down beside the truck. Anne considered this a logical move, as the position of the over-turned vehicle would interrupt her view of the man with his head split open. In minutes the flies would gather on his face, and she had no intention of seeing that happen. Only briefly did she consider advancing toward the man and checking him for a pulse. By the looks of his head, there was little Anne and a first-aid kit could do to save him. Better to wait for the paramedics.

She lowered herself to the ground next to Sally. She put her back against the truck and sat there with her legs straight out in front of her, a phone in each hand.

Sally put a hand on her knee.

Anne relished the touch. Just as she wasn't a woman prone to crying, neither was she given to physical expressions of emotion. Some people craved the handshake, the hug, the arm slung across their neighbor's shoulder. Anne rarely felt the impulse. Perhaps that was why she'd married Barry Greene, who was at times as distant as the stars which he spent so much time observing.

Something occurred to her then. She relaxed her grip on the phones and said, "He's Mexican. He crossed illegally. He was running for freedom."

"Maybe," Sally allowed.

"No, it's true. I'm sure of it. You saw the canteen. He's an immigrant. That's what they do. They put together a kit, food and water and a knife if they're lucky, and then head out across the desert. Many of them deplete their water too early, and they die out there."

"You're probably right."

Anne knew that she was. Sally and Dawn usually deferred to her in matters involving deductive reasoning, crossword puzzles, and balancing checkbooks. She was a taxonomist by vocation—a student of the principles of scientific classification—and was a few months away from taking a doctoral degree in systematics. She didn't think the schooling made her any smarter. She was simply good at arranging things in proper alignment so as better to understand them.

Hard to put this in any order though: smashed truck, fatally injured foreigner, shoes.

From a mile away, across the dust-packed ground, came a low growling sound.

Engines. Several of them.

Anne stood up at once. The sound wasn't coming from the far end of the road, so it didn't belong to the howling motors of approaching highway patrolmen. Rather, the noise originated in the desert itself, out where the rising heat waves distorted vision.

Sally came to her feet, startled by Anne's sudden movement. "What is it? What's the matter?"

"Don't you hear it? Something's out there." She shielded her eyes with her hand.

"She's right," Dawn said, using the truck as a crutch to prop herself up.

The three of them stood in nearly identical poses, fingers providing shade for their eyes.

It might have been a mirage. The desert was like that, coy and deceptive, like the trickster character from Navajo lore. But far to the south, shapes emerged from the mesquite and clumps of wolfberry. The soil was beginning its morning bake, and the sun pulled wavering bands of hot air from the ground and obscured the figures. Beyond the haze, at the outer limits of her vision, Anne thought she saw a human form, several human forms, though from this distance they might have been illusions conjured by the spirits that supposedly walked these lands.

She turned on her heel, went to the truck, and knelt amongst the hunks of rock-candy that used to be the back window. She pulled out her purse and resumed her position at Sally's side.

"I hear it," Sally said, "but I can't see anything. Maybe it's just the echo of a passing plane, or a big truck down the highway."

"I don't think so." Anne reached into her purse and extracted the anniversary gift Barry had given to her a year ago. *So we can do something as a couple,* he'd explained. *So together we can share the heavens.*

It all sounded far more romantic than it turned out to be. Still, Anne enjoyed the occasional comet, and this pair of binoculars gave her a front-row seat. Barry had extolled the instrument's merits with a connoisseur's pride, including its high-res and fully multicoated optics, its compact size, minimal weight, and polarizing filter. Though you couldn't see the rings of Saturn through these dual tubes, Anne was damn certain she could get up close and personal with whoever was out there in the sand. "So let's see who was chasing him." She put the lenses to her eyes and adjusted them by touch.

Instantly it was as if she were standing among them. They came that sharply into focus. Their motorcycles were responsible for the kicked-up dust, five or six motocross-style dirtbikes and what appeared to be a dune-buggy with over-inflated tires. They had driven from the south and, by the looks of them, driven hard. Their goggles were coated in grime as thick as paint.

"What is it?" Sally asked. "What's out there? What do you see?"

"Their faces."

One of them had a red beard. Another couldn't have been older than seventeen. There was a man with a black bandana tied around his head, and the buggy driver was borderline obese; his beef-slab arms encircled the steering wheel, and the straps of his goggles made grooves in the flesh on either side of his face.

"Who are they?"

"I don't know. But I see a standard."

"A standard what?"

"I mean a banner, a flag. It's attached to the back of the dune-buggy. It's an American flag, except I think there's something printed across it, a symbol of some kind."

"What are they doing?"

"Waiting, I think."

And so they seemed to be. They had spotted the wreck and were keeping their distance.

Anne panned them with the binoculars. She saw them talking, firing questions back and forth, gesturing angrily. Though lip-reading was not in her repertoire, she inferred enough to know that they were, to use Jazmyn's lingo, pissed off majestically. The one in the passenger's side of the buggy stood up, gripping the roll bars in black-gloved hands.

"Annie, what's going on?"

"Shit."

"What? What does that mean? Do you mean shit as in they're coming this way or just shit for the sake of swearing?"

"Take me to your leader," Anne muttered. This guy was obviously in charge. His face was deeply grooved with premature wrinkles, as contoured as a topographical map. His hair was nearly as dark as Anne's own, tousled by his ride in the open-air vehicle. His safari shirt was open halfway down his chest, exposing a smooth, sweat-dappled chest.

He wore a pistol on his belt.

The gun was not the kind Anne would have expected, not one of the sleek automatics used by movie cops. Rather it was a revolver, its brown leather holster lashed to the man's thigh a la Wyatt Earp.

"DATFUG," she said, invoking their girlhood acronym: *deep-ass trouble for us girls.*

The others, upon hearing this abbreviated oath, stiffened as a matter of reflex. Though Dawn-Marie might toss out DATFUGs at the slightest provocation, Anne employed them only when she ascertained that matters had degenerated to a point warranting serious concern. Tatyana had first coined that little ditty, and it stuck, and nothing else could have so effectively transmitted Anne's feelings at the moment. "He has a gun."

"Who?" Sally wanted to know. "Who's got a gun?"

"Come on, Kobayashi," Dawn said, her voice hiking up a notch. "Are these people harmless coyote hunters out for a Sunday morning killing spree, or is someone pointing a rifle at my head right now? Either tell us what's going on or pass over the spectacles and let me have a look."

"Wait. They're leaving." Her field of vision circumscribed by the round tunnel of the binoculars, Anne watched them throttle their bikes and throw up long crescents of dirt with their rear tires. "They're making an about-face, heading back the way they came." The man with the gun resumed his seat, the sun flashing off a large gemstone he wore on a chain around his neck. As the dune-buggy turned and picked up speed, its flag caught the wind and unfurled, revealing a black snake stitched across the red and white stripes. After they were gone, dust as thick as fog hung motionless in the air.

Anne lowered the binoculars but continued to stare in their direction. "That's them."

Sally touched her on the arm. "Them who?"

"The ones who were chasing that man." Though she had no need to indicate the man in question, she felt compelled to point him out. "Right there, Sal. The person we just hit. He's a Mexican immigrant who crossed illegally, and for some reason those goons on the bikes were tracking him."

"Why? Why would they do that? If you're right and he's just another alien hopping the border, why on earth would anyone put so much effort into catching him? It makes no sense. Even the Border Patrol isn't going to send out a troop of motorcyclists to capture and deport one ordinary man, so why would anyone else?"

"I don't have an answer for that." Though she hated shrugging—it always seemed like such an impotent and coarse gesture, sort of like the slang of body language—she heaved her shoulders up and down before she could stop herself. "Perhaps he isn't so ordinary."

A wolf cried out across the desert. But Anne knew it wasn't really a wolf.

She tilted her ear to the east and heard the keen of sirens.

Police stations, Sally decided, were hell on the fingernails.

She'd broken the first one simply coming through the front door. She reached back to hold it open for Dawn, who was quizzing one of the patrolmen for information on the Mexican's condition, and the nail of her ring finger on her right hand snagged the door at just the proper angle that, when the pneumatic arm began dragging it shut, a good portion of her nail went with it.

"Can I get you ladies anything?" a young man in uniform asked. They were sitting in a glass-walled office in front of a vacant desk with a nameplate that read *CAPTAIN ALISTAIR IQUI*. "Bottle of water? Coffee?"

Sally smiled curtly. "Water would be nice, thanks."

The second casualty had occurred when she sat down in the chair she now occupied. The pinky of her left hand chipped on the chair's hard metal armrest.

Not a good omen.

Anne cupped her hand over her phone and said, "Barry wants to know if we need him to come pick us up."

"Not unless he plans on trading cars," Sally said, inspecting the state of her cuticles. "Corvettes are two-seaters, last time I checked."

She hoped that an intense examination of her nails would help distract her from the fact that she was sitting in the District 8 headquarters of the Arizona Highway Patrol. Three glass walls offered her a view of men and women she usually only saw from behind the windshield when she passed them on the road. But evidently they were real people, out there right now joking and slurping coffee and generally acting too normal on a day that was anything but. The office's fourth wall was papered with notices, warrants, photographs of AHP barbecues, posters of icons like Lady Justice and Uncle Sam, and a chart showing the annual number of illegal immigrants apprehended here in District 8. The figures on the chart seemed quite high. But for all of those arrested en route, lots of others made it undetected. Minus those run over on the highway.

Sally realized she could no longer see her nails because

she had curled her fingers into a fist.

"Sorry to keep you waiting," Captain Iqui said, hustling into the room and dropping swiftly behind his desk. The young patrolman was right behind him, bearing bottles of cold water.

"Shut the door on your way out, Pete," Iqui said. "And get Surry from Immigration in here pronto."

"Sure thing, Cap." Before he left, Pete stopped to study the wall of photographs and notices from the Arizona Department of Public Safety. "You know what I just realized after all these years?"

"What's that?"

Pete nodded toward one of the posters. "Lady Justice is pretty hot. You know what I mean?"

"No, I can't honestly say that I do."

"Just look at her, Cap. Yeah, you can't see her eyes, on account of the blindfold and all, but have you ever really checked out that body? Woman is built."

"Sure, Pete, Lady Justice is appearing next month spread-eagled in *Penthouse*. Will you please get the hell back to work?"

Pete scurried out.

As soon as the door closed, Iqui leaned his elbows on the desk and took the three of them in at a glance. He was American Indian with a military haircut and eyes as black as onyx. "This is what my daddy would call two pounds of bacon in a one-pound skillet."

To this, Sally could think of no fitting reply.

"What I mean is, put too much fat in the fryer and it jumps out, and then what started out as breakfast turns into a grease fire. Make sense? You three set out to take a Sunday drive, end up with a Mexican national in the ER and the makings of a mighty nice house fire."

"Is he going to be okay?" she asked.

"The truth? I wouldn't bet any family heirlooms on it."

She shook her head. "I just can't believe . . ."

"None of us can," Dawn said.

Iqui laced his fingers in front of him. Sally noticed that his own nails were clipped much too short, uneven, and in need of a good emery board. "That's how these things go. I see more disbelief on the faces of folks like you than you'd ever imagine. Now, I've read your statements, and everything seems to be pretty much in order. It was a tragic thing that happened out there, and I wish that you hadn't been made to experience it. But it was an accident, what they might call a *freak* accident, or even an act of God, and there was nothing you could have done to avoid it. Maybe you were going a few miles an hour over the limit, but even at half your speed, that man would still be lying with his head under the surgeon's knife. You hear me?"

"Yes, but . . ."

"But what?"

"I don't think you can call it an accident."

"Oh? And why is that, Mrs. Jasper?"

Sally didn't bother correcting him on the whole Mrs. thing. In her younger days she'd been a Miss, now she was considered Ms., and a few years from now she'd be whatever you called a middle-aged woman who still hadn't managed to get herself married. Marm couldn't be far down the road. "Captain, I really don't think I would have hit him if he hadn't been running. And the reason he was running was because—"

"Because someone was hounding him," Iqui interjected.

"Yes."

"Uh-huh. I read in your statements that a group of men was spotted by"—he looked at Anne—"pardon me, ma'am, but I'm not sure how to pronounce your name."

Anne was sitting up very straight. She had fixed her hair behind her head in a bun so tight that Sally almost got a migraine just looking at it. "Kobayashi," she said, and then pronounced it by syllable. "Ko-bah-yah-she." Had she a nickel for every time in her life that she'd spelled that name to someone, she could've kept them all in chocolate for the rest of their lives.

"Mrs. Kobayashi, you claimed to have seen some people out there on motorcycles—"

"She doesn't claim," Sally said. "They were out there. She saw them."

Iqui raised his hands defensively, palms out. "I'm not doubting it for a minute. But unless you've got some evidence that . . ." He stopped himself, dismissing the subject with a slight move of his head. "It doesn't matter a hill of beans, really. What I've got is a hospital complaining that they're never going to be paid for the work they're doing on a nameless alien, a public relations department that gets to explain to the Mexican government that we're not intentionally harming its citizens, and two rookie patrolmen spending their morning picking up a million shoes from the side of the road. Needless to say, it's already been one hell of a day."

A knock on the office door saved Sally from having to respond, from gushing forth with all the many dangerous waters she held inside. They would wash her away, those waters, carry her off to reckless decisions if she weren't careful. She wanted to ask Iqui why this country worked so hard to prevent foreigners from entering. She wanted to know why hospitals would complain for tending the sick. She wanted to know why nobody would bother to learn about this man from Mexico, not even so much as his name.

53

Pete, the young officer with a jones for Lady Justice, stuck his head in the door. "Uh, Cap?"

"What is it?"

Pete balked, shifting his feet in the doorway.

"Either spit it out, trooper, or close your mouth before one of these damn horseflies decides to pay a visit to your tongue."

Pete flicked his eyes toward Sally, and in his hesitation she guessed what he was about to say. "Hospital just called."

Sally forgot her nails and gripped the armrests.

Iqui's black eyes were relentless. "Yeah, and?"

Pete only shook his head. Then he withdrew from the door and closed it softly.

Afraid even to move her eyes, Sally stared at the place where Pete had been standing.

Iqui leaned back in his chair and rubbed the stubble of his recent haircut. "For what it's worth, and I know it ain't worth much, I'm sorry."

Sally didn't hear him. She was too busy talking to herself, repeating the same three words in her mind in hopes that she'd eventually accept them. *I killed him.*

I killed him.

I killed him . . .

Chapter Four

When the man from Immigration arrived, Iqui excused himself and let them have his office. He'd likely had his dose of forlorn women for one day.

Him and me both, Sally thought, and then resisted the urge to grab the nearest hand and communicate in that tactile telepathy they'd developed over the years. She wondered why she wasn't in shock. Isn't that what happened to innocent people when they accidentally murdered someone? They were always talking about shock in the thrillers she read—her secret sin, those pulp paperbacks—and shock was supposed to pull the plug on your body, so that you kind of just hummed like a wire but didn't feel much. But instead of a welcome numbness, there was instead a feeling in her chest like a rusty hinge working back and forth. Did that man have a family? Was he coming to this country to secure a place for a wife and children? And how would those little *niños* ever find out their father was dead? The desire to learn small, vital things about his life was surprising in its intensity. She wanted to make him real by knowing his favorite song.

"Hello. Do you mind if I sit?"

No time for swallowing bitter pills. She forced herself to lift her eyes to the voice.

"Hi," he said, and he looked like a freshman being made to stand up on the first day at college and state his name and major. "My name is Leigh Surry. I'm with the Bureau of Immigration and Customs Enforcement. I appreciate your letting me have a few minutes of your time."

Sally experienced a sudden, unnatural clarity. Her powers of observation were tuned to a rare frequency. Damned if vehicular homicide didn't have a way of scrubbing a person's senses shiny clean. She saw Leigh Surry in every detail, down to the turquoise bracelet on his wrist and the puckered round scar on his neck. He wore a scruffy blazer over a hunter green T-shirt that was tight enough to accentuate his torso when he sat down on the edge of the captain's desk. His jeans were new but his boots were not.

Size ten, she thought robotically. It was her curse.

He was a man on lifelong terms with the desert, as evidenced in his skin tone. His hair was like his blazer: dark and soft-looking and in need of a good brushing. Sally tried to imagine who he might have been in a past life, her private game, but nothing would come.

"You mind if we have a little chat?" he asked.

"Chat away," Sally said. "We're all feeling quite chatty at the moment. Probably talk your ear off if you're not careful."

He didn't seem to know how to take that, so he cleared his throat and opened a beleaguered field book. It looked like something that had been carried through a war in a rainy country. "I'd like to tell you first that you've done nothing wrong. As soon as we're finished here, you're free to go. Captain Iqui has assured me of this. Secondly I want to say it's an unlucky thing that happened out there today. It was sheer chance, an intersection of wrong things, and you don't deserve that kind of bad luck. Finally, I just want to state for the record that there *is* justice in this world."

"Prove it." She didn't know why she said it; antagonism just felt comfortable.

"Wish I could, but I can't. It's just something I believe in. Call me the last of the white hats. For starters I'm hoping to trace the man to his home back in Mexico, even though our success rate with Juan Does isn't very good."

Heat flushed Sally's cheeks. "Juan Doe? That's the racist name you're calling him?"

Leigh Surry, clearly mortified, quickly shook his head. "No, it's not that at all, pardon me completely. That's just the local lingo. I had no intention of offending you."

"Never mind. Juan Doe's as good as anything else. Was he somebody's mule?"

"Excuse me?"

"That's what they call it, right? A mule? In my business a mule is a type of shoe. But I think a mule is also what happens when a drug lord or someone down in Mexico pays Juan Doe to smuggle dope across the border. They turn him into a mule. Is that why those men were after him? Because he was carrying drugs?"

Surry stared at her attentively. "May I ask you a question?"

"You're giving me a choice?"

"Have you lived in this area all your life?"

That wasn't the question she was expecting. She answered without thinking. "Sad but true. Some people graduate high school and go. Some stay. Me, I'm a stayer. What difference does it make?"

"Then you're familiar with the term *water station*."

Sally squinted. Where was this leading? "I suppose I've heard the phrase a time or two." She looked at Anne. "Were you able to find us a ride home?"

"Yes."

"Good. Now do you have any idea what this guy's talking about?"

Anne never shifted in her seat, but sat straight-backed with her hands atop the phones in her lap. She had sat the same way when the four of them had been called to the principal's office in seventh grade after Dawn put those firecrackers in Todd Nuttle's sack lunch. "A water station," she said with steady clarity, "is an outpost erected by various altruistic groups who hope to provide a measure of relief to immigrants crossing the desert. Such stations consist of fifty-gallon drums containing fresh water, and perhaps containers of nonperishable food as well. Unfortunately, the random placement of these sites hasn't been committed to any public map, so travelers hoping to make use of them must rely primarily on luck to stumble upon one. Thus the utility of a water station is minimal at best. Is that an accurate assessment, Mr. Surry?"

Surry's blue eyes widened. "Yeah, yes, of course, I couldn't have said it better if I read it straight out of a report. And, incidentally, I *have* read it out of a report. I've written such a report. That's part of my job. Those men you saw out there on the motorcycles? I believe they're among the ones who use water stations as bait. They wait for migrants to happen along, then they ambush them."

"Why would they do that?" Sally asked, though she supposed she already knew.

"Because they call themselves patriots and they think they're acting on America's behalf by rousting aliens, roughing them up, and sometimes worse. The water stations make things easy for them. It's just like the lions in Africa. They stay close to the watering holes, waiting for prey."

"That's sadistic. They lay traps and hurt people just for . . . for fun?"

"I think they'd tell you they were doing it for their country." He took out a pen. "I'd like you to give me a full description of the men you saw, every little bit about them that you can remember. Can you do that for me?"

So Anne did. Her memory being what it was, she gave Surry so much information that he kept having to say, "Hold on a sec," while his pen worked to catch up with her narration. Twenty minutes later, Surry handed each of them a card and told them to call him if they thought of anything else.

"Anything else like what?" Sally asked. She felt surly, and this self-proclaimed white hat was a target of convenience.

"Like a detail you might have forgotten about the incident. Or if there's something you need . . ."

"Oh, well, if it's my needs we're talking about, then the list is long and not easily filled."

"Ease up, Sal." Dawn tapped her on the knee, a little Morse message that said there was no reason to push matters any further: *Let's just get home.*

Sally shied away from the touch. Something was boiling in her. "Here's a need for you, Mr. Surry. I need a sympathy card for Juan Doe's mother or his wife or his son. And now that I think about it, I need the insurance company to pay for the truck I wrecked, because it was a loaner. I need people to stop using patriotism as an excuse to be a bully. I need two hundred bucks extra for rent."

"I really wish I could give you those things."

"I'm not finished."

He held up both hands in surrender.

"I need a salary cap for millionaires so we can use the

extra money to feed hungry people. I need congressmen who are paid only as much as school teachers. I need telemarketers to stop wasting my time." She scooted forward in her seat. "I need a tanning bed that won't give me cancer. I need the Pope to tell people it's okay to use condoms. In fact, I need just one religious denomination that doesn't think it alone is the best and truest way to heaven. I need the return of Steve McQueen, because all the leading men these days are just pretenders. I need a comfortable bra."

Leigh Surry looked like a man at the receiving end of a firing squad.

"I need socialized health care. I need a woman president." She stood up. Because Surry was sitting on the desk, Sally had the advantage of superior elevation. "And do you know what I need most of all, Mister White Hat? I need my friend Tatyana not to be dead. Sixteen years ago she died in childbirth, and on certain days I need her laughter more than I need to breathe."

All at once the fire in her blew out. It left behind a choking smoke that prompted one more need: fresh air. "I've got to get out of here."

She clipped toward the door without waiting for the others.

The sun helped, but not much. When she reached the curb, she stopped and looked up at the sky. Today her life had changed. The exact nature of that change remained undefined. She had murdered a man inadvertently. Maybe it wasn't her fault. What had Leigh Surry called it? An intersection of wrong things. But the fact remained that she'd been driving, and probably daydreaming, and speeding. Paying the lease on the shop no longer seemed very important.

Then what's important, Jasper?

60

Whose voice was that? Though it issued from within, it sounded like someone else.

Well?

"Saving people," she said under her breath. "Just saving all of them."

She heard the others behind her.

Before climbing into the AHP cruisers, they'd collected their personal articles from the cab of the overturned truck, notably their purses and the bright orange shoebox that was a gift from Jeffrey Longbranch. Dawn-Marie held out Sally's big gingham handbag. Her face grave, Dawn said, "Hell of a speech in there, girlfriend, but there's one more thing you should know."

Sally accepted her purse and was glad to feel its familiar, solid weight when she hooked it over her shoulder. "What is it now?"

"Reason eighty-two. A cucumber doesn't leave the toilet seat up."

Sally couldn't help it: the smile came, however slight. It made her feel guilty. But there was nothing to be done about it; Dawn was a carrier of the optimism bug, and you couldn't avoid periodic infection.

A big convertible pulled around the corner and sounded its horn—the first few notes of "Johnny B. Goode." If Sally's purse were an anchor keeping her from floating away, then she was fully grounded by the welcome sound of that horn and the sight of the girl at the wheel.

Jazmyn.

Boys had climbed trees and spied over fences to get a glimpse of that hair.

Jaz had frosted the tips of it, so that now the last inch was wintry white all the way around, making her look fey, a spirit from a fairy wood. But the rest remained a blond storm, lustrous, with just enough natural curl to give it life. It swung down her back as she bounced from the car and jogged toward them.

She stopped ten feet away, fixing her hands to her hips. "Somebody here call a cab?"

"Right on time," Dawn said, going to her and pulling her into a hug.

Sally watched them as they embraced. Jazmyn closed her eyes and gripped Dawn's shirt in her fists, as was her wont when hugging; it had the effect of making you feel as if she had no intention of letting you go, which was, Sally knew, an incredible experience.

"Everybody cool?" Jazmyn asked after they parted.

"You could say we're as cool as cucumbers," Dawn said, and she looked at Sally and winked. "Bring any lunch with you?"

"I thought we could stop on the way home. You guys are buying, of course, and that includes my gas. You know how much this sucker guzzles?" She went through the hug ritual with Anne, but her face became imprinted with concern after only a second. She held Anne at arm's length. "Mother, what's wrong?"

Anne smiled thinly. "I suppose I'm not so good at dissembling my emotions as other people we know."

Tossing Anne's things into the backseat, Dawn said, "I don't even know what dissembling means, so I know you can't be talking about me."

Anne touched the dimple on Jazmyn's chin, that identical little depression another chin had borne in another time. "Honey, that man we struck with the pickup . . . he died."

"Aw, shit . . ."

Simultaneously Sally, Anne, and Dawn made various noises of disapproval.

"Sorry, sorry," Jazmyn said, fending off their reprimands with a flutter of her hands. As always, her feelings were so apparent on her face and in her stance that she might have been the emotive creation of a sculptor who could alter his design at will as the passions moved him. "You're kidding me, right? I can see on your face that you're not, but it doesn't hurt a girl to ask, huh?" She looked from one of them to the next, asking them with her sympathetic green eyes if there was anything she could do; they had but to ask.

Sally opened her arms. "Come here, kiddo."

In the three strides it took Jazmyn to reach the curb, Sally soaked up the sight of her, because she knew her soul's medicine when she saw it. Jazmyn wore Dawn's old denim jacket, the one with the faded patches sewn on it promoting Stevie Nicks's 1982 world tour. Sally recalled seeing the Dawn of yesteryear wearing that very article on endless occasions. Clothes had their own memories, holding them together like stitches. Though the day would soon be too warm for the jacket, Jaz usually wore it when she drove in the cool mornings, as the car was a convertible and she despised having to go anywhere with the top up. Underneath the denim was a black halter top with a message written in silver sequins: *IN YOUR DREAMS*. Her Scottish plaid skirt hit her two inches above the knee, and her ensemble was completed by a pair of surplus paratrooper boots, the buckles of which she'd polished to a high gleam.

Size five. Sally pulled her close. "You've been wearing your seatbelt, haven't you?"

"Please, Mom. What kind of dummy do you think I am? I know I've only had my license for a few months, but duh."

She lifted Sally's hand and kissed her knuckles. "Are you okay?"

"For a basket case, yes, I'm fine."

"What's going to happen now?"

"You mean with the police? They worked the accident and said it wasn't my fault."

"How do they know?"

"I guess they don't think the three of us look like practiced liars. Besides, they can figure these things out with all their gizmos. They use some kind of measuring stick on wheels to determine distances, and they measured our skid marks. That kind of thing."

"And the trajectory of the body," Anne added.

Sally didn't need to be reminded of that. "Yes. That, too."

From the backseat Dawn called, "Let's get this road on the show!"

Anne got in beside her, leaving the passenger's seat to Sally. The three of them had only recently taught the girl to drive, and here they were, captives of their student. Sally slammed the car's heavy door. Accustomed to her own modern subcompact, she marveled at the girth of this brontosaurus, a two-door 1975 Buick Custom with a giant V8 engine and white leather seats. For Jazmyn's birthday they'd tried to talk her into something practical, with favorable gas mileage and a tidy engine, but Jaz had fallen in love with the mighty convertible the moment she saw it. The girl was a sly alchemy of trendy youth and old-school savoir faire.

When the Buick assumed the highway and took on speed, it was not like a dinosaur at all. The sensation was rather like sitting on the bowsprit of a galleon as it rode the open sea.

"Mama?"

64

"Yes, dear?" Dawn said, cranking up her voice to be heard above the wind. Ever since Jazmyn was little, that's how her adopted parents were known to her: Anne was Mother and Sally was Mom and Dawn was Mama because she'd drawn the winning straw all those years ago when they were deciding who should be called by what name.

"Remember our bet?" Jaz asked.

"How could I forget? A midnight run across the blind dangers of my own backyard."

"I want to do it tonight."

"I'm not sure if tonight's such a good idea. Maybe tomorrow. I think I need a solid evening of Alex and the boys, sort of recharge my batteries."

"No, it has to be tonight. The battle of the bands is only two days away, and you're going to need a lot of practice when you lose the bet."

"What on earth are you talking about, girl? If I lose this little wager of ours—which I promise you, I won't—but for the sake of discussion let's say I lose, the price I pay is doing your laundry for three months. Remember?"

"I've changed the bet."

"You can't change a bet. That's a law as old as gravity. You go changing bets on a poker player in a saloon in Tombstone and they shoot you dead for being a mangy dog."

"Will you just listen to me for a minute? If you win—fat chance of that, unless you plan on trying to get away with wearing night-vision goggles—then I have to play with Dakota's band on Memorial Day."

"Yes, that's right. So far you're still alive in Tombstone."

"But if I win," Jazmyn continued, head turned slightly to aim her voice toward the backseat while still keeping her

65

eyes on the road, "then you have to let me play in *your* band."

"Dear, the only band I have is the band of outlaws riding in this car of yours. Unless of course you count my wedding band, which I keep warning Alex I'm going to hawk unless he buys me a new flat iron."

Jazmyn's hair was running like a yellow flag in the wind. A smile had alighted on her face. Sally found this mildly amazing, that anyone could look like that on a day when blood had been spilled.

Past life?

No. Painful to think of that. Sally knew who the girl had been in a previous life.

"I've got it all figured out," Jazmyn said. "You three and me are starting up a band."

"You three and I," Anne said.

"Uh, dear, that would be great and all, really it would, but we have a slight problem in the fact that none of us can play a instrument."

"Not true. Mother plays the keyboard."

Dawn let out a bark of laughter. "I don't think classical piano is going to get anyone on the cover of *Rolling Stone*."

"Are you kidding me? She can sight-read anything you put in front of her. Isn't that right, Mother?" She briefly found Anne in the rearview mirror. "I mean, you're awesome."

"The piano is no synthesizer," Anne said. "I wouldn't know what to do with myself in front of one of them."

"Yeah, whatever. You'd be great. And you, Mama, are going to play percussion."

Dawn laughed again, louder this time. She seemed to be enjoying this. "Uh-huh. The only drumsticks I've ever touched in my life are the kind connected to a chicken. Hey, will somebody give me Ringo Starr's number? I want to tell him I'm free for lunch."

"You can keep a beat, can't you?"

"You can keep dreaming, can't you?"

"Dakota is a percussionist, and he's good. He can give you lessons."

"Okay, sunshine, let's see what we've got in this band of yours." Dawn was leaning forward now, her hands animated. "One, a lead guitarist who is actually something of a prodigy, though to my knowledge she plays mostly folk music and acoustic pop and has little experience with the electric guitar. Still, any band in any garage would love to sign her up. Two, a woman forced in her youth to take piano lessons, who's buddy-buddy with Bach and Freddy Chopin but entirely unacquainted with the makings of electronic keyboard music. All right, still not a bad choice at all as far as musicians go. But our third selection? Whew, this bartender with the split ends can't maintain a steady rhythm at gunpoint. That's what the reviewers will say. Drums for miles around will run terrified when they hear me coming. Cymbals will cry out for mercy. But other than that, sounds like you've got yourself a winning unit on your hands, dear. But what do we need to complete this patchwork symphony? What's Sal going to do?"

At this, Jazmyn looked over at Sally. The girl's eyes were those of a leprechaun.

"Don't say it," Sally warned her, finally sniffing out the conclusion. "Don't you even think it. If you are actually fantasizing that I could ever possibly—"

"Sing," Jazmyn said.

"Never."

"*Sing.*"

"In public? I assume your intention then is to revolt the audience."

"I've heard you sing, Mom. You're good."

"Compared to what? A Siamese cat being drawn and quartered?"

Dawn was crowing in the backseat.

"You're not helping any," Sally told her.

"You've got pipes," Jazmyn said, as if it were an accepted fact. "You think I haven't been listening all my life when you sing around the house? Not only are you always on key, but you've got totally ballistic range."

"Singing along with Linda Ronstadt while I'm running the vacuum cleaner does nothing to qualify me for the stage. I honestly wouldn't know the first thing to do with myself in front of a crowd."

"Easy. Just let it all hang out."

"Yeah, Sal," Dawn said, "just let it all hang out."

"Enough out of both of you."

"So do we have a bet, Mama, or are you chickening out?"

Dawn put on a very serious face. "I've never done any chickening in my entire life. You, my flamboyant, dazzling child, have yourself a wager."

At the exact same time, the two of them feigned spitting on their palms, then clasped hands over the seat. It was a pact-sealer they'd shared for years, and by unspoken vow, neither of them could break it. Come what may.

"You can't bet on my behalf," Sally said.

"Nor mine," Anne added. "I refuse to be someone's poker chip."

"Tonight then?" Jazmyn asked, looking at Dawn in the mirror. She was ignoring the others completely.

"Nightfall," Dawn agreed. "Fifteen seconds across the

yard and up the treehouse."

Sally let them have their game. If they could use it to distract themselves from the day's events, then it was tonic for their hearts and they should drink their fill. If only Sally could take such a bottle and put it to her lips. But the thought of what she'd done made her throat burn, and there was no balm that would soothe it. She kept on wishing ardently for a chance to set things right, to iron out her wrinkled karma, to avenge the dead.

Sitting behind Sally in the backseat, Anne didn't let on that she was afraid. She kept her placid demeanor pulled up tightly near her neck, the way she used to draw the covers close when she was a little girl and the scary things came out.

In her mind she was standing on the highway beside the ruined truck, watching the men in the clouds of dust, their leader with his gun. She kept seeing the man's face, lines like ax marks in his cheeks, a colored stone catching the light as it lay between the slopes of his pectorals. Though hundreds of yards had separated them and the man had employed no binoculars of his own, Anne couldn't shake the feeling that he'd been staring right at her, that he would recognize her on sight, that he would, perhaps, come looking for her when the moon was right.

Chapter Five

Sally could not get the day to end. The sun, despite her best efforts at cajoling, refused to move any faster, so that the hours came as they always did, each one laden with new thoughts of the accident. Guilt, she decided, always traveled in slow motion.

Telephone calls on Sunday were no good. She didn't want to bother her girlfriend Dominique, who waited tables over at the Cheshire Grin, because Domi was trying in a way that was painful for her friends to get that new hunk at the lumberyard to ask her out. So on Sundays, Domi's day off, she was likely to discover a sudden need to talk about two-by-fours and the right type of wood to use when building a birdhouse—this from a woman who didn't know a tape measure from a plumb line. Her chosen target for these carpentry queries was a Swede with shoulders so rounded with muscle they looked like car fenders.

The Gallagans were also off-limits on the Sabbath. They had four children and were some of Sole Mates' best customers. But every weekend they drove off in an RV full of road maps, potato chips, and hand-held video games. And Gina from next door had driven up to Vegas to show off a new red dress.

So in a moment of masochism, Sally decided to ride her bike.

Mostly the bike was a New Year's resolution gone to seed. For the better part of three years it had occupied the same corner of her garage, framework for spider webs, a generally misspent hundred and ten dollars. But by five o'clock in the evening, Sally knew she had to escape, and since she shivered at the thought of operating a motor vehicle so soon after the accident—

—it was no accident—

—it was give her pedals or give her death. She used Jazmyn's old T-shaped air pump to inflate the sagging tires, then trundled the bike from the garage and took a few perfunctory swipes at the cobwebs. Though she appeared intent upon nothing but an examination of gears and handlebars, her inner eye saw a flash of color as Juan Doe appeared in front of her. She thought about Juan and her bike at the same time, in that way humans have of piggybacking one set of concerns atop another, like hiding a comic book behind your algebra text in math class.

Mercifully she finally got going.

The town of Fresh Waters wasn't so fresh anymore. Over the years it had taken on a staleness for her, as she'd lived here long enough to see its paint begin to flake and its eaves begin to droop. She rode straight to the city park, which was undergoing a makeover for Memorial Day. Here at least a measure of freshness had been restored. The jungle gym was newly painted, the graffiti on the trash barrels concealed beneath recent layers of adobe brown and cactus green, the school colors of the Fresh Waters Sidewinders. Someone had finally removed the weeds that had been growing up through the cracks in the tennis court, and the water fountain actually looked safe for human use; for years the spout had been caked with hardened God-knows-what, but now it sparkled. The eastern half of the park also boasted the public swimming pool. The western half, however, had no teeter-totters or sandboxes, but was simply a broad expanse of trimmed grass, a vast field for pick-up soccer games and kite-flying and for spreading your quilts on when the policemen shot fireworks into the air on Independence Day. The sward surrounded a raised wood platform, the back half of which was semi-enclosed in a wooden roof. This dais served as a stage for local plays and high school music recitals when the weather permitted. During election years, touring congressmen used it as a podium and sometimes a soapbox, but its claim to questionable fame was its renown as a make-out spot for the young or rebellious of heart. It was known to everyone as the Ampi, meaning the amphitheater, though Reverend Smithson had once referred to it as the Den of Illicit Assignations and Premarital Copulation.

That's what I need, she thought as she pedaled through the grass, *an illicit assignation.*

Not to mention a little premarital copulation.

The last time she'd had sex—

—no accident, they were chasing him—

—she'd been seeing Louis the literature professor, whom Dawn called Lou the Blue Gloom. Lou had taken his neo-romantic poetry very seriously, very broodingly, so Dawn had composed raunchy couplets behind his back and recited them whenever his pretentiousness overwhelmed her. Sally had given them the details when they asked how he was in bed, told them even though she would have hated it had he been the one doing the talking about her, because the kiss-and-tell rule had always been different for women. Unfortunately she'd had little more to report other than the fact that Lou's quest for coolness knew no bounds, and it rendered him an inhibited lover.

Something was going on at the statue.

Sally rode up to the statue's base and stopped where the yellow tape marked its perimeter.

"Howdy, Sally!"

"Good evening, Zeb. Since when are parks-and-rec people working on Sundays?"

Though Sally didn't know why, Zeb laughed. It was the sound an old 'forty-niner might have made when asked why he spent his life panning for gold. "I ain't working, Sally. I'm *measuring*."

This did indeed seem to be the case. The statue around which he bustled was encircled by bands of fluttering yellow tape borrowed from the county sheriff's office. *POLICE LINE DO NOT CROSS*. This barrier was a matter of public safety, as the statue had been marked for removal and was now an obvious danger to bystanders. The statue itself was cast of bronze. It was nine and a half feet tall and probably weighed a thousand pounds. The figure depicted was none other than Farrington Schatz, famous army scout of the 1800s, trailblazer, prospector, desert survivalist, and reported rattlesnake hunter. For a hundred years Schatz had been part of local mythology. But his legend was dealt a death blow when a grad student in Tempe unearthed details of atrocities perpetrated against the Indian population, with Schatz one of the primary offenders. Evidence was found implicating the man in a variety of anti-Indian endeavors, so the town council took swift and politically correct action and voted to have the statue removed. A week ago the workers had loosened its foundation and toppled it.

Except it hadn't quite fallen over. Not yet.

"Sal Jasper?" It was Mark Cheevey, insurance salesman

and unofficial Keeper of the Leaning Statue. "I don't believe you've bought a time slot yet. What can I write you down for?"

Sally was straddling the bike, watching Zeb hunker down near the effigy's uprooted base, taking rapid measurements. She turned to Mr. Cheevey. "I'm sorry?"

Cheevey gestured with his pen. "Farrington here is currently tilted at a twenty-one-degree angle. As you can see, much of the old guy's base is still rather solidly connected to the ground, so it's going to be awhile before his weight tears him free. The physics teacher over at the high school predicts good Farrington will lose the fight to gravity in the next seven to ten days. Poor gent can't lean that way forever. Four days ago his angle was only eighteen degrees. Eventually he's going to drop and make a most spectacular noise."

"So you're taking bets?"

"We're selling tickets. Buy a ticket and pick a time slot. The proceeds from the tickets go toward buying a new piece of statuary. Whoever picks the slot in which Farrington actually falls will win themselves a mess of coupons from area merchants. A free dinner at the Cheshire Grin, an oil change, a discount at the dry cleaner's, that sort of thing. So what do you say? Each time slot is five dollars."

Sally looked back at the statue.

—*he came out of nowhere*—

Farrington Schatz was a dashing figure, and somewhat handsome, despite his swooping sideburns. His shirt was open at the chest, and he wore his famous necklace, the one festooned with rattles taken from the snakes he killed. His right arm was extended high over his head. He gripped his hat in his hand in an eternal wave. Apparently the Sidewinder marching band had donated one of its cymbals to the cause, because when the statue finally collapsed, Farrington's big bronze hat would strike the cymbal, alerting anyone nearby.

Something was troubling her. What was it? Was there a message hidden in the statue?

"How about Thursday night between nine-fifteen and nine-thirty?" Cheevey suggested.

"Each slot is only fifteen minutes long?"

"Yep. So the more tickets you buy . . ."

"Has Horace bought a slot yet?"

"Horace Shine? Well, let me see." He scanned the pages of his thick register. "Ah, yes. Here he is. Mr. Shine has opted for twelve-fifteen on next Saturday, seven days from now."

"What if it never falls?"

"Pardon?"

"Schatz here. What if he just keeps hanging on? What if he says to hell with you all and just leans there forever? I hear there's a tower in Pisa that does that."

"He'll fall, all right," Zeb promised from his spot on the ground. Then he laughed again.

"Uh, it's a matter of science, I think," Cheevey said. "Farrington's on the move. It may take a week, it may take two, but sooner or later, he's going to go bang."

Sally continued her examination of the statue. To the west, the sun slid closer to the horizon, much as Schatz was sinking toward a cymbal crash. The Ampi, directly in front of the sun, unrolled a shadow that seemed much too long for a structure of its size.

"I want the slot right in front of Shine's," Sally decided. "Next Saturday. High noon."

"A fine choice." Cheevey carefully printed her name in the register, and she dug some crumpled bills from her pocket and handed them over. "Care to buy a slot for your daughter? Might as well keep the winnings in the family, right?"

She suspected there was a time just after impact that Juan Doe was also tilted at a twenty-one-degree angle. She tried not to think about that.

"So how about it?" Cheevey prompted.

"No thanks. Jazmyn places her own bets."

"Very well. I suppose it might be illegal for her to buy a slot, anyway, as she's only a minor. I'm not certain about the laws governing lotteries like this, but I think . . ."

Sally stopped listening.

Farrington Schatz was calling her.

See me, he said.

I see you.

I'm wearing chaps and a gunbelt.

Yes, I noticed.

But that's not all.

What are you talking about?

Look.

I am.

Look.

I'm looking, dammit, cut me some slack.

And?

And I see boots, size twelve, which means you had really big feet when you were alive, the better to crush the skulls of bobcats and Indian resisters, and the gloves on your hands have little wrinkles carved into them, which means the sculptor was one talented dude, and there's a band of conchos around your hat and a necklace at your throat—

Yes, there is.

". . . but if folks can play bingo on the Navajo lands then I don't see why certain old biddies here in town can say

76

anything about a harmless raffle. Don't you agree?"

"Hell," Sally said. She'd finally seen it.

"I beg your pardon?"

"Around his neck. Annie said he wore a necklace."

"I don't believe I'm following you."

Sally still paid Mark Cheevey no heed. "That man in the desert. She saw the necklace he was wearing. She also saw his flag. We find that flag, we find the man."

"Find who? Sally, what the devil are you talking about?"

"Saving people," she said. "I'm talking about saving people."

She heaved hard against the pedals and built speed through the grass, wondering if she'd kept Leigh Surry's business card and wondering—at least in the back of her mind—what she would do if she ever met the man who had chased Juan Doe to his death.

Anne found her son at Scorpion City.

The old placer mine had long played out, and nothing remained but a ring of condemned shacks along the edge of a pit full of broken sandstone and three feet of stagnant water. On geological survey maps it was known as B. R. Silver Number 3, but due to the alarming population of poisonous arthropods, everyone called it Scorp City.

As she guided the car onto the gravel access road that serviced the mine, Anne counted two big fears. One, she'd find Trevor out here risking suicide on the motorcycles they liked to race. Or two, he was holed up in one of the tumbledown buildings with a bong to his lips or a scattering of pills in his lap. She'd never seen him using drugs. And he swore he didn't. But what did that prove? Boys had not attained their reputation as boys by always telling their mothers the truth.

Anne's grandmother had been a *kyoikumama*. In Japan a *kyoikumama* was a woman who envisioned the ultimate education for her child and then used threats, charm, spankings, love, anger, tricks, and the occasional crowbar to get said child moving toward this goal. Ashiko Kobayashi and her husband Ichiyo had been released from the California internment camps in 1945 and systematically kept their son on a fast train to fame and fortune. Michael Kobayashi was now a professor of applied mechanics at Caltech. He'd married a white woman who happened to hold an advanced degree in adultery. Anne hadn't seen her mother since she was three years old.

With Trevor, then, Anne was striving for balance: not so unbending and single-minded as her grandmother, but not so delinquent as Anne's own sweet mum. Somewhere in between must reside the secret to child-rearing.

Too bad her plan was disintegrating.

Her tires crunched to a stop beside a sign that warned of the abandoned mine and its attendant dangers. Most of the sign was hidden behind a pleasing shrubbery of Apache plume, its round white flowers with their bright yellow centers seeming to contradict any message of peril.

"Fallugia paradoxa," Anne said to herself when she spotted the flowers. Barry said she had a memory like a black hole, so powerful that even light couldn't escape. The Latin names of an embarrassing number of plants and animals were inscribed forever in her mind.

There once was a nerd from Japvilly, the kids had said, *whose brain was so big it was silly.*

It blew up one night,

And the town lost the fight,

Like Tokyo mashed by Godzilly.

She got out of the car and made her way up the trail that

led through the brown grass. She identified other types of flora as she went, making a mantra of it so as not to think about what Trevor might be doing out here. She'd always thought that desert chicory looked like a pinwheel, with its straight gray stem and big fanfare of white flowers.

"*Rafinesquia neomexicanak.*" God, she was sick. Who possessed such ineffectual knowledge?

She reached the first building. Its roof of corrugated metal was so rusted that big flakes of it had begun to drift away in the occasional breeze. Weeds had claimed it. Spray paint covered it.

MONA HUMPS FOR PESOS, she read.

She skirted the building, watching where she placed her feet. She'd put on her most expensive pair of running shoes, thinking she was going to jog and jog until she sweated out the visions of the dead man on the road, but instead she'd gone looking for Trevor, and now her shoes were coated in red dust.

Then she heard them.

Beyond the building, probably out near the cusp of the mine crater, were at least two boys, and one of them had just said something about boobs.

She heard Trevor laugh.

Though she couldn't have explained it, she felt the need for stealth. She hated the thought of sneaking up on her son, but ever since that episode this morning, wariness seemed the order of the day.

She stepped around the corner.

They saw her immediately and froze.

Bathed in sunlight, out in the open and away from the shelter of the buildings, the boys were completely revealed. They had nowhere to duck for cover. All they could do was nothing at all, simply hang there, captured like figures in a photograph.

"Mother?"

When she realized what they were doing, Anne sighed and almost laughed. They were up to their elbows in grease and fixing an overturned motorcycle.

"Mother, what are you doing out here?"

Relief flowed down Anne's body the way an icy drink leaves a cold trail down the throat on a hot day. "Hey, mister. I wanted to see if you'd like to take a ride with me. If you're not overly busy."

A special vibe must have been transmitted then. Trevor picked up on his mother's distress—will wonders never cease?—and he quickly gathered his tools and said goodbye to his friend.

"Everything cool?" he asked as they got into the car.

"Not really."

"What do you mean? Is it Dad? Is he okay?"

She told him before he could ask another question. Told him about the trip to Tucson. Told him about the man in the Chevy Cruisin' ballcap. Told him about the police. The only detail she omitted was that of the men with the strange American flag. The ones that reminded her of human coyotes.

Trevor sat wide-eyed through it all. The story seemed to impress him, because boys his age find wonder in disaster, and she couldn't fault him for his reaction.

They drove for an hour while the sun fired the western horizon like pottery in a kiln, hardening it from a burnt orange to a shade of pre-night purple. She bought him fast food for dinner, and this also impressed him, because Anne despised such cuisine and by chomping down fries she let him know that she was truly distraught. They spent the evening in rare companionship, and by the time they pulled up at Dawn's house, full darkness had settled around them.

"I thought we were going home," Trevor said.

"We won't be long," she promised. "I just want to check in, ensure that everything is all right." How could she explain to him the need to be with one of them, either Dawn or Sally? At times she could almost see the strings that laced them together—the soulstrings, she had named them—but this evening she needed affirmation. Hours had passed since they had returned to Fresh Waters. Things happened in hours.

The kids, Caleb and Coy, were playing in the front yard, zapping flashlights at each other like laser guns. The garage door was open and Alex's music spilled out. And on the front steps, Dawn-Marie and Jazmyn sat side by side. Jaz had her guitar across her lap. Dawn wore a Band-Aid across the bridge of her nose.

"If you want apple pie," Dawn said, "you're too late. Lex just ate the last piece."

"We've already eaten, thanks."

"Real food, or that weird organic fare you occasionally force us all to eat?"

"I'm not sure you can call french fries real food. I just wanted to stop by and—"

"I know why," Dawn said. "But we're just jim-dandy at this end. Been a doozy of a day, I guess, but we're good. Ain't that right, Jazzy?"

Jazmyn strummed the guitar with no particular intention. Her free-flying hair was currently at parade rest behind her head, and she'd put on a long cotton skirt that made her look like a gypsy's child. Looking at Anne she said, "I won the bet."

It took Anne a moment to remember. A bet? Then she made the connection between the bandage on Dawn's nose

and the wager involving a night-blind trip across the backyard and an ascent up a treehouse ladder.

"I really tried to pull it off," Dawn said in way of explanation. "I even tried to cheat. That was my whole plan, see.
Before dark I climbed into the treehouse and put a radio up
there, with the volume down really low. You know how I
can hear better than anybody, so when the time came for
the challenge, I figured I'd be able to barely hear the radio,
really faint but just enough to guide me to the treehouse,
and nobody would know how I did it. But I guess the radio's stupid batteries went dead. And as you can see, my
nose paid the price."

"Cheaters never win," Jazmyn said.

"You could have seriously hurt yourself," Anne told her.

"Ah, heck, Annie, you only live once . . . unless you're
one of those characters in the movies who gets amnesia and
has to start life all over again with a new identity, but we
can't all be so lucky as that, huh? Anyway, I lost."

"So it's drumsticks for her," Jazmyn said, plucking out a
few notes as light and lyrical as a windchime. "Dakota's
coming over tomorrow for her first lesson."

"What are you guys talking about?" Trevor asked.

Jazmyn was eager to explain. She accompanied her
tale with a casual guitar score. She finished with a dis-
cordant clash of notes to represent Dawn's collision with
the tree.

"So you're going to play in a band?" Trevor's expression
was one that Anne could not recall seeing in years. "Like, a
rock band?"

Anne briefly imagined herself pounding out electrically
amplified melodies while the greater part of Fresh Waters
watched her make a fool of herself. "I never actually agreed
to anything . . ."

"But Mother, that would be so totally tight. You know what I'm saying?"

Though she hated to utter anything that might dispel that look of innocent delight, Anne shook her head. Her inner geometry was too logically arranged to accommodate such a shapeless notion as performing onstage at the town's music festival. "At the risk of being my notoriously unfun self, I'll have to decline. I don't really think I have what it takes."

"He's right, Mother," Jazmyn said. "Everybody would love it."

"Love what, exactly?"

"If you guys and me formed a band and competed."

"You guys and *I,* and I thought this afternoon we concluded the discussion on the infeasibility of this mythical band of yours."

"But it would be so *cool,*" Trevor said, apparently having forgotten his self-assumed role of the disgruntled and intentionally dispassionate teen. He was just a kid again, and this thrilled Anne in a way that she almost gave in and said yes. But then she remembered who she was and promptly discarded the fleeting notion. Perhaps that was her trouble: she always remembered who she was. Her bills were always paid on time, her dental appointments as regular as the moon phases. Even her period came and went with an infallible rhythm, never faltering. The only uncertain thing in her life was standing beside her.

"Mother, at least think about it."

Dawn said, "Yeah, scaredy cat, at least think about it."

"What? You mean to tell me that you've agreed to this . . . this fiasco in the making?"

"I lost a bet. Got no choice. Don't you remember that day behind the drugstore? Tatyana made us all promise not to tell about the stolen licorice, and she said she'd call us all welchers if we reneged. I've never forgotten how important it was to her to keep a vow. You taught Jaz the Pythagorean theorem and how to carry herself like a lady. I taught her to shoot nine-ball and to never be a welcher."

"Fine, I understand you made an oath, even though you had no right to make one on my behalf. But that aside, today is Sunday. The performances are scheduled for Tuesday night. That's only two days. You honestly believe you're going to be playing the drums by then?"

"How hard can it be? I won't be doing any solos. I don't have to read any music, just keep the beat."

"Perhaps, but I've known you since the third grade and I don't recall ever witnessing any evidence suggesting you possess even a single musical bone in your body."

Dawn scoffed and made a dismissive gesture. "Musical, schmusical. Have you seen those jokers on the videos these days? Some of them may be musicians, but a big heaping spoonful of them simply beat the hell out of the drums and toss their hair around. Don't you worry about me, sister. Have drumsticks, will travel."

"See, Mother?" Jazmyn persisted. "Mama's going to do it."

"Your mama's done a lot of things in her life that I wasn't about to do."

"Watch it, Kobayashi."

"What kind of stuff will you play?" Trevor asked. "Modern stuff or the oldies?"

Anne shook her head again. "I really wouldn't know, Trev."

"We'll play it all," Dawn said, throwing out her arms as if to encompass the full range of music history. "The old boy may be barely breathing, but the heart of rock 'n' roll is still beating."

"I have no desire to be a laughingstock."

"You play piano not quite like a virtuoso, but close. So put your modesty in the closet where you keep the leg-warmers you used to wear in high school. You're the cat's meow and you know it."

"Just say you'll try," Trevor pleaded. He tugged on her sleeve, which was something he hadn't done since he was six. "Just do some rehearsing and see how it goes."

"No, I'm sorry, but I don't think so. And I never wore leg-warmers, by the way."

Dawn shot to her feet and cupped her hands around her mouth. "Hello out there! There's a woman on my lawn who's a liar! I swear to the god of all the material girls of the eighties that Anne Kobayashi wore leg-warmers!"

"Please, enough." Anne felt the warmth in her cheeks. Dawn had always been able to embarrass her into admitting the truth. "How about we discuss this in the morning? Let me sleep on it. Can you permit that, please, and stop shouting?"

Jazmyn put the guitar aside and scooted forward on the porch. "Mother, I'd love to have you up there with me on the Ampi stage. You're the one who taught me the notes and the scales in the first place. *You*. We've played together lots of times. Haven't we always sounded great?"

"Jaz, it's not the same."

"It is the same, only with an audience."

"Sis is right on," Trevor said. "You've got the skills, you know? Just please say you'll do it."

Anne bit her lip. Though illuminated only by the porch light, their fervent faces were all too visible. And she had invested too much of her life's energy into these three souls to deny them that for which they so obviously longed. But still . . .

Dawn broke the silence. "So what do you say, Annie? Wanna be a jukebox hero?"

In the end, it was her son that moved her. Days later, in the middle of the hurly-burly, Anne would retrace her steps in an effort to find the catalyst, the spark that birthed the bonfire. It was Trevor's smile.

"Okay," was all she said.

Chapter Six

Sally woke up hard.

The dream shattered at once, leaving her alone in her room with the clock showing 5:51 a.m. and tiny pearls of sweat on her neckline.

Monday morning, she thought. *Memorial Day.*

Fragments of the dream persisted. Shards of the past. Visions of that day in the rain when she and the girls heard the noises out at the mine. The day they became locally famous. The elementary school track meet had just ended, and the four of them were taking the long way home . . .

Sally swung her legs out of bed and reached for her notes.

Leigh Surry's number was printed six pages deep in the yellow legal pad. The top five pages were curled back over the pad's spine. Though Sally craved a shower and something to eat, she knew that the dream would haunt her unless she occupied her mind. It always did. She took the cordless phone from its base and dialed.

There had been a car parked on the macadam in front of the mine. A rangy old Impala with polarized windows. Sally could see its bumper sticker as clearly as if she were eleven years old again and reading it for the first time.

DON'T TELL MY FOLKS I'M A TRUCK DRIVER. THEY THINK I'M A PIANO PLAYER IN A WHOREHOUSE.

She hadn't understood this message the day she saw it on the car's rusted rear end—she didn't even know the meaning of the word *whorehouse*, knowing only vaguely that it was not to be used in front of adults—but for some reason the lines had stenciled themselves in her mind, inscribed there permanently by the knife-edge intensity of the day's events.

The phone picked up at the other end. Groggily. "Yes?"

"Mr. Surry?"

"Uh, yes. At least I think so."

"This is Sally Jasper. We met yesterday. At the highway patrol headquarters."

She heard him moving around, probably sitting up in bed, rubbing his face, checking the clock. "Yeah, sure, Sally Jasper. The one who needs Steve McQueen and a comfortable bra. How could I forget?"

"I'm sorry about flying off the handle like that. It was a rough day."

"And apparently a rough night after that. Have you slept?"

"Here and there."

"Why are you calling me at not even six in the morning?"

"I would have called last night, but I couldn't find your number."

"I gave you my business card."

"Yes, I know, but I threw it away. When we got back from Tucson yesterday afternoon, I went to my store to try and figure out what I was going to do about the shipment of shoes I'd lost out on the highway, and I must have tossed the card out with the store trash. I called the Border Patrol, thinking that maybe they knew how to get in touch with you, but I didn't have any luck. So I stared at a movie that made no sense, tried to read, tried to sleep, and ended up on the phone with Captain Iqui, who gave me your number around midnight. I didn't want to call then because I thought it was too late and you might have a wife and family who didn't want to be disturbed at that hour on a Sunday night, so I put another movie in the VCR and this one was worse than the first, so I went to bed and stared at the water stain on the ceiling and somehow managed to fall asleep. And here I am, waking you up. I want to know what you can tell me about that gang we saw out in the desert."

"Wait a minute. I'm offended."

"Why?"

"You threw my card away."

"You'll get over it."

"I keep giving those things out in hopes that someone might actually call."

"So I'm sorry already."

"Don't sweat it. Story of my life."

"What do you know about those men who were chasing Juan Doe? Is this too early? Is your wife giving you the evil eye as we speak?"

"My wife *invented* the evil eye. Has a patent pending on the damn thing. But she's my ex. Now she's giving the evil eye to a broker in Denver. Hang on a minute, will you, and I'll see if I can find some pants around here." He put the phone down, and Sally could hear the imprecise sounds of his house: footsteps on a hardwood floor, morning birds through an open window, the distant barking of a dog. "Okay, I'm back. You do know this is a holiday, don't you?"

"Not for me. The store's open as usual today. We're having sort of a festival in town this week. Lots of shopping going on, I hope."

"I'm off."

"Pardon?"

"Work. I'm off. Government holiday. Usually I sleep in."

"I'm sorry, I'm not really like this. I don't call strangers at the crack of dawn and ask them for a favor. It's not my style. If you want, I can ring back at a more respectable hour."

"Let me ask you a question."

"Okay."

"These thugs you're talking about, why are they so important to you?"

"Because they're not important to anybody else."

"Come again?"

"Forgive me, Mr. Surry—"

"Leigh."

"Forgive me, Leigh, if I assume that the government isn't going to expend a lot of resources in bringing these men to justice. One more dead alien doesn't matter to anyone. Somebody's got to care."

"And that somebody's you?"

"Looks that way. Have you ever played musical chairs?"

"It's been awhile, but yeah, I know the game."

"The tune stopped and I was the only one left standing. So I get the job of caring about Juan Doe when no one else does."

"Is that how it is? Well, you're right when you say that Johnny Law isn't about to waste any officers in the pursuit of whoever Ms. Kobayashi saw out there on the highway. There's no evidence that a crime was committed."

"I think they might have killed him had I not done the job for them."

"It wasn't your fault."

"Then why does it feel that way?"

"Because that's how it works. I wish that I could . . . I don't know. Never mind. But like I told you yesterday, certain groups of sickos get their nationalism kicks by laying traps out at the water stations. They're trying to send a message back to Mexico."

"You mean don't come up here because we'll cut your heads off?"

"Something like that."

"That's not right."

"Welcome to the real world."

Sally swallowed her next words before they stung a man she hardly knew. Strangely, the longer she abided with the knowledge of what happened out there, the more prominent it became, fused between the seconds of her day like mortar between bricks. She couldn't turn her thoughts without running into it. And that was beginning to irritate her. "Listen. I know there's nothing I can really do to help. I'm sure this is just my guilt getting the better of me, trying to reset the silverware after the dinner guests have all left. That happened to me once. I hosted a party, and it was a flop, and that night after everyone was gone, I stood in my dining room arranging all the flatware according to perfect table etiquette, like that would turn back the clock and make me a winning hostess. It doesn't work that way. I know. But I need to learn about these men, Leigh, and you're the best shot I've got. So what do you say?"

Silence while he considered. Then: "Did I mention that I'm off work today?"

"Does that mean you're not going to help me?"

"No, it means I have nothing better to do. If I spend too much time alone in my house with only my roommate Francine for company, I get so bored I almost start cleaning. And that's the last thing I want to do on my day off."

"Is Francine the dog?"

"How do you know that?"

"I'm psychic."

"Does that mean you're charging me three-ninety-nine per minute for this phone call?"

Despite her irascible mood, Sally laughed.

"Tell you what," Leigh said. "I'll get myself together and run a few errands. After that I'll take a drive over to Fresh Waters. I hear they've got some good shopping over there."

"Are you in the market for a pair of loafers? I could use the business."

"Do you sell hiking boots?"

"Will that be cash or credit card?"

Now it was Leigh's turn to laugh. "I'll see you this afternoon."

"I'm penciling you in."

"And Sally?"

"Yes?"

"I'm bringing you a file."

She felt a tiny squirt of relief. "Thank you."

"Don't thank me. There's nothing in this file but seriously bad news."

Hours later, while she was in the Sole Mates storeroom searching for a size-five rope sandal, the door chime sounded—it never failed to ring when she was on the ladder; hell, she should climb the ladder more often and improve business—so she gave up her search and swept through the red curtain—

Dawn-Marie said, "Boo."

Sally drew back with a small intake of breath.

"Jumpy today, ain't we?" Dawn thrust something at her. "Here. This is from us to you."

Sally had her palm flat pressed against her chest. Why did she always do that when something scared her? It was such a silly, girly thing to do. "What is it?"

"In some parts of the world they call it a microphone."

"You know there's a fine line between comedienne and smartass."

Dawn smirked. "So true."

"Why do I want a micro . . . oh, right. You must have lost the bet. Nice Band-Aid, by the way." She returned to her ladder and her quest for the sandal.

"It's after twelve. Have you eaten? I was thinking I could bring us takeout and we could talk about what songs we're going to perform. You know, Americans call it takeout and the British call it takeaway. Why is that, do you think?"

"Shouldn't you be at work right now?"

"Are you changing the subject? I think maybe you're trying to avoid talking about our entry in Tuesday night's battle of the bands. But as long as we're subject-changing, have you had many customers this morning?"

"The usual. Old Mrs. Buckley demanded that I measure her feet again, even though they've been the same size since she was our fifth-grade math teacher. I think she'll be in a nursing home before long, poor thing. And the highway patrol called to say I could come pick up the shoes at my convenience, at least what's left of them. I hate to see what condition they're in. Ah, here we go." She extracted the proper box and handed it down to Dawn. It was only then that she noticed she was a foot taller than her friend, thanks to the ladder. It was an unusual perspective. Ever since they were eight years old, Dawn had been what the kids called a beanpole. She'd always been at least a head taller than Sally. But now the elevations had changed. "You've been dyeing your hair."

"Only a shade or two. Why?"

"Your roots are showing."

"Yeah, so I'm a slacker in hair-dyeing and all other aspects of life. Not all of us were born with such a cutesy head of curls."

"Remember when we all decided to be redheads?"

"Ghastly, wasn't it?"

"And to answer your question, no, I haven't eaten, but I'm holding out. I think there's a tiny, all-but-nonexistent chance that I'm going to have lunch with a representative from planet Man."

Dawn plunged fingers into both of her ears and wiggled them vigorously, as if to clean them out. "Okay, say that again. It sounded like you said something about a lunch date. And Sally Jasper being on a date is, if I remember my Bible correctly, one of the signs of end times. Let me know so I can confess my sins and tell my boss to take this job and shove it."

Sally swept by her, tossing aside the curtain that divided the walk-in storage closet from the main showroom. "Don't bother asking for details, because there aren't any to divulge. I'll fill you in if anything happens worth talking about."

"I have only two questions, and then I shall bother you no more."

Sally went to the window and began fixing the display; she'd just sold the pair of rope sandals that had been so artfully arranged on a bed of sand-colored velvet. "Before you ask, I have a question of my own."

"Shoot."

"How did you sleep last night?"

Dawn quieted for a moment. "I didn't dream about it. But . . . but I stayed up late with Lex, telling him the story. Juan Doe looked right at me, Sal. I saw his eyes."

"But you're okay?"

"I guess. But it's iffy. *Y tu?*"

"Not so okay. So ask your questions and take my mind off it."

Dawn took the new sandals from the box when Sally motioned for them. "First, who is he?"

Sally considered playing dumb or fibbing, but today she didn't have space in her life for any games. All the empty slots of herself were taken up by thoughts of what had happened out there, with only the sun and the snakes to bear witness. "He happens to be Leigh Surry, the Immigrations agent from the highway patrol office yesterday."

Dawn blinked. "Who?"

"Is that your second question?"

"No, it's just . . . whatever. You just met the guy and . . . forget it." She shook it off. "My second question is, do you still remember the lyrics to 'Walk Like an Egyptian'?"

"I'm not singing in any band."

"But you have to."

"No."

"Annie is."

Sally looked up. "You're kidding."

Dawn held up three fingers. Then two. Then four, when it became obvious she was unsure as to the proper number. "Girl Scout's honor, or at least as close as I can manage."

"What did you do to convince her? Threaten her life?"

"Jaz really wants this to happen. You know she does.

Erin O'Rourke

Let's do it for Jaz the Gipper."

"I'm thrilled that Jaz wants to be part of a band, a part of anything. You know what a loner she is. I suppose she inherited that from me. Neither of us has ever felt like we truly fit in, except with you guys. But if she wants to perform live then there's always Dakota's band—"

"Jaz says Dakota's boys only play neo-punk. I have no idea what that is. But I do know that Jazmyn hates it. We raised her on Bruce Springsteen. I thought it'd be a rush to play that kind of thing with her in front of people."

"I'm sure it would be, but ever since you started doing stand-up, you get all kinds of practice at performing in front of people. Have you forgotten the Christmas program when I threw up?"

"You were twelve, for God's sake."

Chime! from the door.

Both women looked over.

Leigh Surry stood on the threshold, hand on the knob. He wore a rugged green sport coat and khaki pants. His dark wavy hair brushed his collar, a little too long to be considered proper for a man of his age—forty?—but boyishly charming.

He said, "Am I too early?"

"You're just in time to save me," Sally told him. "This strange woman here was in the middle of making me a shady offer."

Dawn tossed up her hands. "Shady? There's nothing shady about it. It would be so fun, Sal." She fired a smile at Leigh. "Howdy."

"Uh, hi."

"You're with the Immigration services, right?"

"Yep."

"Deport anyone this morning?"

96

"No. But it's been a slow day."

"Could you do a girl a favor, Mr. Surry?"

He looked uncertain. "Sure."

"Will you please tell my friend here how exciting it would be, not to mention how much the town would enjoy it, if she joined me and my band onstage Tuesday night to play a little rowdy music."

Sally snatched the empty box away from her and tromped across the room. "Dawn, please."

Leigh came fully into the store and let the door close behind him. "I . . . I'm not sure I know what you're talking about."

"I'm talking about rock music, country music, and all musics in between. I'm talking about Sally being lead vocal in a band. Personally I think that kind of publicity would do wonders for her sales here at the store, and I was wondering if you could help encourage her."

"Well, that does sort of sound interesting."

"So you'd buy a ticket then?"

"Yeah, I guess. Of course my social life on Tuesday nights isn't much to speak of . . ."

"See there?" Dawn looked at Sally but pointed at Leigh. "Already got your first groupie. What do you say, Sal, will you please just come over tonight and give it a try? Alex has got a karaoke machine. If you totally suck then you don't have to do it. Sound good?"

"Sounds like now it's two against one." She blazed Leigh with her eyes.

He held up his hands in mute defense.

"A trial, Sal, that's all I'm asking. No obligation. Money back guarantee and all that crap. Come tonight. I will attach this very microphone to the karaoke machine. You sing as the spirit moves you, and then if you puke like you did

97

when we were kids, if you even sense that puking might be a possibility, we can shelve this pipe dream and get on with our humdrum lives. So what say you, woman?"

Leigh looked back and forth between them. His gaze settled on Sally.

What's he thinking? she wondered. *That I'm wishy-washy and no fun?*

"Sal, the polar ice caps melt faster."

Looking right at her, Leigh said, "I'd buy a front-row seat to a show like that."

"There you have it," Dawn said, sounding more like a car salesman every time she opened her mouth. "Let's hear it, then. It's nut-crunching time, as the Marines say. Step up or shut up. Will you or will you not attend our jam session tonight?"

Sally didn't know what to say.

Dawn held out the microphone, waiting for her to accept or decline it.

"You may be the only man I know," Sally said, "who doesn't like beer."

Leigh saluted her with his glass of lemonade. "There's a story behind that. But it involves my old man and what he did when he came home drunk, so I assure you that it's much too heavy for a first date."

"Is that what this is?"

"I don't know. We're sitting in a restaurant, I'm planning on paying the bill, and I'm wearing clean socks. For me, that qualifies."

Sally briefly looked away from him, scanning the other lunch patrons. The Cheshire Grin was busier than usual for a Monday, with most of the customers being folks she didn't recognize, out-of-towners here for the Indian art exhibit or maybe the Arizona Quilters annual show. They all seemed so normal. Sally felt detached from her surroundings in an unfamiliar way. "So how long have you been with the INS?" she asked to keep herself grounded.

He wiped the moisture from his lips. "Name's changed. Immigration and Naturalization has been incorporated into the Department of Homeland Security. Since it was created a few years back, DHS has created, disbanded, and reorganized dozens of government agencies. I can't keep 'em all straight anymore. Technically I work for the Bureau of Immigration and Customs Enforcement, or the ICE. One of the many components of the ICE is Immigration Investigations. I'm a criminal investigator. Sort of like being a plainclothes policeman."

"You're a cop?"

"Shameful, isn't it? When I was seventeen I hated cops."

"You have a badge?"

"Why do I get the feeling this makes you nervous?"

"I just . . . good question. One minute I'm sitting here with a pencil-pusher from some stuffy office that processes green cards, and then next minute you're a detective."

"It's better than a detective."

"Oh?"

"Officially I'm a special agent."

Sally raised her eyebrows. "Like the CIA?"

"No, that's *secret* agent." He grinned but tried to hide it behind his glass.

"So like the FBI then."

"More or less. We go after the people operating alien-smuggling rings, like those boats you hear about full of starved Chinese nationals. We also investigate document counterfeiting, immigration benefit fraud, and alien gangs and terrorism."

"Do you carry a gun?"

"Everybody asks that. And the answer is that we're trained in everything from constitutional law to a course called Shotgun Safety and Judgment. So, yeah, when I'm working they make me carry a sidearm."

"But not today."

"Like I said, this is a holiday."

"Have you ever shot at anyone?"

"I've never even drawn my weapon in the line of duty. I like it that way. Do we have to talk about this?"

"Yes. Why did Captain Iqui call you in to talk with us yesterday? Consoling three blubbering women doesn't sound like it would be in a special agent's job description."

"First of all, I don't recall any blubbering. Secondly, what happened out there might have fallen under the jurisdiction of the ICE, so the captain was doing everything by the book just to make sure."

Sally noticed, quite randomly, that Leigh Surry had nice nails. Men's cuticles were usually a wreck.

"And as it turns out," he said, "the captain was right, almost."

"Almost?"

"No crime was committed, but I think those men intended otherwise, just like you said. Had they caught up with Juan Doe, we probably never would have seen him again."

"They would have killed him?"

Leigh thought about it for a moment. "Immigration Investigations also works *for* the immigrants, not just against them. Take cases of involuntary servitude and forced prostitution. These are getting more common all the time. Someone pays to import women from Eastern Europe, Asia, or South America, and then turns them into slaves or call girls. We bust those people. Then there are the cases of the right-wing radicals who hunt immigrants like prey."

"The men Anne saw. That's what they were doing?"

"I couldn't swear on it, but yeah, I think so."

"Who were they?"

"Why does it matter so much to you?"

"Because it's got to matter to somebody. Haven't I answered that question already? Where's the file?"

"In my car."

"I need to get back to work. May I take it?"

"The papers in there aren't public records. I can't let you borrow them."

"So sit there in the shop with me while I read. Look over my shoulder. Put me under surveillance. Handcuff the thing to your wrist so I won't steal it. Come on, Leigh, if you were that worried about breaking the rules, you wouldn't have brought the file in the first place."

"It got me lunch with you, didn't it?"

"That's the only reason you agreed?"

"Do you want dessert?"

"No, I want you to level with me. What's in this for you? Why are you doing it?"

He glanced at his glass, but it was empty of everything but a few ice cubes, so he couldn't find the distraction he apparently sought. He had no choice but to look her in the eyes. "I want you to know I'm strange."

"Join the club. You don't know strange until you've spent a little time with my friends." Then she reconsidered. "What do you mean by strange?"

"The reason I do what I do . . . why I took this job . . . it's not the standard philosophy."

"You're not out there righting wrongs just on general principles?"

He leaned forward on the table for the first time. As the distance between them closed, his voice softened, and the instant intimacy this established caught Sally unprepared. "Do you want to hear a story? I don't know why I'm telling you this, but would you like to get a piece of my admittedly atypical worldview?"

"Yes." She was, she realized, interested in nothing else.

"I guess it goes something like this. The Navajo have a word, *hózh'q*, and there's really no adequate English description. To Anglo eyes, beauty is something on the surface, an ornamental thing, nice to observe but not as important to civilization as economics, stability, and achievement. But to the Navajo, the concept is reversed. Beauty isn't secondary, but fundamental to civilization. It's not an ideal that exists only on the surface. *Hózh'q* is beauty that involves the observer as much as the object that is observed. It's a way of life, in which all things are connected to form a beautiful whole. Everything else is but a smaller piece of that whole. A Navajo elder told that to me a long time ago, and it changed everything. Americans have it all backwards. Beauty isn't a fringe benefit of life, something we get to enjoy during our leisure time. Our careers and cars and legislation are as important to *hózh'q* as our paintings and our ballet recitals."

Sally could not begin to construct an adequate response.

"*Hózh'q* begins with people," he said. "The ICE deals with crimes against people. That's why I brought you the file, Sally. Because you want to help people you don't even know."

"I wish it were so noble. Actually I want to beat the bad guys to a pulp." She nudged a finger at her purse, from which the microphone jutted like a magic wand waiting to be called into action. "At the same time, I have to practice my Janis Joplin. Can't wait to see which activity will be the first to blow up in my face."

Chapter Seven

"Incoming!"

Dawn pounded the sticks across the drum heads like hard rain striking a series of puddles. She smote the cymbal as if trying to leave a dent. She hollered again, whipped her hair around her head in imitation of all the drummers she'd ever seen, and drove the sticks back across the drum array, ending with another jarring cymbal explosion.

"God, that's obnoxious," she said to herself. "I'm setting my own teeth on edge here."

Dakota laughed.

"You find my lack of rhythm funny?"

With the hand that wasn't encased in a plastic cast, Dakota gripped the buzzing cymbal to cease its ringing. "You're not so bad. You'll get the hang of it. Like everything else good in life, it just takes practice." He was young and blond and cute as hell, at least if you were into lean country-boy bodies pressing against the white cotton of their T-shirts. "Just don't worry about anything fancy. What you just did there? Forget about it. No tricks. No drum rolls. Just keep it—"

"Keep it simple, stupid. Yes, I know." She worked the foot pedal a few times, causing the bass drum to send little shockwaves through the garage. "You know something, Dak?"

"What?"

"This is fun."

He grinned. "Just wait till you get up there in front of people. Then fun becomes scary."

"People I can handle. It's embarrassing Jazmyn that I'm worried about. I don't want us senior citizens doing anything to make her ashamed. What time is it?"

"Almost eight."

"We've been at this for four hours?"

"I think your husband doesn't like me."

"Why? Because you're hogging up all my time? He can fend for himself for awhile. Contrary to local lore, he does indeed know how to operate the microwave. Although all those dials on the stove shall forever confuse him." She kept her foot moving: *boom-boom-boom!* She'd quickly learned the hardest part about playing percussion was maintaining a steady beat with her foot while her hands carried on with other, differing tempos. It was like when they were kids and tried that old stunt of simultaneously rubbing your belly and tapping your head. And Dawn-Marie had never been the most coordinated chick in the henhouse. "Okay, let me try again, at least one more time before we call it a night. Can you turn the music back on? I want to see if I can keep up."

"My pleasure." He reached over and pressed *PLAY*.

Upstairs in Jazmyn's room, Anne lifted her fingers from the keys and stretched. Over the course of the last few hours she'd tried her hand at a dozen numbers from a variety of songbooks—mainly stadium rock from the seventies and hair-band power ballads, but also a sprinkle of bluegrass and something Jazmyn referred to as *ska*. To Anne, ska sounded like a term from ancient Egyptian metaphysics, or the name of a character in one of the sci-fi novels that Barry liked to read. Each generation, she noted, added to the English lexicon before growing old. She tried to think of a word her own peer group had coined. . . .

"Mother?"

"Hmmm?"

Jazmyn rifled through the stacks of sheet music. "Do you think we should go with country or rock or pop or what?"

"We only have to play a single song, correct?"

"Yeah."

"Then I suggest we find something that we all enjoy, regardless of genre. It must be fairly simple, not to mention entertaining. We're walking a very fine line as it is, so we should take pains to keep the audience pleased. Let's select a number that we're sure they'll enjoy."

"Modern or classic?"

"Consider the listeners. This week's festival is a family-oriented event. Granted, there will certainly be young people in attendance specifically to watch the battle of the bands, but it won't be your typical concert crowd. If we play something from the current top forty, we're likely to overlook a large percentage of the audience."

"But if we play an oldie, like from the fifties or something, then the kids won't get it, and we need them, too."

"Agreed. Conclusion?"

Jazmyn thought about it, assuming that distant look that said she was forming pictures in her mind. Anne was drawn to that look. It spoke of imagination, an underlying depth that other girls Jazmyn's age didn't bother exploring. In so many ways, Jaz defied her demographic. She could knit and arm wrestle with equal proficiency. Each of her three mothers possessed her own set of talents, hobbies, and desires, and they had passed these gifts to Jazmyn, in whose

mind and body they'd been distilled and—in ways—per-
fected. From Dawn she'd learned a brazen self-confidence
that helped her to shine when meeting new people and in-
teracting with strangers, but in her moments of quiet intro-
spection, she was Anne through and through.

Anne saw this, saw herself, and was warmed by it.

"I've got it," Jazmyn said with a snap of her fingers.

"You *have* it."

"Yeah. I have it. Something not too old, not too new.
Upbeat but not too complicated."

"A crowd-pleaser, then?"

"Definitely." She hunted through her reams of music. "I
know it's in here somewhere."

Anne let her search for a few seconds, then said, "Dakota really likes you."

Jazmyn shrugged.

"I admit that I was displeased with him for awhile after
his encounter with the police, but I suppose boys have been
trying to pass fake IDs for as long as there have been laws
requiring them. He redeemed himself in my eyes by assisting the police with their investigation of the forgers. At
any rate, I believe he likes you. At least that's my observation. There are certain signs."

"He hardly speaks to me."

"That's one of the signs."

"I don't know. He's shy. I don't think he's my type."

"Is shy so bad?"

"Girls like gutsy guys, Mother. Dakota's a hottie, but he
can't crow."

"Crow?"

Without warning, Jaz threw back her head and cawed
loudly. The sound that issued from her throat was a harsh
lusty raven noise that no doubt carried throughout the

house and into the yard beyond. Then she looked squarely at Anne. "To crow. A verb meaning making a sound from the pit of your soul that basically tells the world to kiss your—"

"I get the point."

Jaz grinned like an elf and went back to her sheet music.

Perhaps that's what is missing from my life, Anne thought. *A good long crow.*

"Ah-ha!" Jaz whipped out three pages and flung them, so that they wafted through the air like drifting leaves. One of them settled atop Anne's digital keyboard.

She picked it up. Studied it. Nodded. "I think this will do nicely."

"Hey."

"Yes?"

"Do you really think he does?"

Anne gave her a conspirator's smile. "He's no expert flirter, but he watches you."

The door opened suddenly. Sally stood there with a mass of papers clutched to her chest. "We've got a problem."

"We *have* a problem," Jazmyn said.

As soon as Jazmyn left to give Dakota a ride home, Sally turned over the top page.

"What is that?" Dawn asked. "A graph?"

"It's from a grad student's thesis, out of the file Leigh gave me. His office compiled it as part of a comprehensive study of the causes and effects of illegal Mexican immigration. Like why it happens in the first place, what makes them want to get here so badly, how they go about doing it, and what happens when they arrive. What's their success rate for establishing a decent lifestyle once they're here?

How many of them end up on welfare or destitute or dead? Do they enrich society or detract from it? It's all here. Everything."

"What you're telling me is that you haven't been spending all this time working on your singing voice."

"People are dying because of this, Dawn. It's like a war. Both sides believe in a different cause, and America is the battlefield. Millions of dollars are being spent. Families are being torn apart. Crimes are being committed. And nobody knows."

"Or cares."

"Here, look at this. See this first comparison? That's the number of jobs provided to Mexicans by American companies in Mexico. Beside it is the number of jobs worked by Mexican-Americans here in the U.S., and the next column shows the pay rates."

"It only stands to reason," Anne said, "that employees in Mexico will earn less in wages than those here. It's all a matter of the economy."

"True, but look at the third column. That's the poverty level in Mexico. And the fourth column represents the amount of dollars those companies put into the Mexican economy. As you can see, the U.S. corporations are paying workers in Mexico slave wages for products their countrymen will never have access to, and to make it worse, they're not spending much money inside the country, meaning that they contribute absolutely nothing to support the economic livelihood."

"Damn leeches," Dawn said.

Anne reached over and forced Sally to lower the paper. "You can continue with this diatribe until you're blue in the face, but there's nothing we can do about it. If you'd like, I could begin quoting you facts about the evils of the death penalty and conclude with a rousing call to arms against capital punishment, but we would still be sitting here in Jazmyn's room when I finished, death row would still exist, and the world would move on."

"I'm not suggesting we start boycotting these companies or firebombing them."

"So?"

"Bear with me, I'm getting there. I just had to get that off my chest. The United States is running that country into the ground when we're rich enough to save them, but that's not my point. Maybe I'll fight that battle in my next life." She'd dog-eared certain pages, permitting her to move quickly to the salient issue. "One section of this huge report deals with the plight of the immigrants as they're crossing over. Certain groups are making a lot of noise about tighter border control. They want tighter trade restrictions. And they want armed patrolmen constantly buzzing along the border with orders to shoot to kill."

Dawn frowned. "Isn't that a little extreme? Why not just bag 'em up and ship 'em back?"

"Because the Mexicans are a danger to the fabric of American culture. They should be considered an enemy as dangerous as terrorist organizations. They pollute our society with their language. Already they've made white people a minority in Texas and California and even here in Arizona. Spanish will eventually pass English as the country's dominant language. Hard-working white people are losing jobs to Mexicans willing to work for less. Unions are suffering. Crimes are increasing, because we all know that Mexicans are rapists and thieves. Our daughters aren't safe, our jobs aren't safe. Let's not worry about men with missiles from the Middle East because we're already being destroyed by scum from the inside."

110

"Always there have been men who think that way," Anne said. "All of the statements you just made comprise the truth for many people in this country. But as sad and pathetic as that may be, people have always held such beliefs throughout history. There will always be bigots, Sal. There will always be ignorance."

"Granted. But I still haven't made my point."

"Can I get anyone a cup of coffee?" Dawn asked. "Personally there's some cherry cheesecake down in the fridge that's really calling my name."

Sally ignored her, jumping to the next group of marked pages. "To some people, prejudice is just a philosophy, but to others it's a plan of action. I give you the Sonora Partisans." She placed a single page flat on Jazmyn's bed.

Paperclipped to one edge was the picture of a flag with a snake sewn on it.

"That's them," Anne whispered.

"They've been around for almost ten years now. The Sonora Partisans. They've taken it upon themselves to assist the Border Patrol, their methods ranging from letters to Arizona congressmen to what they call *capture and coerce*. They forcibly return captive immigrants to Mexico. But only after beating them half to death as a warning to others."

"Jesus, what about the cops?" Dawn said, waving her drumsticks for emphasis. "What the hell are the police doing about these guys? You can't just go around beating people up and getting away with it." Then she thought about it. "Can you?"

"The Partisans are patriots," Sally said. "They support their communities, donate money to schools, and probably have supporters in the Border Patrol. Eight months ago somebody found a Mexican national who'd been dragged behind a pickup. The man died. No charges were ever filed. Last year alone, three bodies were discovered in the desert between Highway 86 and the Mexican line. The report says they were in various states of decomposition. They find a lot of corpses out there, because the desert kills way too many aliens who try to cross it, but these bodies had signs of physical injury. From things like knives."

"And these assholes are responsible?"

"One of their members did time for assault. Another has links to a radical militia group from Idaho. One has ties to something called the Aryan Brotherhood."

"How do you know all of this creepy stuff?"

"Leigh Surrey's department conducted an investigation. It's all here."

"And these were the ones chasing Juan Doe?"

"Yes. They're based in Maxon. Or at least their leader is."

"Their leader? You actually know who's in charge of these freaks?"

Sally had been waiting for this. She'd already stared at the picture for quite some time, writing its details in her memory. She had never had an enemy before, other than the brief time she'd hated God for taking Tatyana and that didn't count since you couldn't make an enemy of someone who refused to do anything but love you. But this guy . . . "I not only know his name, I have his photograph." She placed it face-up on the bed.

Anne looked away.

In the picture, he was turned to the side, so that his lean profile was cast against a distant mesa. His nose was hooked like a weapon, but other than this facial anomaly, he was handsome. His cheeks were burnished from the sun and his eyes bright, lively even. He might have been fifty years old but fit, likely able to hold his own in the games of touch football he played with his sons and their college friends on Sunday afternoon. He had an old canvas satchel over his shoulder and a leather-bound book in his hand. He seemed about to set off down a rocky trail into the badlands, a hiker or explorer out for a day in the desert.

"He's a metallurgist by trade, but also a fairly talented amateur archaeologist. His specialty is finding and cataloguing relics of the Southwest. His name is Isadore Presper."

"I need some of that cheesecake now," Dawn said.

Anne picked up the photo by its corner, as if it were painted in acid. "This is the one. I saw him out there. His eyes. The chain around his neck. Isadore Presper."

"Screwy name, if you ask me. Here, let me see that." Dawn snatched the picture away. After a moment she tapped it with the tip of her stick. "You know, I really can't see this man dragging anyone behind a truck. He looks too . . . I don't know, educated."

"I'm still not certain I see your intention here," Anne said. "Are you wanting us to find evidence of this man's guilt? Are we trying to put him in jail?"

"No, no, nothing so dramatic as that, I'm afraid. I wouldn't know where to start on a project like that. I just sell shoes. I'm nobody's bounty hunter."

"Then what?"

A pause. Then: "I want to go out to the water stations and help those people."

Anne and Dawn exchanged looks: *Pardon our loco friend.*

"I'm serious. I want to do everything I can to make sure those desert runners make it to safety. I want to keep them from being tied to pickup bumpers. I want to give them every chance to stay alive and to get their families here. No one should be treated like game to be hunted by safari guides like Isadore Presper."

Anne touched Sally's hand. "If they want to enter this country, they need to take the proper legal action. Anything we do to assist them outside the legal parameters is unlawful."

"But proper legal action doesn't work. The truth is that those people, the runners, they're coming. It may not be lawful, but they're coming anyway. And if the Partisans are working against them, then someone needs to be working *for* them."

"There are other means of helping them."

"Oh, like calling my state representative? Writing a letter to the editor? Sorry, Annie, but I think I'm beyond all that now. I have a debt to pay. Getting an op-ed piece in the *Fresh Waters Trumpet* isn't going to do Juan Doe a damn bit of good."

"Juan Doe is dead, Sally."

"Really? Thanks for the news flash. I wasn't aware."

Anne withdrew her hand.

"I'm sorry." Sally exhaled. "You know I didn't mean that. But I need this. Maybe it's guilt, maybe it's just the desire to get off my butt finally and make a difference. I've spent the last sixteen years telling Jazmyn to leave her mark, stand up for what she believes in, always do the right thing, blah blah blah, and I think that's been sort of hypocritical on my part. Those runners out there need help."

Dawn said, "You're talking about smuggling people."

"Right now I'm only talking about making sure those water stations contain adequate supplies. And making sure that no one is using them to set up an ambush."

"And what if someone is lying in wait? Then what? What if Presper and his Nazi henchmen are out there with their billy clubs? Sure, I carry a can of pepper spray just like the next girl, but it has its limits."

"I haven't thought that far ahead."

"Get to thinking."

"Do you realize the risk involved?" Anne asked. "If the Partisans and those like them are half as dangerous as you claim, they'll feel little compunction about dealing with anyone they feel to be meddling in their business."

"I've considered that."

"And?"

"And I never thought I had much in the way of courage. But that's what it is, courage, going through with something even though you're afraid. Up until now, the bravest thing I've done is wear a two-piece to the swimming pool last summer."

Dawn shook her head. "Not true. That day in the rain out at Scorpion City all those years ago, you had balls of cast iron."

"We were kids then. Girls outgrow their balls."

"So you're saying that you want your balls back?"

Sally smiled, but only with effort. "Something like that."

"And when are you proposing to go through with this daredevil scheme?"

"I don't want to wait."

"Okay."

"Do you two have plans for tonight?"

Anne got up and went to the window. The yellow leaves of a palo verde tree made scratching noises against the glass, as if something outside were trying to get in. "We promised Jaz we'd form this band and play. The concert is tomorrow. We have less than twenty-four hours to practice. The thought of appearing onstage at the Ampi with so little rehearsal time is preposterous. I only agreed because

Trevor won't let me say no. However, if we spend our evening driving across the sand and setting up oases for refugees who may or may not make use of them, then I seriously doubt our ability to avoid disgrace at tomorrow's competition. We must practice even to sound minimally musical."

"You and Jaz are better than any other two performers who will be at the Ampi," Sally told her. "Granted, Dawn and I could use some pointers—"

"You don't even know what song we've selected."

"Then tell me now so I can start learning the lyrics." Sally stood up and went to Anne's side. Outside the leaves of the palo verde looked made of filigreed gold in the sun. Sally brushed an errant hair from Anne's cheek. "I don't know where I got these sudden guts. First the band, now the water stations. Give me time and I might lead a charge across the beaches of Normandy. But if I don't follow through, if I don't go out there tonight and see if I can help those runners, then I never will. I'll get up tomorrow and act like nothing ever happened, and Juan Doe will go on being dead for no reason. Do you understand what I'm feeling here? It's easy to be a decent human being. It's a passive state and doesn't require much except that you're kind to strangers and give blood on Tuesday afternoons. But it's hard taking the next step. And scary. But that next step is where heroes live. And those runners need a hero. So I'm going to leave now and drive to the shop and take from the shelves the best pair of cross-trainers I can find, and they're going to lead me out there into the sand. And then we'll see what happens next."

Anne kept staring from the window. Half a minute later, she wove her fingers into Sally's and held on, a tacit agreement that Sally would not be alone in her night journey.

"Well," Dawn said after awhile. "I have only one more

thing to say to all of this."

Sally looked at her and waited.

"Reason thirty-two. Cucumbers won't ask to have sex when your nails are wet."

They made plans to go that night.

Chapter Eight

Dawn hated the dark.

She rode in the backseat of her own SUV, eyes straight ahead because she could see nothing through the windows. Her nyctalopia was such that, at night, she could discern only very bright lights, and even these disappeared if they moved from her central field of vision. For the most part, she was completely sightless. As they drove south and passed oncoming cars, the headlights appeared as faint as fireflies. She knew the dashboard glow was green because someone had said so, but all she could see of the panel instruments was a dim blur.

Her secret was this: the darkness terrified her.

You'd think that after a lifetime of night-blindness she would have gotten a grip on it; Stevie Wonder seemed to do okay. But she still felt the bolts of fear that had charged her small body when she was young. Back then, turn out the light at bedtime and she'd go crazy, a cornered animal, the occasional victim of hyperventilation when she lost control. She'd read a lot about it since then. Conducted sessions of self-psychology. Tried Buddhist meditation. But all she got was her hand groping for the lamp every night. Alex, God bless him, had learned to sleep with the light on.

"Are we there yet?" she asked. Her oldest defense: humor.

"No," Anne said. She was driving. Sally had refused on the grounds that she was the one with the map from Leigh Surry's file, and someone had to be the navigator. But Dawn suspected that Sally wanted to avoid the steering wheel at all costs. "We haven't even left the main highway yet."

"Yeah, I can tell. Like the princess and the pea, I can feel the road with my ass. What's happening right now? Sal, what's the map say?"

"Surry's people have marked roughly where the primary water stations are located. To get to the nearest one, we've got to drive at least another forty miles south, and then get out."

"Get out. Like, walk, you mean."

"I already explained this to you. You know we're walking a little ways."

"How far is a little ways?"

"About three miles, give or take."

"Sounds like a hell of a fun trip to me."

"I told you not to come. Stop complaining."

"I know what you told me, Captain Jasper, and I immediately told you to stick your concern where el suno don't shine-o. Complaining is to me what whistling is to others. I do it when I get nervous."

Lex had scratched his nose when she told him she was taking a drive. He'd spent a long time at it, scratching and scratching, probably trying to decide who had tricked him into marrying such a total spaz. He loved his hot rods and his tools and his sons. Nothing else seemed to make sense to him, least of all his madcap wife. But before Dawn left, Alex pulled her into a hug, and this surprised and elated her so much that she almost said to hell with it and stayed. And she would have, if not for a promise she'd made to Tatyana,

119

vowing to keep Sally safe and to keep Anne from being too serious.

Miles passed under the tires.

She imagined the journey she couldn't see. The soaptree yucca plants along the shoulder of the road. The wind-carved arroyos full of night predators and the spirits of dead Indians. And high overhead, something she had never witnessed: a starry sky. The stars were a myth to her. She assumed they existed only because so many people talked about them and Anne's husband made a living by studying them. But there was a word Dawn loved—chimera—and that's what the stars were to her. A chimera. An unlikely but enticing dream. A notion that somewhere beyond the unpierceable darkness burned the light of ancient suns.

She felt the continued hum of the highway beneath her.

"Are we there yet?"

Sally clicked on her flashlight and led them away from the car. Already the air had shed most of the day's heat, so she was glad she'd tied the denim shirt around her waist, just in case she needed it. More importantly, she was wearing her backpack. Anne and Dawn both wore similar rigs. The packs were stuffed with saltine crackers, protein bars, matches, water, and socks. They'd chipped in and bought a hundred bucks' worth of supplies. Sally had learned one thing after having the pack slung on her back for only three minutes: water weighed a ton.

"Campers have always confounded me," Dawn said.

Sally didn't take the bait, just kept walking, listening to the bits of sand crunch beneath her new white shoes.

"Why anyone would intentionally strap gear to their back and traipse out into the wilderness is beyond me. I'm all for getting back to nature, but what's so bad about an

RV and running water? That's all the camping this girl will ever need."

Sally panned the light across the ground, a hardpan expanse sprouting gristly bushes and a variety of cacti. Now that she considered it, there was no reason they couldn't drive the car out here. Dawn and Alex owned a 1957 Pontiac Chieftain. The Chieftain was a sport-utility vehicle long before anyone ever coined the term SUV and decided to market them to housewives. The car was a rugged ground-gobbler, restored by Alex's talented hand, and it should have been hauling them across this wasteland instead of sitting back there on the shoulder of the road.

"Here's an idea," Dawn said. "We can make a game of it. We can be famous explorers on a grand expedition to chart the deserts of the American West. How does that sound? Sally and I can be Lewis and Clark. Which I guess makes you Sacagawea, Annie."

"A Japanese Sacagawea," Anne mused. "How nice."

Their plan, such as it was, involved visiting three water stations before sunrise. The stations were placed dozens of miles apart in the middle of the trackless Sonora. Once they unloaded their packs at the first stop-off, they'd hoof it back to the Chieftain, drive to the next point, resupply themselves, and head back out. As far as social charity was concerned, it wasn't like they were walking the streets of Calcutta and dispensing medical supplies and bags of rice, nothing so grand as that, but Sally comforted herself with the thought that it was more than she'd been doing yesterday. Did it take Juan Doe's death to make her look beyond her own comfort zone?

". . . and if we run into any hostile natives out here," Dawn was saying, "then we can negotiate an unfair peace treaty with them, kill off half their population with smallpox, buy their land for a wagon load of pickled fish, and march them off to a reservation. How does that sound? You know, sometimes I'm embarrassed to be Caucasian. You know what I mean?"

Sally realized that Dawn was jabbering out of anxiety.

No point in trying to shut her up. Sally focused on the act of walking. Every so often she'd jab the flashlight's beam at her feet. Already her new cross-trainers with their air-cushioned soles and breathable weave were coated in a thin patina of dust. It was everywhere in the desert. You couldn't live within ten miles of a place like this without investing heavily in feather dusters; the stuff permeated your house, your clothes, your life. But at least her feet were comfortable. She kept up a determined pace, stopping only occasionally when someone needed to shift the weight of her backpack. The constellations appeared all at once, a fabulous painting across the heavens. The sky seemed without end.

Because there was nothing in front of her she might trip over, Sally was able to keep her eyes on the firmament while she walked. "Annie, which one is the North Star?"

"Mmmm, see Ursa Major there? The Big Dipper?"

"Uh, yeah, I think so. That's the only one I know on sight."

"Find the two stars in the bottom of the Dipper's pan."

"Okay."

"Now from these two pointer stars, draw an imaginary line to your right. That's Polaris. It isn't the brightest star, nor even a particularly impressive one. But it never moves."

"Ever?" Dawn asked.

"Mariners have used it for centuries to chart their way home. I've always found it comforting to know there's at least one constant in this universe."

"My hatred of Pap smears is a constant in this universe."

Three miles was longer than anybody imagined. Their shoulders began to chafe. Halfway there, Sally called a halt, pulled out the map, and consulted the GPS unit that Anne had brought along. Barry owned a surplus of gadgets such as this hand-held computer that was linked to a network of global-positioning satellites. With the touch of a button, Anne knew their precise coordinates and could steer their trek in the proper direction. Personally, Sally didn't know Mr. Longitude from Mr. Latitude and would not have been able to tell them apart had they invited her to tea at their home in Greenwich, England. For the millionth time in her life, she gave thanks for her friends.

Then they set off again.

Even without the cone of light in front of her, Sally could see fairly well, now that her eyes had adjusted. The stars rained down illumination. Sally imagined this was like walking on the moon. It even smelled rather moonlike, with the dust and mesquite. Sure, there wasn't a lot of mesquite growing on the moon but—

"We're almost there," Anne announced.

"Can you see it?" Dawn gave a tug of the line which ran from her hand to Anne's belt. The tether was actually a leash belonging to Caleb and Coy's black Labrador. "What's it look like?"

Anne said nothing. She touched Sally on the arm to indicate a slight turn in their trajectory. Sally altered course, and a few minutes later, a dark shape materialized in the gloom.

"Somebody say something."

It rose like a ghost ship from a foggy sea, a bulk made of shadow, shapeless and without sound. Sally felt a frission of apprehension. They were forty miles from the nearest town in the middle of no-man's-land. They were unarmed. They had four phones between them, but this did nothing to assuage Sally's trepidation. Here on the moon, all bets were off. Out beyond the reach of her flashlight, periodic animals called out—coyotes yipping at one another and rodents screeching as owls plucked them from the ground.

"I'm about half a second away from yanking the hell out of this leash."

"We're fine," Anne said softly. "I think we've arrived."

"It's about time. My lower back is ki—"

"Shhh." Sally felt the need for covertness, but couldn't say why. If some of Isadore Presper's goons were waiting out here . . .

Sally gave the word, and the three of them advanced.

The dark mass awaited them.

Whatever it was that had bestowed courage to Sally that day at the placer mine when they were kids, it rose again, and it warmed her. Twenty-five years ago a policeman had interviewed them. A big German named Horst. In his fading accent Horst had said something to her that Sally had never forgotten: *You are a very plucky girl. Pigtails must be antennas for bravery.*

She thought about this as she investigated the water station.

Ten or twelve fifty-gallon barrels stood on their ends, and one more lay on its side. Each was clearly marked *FRESH WATER* and *AGUA FRESCO*. The central barrels were lashed together with thick nylon straps. They formed a kind of cave, a recess in which a man might take shelter from the sun. Sally probed this hollow with her light.

"What is that?" Anne asked.

"What's what?" Dawn wanted to know.

"I saw it, too." Sally swept the corner with her light again—there. Something glittered in the sand.

Dawn gave a tug on the leash. "Is it alive?"

Sally dared to move closer. "No. Probably just junk. I'm not sure yet."

"What's this place look like?"

"There's a flag on top," Sally explained. "In the center of the water containers is a steel pole maybe fifteen or twenty feet tall. There's a big flag attached to it, probably so that people can see it from far away. Looks like it might be red, but I'm not sure. Hard to be certain in the dark."

"You're telling me."

Sally was near enough to see the footprints. Dozens of them marked the hard soil. Every time she moved the light, the shadows shifted, pulling back and lashing out in a disconcerting pattern. More footprints revealed themselves whenever the light dispelled another patch of darkness.

The coyotes sounded vaguely human when they chattered.

"Suckers are getting closer," Dawn observed.

Sally crouched and stabbed her light between the barrels. Lying there, half buried in the dirt, was a metallic object. "You two start unloading the stuff."

Dawn shrugged off her pack immediately. "My pleasure. Damn thing's about ready to break my back. Do we really need to do this three times tonight? Can't we just call it good at one of these places? And by the way, if I suddenly disappear, it's because those wild dogs out there have drug me off and eaten me."

"Dragged," Anne said.

"Yes, Mother."

Sally edged closer, so that now she was partially enclosed by the barrels. The smell was no different than elsewhere in the desert, earthy and unsullied by man, but here the evidence of man's intrusion was prominent. Small holes had been dug in the ground. The ruins of a campfire crumbled when Sally nudged them with the flashlight. Marks had been scratched on the barrels, symbols of those who had bivouacked here, as indecipherable as prehistoric cave-writings. Sally noted a torn strip of cloth, a few blackened matchsticks—and something else.

She brushed away the layer of dirt, revealing a locket on a silver chain.

From the other side of the barrels Anne said, "Trevor wouldn't believe I was out here doing this. I almost wish he could see me. One time he told me I needed a cause, a social issue to support. I said Ph.D. students have no time for causes. I suppose I was wrong."

Dawn was pulling boxes of saltines from her pack. "Annie, what's the official name for a group of coyotes?"

"A band, I believe. Why?"

"No reason."

Sally held the locket before her face. It was heart-shaped. It hung from a tarnished chain and was hinged along one side.

"How about snakes?"

"Snakes? Variously known as a nest, pit, or knot. Unless you're talking about rattlesnakes in particular, in which case they're called a rhumba."

"A what? Rhumba? Like something you do at a Latino dance club? Who names these things, anyway?"

Sally adjusted her position so that she was able to place the flashlight against her knees and free her hands to inspect the locket. Odd to find such an heirloom out here. Those who made use of this place didn't have the resources for adequate food and clothing, yet here was a piece of jewelry, as chintzy as it might have been. Carefully she pried open the cover.

"Here I am," Dawn said, "surrounded by a band of coyotes and a rhumba of rattlesnakes, and I'm as blind as whatever you call a shitload of bats."

Sally had expected to find a picture. Isn't that what lockets usually protected? But instead of a tiny snapshot of a child or a daguerreotype of an ancestor, there was a note neatly pressed into the locket's shallow bowl. A single word was written upon it: *LIBERTAD.*

Sally's command of the Spanish tongue was limited to asking for the bathroom and saying thank you. But Anne was proficient and had been teaching the language to Jazmyn for years now. Sally withdrew from the nook and offered the treasure to Anne without a word.

Anne had just finished wedging a box of strike-anywhere matches into a crevice between one of the barrels and a flat piece of sandstone. She trained her flashlight on the locket. "You found this?"

"Found what?" Dawn wanted to know. "God, I hope it's money."

"A pendant of some kind," Anne said. She held it up to the light. "It says *liberty.*"

Sally nodded to herself. She had guessed correctly.

"Liberty? What are you talking about?" Dawn used the leash as a belaying line, pulling herself toward Anne like a spelunker in a catacomb. "Will you two quit being so damn mysterious? You forget that I'm pretty much helpless out here, which is too much like being a man for my tastes. Describe what you found."

"It's a locket," Sally said, turning away and resuming her tour. "There's no picture inside, only the word liberty."

"Or *freedom,* if you prefer," Anne added.

"I don't get it. Why would anyone leave that behind?"

"I'm sure they didn't intend to do so. Obviously it was misplaced."

"Who do you think owned it?"

"One of the migrants, I imagine."

"Well, hell, finders keepers, right? That's what we always used to say."

"We used to say a lot of things."

"Ain't that the truth. Sal? Can we please go now? I've unloaded all my crap."

Sally was walking the perimeter. She didn't know what she expected to find. Tire tracks? Signs of a struggle? There was an itch in the center of her back and she realized this was intuition. She'd lived thirty-six years and never felt it, yet here it was, a gentle nudging along the middle of her spine, a hand that pressed her forward. She swung the light all around. There was nothing to see save a single bright desert marigold clinging stalwartly to the sand. She turned away, clicked off the light, and stared into the darkness. Miles from urban development, the land was shrouded in such stillness that it seemed surreal. The world had stopped and all that was left was Sally Jasper and a German-accented voice saying, *Pigtails must be antennas for bravery.*

"Sally, what's up? Did you get bitten by a rhumba?"

"I'm fine." Her words seemed to carry too far. "Let's head back to the car."

"Best suggestion I've heard all night."

The return trip was swifter, in part because their loads were considerably lighter, but also because Sally wasn't alone in her premonition that the night had yet to divulge its full story. Eighteen miles later they drove the Chieftain away from the highway and tested its off-road ability. Guided by satellites she couldn't see and an impulse she couldn't name, Sally led them to the second water station. This one was much like the first, except the flag was lying on the ground, its staff snapped like a broken bone. They left another deposit of water and bandages. Sally began to take heart because this drop-off was also a success, as they were assaulted by neither rhumbas nor bands nor flocks nor herds—she even laughed when Dawn told a joke about a priest and a dyslexic duck—but at the third station everything changed because that was where they found the body.

Chapter Nine

The man lay on his back between the barrels.

He was Mexican and young and blistered from the sun. He had lost much of his color in death, so that his skin looked no different than the dust. He wore cowboy boots so old and tape-repaired they must have been hand-me-downs from at least two previous owners. He was as skinny as a stick figure.

"DATFUG," Sally said.

Dawn stiffened. "What's wrong?"

"There's a . . . a person."

Dawn wet her lips. "I guess dead, right?"

Sally was at a loss. Up until now everything had gone so smoothly. She was getting her Mother Teresa fix by helping the needy and she was going to go home and enjoy a self-righteous sleep. But now her stomach began to tighten, and she was thankful there was nothing inside of her worth throwing up. She had seen only two dead bodies in her life. One was Juan Doe, though technically he hadn't been dead until later. Before that was Tatyana; the open casket was the worst idea in history, for now that image was part of the Tatyana portfolio Sally carried in her mind.

"Should I call someone?" Anne asked.

"I can't smell anything," Dawn said. "Is it a man or a woman?"

Sally kept the light fixed to the youthful face. "A man."

"There's no stink. He must not have been dead for very long. Otherwise the scavengers—"

"I'm calling." Anne slid a phone from its case on her hip.

Sally went closer and knelt over the body.

"Uh, Sal? I hear you moving around. You want to give me the play-by-play?"

"I just want to see if anything . . . happened. To him. Before he died."

"Right. The cause of death."

"I suppose so."

"Jesus, Annie, Sally is searching for signs of foul play. Suddenly I'm living a movie."

Sally moved the light around, looking for just such signs. She saw no knife gouges, no splotches of blood that were tell-tales of bullet holes. It occurred to her then that a change had taken place inside her. This moment of her life was different than those before it. A few hours ago there had been only the ordinary, and here was something else. There was selling shoes and there was examining corpses for exit wounds.

The man opened his eyes.

"Shit!" Sally recoiled, falling back on her butt and losing her grip on the light.

Dawn yelled when Sally crashed into her legs. Anne gasped and dropped the phone.

The flashlight rolled and threw lopsided yellow circles into the darkness. Sally groped for it without looking away from the now invisible figure between the barrels.

Dawn bent down and grabbed her. "Sally, what's going on?"

"He's alive."

"The hell you say."

Anne was the first to find a light. *Click.* A fresh spotlight appeared on the man.

He was sitting up. He was not moving to attack. He blinked and shielded his eyes.

Sally scrambled to her feet. She recovered her flashlight and swung its beam at him like a sword.

The man pulled deeper into the recess and drew his knees against his chest.

"What's he doing? Is he moving? Is he coming this way? What should I do?" Dawn had assumed a defensive posture, an awkward, bent-over stance that Sally would have found humorous under different circumstances. As it was, she hardly noticed.

"Take it easy," Sally said, though she wasn't sure if she was talking to Dawn or the Mexican or her own raging heart. Sweat already creased her shirt from all the walking, and now droplets of it appeared on her forehead and along the hollow of her neck. She could see by the wavering dance of her light that she was shaking. "Everybody just calm down."

Anne picked up her phone and put it to her ear. "Hello?"

"Annie, hang up."

"Why?"

Sally didn't look away from the man cowering beneath the barrels, though she felt Anne's black eyes searching her face, trying to find answers that the darkness wasn't revealing. "Just disconnect, okay? If the police come, they'll take him into custody, and I don't want that. At least not yet."

Anne complied without another word. She returned the phone to her belt.

Has their trust in me always been so blind? Sally wondered.

The Mexican spoke: *"Necesito agua, por favor."*

Anne said, "He wants—"

"I know what he wants." Even with her negligible grasp of the language, Sally understood, and she was already coming forward fearlessly with her canteen.

Someone had put holes in the barrels.

Anne noticed this as Sally offered her water to the stranger. The long, narrow rents along the bottom edges of the big drums looked to be the work of an ax or shovel or similar tool.

Sabotage.

So it was true. Groups of grown men actually tormented helpless immigrants. They perpetrated these little crimes in the name of their country or their god. And they were sick. If Anne's problem was that she always remembered who she was, then perhaps it was time to forget for awhile and see what the new her was capable of doing.

"Go slow," Sally said when the man tipped the bottle to his lips.

He drank deeply—too much so: he spit it up and bent over in a series of harsh coughs.

"Easy now." She touched his sun-burned shoulder and he didn't pull away. "Straighten up and let's try that again." She got him upright and used the sleeve of her denim shirt to pad the sweat from his forehead. "Not so much at once." She looked back at Anne.

Anne read the soulstrings between them before Sally spoke. She knew what was required of her. Barry liked to

say that Anne and her friends were precognitive, antici-
pating one another's needs, but Anne wasn't into metaphysics and wrote it off as simply knowing someone for so
long that they became predictable. Either way, she understood that Sally wanted her to translate.

"I'm a little out of practice," she said. But she came forward anyway, keeping the light squarely in front of her, as if
it were a ward against possible attack. She'd studied
Spanish for four years in high school and two semesters as
an undergrad. "What do you want me to say?"

"Tell him not to be afraid."

"No tenga miedo."

His eyes changed. All at once he was not alone. Anne
saw his face alter as he realized he was no longer among foreigners who spoke only in code.

"Tell him to take it slow with the water."

"Beba lentamente."

"Tell him we're here to save him."

Anne shot Sally a glance.

"We're here to what?" Dawn demanded. "Speak for
yourself, sister." Apparently Anne wasn't alone in her apprehension.

"Just tell him."

But Anne wasn't ready to relent quite yet. This was too
unSallylike to accept without discussion. "Are you planning
on taking him home and caring for him? Rather like a lost
puppy?"

"I haven't thought that far ahead yet. But I'm not
leaving him out here on his own."

"He has supplies now. He can easily make it to a city."

"And then what? They aren't going to roll out any red
carpet for him."

"He'll find work. They always do."

134

"That's not true and you know it. Please, Annie, stop arguing just for the sake of arguing and think about the opportunity we have here."

"Opportunity? To break the law by abetting an illegal alien?"

"We can either walk away, or we can get this man to safety."

"Safety in this case means breaking the law."

Sally had no response to this, but let the words hang in the air. During this exchange, both Dawn and the Mexican had looked back and forth between Anne and Sally, mouths shut but eyes alert. Now Dawn, perhaps sensing an impasse in the debate, squatted beside the Mexican and said in his general direction, "Howdy, I'm Dawn. *Buenas noches* and all that."

The man watched her over the lip of the canteen. Softly: *"Hola."*

"Hey, that means hello, doesn't it?" Dawn slapped her knee, proud of this bilingual feat. "Hell, I'll be working as a translator at the U.N. pretty soon. I wonder how you say 'I sure love your country's tequila. . . .' "

"Is this the right thing to do, Sally?" Anne asked. She couldn't remember the last time she'd done anything even slightly illegal, except breaking the speed limit, and then only by a little. Her mind was such that she was able to envision the ramifications of taking this man in, how she would have to explain things to Barry and Trevor, how they would respond, what Jazmyn would think and what the police would do if they caught wind of it. "If you believe in this, I'll do it. You know that. We may have to face up to it later. It may cost us. But I'll tell this man we're going to feed him, protect him, and smuggle him to a safe place, if you give the word."

Sally's eyes were fixed to the man's dilapidated boots. "The word is given."

Anne sighed and thought, *So be it.* What had Caesar supposedly said? The die is cast. Whatever happened next was up to providence. She met the stranger's gaze; he was wary, and his muscles twitched. She told him her name and that she and her friends had come to deliver provisions to the water station. She said he should eat a little and keep drinking so as to hydrate himself.

He interrupted and asked if she was going to turn him over to *la policía.*

She assured him that wasn't the case, and she saw that he caught the quick look she gave Sally. Plainly he knew they had discussed what to do with him. There was an intelligence in his narrow face that belied his ragamuffin state. Anne explained their intention to take him back with them, to give him a place to spend the night. As for what Sally would to do with him in the morning, Anne couldn't begin to guess. She had to trust that a plan was even now being developed behind her friend's suddenly secretive eyes.

Anne asked the man's name.

He hesitated only a moment. "Crespin." He took a sip of water and cleared his throat. "Crespin Onofre y Ramos."

"His name is Crespin," she announced to the others.

Though Dawn could see very little of what was transpiring, she had by now situated herself so that she was facing the man. When she extended her hand, she was more or less on target. "Pleased to meet you, Crespin. I'm Dawn. Welcome to America."

At this, Crespin's chapped lips parted in a smile, revealing teeth as white as soapstone.

They shook hands.

★ ★ ★ ★ ★

Sally brought him home and locked him in the garage.

They discussed it along the way. Dawn-Marie had Alex and the boys; Anne had Barry and Trevor. Explanations would be required from wives who showed up at three in the morning with ill-clad, unlawful aliens in tow. Anne said that Sally was the reasonable choice, and as usual her logic was bulletproof.

Sally had only Jazmyn to explain things to, and she was asleep when Sally got home. The girl roamed from one of her houses to the next, keeping rooms at all three and somehow managing not to be a spoiled brat from all the stuff that three mothers could supply. This arrangement had worked well for all concerned ever since Jaz was a baby, as it was a lot easier to buy diapers and bicycles and class rings when you split the bills three ways.

After checking on her daughter, Sally returned to the garage, where Crespin was waiting. Anne had spoken to him at length before she left, so Sally didn't have to go through the trouble of pantomiming instructions with her hands. Crespin knew he was to sleep on a cot in the garage, and he seemed devoutly appreciative of such lavish accommodations. Sally could've let him have the couch, but she wasn't about to set a stranger loose in her house, be he Mexican or Armenian or a long-standing member of the Mormon Tabernacle Choir. The garage was in effect a cage, as its doors could be locked from their opposite sides. Sally quickly unfolded the musty cot, put down a pillow and blanket from the linen closet, and as Crespin watched in silence, she added a bag of barbecue potato chips, two apples, and a carton of orange juice, pulp free.

This offering, too, amazed him.

"Don't get used to it," she said, though she knew he

couldn't understand her. "You're not likely to find much generosity in this country. Enjoy it while you can."

"*Gracias.*"

"Don't mention it. Do you speak any English at all?"

He held up his hand and put his thumb and index finger an inch apart.

Sally smirked. "Yeah. That's about the size of my Spanish." Standing this close to him was incentive to ask if he'd like to take a shower—he'd been running through the desert for days and smelled like it—but she figured that could wait till the morning. "But you can say work, right?"

"Work? *Sí.* I look for work." He said it almost perfectly. Obviously he'd practiced.

"Then work you shall. I've got a job for you."

"Job?" He cocked his head to the side.

Sally was struck by the sharpness of those eyes. Curiosity dwelled there, side by side with desperation, and the union of the two had a mesmerizing effect on her. "We'll talk about it tomorrow—*mañana*—when we have a translator. Until then, goodnight."

He nodded. "*Gracias tanto.*"

Sally went from the garage into her kitchen, careful to lock the door behind her. She showered and thought continuously about her fragile plan. She was not only harboring a man who was in this country illegally, she was intending to give him a job without worry about green cards and tax forms and other bothersome paperwork. The employment she had in mind for him didn't involve her shoe shop, but was something a bit more . . . she searched for the right word: Elusive? Shady? Completely kooky? Regardless, she was about to become just the type of person that Leigh Surry prosecuted. Could she pull it off without him finding out?

"Just like me to do something such as this," she said to herself as she toweled dry. "Finally meet an above-average guy and then you have to go and make him arrest you."

If she carried through with this scheme, she risked legal consequences, but she also stood to lose the chance for a relationship with a man who so far seemed to be what her mother would have called a Conditional Keeper; in other words, you keep him if he folds his own clothes and isn't embarrassed to buy tampons for you. Was Leigh such a man?

Were there such men?

"Somewhere," she said as she pulled on her robe. "Somewhere."

She double-checked the bolt on the garage door, looked in on Jazmyn a second time, and then lay in bed trying to remember the Navajo word for beauty that meant so much to Leigh. But, incongruously, the word that kept returning to her was the one from the locket—*libertad*—and she fell asleep an hour later thinking of nothing else.

Chapter Ten

At ten the next morning, Crespin Onofre y Ramos still occupied Sally's garage, although now he sat wide-eyed atop the deep-freeze while four senseless American women shouted at one another and occasionally banged a keyboard, bumped into a drum, sent a squall of static through an amplifier, and produced other, equally stressful noises.

"Will you please for once listen to what I'm saying?" Dawn pleaded.

"Will you please for once say something intelligent?" Sally fired back.

"Intelligent? What does that mean?"

"Mama, she means you're being a smart-aleck again."

"You stay out of this."

"I just hate to see you two fight. Can't we just rehearse?"

"Your mom and I have been fighting for decades, Jaz. The Arabs and Israelis have nothing on us. We've been fighting ever since that day in the fourth grade when she splattered Kool-Aid all over my new birthday outfit. So don't lecture us about fighting."

From her position behind the synthesizer, Anne said, "I called Rachel over at the Chamber of Commerce and got our names on the list for tonight's show. They tacked us on at the end. So we have less than twelve hours to pull ourselves together. May I suggest that we make an effort to get through the piece at least once?"

Sally pointed the microphone at Dawn. "I'm just saying she should try to take it easy over there. She doesn't have to be so fancy, just keep the beat. All I can hear are drums, drums, drums."

Dawn met the outthrust microphone with a similarly advanced drumstick. "You haven't even sang a single note yet!"

"Haven't sung," Anne said.

"Who gives a damn, Annie?" Dawn waved her sticks. "Musicians aren't noted for their terrific grasp of English grammar."

"It's a habit. Sue me."

"Is Sally right? Am I playing too loudly? Or too often? Or what? You want me to just sit back here and run the bass drum? Is that what you want? Because what I thought we were doing here was trying to have some fun."

"Without mortifying ourselves," Sally said. "Fun without humiliation. And since you expect me to sing, then it's me the crowd is going to be staring at, and I'd rather not look like a total idiot."

"Don't flatter yourself, Jasper. Just maybe they might every once in awhile look away from your rapturously glorious face and take a gander at the rest of us, plain peasants that we are. I don't want to look like a total idiot, either, which is exactly what'll happen if I'm just sitting on my ass using my foot to tap out the beat. I want to appear at least halfway like I know what I'm doing."

"Then stop being so . . ."

"So what?"

"So wild over there."

"Drummers are wild. Part of the job description.

Haven't you ever seen Animal from *The Muppet Show*? He's
so wild they have to chain him down. *Chain* him. Or did
you ever hear of a guy named Alex Van Halen? You might
remember that when the four of us saw him in concert our
junior year, he wasn't what you'd call a tame and polite
fellow."

Anne said, "There *is* something called a happy medium."

"Sal, for pity's sake, just sing and let me do my thing. I
think you're just stalling."

"Stalling?"

"Yeah, 'cause this whole idea scares you to death."

"So what if it does? All that clatter you're making isn't
helping my nerves any."

"Maybe it would help you if I took this stick and—"
Jazmyn laughed.

The sound shut them up. Electric guitar slung across her
front and hair hidden in a red bandana in pirate fashion,
Jazmyn laughed and in her laughter shamed them all. "I
think you guys are scaring poor Crespin to death." She
looked at him, smiled hugely at his bewildered expression,
and assured him in broken Spanish that not all American
women were lunatics.

Crespin still seemed uncertain.

"Now let's cut the crap and take it from the top,"
Jazmyn commanded. "Ready? Two-three-four!" She laid
into a riff so laced with sweet funk that the others couldn't
help but lose themselves in the sound.

A few minutes later, Crespin was bobbing his head.

Noon.
"Uh, Sal?" Dawn said.
"Yes."

"I guess you've decided not to open the shop today."

"Are you kidding? I need all the business I can get. I asked Dominique to mind it for me. She's done it before when I had to be away. I'd have her in there more often if I could afford to pay her. She attracts male shoppers."

"How's her quest for the Swede at the lumberyard?"

"I haven't asked."

"What about your own quest?"

"Huh?"

"Mister immigration man."

"That's no quest."

"He has what you call rugged good looks."

"If you say so."

Dawn broke into sing-song: "Sally and Surry sittin' in a tree! K-I-S-S-I-N-G!"

"How do I shut you up?"

"Better women than you have tried." Then she shook her head. "On second thought, there are no better women. How about you shut me up by singing? Do you remember any Pat Benatar?"

"Shall I hit you with my best shot?"

"Fire away."

Three-seventeen.

Dawn traded her sticks for a shot of bottled water. "What time does this shindig start, anyway?"

"The day's festivities have already begun," Anne explained, her cheeks flushed from the exertion of practice. She operated two electronic keyboards, one mounted atop the other to permit her to play them in tandem. "They're throwing horseshoes at the park, eating hotdogs, having sack races . . ."

"And enjoying Mom's dunking booth," Jazmyn said.

"Yeah, Sal, what about that thing? I thought you were in charge of it."

"Was. Farmed it out. Two girls from Jaz's class."

"Michelle and Molly Baker. They're twins." Jazmyn was fine-tuning an amplifier with veteran skill. "The only two girls in my grade who aren't total snots."

"Damn total snots," Dawn said. "We've all had to deal with 'em."

"You had a lot of them when you were in school?"

"Honey, you couldn't throw a spitwad in that classroom without hitting one. Those prissy little Sunshine Suzies with their lookalike hairdos and sixty-dollar jeans—God, how I loathed them. There was this one girl who was especially wretched. I think the word is *aloof*. Smart as hell but sometimes too smart for her own good. And to make matters worse, she was also a killer athlete and the teacher's pet. What was her name again, Annie?"

Anne's black eyes were chiseled to fine points. "If you're not careful, Dawn-Marie, I'm going to show you the myriad means of inserting a drumstick into various bodily orifices."

Dawn looked at Jazmyn. "See what I mean? Total snot."

At half past five, entirely out of the blue, Crespin spoke up for the first time since Anne had asked him what he wanted for lunch. Throughout the afternoon he'd sat quietly in the corner, listening to them bicker and play, thinking his thoughts. He was wearing a pair of Trevor's cargo pants and one of Alex's few collared shirts. On his feet were brand-new, lightweight, air-sole running shoes that he couldn't stop looking at; they were gifts of staggering value. He was clearly humbled by the riches in this land and the queenly generosity of its inhabitants.

"*¿Qué es el nombre de este grupo musical?*"

144

His sudden words surprised them. Sally had been about to launch into one last attempt to nail the chorus on key, but instead she glanced at Anne. "What was that?"

"He's asking what our name is."

"Our names? He knows our names."

"The name of the band."

"Oh." No one had given the matter any thought. "Good question. Dawn?"

"Beats me. But we better think fast. The first act goes on at eight. We've got to get our gear loaded up and get over there. Jaz, name the band, please."

"How about The Blind Leading the Blind?"

"Funny girl."

"Jazmyn and the Old Fogeys?"

"Did you get that so-called wit from me? If so, let me apologize to the world."

"Mom, what do you think? Any ideas?"

"Why don't you ask Crespin? All we know about him so far is that he comes from a small town where his father works in a paint factory. Maybe he has a knack for names."

Anne posed the question, and Crespin replied.

"He wants to know what kind of music we like."

"These days I'm not picky. I listen to whatever's on the radio."

Anne relayed this to Crespin, who thought for a moment, looked at all of them shyly, then made a suggestion.

"He says if that's the case, then we should call ourselves Radio."

The women looked at one another, transmitting their thoughts.

"So be it," Sally said. "What's in a name, right?" She shrugged nonchalantly, not knowing the gravity of this one decision and what would soon become of it. "Good job,

Crespin. I knew I hired you for a reason."

Jazmyn cranked up the volume on her amp. "Okay, Radio. Let's do one more run-through, and then we'll get our show on the road."

So one final time before they faced potential disgrace and disaster, they poured themselves into it, and Crespin sat in monklike stillness and listened to an increasingly musical rendition of their choice for this battle of the bush-league bands, a number by one of Dawn's eternal heart-throbs, Mr. John Cougar Mellencamp.

By now Crespin knew all the words, and he sang with the fervor of a man saved from death.

"All right, Crespin, time to earn your keep."

Having been briefed by Anne, Crespin was ready. His newest word in English: roadie.

He loaded their gear into a borrowed van with an enthusiasm that bordered on the sycophantic, if not the downright insane. His glee was visible in his walk and on his face and in the way he dove into every new task as if it were the key to his salvation. He was lean—what Dawn called sexy skinny—but what he lacked in muscle he compensated with lumberjack stamina. He made a dozen trips from garage to van without pause, happy to set his able hands to a task he understood, even if he didn't understand the women behind it.

"Boy must think every woman in America has a life as crazy as an episode of *I Love Lucy*." Dawn gestured vaguely southward. "He's going to write home to Mexico and tell the men not to bother, because dames from this country are even scarier than the ones back home."

Crespin's shirt bore a V of sweat. He caught them watching him and waved.

"So do you want to hear the secret of the ages?" Sally asked.

"I'm all ears. Except for my ass, which is also a considerable part of me."

"I'm going to pay him fifty bucks for helping us tonight, and then I'm taking him back."

"Back? Across the border? Why?"

"To get his friends."

"Pardon? I think I missed that one."

"His friends. I'm going to help them. They need a foothold in this country. They need a good place to start so they can get their balance before making a go of it as a citizen. And please refrain from the wisecracks, because my mind's made up. Besides, the equipment's loaded and we need to get going."

Dawn obediently said nothing. She crossed her arms, her face uncharacteristically serious.

Sally looked at her watch. "You ready for this?"

"I'm scared poopless."

"Poopless is a terrible way to be."

"No shit."

They arrived at the park at dusk. More townspeople had gathered here than Radio's four members had anticipated, and as the daylight faded, so too did the women's bravado. The audience at the Ampi would be larger than expected. Only Crespin seemed without worry.

The games were in full swing, horseshoe tossing and Croquet for Dollars, with the two most popular sites being the kissing booth—the kisser being Nicole Akers, a bubbly redhead whose powers of effective flirtation were almost supernatural—and the dunking booth sans Sally. Families wore matching T-shirts bearing the image of Old Glory or a brand name rendered in patriotic colors. Most of them had on sandals or white tennis shoes.

Sally's crew wore boots. This decision, monumental as it was, had not come easily. They'd battled over shoe selection with the zeal of the founding fathers debating the fledgling Constitution. What image did they want to project onstage? Sally said she wasn't thinking of projecting any image, just being comfortable, but Jazmyn argued for style and Dawn agreed. They used words like pizzazz and punch, and Anne supplied panache. Jaz said they had to have a certain look. Anne concurred. In the end, they'd driven to Sole Mates and selected four pairs of low-heeled cowboy boots called Ropers. Sally's were black. Dawn and Anne wore navy blue. Jazmyn brimmed with moxie in bright red.

"I'm going to go check our registration," Anne said. "I'm sure everything's in order, but it doesn't hurt to ask. I'll also find out where Crespin needs to unload our paraphernalia."

"And I'm gonna buy a snow cone," Dawn said. "No use standing around letting my nerves chew a hole in my stomach. And Lex and the boys should be around here somewhere. Maybe I can beg a little moral support." She veered off into the crowd.

"Mom?"

"Yes, dear? Are you abandoning me too?"

"I want to go meet some of the other bands. See what they're up to."

"Spy on the competition?"

"Nah, just make some friends, maybe. Is that cool?"

"Go. I'll be fine."

Jazmyn kissed her on the cheek. "Thanks for doing this, Mom. You're one of the three best mothers a girl could have." She dashed off with the new red highlights in her hair looking like bands of copper in the fading sun.

Sally stood there for a moment, searching the crowd. These were people she knew, that she had grown up with, that she'd served on committees with and attended funerals with, and now—incredibly—they were the people she was about to entertain. She had performed a vocal solo on the occasional Sunday in church, and two years ago she'd sung at Lindsey Hong's wedding. But this was different. This was the kind of thing that introverts like Sally Jasper didn't do. Show-off stuff. Fairy tale stuff.

Leigh Surry was nowhere to be seen.

So Sally went to check on the status of Farrington Schatz.

He was tilted at a precipitous angle. A small group had gathered around the yellow tape. The statue looked absurd jutting from its partially ruptured base like that, bronze hat thrust high, leaning mightily but not yet falling. Mark Cheevey kept a position inside the warning tape, notebook in hand, selling raffle tickets and chatting it up with the onlookers like a snake-oil salesman hawking his latest miracle brew. He was explaining how Farrington had been a rich man in his day, owner of his own gold mine, and to bet on such a man's demise would take guts, so only the daring need buy a ticket.

"Ms. Jasper! How's the world treating you tonight?"

"What's the angle, Mark?"

"Ah, yes, I'm happy to report this afternoon's measurement recorded an angle of twenty-two degrees."

"That's only one degree more than the last time I was here."

"Rome wasn't built in a day. Nor did its empire fall in a day. Emphasis on fall."

Others stepped forward to buy time slots, and Sally let

them take her place at the tape. She melted into the crowd, while over at the Ampi, workers set the stage for the night's first act. A painted Mardi Gras mask glared from the head of the bass drum.

A disembodied voice announced through a loudspeaker: "Testing. Two . . . three. Twenty minutes till showtime, folks."

A few people cheered.

Dawn-Marie grabbed Sally's elbow, giving her a start. "Let me ask you a question."

"Don't do that, you scared me to death. Is it too late to back out of this?"

"Way. Now listen." She put her mouth to Sally's ear. "I've been wondering, these Mexican immigrants of yours, how do you intend on getting them jobs without Johnny Law slapping the cuffs on them? These people are going to need the proper legal documents, you know."

"Would you believe I have a plan for that?"

"I was hoping so. I'll let you explain it to me later. Here, I bought you a snow cone. Now let's go to the van and check on Crespin. The first act is getting ready to go on, so we have maybe an hour until we become the belles of the ball."

"An hour."

"And counting."

"Do you think Jaz would hate us forever if we changed our minds about this?"

"Tick-tock, tick-tock."

The first of the night's six bands was called Frogbox.

The crowd was in a favorable mood, so they were merciful, even a little supportive, when Frogbox offered blaring, toneless guitar work and incomprehensible lyrics.

Sally and the others watched from beyond the seats, standing in a tight cluster behind the last row of chairs. They were no longer dressed in mufti, but were clad in what Jazmyn had called their stage clothes. Their Ropers were the only articles they had in common. Anne wore a scarlet silk blouse that exposed more of her neckline than she was used to, her hair free-falling over her shoulders. She'd permitted Jazmyn to add sparkles to her hair, so that when the lights fell on it in a certain way, constellations happened.

Dawn was drummer to the bone. Her hair was tossed and solidified with mousse. Her jeans were ripped, her tank top a relic from their high school days, bearing the faded image of a boy angel toking on a cigarette and looking over his shoulder so as not to get caught.

The second and third acts were rather indistinguishable from Frogbox, being comprised of college sophomores who performed covers of current top forty hits. The audience applauded but seemed unimpressed. Neither of the two bands projected either a look or a sound that set them apart. Thirty minutes passed while the bands quit the stage and the next shuffled on with its own assortment of pawn-shop amps and wannabe attitudes.

"Tick-tock," Dawn said again, which did nothing for anyone's nerves.

Sally's attire had not been donned without a fight. Had it been up to Jazmyn, Sally would have pranced onto the stage in a sleeveless top and size-four suede pants, and maybe there had been a time when size four wouldn't have hugged her so snugly, but alas, that was Dark Ages stuff, so long ago that records of it no longer existed. After trying on everything in everyone's closet, Sally had surprised herself by consulting her new oracle: Crespin.

Following a spell of quiet thought, his dark, lambent eyes staring into space, Crespin spoke at length to Anne, who nodded, went off to search her son's closet, and returned with a simple white cotton T-shirt. The shirt was small enough that Sally's navel showed if she raised her arms, so Jazmyn pronounced it to be perfect. Coupled with a pair of faded jeans—a few digits higher than size four—it had the magical effect of making her feel at once frumpy and magnetic.

The fourth band kicked ass.

That was how Dawn so bluntly put it, in typical Dawn lingo. In every contest there had to be a ringer, and in this case it was a band that had traveled all the way from Minnesota. They were known as Seven Against Thebes, and they were fronted by a woman with hair like flames and a stage presence that had every man in the Ampi thinking secrets to himself. Though they had yet to snag a record deal, they looked professional, with a big, streaming sound that was all the more appealing because it seemed effortless. These kids were good.

"Punks," Dawn said when they were done.

The crowd's response was the loudest yet. Seven Against Thebes was likely in the lead after this display, as audience reaction counted for fifty percent of their final score in the contest. The other half depended on the majority vote of the three judges, the panel consisting of the high school band instructor, the mayor's wife, and a popular late-night deejay from the local FM station out of Maxon. The judges based their decision on technical aptitude and overall effect.

"Amateurs," Dawn said. "Pathetic. All that applause is just mercy clapping."

"We better get moving." Anne started toward the Ampi's backstage area.

152

"I was stupid for making that bet. Sal, let's make a run for it. I'm chickening out."

Sally didn't hear her, because at that moment she saw Jeffrey Longbranch watching her.

The boy stood on the edge of the crowd, grass stains on his pants and yellow hair hanging carelessly in his eyes. At his waist he wore the small pouch that Sally knew contained his emergency syringes, lest he be caught in a diabetic paroxysm away from home. While she watched, Jeffrey held up his hand and made a strange sign: pinky and index finger extended, middle fingers held down with the thumb.

Only then did Sally remember the box. She'd forgotten all about the shoebox that Jeffrey had given her. In all the recent tumult she'd overlooked it.

"Salster, come on." Dawn took her by the elbow and dragged her through the mob.

Jeffrey was lost somewhere behind.

"What happened to chickening out?" Sally asked.

"I chickened out on chickening out. Jaz and Lex both would murder me in my sleep if I try and cop out at this point. Do you know that Lex brought his camcorder? I begged him not to, even threatened to divorce him, but he called my bluff. Hey, are you all right?"

"No."

Somehow she made it backstage without fainting.

Sally felt.

All day she'd been disconnected. All day events had rolled on without provoking any inner commentary. All day she had gone through the motions and rehearsed without thinking and now here she was, fractured with sudden emotion.

She was crouched in the corner amongst old stage flats

and sawhorses, mostly hidden in shadow, experiencing such a tide of apprehension that it bordered on nausea. In her life she had done only one truly risky thing, and that had been years ago and her friends had been with her to give her strength. More to the point, Tatyana had been there, and that was like having Excalibur in King Arthur's hand.

Pigtails must be antennas for bravery.

Now two more chancy endeavors were upon her. First this performance, then her gambit with the immigrants.

With this on her mind, she glanced over at Dakota. He was giving Dawn a few last-minute reminders. ". . . and remember, when Sally sings 'crack, boom, bam,' you stomp the bass pedal extra hard and give a rimshot on each beat."

"Rimshot, right. Got it. I hope."

Sally would have to enlist Dakota if her plan had any hope of working.

Meanwhile, Anne was pacing and Jaz was sitting in the lotus position. Sally found this mildly ironic, as Anne had been the one who taught Jaz yoga and meditation in the first place, and now the student was at peace while the teacher was talking to herself.

When it comes time to do this thing with the Mexicans, she wondered, *will they back my play?*

And then a rogue thought: *Anne and Dawn have imparted so much of themselves to Jaz, what have I ever given her but a savvy for choosing chic shoes?*

Surely there was something. Surely she'd managed to—

"Are you folks Radio?" asked a man wearing a headset and bearing a clipboard.

"No," Dawn replied, "we're Aerosmith in drag."

"You're on in five."

Out on the stage, Spur Nation had just finished their

number. The sound of the crowd was a muffled rumble through the wall.

As she got shakily to her feet, Sally's heart was a not-so-muffled rumble in her chest.

Chapter Eleven

Waiting in the wings was the worst.

The Ampi stage had no curtain, no divider to mask its players from the audience they would entertain. A broad proscenium extended toward the front row of seats, and the stage floor itself was twenty feet deep. But no screen stood between these two territories, so that Dakota and Crespin were in full view of the crowd as they tightened the last drum stand and positioned the last mike.

Most people ain't even realized they're alive.

Sally heard Jazmyn's words again, thinking that finally she wasn't one of most people. Her palms were resting lightly against her chest, which rose and fell rapidly to the beat of her quickened breath. After a minute she lowered her arms and found a hand waiting on either side of her. She knew these hands by touch, slipped her fingers into them, and held on.

The mayor was going through his spiel. He stood under one of the two spotlights, admonishing his listeners to give freely to the city's ongoing blood drive, interspersing his monologue with jokes he probably stole from the late show.

Sally's hands started to ache, another's fingertips pressing hard dimples into her skin. When was the last time they'd held one another so tightly?

She knew the answer to that. Her hands had cramped like this sixteen years ago at the funeral, so determinedly had she and Anne and Dawn supported themselves beside the casket. For days after, the three of them had lain across one another like beaten animals, not wanting to rise from bed, but just remain entwined in hot, sympathetic limbs, because the world beyond that tangled embrace could not begin to understand.

The mayor reminded the audience not to miss the upcoming meteor shower, which the watchers over in Maxon predicted would be one of the finest ever, and then he segued into a yarn about a sailor who walks into a bar with a fallen star under his arm.

But now a fourth hand was joined to their line, and the chain was again unbroken. Sally had but to turn her head the slightest bit to see Jazmyn on Dawn's right side, holding on, holding on. A current passed across Sally's shoulders and caused the fine hairs to dance on her arms. Maybe it wasn't Jazmyn standing there at all. Maybe it was Tatyana's ghost returned to settle some unpaid account or impart a last morsel of girlish wisdom. Sally's mouth went dry. The sense of déjà vu was so potent that it staggered her, and she took a quick step back to keep her balance.

"Easy does it," Dawn said, tugging her back into place.

". . . which means we've come to the last of tonight's performers, a band right here from our own town of Fresh Waters."

"Just please get it over with," Anne quietly implored.

But the mayor wasn't through. "Now, when I heard that these ladies were signing up for the show, well, I have to admit that I raised a curious eyebrow. I've known them all my life and honestly I didn't think they had it in them. But as you're all aware, I have a habit of being proven wrong."

Bubbles of laughter burst through the crowd.

"So it's with sincere respect, ladies and gentlemen, that I present to you the final act in our battle of the bands"—he stepped aside and pointed right at them—"Radio!"

Had no one else moved, Sally doubted she could have done it. But almost as one, steps were taken, and Sally looked down to see her boot, her new, polished, fearless boot, setting its heel upon the stage.

Silence.

Sally stood before the silver staff of the microphone and stared.

A thousand faces stared back.

More than she had thought. More than seemed proper for such a minor-league event. So many that her breath shriveled in her throat. In front of her lay a tapestry of humanity, each individual thread equally bright, so that she was unable to behold them as the anonymous piece of fabric like she had hoped. Face after face she recognized, patterns in the tapestry, women from the PTA and men from the garage where she took her car. Hank the mailman. The Pakistani grocer with the unpronounceable name whom everyone called Bob. They were all here, their upturned faces waiting for a gift Sally didn't think she had the courage to bestow. Those closest to the stage were seated in long wooden pews, while the ones farther back occupied lawn chairs and, more distant still, quilts and the occasional beach towel. More stood on the fringes, but their eyes were no less recognizable than those up front. Sally saw them all.

And they saw her.

Granted, not all of them were paying attention; they held beers in plastic cups and talked in little groups, or they chased their errant children, or they traded gossip or cuddled in the shadows and necked. The air smelled of pop-corn and sweat.

But they saw her.

Never before had so many people watched her at once. Their stares had pressure, and with each new set of eyes that turned her way, the pounds per square inch increased, and in those first few seconds Sally thought she might im-plode. The tapestry was too heavy, and it was smothering her.

She was unaware of the women taking up their positions behind her, Dawn ensconced in her circle of drums, Anne at her keyboard, Jazmyn adjusting the strap of her guitar . . .

Someone gave a wolf whistle. Others laughed.

Sally's skin burned. It wasn't the spotlights and it wasn't the spring heat. Her underarms were swampy, which didn't say much for her extra-dry deodorant. She caught sight of Leigh Surry. He wore a tennis player's shirt and held a longneck. His tan skin stood out boldly against the white of his shirt. The man beside him was talking his ear off, but Leigh never took his eyes from Sally.

She couldn't bear it and looked away.

"Any day now!" came the cry.

Sally curled her fingers around the mike stand.

"Sal?" That was Dawn, from a place way back, isolated behind her drum set and unable to lend any meaningful support. Sally was alone and the world was watching.

"Sal, I'm counting to three and then we're starting, okay?"

So this is stage fright.

That was her last thought before the tapping began: Dawn stroked the steel rim of the drum three times—

—*Oh shit, I'm not ready*—

—and then Jazmyn pranced to the front of the stage, guitar like a weapon in her arms—

—*God, just don't let me pass out*—

—and the sound issued suddenly from those six strings like a sonic blessing, showering the crowd with the divine favor of music. It was pure and loud and took Sally by surprise with its power to strike at her own core and ignite her in the same way it was setting fire to the tapestry before her.

They love her.

That was what at last shook her from her trance: the sight of Jazmyn on the lip of that stage with every eye in the joint upon her. Jaz stood before a microphone stand to which were clipped a dozen spare guitar picks, each of them imprinted with the colors of the Union Jack; she had inherited Dawn's love of British rock, from Bowie to the Sex Pistols. She played the song's opening bars with her heavy locks of hair shimmering stormlike around her and her hips rocking sensually against the guitar. With her red Ropers she wore a white skirt that hit her three inches above the knee. Sally had never been more aware of the girl's sexuality. Jaz slid her hand along the instrument's neck, cranking out deliverance, and the crowd could not help but respond.

It occurred to Sally then that a girl with a guitar could own every heart that beat in a male chest.

The moment came. Sally leaned toward the mike, mouth open, thinking only of Jazmyn and the fearsome pride that swelled her own heart, and without realizing it, she heard her cue and, miraculously, summoned the nerve to sing. "They come from the cities and they come from the smaller towns . . ."

Her words, electrically enlarged, soared into the night.

But her voice sounded strained and frail, even to her

own ears. Already she was screwing this up. Her face burned all the hotter. Fortunately Anne's light-fingered keyboarding spiraled into the notes from Jaz's guitar and formed a conjugal triumph of sound.

"Beat-up cars with guitars and drummers goin'—"

All four women chanted as one: "Crack! Boom! Bam!"

And because she had no recourse but to stand there and hold up her end of a four-way bargain, and because somewhere she believed that Tatyana was watching and cheering her on, Sally said to hell with it and followed that last *Bam!* into the cavalry charge of sound.

The fetters around her heart came undone. Instantly her voice strengthened and assumed a purity, and the threads did indeed meld into a single, shifting cloth, and when they did Sally found herself tumbling headlong into the role she was playing, letting loose her final, obstinate qualms and permitting the heady thrill of performance to lift her practically off her feet. The feeling of release was as intoxicating as any she'd ever known, save that of watching Jazmyn's birth, and when she gave herself fully to it, like a lover, she slipped free of earth's grasp. Paying the lease on the shop, growing old, even the death of Juan Doe—these were but wisps, and she flew through them.

She screamed, and her voice was thunder: "R.O.C.K in the U.S.A!"

The others sang the same words in perfect echo.

Sally tore the mike free and flung away its stand. "Rockin' in the U.S.A!"

A mountain range of guitar riffs rose to take the place of her voice, and Sally, without thinking, ran halfway down the stage and stopped at its edge, staring boldly over the crowd like a captain on the prow of her ship. Subliminally she heard them, howling the war cries that only concert-goers can muster. They should not have been so loud. They should not have yelled like that in response to a group of blundering, shameless women on the brink of middle-agedom. They should've been laughing their asses off.

But instead they were cheering.

Their energy suffused Sally's body and she reciprocated with an energy of her own, bleating out the second verse with a wildness that kept pace with the crowd's rising frenzy. Not even when she was in her car, driving alone with the windows rolled up, did she sing with such abandon. The matter was out of her control. The stage was a site of emancipation.

"Rockin' in the U.S.A!"

She wasn't sure what happened next. Afterwards she'd replay their performance in an effort to find the pivot on which the crowd had turned. What made them change like that? What altered their mob mind so drastically? Sally never knew for certain, but at first the audience was simply having a good time watching this unlikely ensemble cavorting around on the stage. The band called Radio was a novelty act, a gimmick, and the onlookers ate it up with polite merriment and cheered obligingly. But somewhere along the way, the poles shifted, and what had started out as jocular acceptance transformed into honest, reckless adoration.

People surged against the stage.

Hands reached for Jazmyn as her hair hung in her face and her fingers attacked the guitar.

Arms shot into the air when Dawn pounded out a drum roll and a dual cymbal smash.

Voices cried out for more when Anne completed a wicked keyboard solo.

And when Sally sang the words they joined her. This

time when she hollered out the title line, she was joined by rising voices from the tapestry and a thousand pumping fists.

Then it was over.

Jaz struck the finishing note, whipping her arm in a full circle and giving the strings one final stroke. That last note rang out, and the people seemed to grasp for it, fingers clutching at it as if it were a comet tail that might grant dust from the stars to those lucky enough to touch it. Sally stood in its wake, so near to the cusp of the stage that the toes of her boots extended a full inch beyond it. Amazingly, a hand reached up and touched that boot, just as she had seen fans do at concerts since she'd attended her first in junior high. Crowds always wanted the blessings of passing saints, a boon taken by brief contact, and to think that Sally herself was the giver of such favors was beyond her ability to comprehend.

The note faded.

Raucous applause took its place.

Baffled by their reaction, Sally could do nothing but stand there, feet welded to the stage. The tapestry fell apart, revealing all the sundry threads, all the faces she'd known since girlhood, and the blush in her cheeks was so hot and sudden it made her dizzy. She started to fall . . .

Anne was there to catch her. "Can you believe this?"

Sally's stomach was bound up like a wet dishrag. She couldn't speak for fear of throwing up.

Whistles continued to assail them, along with the random cry for encore.

Sally could not have managed an encore had her life been at stake. Everything was gone from inside her. It was all she could do to get her feet moving as Anne led her away. She sagged in Anne's embrace just like she had on those few occasions she'd been blazingly drunk. Her distress must have been apparent, because Dakota and Crespin appeared, one on either side, chaperoning her backstage like bodyguards escorting a rock star.

Jazmyn and Dawn embraced, laughing exuberantly, flushed with victory.

The mayor pounced onto the stage, arms above his head, leading the applause.

And all Sally could do was lean on her friend and wonder who she herself had been in a past life, not knowing for sure but thinking it must have been something with wings.

Anne had just settled Sally into a folding steel chair backstage when she heard the call.

Coyote, she thought, how odd to hear one in town.

But that wasn't right at all. It wasn't a coyote.

Wolf.

She left Sally with a damp compress against her forehead and hurried to the wings off stage-left. Her pulse was still strumming, her skin slick with the kind of sweat she got after her morning run, a thin sheen that always had the effect of reminding her she was alive.

What was that sound?

She often imagined that her sensibilities were inscribed in her bones like winding oriental ideograms, a careful calligraphy of logic that, when read thoughtfully, permitted her to solve any algebra problem and complete the most complex of jigsaw puzzles. She had an uncanny eye for patterns, hence her success in the field of systematics. Sally had once suggested that—in another lifetime—Anne had lived on Baker Street and answered to the name of Holmes. Whatever.

But underneath those letters of reason, down in her marrow, her true gift was buried. Through meditation and personal exploration, she had learned to listen to her own intuition, what popular culture called the sixth sense, and now, as she studied the crowd from the edge of the stage, she ignored the immaculate penmanship of common sense and read instead only the messy scribbles of a hunch.

When she saw him in the crowd, her elation withered like a petal in the sun.

Perhaps she had noticed him during her performance and only now, in adrenaline's wake, did she recognize his face. There had been no mystic wolf-cry that alerted her, no sixth sense, only her mind processing the data a bit belatedly. Either way, it didn't matter. The fact was that he and his companions were out there in the grass in front of the Ampi, enjoying the show with everyone else.

Isadore Presper.

He wore a white linen sport jacket and matching trousers, and his smile was radiant. He was laughing at a friend's joke, tossing back his head in mirth. His abundant black hair tumbled around his shoulders when he shook his head and saluted the joke-teller with a bottle of imported beer. He seemed the center of a small cluster. Those around him appeared to appreciate his presence; they followed his eyes when he spoke.

Anne looked away, for fear her stare was tangible and would warn him with its weight.

She had no time to recover before the mayor, folded card in hand, stepped up to the mike and announced, "Looks like we have a winner!"

The cheers returned, but only for a few seconds. Then everyone quieted, waiting.

Anne dared another peek, gazing up through her lashes.

165

Presper and his band had left off their banter and stood facing the stage, as hushed as all the others. Presper softly tapped the neck of his bottle against his lips.

"Remember, folks, the final decision depends not only upon the judges' vote, but also on how you responded to the bands. Our decibel meter never lies. Now then . . ." He opened the cardstock note, scanned what was printed there, and smiled.

Anne wanted to run but could not. Between the rush of live performance, the anticipation of the mayor's pronouncement, and the sight of that man-wolf in the crowd, she was stricken immobile by conflicting emotions. Isadore Presper had seen her onstage. Had he known her? Was there a way he could have spotted her out there on the highway two days ago? No doubt he'd seen her vague form, hazy through the desert heat, but had he noted her distinctly Asian features and made the connection with the woman at the keyboard?

And if she reported Presper's presence to Sally, what would happen then?

Down in the grass, Presper stood unmoving, and ever watchful.

Anne remembered that the last time she'd seen him, he'd been wearing a gun.

The mayor held the card aloft and spoke.

Chapter Twelve

Exactly four minutes later, Dawn-Marie stopped guzzling and pitched the empty water bottle at Crespin. "Heads up!"

Crespin ducked with a dancer's agility and came up smiling. He was glad to be included in the antics, a part of the team.

"And the angels sang hallelujah!" Dawn cried. Then she belched.

This time no one noticed. They were all too absorbed in their post-performance shock. Dawn surveyed them with her hands on her hips, her smirk still screwed tightly to her face like an ember glowing after the fire had gone out. Jazmyn was surrounded by a group of her friends, playing teen idol. She was a natural. Dawn knew It when she saw it, that spark that made a Hollywood flame. Jaz had It, the presence or charisma or whatever you wanted to call It, and others were drawn to her. Dawn noted this smugly, mentally patting herself on the back for her small part in Jazmyn's acquisition of the mythical It.

"Hell of a show, Dawn!" someone called.

"You ain't seen nothing yet!" she fired back. They had gathered on the steps behind the Ampi, and as the crowd disbanded and folks headed home, more than a few veered close to offer their appreciation. And Dawn loved them for

167

it. She enjoyed taking the stage at the Cheshire Grin with her comedy act, but it was nothing compared to the rocket ride of live musical delivery. The goosebumps still stood on her arms.

"Don't you let her pass out, Dakota!" she shouted, noticing how Sally was still sitting with her head between her knees. "I don't want to have to give her mouth-to-mouth."

"She's okay," Dakota assured her. He was crouched down in front of Sally, fanning her with a folded program.

Then something odd happened.

As Dawn watched from thirty feet away, Sally reached out as quick as a striking snake and took Dakota by the arm. She grabbed the wrist that was encased in a cast, snaring Dakota and tugging him close so that only inches separated them. Sally said something, looking the boy right in the eyes. Though Dawn couldn't hear what Sally told him, the expressions on their faces bore no shine of exhilaration, no light-hearted twinkle, and in their somberness they were alone.

Dakota listened carefully. Then nodded. He looked like a solider who'd just accepted orders to charge an enemy machine-gun emplacement.

"What the hell?" Dawn asked herself.

But she had no time to think about it because Anne appeared in front of her, a sheen of perspiration on her cheeks. "Dawn, it's him."

"What? Him who?"

"Come on."

Suddenly Dawn found herself being dragged around the Ampi's perimeter, under tall-necked lamps that swarmed with insects. To her nyctalopic eyes, it was as if she'd plunged into the sea and several hundred tons of dark saltwater now blocked all but a few patches of light. She hated that sensation, but had learned to live with it. "Hey, hold your horses, sunshine, I'm too worn out to gallop."

"He's here. I saw him."

"Unless you're talking about Tom Selleck then I don't give a damn. Something's wrong with Sal. Did you see how she's acting? Personally I think she needs a good long—"

"There." Anne drew them both against the Ampi's high curving outer wall so as not to be seen. With her back flattened against the building, Anne tipped her head just enough to get a view of the grassy field in front of the stage, where the last of the concert attendees milled around drinking and shooting the breeze. "He and his goons are walking away. They're heading to the parking lot. Can you see them?"

Dawn had only grown more agitated by the second. "For starters, your hair's in the way so I can't see a thing. And unless this mystery person of yours happens to walk directly under a light source, then he might as well be the invisible man. See? I'm looking, okay? And you know what I can see? I see a big bunch of blackness interspersed with hazy yellow spots. Does that help? Wait a sec, I see some dudes passing in front of a car's headlights . . . oh shit."

"Yeah. That's what I thought."

"Is that really him? Are you sure?"

"I will never forget his face. I dreamed of it last night."

"Damn, lost him again in the dark. But he looked just like he did in that picture Sally showed us. You think he was here to watch the show?"

"Yes. But I don't think he recognized us."

"How could he? When you spotted him after the . . . the accident, he was out in the desert and we were on the road. Too far away."

"Maybe."

"Maybe nothing. Was he using binoculars?"

"No. But I have this feeling."

"What's he doing here in town, do you think?"

"I wish I knew."

"Should we go find somebody? The cops or something?"

"And tell them what?"

"Hell, Annie, I don't know." She watched the dimly lit circle through which Isadore Presper had moved before disappearing from sight, lost to the eternal darkness that was Dawn's night vision. She gathered a breath and tried unsuccessfully to think with a clear head. "We've got to tell Sally."

"Bad idea."

"I know. She'll freak out and go chase him down, maybe attack him and get us all thrown in jail, because damned if I'll let her fight alone."

"Me too. So what do we do then?"

Dawn didn't get the chance to reply. "Excuse me, gals."

Dawn turned around. Even this close to the overhead lights, her eyesight was grainy and sepia-toned. But she could see well enough to make out the young lead singer of Seven Against Thebes. The girl's red leather pants were the same color as her hair. The rest of her band was behind her, and they held a trophy. Atop the trophy was a shiny brass number 2.

"You guys totally rocked," the girl said. "Congrats."

And then Seven Against Thebes walked away.

"Here that, Annie? We rocked."

"Fat lot of good that does us now."

The trophy Jazmyn thrust into the air was capped with a gleaming number 1.

The Ampi field had nearly cleared, leaving only paper cups and flattened grass.

"Victory!" Jazmyn yelled, brandishing the award like a spoil from war. She spun a pirouette on the toe of her boot, her skirt spiraling around her so high that anyone watching got a decent glimpse of her panties. "All hail the champions!"

Sally walked behind them. Anne was a few steps ahead, Dawn hanging to her arm like someone thrown overboard and depending on a floating spar. Jazmyn flourished between them, weaving here and there, a creature of bright caprice who time would never tarnish and worry never wrinkle. The sparkles she'd added to her hair were tiny jewels in the moonlight.

But it's not really the moon, Sally reminded herself. What had Anne said? *It's the moon of one-point-three seconds ago. Every time we look up, we see only the past.*

The same could be said for Sally's life. Whenever she studied these women, she tended always to see them with a child's eye. As if they were still leggy adolescents with too much lipstick and remorseless hormones. She had thought the four of them unbreakable then.

"Aren't you guys completely psyched?" Jazmyn touched Anne on the cheek. "Mother, we did it! We totally wiped them out."

"We did okay."

"Okay?" She rolled her eyes with such drama that Sally thought her pupils would remain stuck up there in her skull. "Are you kidding me? Didn't you hear the crowd? They craved us. They . . . they *lusted* after us like . . . like prison inmates who hadn't seen women in thirty years."

"Uh, dearie," Dawn said, "half of the audience were women."

"Yeah, I know, and they wanted us just as badly."

"If you say so."

"They worshipped us, Mama."

Dawn offered no witty rejoinder, only leaned a bit closer to Anne.

"Victory!" Jaz shook the trophy in challenge at the black sky. "All hail the queens!"

Sally still had the taste in her mouth, savoring the feeling of being onstage and letting go. But as rich as it had been, the sentiment was fading quickly, now that she'd dispatched Dakota on this perilous errand. She'd sent Crespin with him. Maybe they would return and maybe they wouldn't. The Border Patrol cast the occasional eye on Fresh Waters, which had seen its share of illegal transients, so there was always a chance that Crespin would be apprehended and Dakota would rat out Sally's tenuous scheme.

Leigh Surry was waiting at the parking lot.

A miracle must have happened, because Dawn looked right at him but didn't say one smart-mouthed word, not even a playful quip. Leigh nodded to them as they passed. Anne said, "Good evening," with her usual monarchial benevolence, and Jazmyn burst out: "Hey, Mr. Surry, did you check us out or what?"

He fetched a grin to his face and gave her a thumbs-up. "Tom Petty and the Heartbreakers had better be looking over their shoulders."

That pleased her. Her smile was so unsullied, so full of happy truth, that Sally gave silent thanks that she had been present to witness it. The fountain of youth lived in such sights.

The others walked by, leaving Sally facing him. All she wanted was to get home, undress, and feel cool sheets against her body. As interesting as Leigh might have been, he was nothing for her at this moment but another reminder that she wasn't actually a winged creature with the ability to fly away as it pleased her. She didn't know what to say, so she opted for silence, looking up at him and taking in the breadth of his shoulders and the ocean color of his eyes.

"I slept with a hairy woman last night," Leigh said.

Sally raised both eyebrows. "I'm happy to see you, too."

"She twitched when she was dreaming."

"Maybe you should spare me the details."

"You remember Francine?"

"You sleep with your dog?"

"My twitching dog. Kept me up half the night."

"But you didn't evict her from bed."

"She's fourteen. The old bones don't take kindly to the floor."

"Is there a point to this charming man's-best-friend story?"

"I couldn't sleep because Frank was chasing pheasants in her dream. So I laid there staring up at nothing and thought a lot about what you were doing here tonight, about how I'd never have the guts to do such a thing, about how sometimes people surprise you, about—"

"Does Francine wear a flea collar?"

"I'll have you know that my bed buddy is completely, one hundred percent pest-free."

"Just checking. You were saying?"

"I was saying that I'm duly impressed. Part of me expected that you four would get up there and . . . I don't know, get laughed off the stage, I guess. You'd end up as a gag on somebody's home video. So this is what you'd call an unexpected surprise. I like those."

Sally wondered if her thoughts showed on her face: *My young friend Dakota was once arrested for bearing a bogus driver's license, and I've just sent him to scare up just such an unlawful document for a Mexican national, and if that works*

*out okay then I'm going to start buying fake IDs by the dozen
and giving them to all the aliens I plan on smuggling into the
country.*

Fortunately Leigh didn't notice this admission of guilt,
even pressed as it was to the surface of Sally's skin. He
simply said, "Anyway, I just wanted to say good job. You
looked great up there."

"Just great? I was trying for stunning."

"That too."

"And sexy wouldn't have been bad, either."

"If you would've heard some of the comments down
there, you wouldn't be worried about whether or not you
were sexy. It was locker-room talk without the lockers."

Sally might have blushed at this a few hours ago, but
that was the distant past, before the stage had liberated her,
and also before she'd commissioned a criminal act. Currently she was blush-proof. "I'm glad you liked the show.
I'm sorry I can't stick around . . ."

"Why can't you? Got another concert in the next
town?"

"I'm tired, Leigh. I paid someone to load our equipment
because I don't have the gumption to mess with it. Right
now I'm taking the shortest route possible to my bed. Being
stunning and sexy takes a lot out of a person."

"Hey, sure, I understand." He retreated a little, not
much, but just enough to give notice that he had no intention of trying to convince her to change her mind. He
looked a little clumsy standing there, as if he were more
properly fitted to the woods and trout streams than gravel
parking lots. Though he had been a man for many years
now, the boy in him didn't seem so far behind. And this was
endearing and not the kind of thing a woman should let get
away.

Sally let it get away anyway. At least for tonight. "I'll see you."

"I look forward to it."

"Maybe you can introduce me to your mistress."

"She'll slobber all over your hand."

"My hand has been through worse." Letting that be her parting line, she turned and left him standing there, hurrying her step to catch up with the others.

But someone shouted, "Yo, ladies, hold up!"

The four of them stopped. "Who's that?" Dawn asked, turning her body toward the sound like a blind woman.

Anne shook her head. "I don't know."

Though Leigh was walking away, another man was jogging up to them. He was fiftyish, with a sloping sandbag of a belly and snakeskin boots. His mustache was gray and formidable and waxed at the tips. "You ladies got a second? Name's Jude Yarbuck." He proffered a hand to whomever was in the mood to take it.

Sally couldn't leave his hand hanging out like that. She didn't know who Jude Yarbuck was or what he wanted, but her dreamlike state persisted, and she wouldn't have been entirely surprised if he claimed to have arrived in a hot-air balloon from Singapore; the night resonated with such wonders.

She shook his hand. "Sally Jasper."

"Yes, ma'am, I know. Just caught your act up there and, by jiminy, it was a show-stopper if I ever saw one."

"Glad you enjoyed it. It was our first."

Jude dashed a thick hand to his cowboy hat, made a slight adjustment, and fixed Sally with a gaze that reminded her of when Tatyana's grandfather would call them all over and tell them a story about riding the railroad or plowing a field behind a mule. "All them folks out there really got a kick out of watching you all tonight. Myself included. Now them kids you competed against, they may have been a sight better at their instrument-playing and all that, but you ladies, you got the sand."

"Sand?"

"Yes, ma'am. And I ain't the only one who thinks so." His eyes left her long enough to take in Anne and Dawn, then swung back at Sally. "I own the Texanna out on Interstate 10. Maybe you've heard of it."

"The bar?"

"We call it a roadhouse, ma'am. Or a dance hall. It's one of the biggest in the state. Cow-punchers, bull-riders, ranchers, and just plain good-hearted folk from all over have themselves quite a time out at the Texanna on the weekends. We like rock 'n' roll as much as we like our country-and-western. We've got hot food, cold beer, a mechanical bull, pool tables, and sawdust on the dance floor. And we've also got live music. I was wondering if maybe you gals would like to make some honest *dinero* and come play for us this Friday."

"A real live gig?" Jazmyn said. She pushed between Sally and Dawn and confronted Jude Yarbuck. Facing each other, they made an odd pair, one of them like a character from *Gunsmoke* and the other a sprite-child from Never Never Land. "Are you serious? You're offering us a paying gig?"

"Well, missy, I'm afraid you've got to be twenty-one to get through the door."

Jazmyn stiffened. "But if I don't play—"

"Easy now, sugar." Yarbuck laughed, the sound like a rolling timpani drum. "If you're part of the band, I'm sure we can make allowances."

Jazmyn squealed—in that second far less a woman and

entirely a girl—and spun toward Sally. "Mom, you've gotta say yes, please don't say no, this would be totally the best thing *ever*."

Sally thought, *Pigtails must be antennas for bravery,* though she didn't know why.

"How much?" Dawn asked, looking in Yarbuck's general direction.

"The same we pay every local band for a one-nighter. Five hundred cash."

"Five hundred dollars for one evening's work?"

"You'll play for about two hours. Can you do that?"

"Mister, for five hundred bucks we'll spit-shine the mechanical bull."

Jazmyn's joy was an Impressionist painting, dappled all over her in bright shades. "Thanks, Mama, I know we can do it and it's gonna be a blast."

"Need I remind everyone," Anne said, "our repertoire consists only of a single song."

"But Mother, you can read any music we put in front of you. And so can I. So we just go buy a ton of sheet music and we can play all night. Right?"

"And Dawn? What about her?"

"Don't you worry about me, Annie dear," Dawn said. "I don't have to be fancy behind those drums, just keep the beat. Besides, Dakota says I've really got a knack for it. Maybe I might just surprise you."

Jazmyn spun back to Yarbuck. "Do you mind if we have sheet music up there with us?"

"Little lady, if you and your six-string shake the Texanna like you did this joint tonight, then I don't care if you have a litter of polecats on stage with you. I can guarantee that the kind of folks who come to my roadhouse are just the kind who'll go apeshit over an act like yours, if you'll pardon my French."

"Pardoned." Another spin on the heel of a red Roper, this time toward Sally. "Mom, what do you say? Can we do it? We'll only pick songs that you already pretty much know, so it won't be any trouble for you to learn the lyrics. And it's five hundred dollars and you need the money for the lease on the shop, so please just say it's okay, please."

The speed of the whole thing was too much. Sally had not yet recovered from her brief butterfly transformation, where she'd taken to the air currents above the Ampi, nor had she completely come to terms with her decision to break the law. Earlier she wouldn't have dreamed of accepting Yarbuck's offer, but now, with the very molecules in her blood transforming . . .

"Let's make it six hundred," Yarbuck said.

Later, Sally would tell herself that it had been for the shop; Jaz was right when she said that Sole Mates needed the cash to make ends meet. But maybe that wasn't the only reason she told Yarbuck, "You're quite the horse-trader, sir. I guess we've got a lot of rehearsing to do."

Jazmyn's shout of exaltation carried all the way to the stars.

Chapter Thirteen

Phony IDs didn't come cheap.

Dawn-Marie realized she was doing something she'd never done before: watching someone purchase the products of a forger. She'd seen kids steal cigarettes, seen college students buy weed in little baggies, seen a variety of other petty criminal exchanges, but never this. To make the sight even more unbelievable, the someone doing the buying was no one less than Sally Jasper, eternal friend, soul-sister, and captain of their collective destinies.

"There's sixty-five," Sally said, handing Dakota a few folded bills from the shoebox where she stored her emergency money. They were currently huddled like plotting thieves in the little storage room at the back of Sally's shop. The lights in the main showroom were dark. "How much for the Social-Security card?"

Dakota accepted the money without counting it and pressed it into the pocket of his faded jeans. "Rudy says a hundred for a card, but if you want a legit number, then it's going to be at least five."

"Legit number?"

"Yeah, an actual number in the system. Rudy can either work up an imitation card with a made-up SSN, or he can have his staff do some computer work and give you the number of somebody recently deceased, along with that person's name, if you want."

"This counterfeiter has a staff?"

"So to speak. He's an artist, not a hacker. But he knows people who are."

"I'm sure he does."

Dawn looked back and forth between them, a spectator at this weird tennis match, wondering why she wasn't laughing out loud. Dakota was a good kid, with blond hair, painfully blue eyes, and a butt that Dawn had on one occasion dreamed she was squeezing. He'd had a brush with the law awhile back, but now he was on the right track, attending night school to get his business degree. One arm was still ensconced in a cast, otherwise he'd be drumming up a storm and maybe Radio wouldn't have walked away with the first-place award tonight. Now, standing there inches from Sally and giving her the scoop on modern forgery, he seemed the perfect rogue. A glint in those sea-blue eyes marked him as a knave, a lovable rascal who should have been taunting authority in Sherwood Forest.

Sally studied the Arizona driver's license, which featured a picture of Crespin, along with accurate vital statistics and a little check mark in the organ-donor box. "I'm going to need more."

"How many?"

"I don't know yet."

"Give me a number so I can tell Rudy. He'll need to get materials."

"A dozen maybe. I don't want anybody else dying in the desert for something they should be given for free."

Anne said, "Can we please hurry this up? Barry's going to be home any minute now, and Trevor will be wondering what's keeping me."

"Can you get green cards?" Sally asked.

"For the right price, I can get you a hand-written note from the governor."

"I think that would be going a little far."

From the showroom: "Hey, what's taking you guys so long in there? A girl can't stand guard duty all night, you know."

They'd left Jazmyn and Crespin hiding in the shadows at the front of the store, as lookouts to watch the street. Dawn found it all mildly amazing. So she sliced into the tension the only way she knew. "Anybody want to hear a joke?"

"Not now," Anne said. Even those two words were edged with apprehension.

"Too bad. There's always time for humor. So the story goes like this. The CIA was looking to fill a vacancy in their assassination department. They'd narrowed their search to three prospects, two men and one woman. They had one last test to administer in order to select their new assassin. Everyone still with me?"

Anne was looking at her without expression. Sally's eyes, like distant moons, were far away.

"The CIA officer says, 'Listen up, people. We need to be sure that you can eliminate your target without hesitation, regardless of the circumstances. Understood?' And then he takes the first man to a plain wooden door and hands him a gun. He says, 'Behind this door, sitting in a chair, you'll find your wife. You must kill her to pass the test.' And the man replies, 'Are you kidding me? I could never, ever kill my wife.' So the officer tells him, 'Fine, that's very touching, but you're obviously not CIA material,' and he has the man escorted from the building."

Anne crossed her arms tightly over her chest. Sally

played her fingers along the edge of the freshly laminated driver's license.

"Now the officer takes the second man down the hall to a similar door and says, 'Your wife is behind this door, sitting in a chair, waiting. You must go inside, use this gun, and shoot her.' The man nods, takes the gun, steps through the door and closes it behind him. But no gunshots are heard. After a minute, the man comes back out, shaking his head. 'I couldn't do it. I'm sorry. I can't kill my wife.' The officer sighs and takes back the gun, dismissing the man. Then he walks the woman down the hall to one last door, and says, 'Your husband is sitting in a chair behind this door. You must go inside and kill him.' Then he hands the woman the gun, and she steps inside."

Finally Sally lifted her eyes, the nearness of the joke's conclusion lulling her back.

"Suddenly from behind the door, a gunshot rings out. This shot is followed by several others. The CIA officer waits. Seconds later, he hears a crash, followed by screams and a bunch of violent smashing sounds. Then there's only silence. A minute later, the door opens, and the woman is standing there, breathing heavily. Wiping the sweat from her face, she says, 'You didn't tell me the gun was filled with blanks. So I had to beat him to death with the chair.' "

No one said a word.

And then, like a sunlight crack in the clouds, Anne smiled.

"So there," Dawn said, and then Sally grinned as well, and the pressure eased from the room like a spigot had been opened. It was just what they needed. Everyone relaxed.

Before they left the cramped closet and its plain wooden shelves of waiting shoes, Sally tapped Dakota's cast as if sending a telegraph message. "How soon?"

"Depends on what you need."

"Forget the computer hackers. Just licenses and Social Security cards, enough to get them jobs when they get over here. A dozen of them to begin with."

"A week. And it's probably going to run you at least a grand."

"Fine. Make it happen." She put her hands in her hair and did a little automatic arranging, gathering herself now that their shady deal was concluded. "So let's go home and get some sleep. We've got a lot of practicing to do between now and Friday."

They adjourned. Jazmyn and Crespin were sitting on the floor in the showroom, speaking in Spanish and gesturing broadly. Though Jaz worked her way slowly around the language, her gusto was undiminished as she plied Crespin with one story after the next in the manner that Dawn had come to cherish. Jaz could talk a person's ear off, and Dawn would gladly be earless the rest of her days if she were so lucky as to listen to her daughter's unbounded zest for life.

"So how's it feel to be criminals?" Jazmyn asked them.

"Don't say that," Anne said in such a way as to brook no rebuttal.

Jazmyn made a show of zipping her mouth closed, then she leaned close to Crespin and whispered something that made his eyes widen.

Before they left the shop and went their separate ways for the evening, Dawn stopped Sally at the door. "I have one question and one statement."

"Make it fast."

"Question. How do you plan on paying for all these sham documents?"

"I'm not sure. I guess I'm hoping Jude Yarbuck will make us an offer to return."

Dawn absorbed this without reaction, deciding it best

not to consider the ramifications until later. "Fine. Statement. Isadore Presper was at the concert tonight."

Sally's face was only half revealed in the crooked light from the sidewalk lamps. "I know."

Dawn was momentarily at a loss. "Uh . . . you already knew that?"

"Suspected. I saw you and Annie, how you talked close to each other, how you kept glancing around. You both looked as pale as ghosts. I knew something was up, and I was betting on a Presper sighting. But I wasn't certain until you just confirmed it."

"Shit, why didn't you say something?"

"Why didn't *you?*"

"Well, we didn't want you to do anything—"

"Rash?"

"Yes."

"Too late for that, I think."

Anne was mugged in her driveway.

The body dislocated itself from the socket of darkness beside her car, and it fell upon her even before she'd gotten both feet on the gravel. Her thoughts at the moment of impact were of the police and the nightly news, and how the former would arrest them and the latter exploit them when the inevitable happened and Sally's plan was exposed. Anne was trying to come to terms with herself and the possibility of jail when the form emerged from the shadows beside the garage and the arms encircled her waist.

She was lifted off her feet. Fear forked through her. She opened her mouth to scream.

"I love you!" her attacker cried. Then he spun her around and gave a happy yelp.

"Trevor?"

"You were awesome tonight! Utterly rad!"

Fear's fork was replaced by a cooling torrent of relief. Pleasure followed quickly after, as the feeling of her son's arms around her was bliss in its purest form. She hugged him back.

Trevor lowered her to her feet. The porch light, in the shape of an antique miner's lantern, shed sufficient light that Anne could see the smile fixed to her son's face. Trevor's lower lip was pierced with a sterling silver stud. His eyes were darkened and granted unnatural mystique by the eyeliner he wore. His skin was clear and unblemished, rare for a boy his age, the color of creamy alabaster. In another era, that skin would have been chronicled by poets.

"I'm glad you came and watched," Anne said. She couldn't resist the urge to touch his chin, however briefly. They were not a family given to casual contact, but as Trevor had just smashed through his unspoken injunction with his ambush-embrace, Anne was not about to miss the chance to reciprocate. "I didn't see you in the crowd."

"I was way in the back. But I saw. And it was tight, Mom, way tight."

"Tight is good, right?"

Trevor rolled his eyes at her as if to say, *Please forgive Ma, she's not up to speed.*

"A thousand pardons," Anne laughed, "but I'm a slacker in the modern slang department. Maybe you and I can go inside, crack open a gallon of French vanilla, and exchange knowledge of street jargon. What do you say to that?"

"The ice cream sounds great, but I don't think you want me repeating a lot of the jargon I hear at school."

"What—you think your mother has virgin ears? You think I've never heard a swear word? You think I've never used one?"

Clearly Trevor did indeed assume these very things.

"I was a kid once too, you know."

"Yeah, but . . . you cussed?"

"Only when I had to."

"Do you still?"

"No, dammit, never, now get your ass in the kitchen and let's eat the hell out of that ice cream."

Trevor was taken aback, but pleasantly so, his smile trying to muster on a face that seemed uncertain as to whether or not such emotions were appropriate.

Anne laughed again, and after a moment Trevor joined her.

She raced him to the door and had no intention of letting him win.

Sally found the tapes at midnight.

Cassette tapes, the kind they likely didn't make anymore, the kind that had defined her life as a teen, the kind that—when held in the hand at this late hour—were quaint and obsolete yet maintained a kind of magic for her, amulets to conjure the past. Sitting cross-legged on the floor in front of her closet, she heard the voices of her bygone days as her hands drifted through the tapes.

Sal, you got that new Eddie Money record yet?

Oh, please, Dawn, nobody buys records anymore. Get a tape player already.

What about you, Annie-cakes?

Sorry. If it isn't Cyndi Lauper, I'm not interested.

Yeah, okay, Cyndi's cool and all, but what about . . . what about . . .

All the girls finished the sentence together, along with Tatyana who'd been lounging on the bed with a teeny-bopper magazine, and now Sally said it here alone on the floor, in synch with the voices in her head: "What about . . . Prince."

The four of them, regardless of their other differences, agreed unanimously on Prince.

Some of the cassettes Sally discovered had been handled so frequently that the print had been worn from the plastic, so that she could no longer read the arrangement of songs on side one of Foreigner's *Double Vision*. And a Phil Collins tape at the bottom of the box had been eviscerated, a long black ribbon pulled from its reels like a skinny intestine and tangled inextricably around itself. So much for Phil. There was a song on that album called "Sussudio," and Sally had yet at this advanced age to figure out just what the hell a Sussudio was.

She pored over these artifacts for half an hour, selecting songs that she would present to the others for their approval, songs that she would sing as camouflage as furtive Mexicans crept behind her, like an illusionist using music as misdirection to keep unwanted eyes away from what was really going on. One thing troubled her. She had no plan of escape. Unlike a stage illusionist, she had no trapdoor, no hidden point of egress should the trick go sour and her true intention be revealed. When some attentive Immigrations investigator or Border Patrol officer caught word of the operation and traced it to its source, Sally would have no defense other than the visceral need to avenge Juan Doe in the only way that seemed appropriate.

From deep in the house: laughter.

Sally knew that laugh like she knew the sound of her own breathing. Jaz was still awake and not getting to bed as Sally had suggested. The girl was in the living room with Crespin, and by the sound of that laugh, they'd be awake for awhile, talking about whatever young people talked about these days. At the moment, surrounded by anti-quated cassettes and thinking thoughts of dead men, forg-eries, and freedom, Sally had never felt further removed from her youth.

She wondered if they'd be able to prepare a set of songs and manage not to embarrass themselves on Friday night at the Texanna. Was tonight's victory a fluke? Had Radio won the contest because they were a gag act? A joke? And more importantly, would she actually be able to maintain her self-appointed role as people-smuggler without getting arrested? Leigh Surry was no dummy, and if he were nearby—and Sally sensed that nearby was where he wanted to be—then she'd have to tread lightly, lest he stumble upon her risky game. And don't forget Isadore Presper and his band, cir-cling the desert sea like sharks, waiting to pick off the weak.

This whole mess had potential DATFUG written all over it.

In an effort to forget about it until morning, Sally dug out her lovingly worn cassette player, turned out her bed-room light, and fell asleep listening to Prince explain to her the mysteries of purple rain.

Chapter Fourteen

Wednesday morning a freak sandstorm blew out of the wasteland. Black and angry, it coruscated through Fresh Waters with vindictive force, curling its grainy tendrils up rainspouts and down chimney flues. While the winds brayed like wounded dogs against the window, the skies darkened from the buildup of silt in the air, and the garage belonging to Alex and Dawn-Marie Johnson shook with a storm of its own.

Anne danced her fingers across the dual electronic keyboards, saber-shaped eyes on the music in front of her. Jazmyn, perched on a barstool, barefoot, hair in a French braid, melded into her guitar with a soulfulness that belied her age, coaxing it to places it had never been. Dawn drove her foot against the bass drum's pedal, as steady and pounding as a locomotive, and used her drumsticks to make soft *click-chink* noises on a dual cymbal that Dakota had told her was called a high-hat. And Sally, she seemed unaware of them all, shelled in a self-woven cocoon of solitude, as she put her mouth against the mike and sang of buying her first six-string at the five-and-dime and playing it until her fingers bled, back in the summer of '69.

Talons of sand raked at the glass.

An hour after it had arrived, howling, sowing fine seeds

of sand in the sidewalk cracks, the storm lost all strength. It faded quickly, its sands whispering as they settled, revealing the sun and leaving everything covered in a faint patina of dust.

People emerged from homes and offices, rubbing the granules from their eyes.

That evening the town would make the news on the big stations in Phoenix and Tucson, and even receive mention on the nationally broadcast Weather Channel. Storms like this, misbegotten and completely unpredicted, were notable not only for the abrasive damage they dealt to cars but also for their capricious origin. This particular meteorological anomaly was sudden and unshakably eerie, packed with equal shares of grit and wonder, like something out of Arabia.

As far as anyone could remember, it was the first time the town of Fresh Waters had made the national news since the incident twenty-five years ago at Scorpion City, when four local girls had found all that blood and then thwarted the man responsible for it.

"So who's minding the shop for you, Sal?"

"Do you know Jill from the bank?"

"The one with all the liposuction?"

"She's willing to work for minimum wage. That was my sole criterion when hiring."

"Lex says along with the lipo-work she also got a boob job, but how can you tell aside from grabbing the things?"

"Alex has been grabbing Jill's boobs?"

"No, but his mechanic buddy Matt used to date her. Jill, I mean. And he grabbed."

"Can we get back to the songs, please?"

"Sure, practice makes perfect and all that. Slave-driver."

"I'll settle for practice makes passable. Now let's try the Joan Jett number."

"Wait, one more thing. Very important."

"Let me guess. A cucumber update."

"You bet. Reason fifty. Cucumbers never tell you they liked you better with long hair."

"Long live cucumbers."

"Amen, sister Sally. Let's rock."

For dinner they ate takeout burgers, except for Anne, whose health-food sensibilities forced a raid on Dawn's fridge, where she found the makings of a salad and a single, bruised pear that looked like a dud grenade found at the scene of a battle. Dawn had called in sick, so as to escape her shift at the Cheshire Grin. Alex was a dear and, muttering about his wife going off the deep end, kept the twins occupied and stunned everyone by making a chocolate cake, two layers, messy but edible. So what if his frosting came from a can? The cake was a gesture of support for whatever his wife and her friends thought they were doing. He'd known them long enough to appreciate their eccentricities, even if he didn't understand them. His second moment of brilliance, after the cake, came when he suggested offhandedly that Radio add to its song list the immortal "We Will Rock You." He loaned them his old Queen record, and Sally studied the lyrics printed in the liner notes while Dawn mastered the simple yet primitively powerful three-beat rhythm.

By eight o'clock the sun was turning to orange liquid on the horizon, drenching the western mesas in lavalike color. The dust motes that still hung in the air from the morning's storm appeared in that burnished light like flecks of floating prospector's gold.

At eight-fifteen, on impulse, Sally called Mark Cheevey to ask about Farrington Schatz.

The statue remained standing despite the storm winds, according to the latest eyewitness report, taken at 8:02. This was good, since it was only Wednesday, and Sally's money was on a Saturday fall. Members of the high school science club had gotten permission to replace the cymbal under Farrington's upraised bronze arm with a Rube Goldberg contraption that would sound an air horn when the monument finally toppled. The air horn, Cheevey assured her, was not so loud as a military klaxon, but close. When it ultimately went off, she'd be able to hear it from nearly anywhere in town, unless she was in the shower, watching a loud movie, or otherwise engaged in a high-decibel activity.

Which, at the moment, she was.

An hour later, fingers abraded from guitar strings, nails split from keyboards, backs aching from sitting behind drum sets, they left off their practicing and flopped onto the sofa in Dawn's living room, as they had flopped countless times before on countless sofas, eyes closed and arms draped over weary foreheads.

"Bedtime," Dawn said to the ceiling.

"I second the motion." Sally got to her feet, said her goodbyes, and drove home. She left Jazmyn, who had already run up the stairs to her bedroom across the hall from the twins; with three mothers, three homes, and three beds, Jazmyn was never far away from a decent night's rest. The girl owned three of all the essentials, one set at each house, and Dawn had once called her Noah-and-a-Half, though it had taken everyone awhile to get the joke.

Crespin and Dakota were waiting in Sally's driveway.

Despite the barricade of language, the two young men

had come upon the partnership common to those of their age, facilitated by Jazmyn's translations and cemented by their shared love of soccer. And of girls.

Sally, facing them as they stood up to meet her, felt ancient. She didn't know why. Though she was—what?—maybe sixteen years older than them, she felt like a grandmother, her skin a wrinkled road map next to these fresh faces. "Normally I'd be thrilled to find two hunks camped out on my doorstep, but it's been a long day."

"Can we go inside and talk?" Dakota asked.

"Is this the kind of talk that needs to be done inside?"

"Probably."

Realizing that those types of talks were blessedly rare in life, Sally led them into her living room and turned on more lights than usual. Had she been alone, she likely would have patrolled the house for intruders, but in the company of these strong squires she felt less threatened by things unseen in the dark. Ever since she'd made the decision to cross the legal line, she'd sensed a rising of the old paranoia barometer. Carrying a can of Mace couldn't be far behind.

"Show her the new you," Dakota told Crespin. There was something ominous in the way he said it.

Crespin's ruddy good looks were haunted by a slyness that Sally had never seen in him before. And apparently his grasp of English was improving rapidly, because he responded to Dakota's suggestion without pause, digging into his back pocket and extracting a new bifold wallet of imitation leather. He opened it with care. The wallet's little credit card slots held only two items, and he removed them one at a time and held them out toward Sally with the confidence of a cop displaying his badge.

"So now you qualify to receive Social Security checks," Sally observed, reading the name printed on the little card.

"Which means when you turn sixty-five, after a lifetime of working your butt off, paying your bills, and raising a family, you'll get just enough retirement money to buy TV dinners and maybe if you're lucky you can pay the electricity bill every month."

Crespin knotted his brow.

"Never mind. My recent awareness of social injustice is causing the sarcasm to leak out. Congratulations on your new life as an American citizen and your license to operate a motor vehicle in the state of Arizona." She turned to Dakota. "What about the others?"

"Rudy can't do much work in advance. He needs passport-style IDs of everyone."

"He wants me to march a line of illegal Mexicans into his studio?"

"Can you get pictures of them somewhere else?"

"I don't even have them yet. As far as I know, they're still down Mexico way, waiting for me to rescue them. Besides, I'm not much of a photographer. Everyone always ends up with red demon eyes. But, yeah, I guess I can manage to get pictures of anyone I bring across the border. Anything else I need to supply?"

"Just the *dinero*." For a moment he looked uncertain, but then a wisp of a grin ghosted across his face.

"What?" Sally demanded. "What are you thinking but not saying?"

"Who says I'm thinking but not saying?"

"Your smirk says, that's who."

He thrust his unbroken hand into a back pocket of his jeans and looked like a schoolboy when he did it. "It's nothing. I just . . . I just didn't think you'd ever do something like this. I've known you and Jaz for almost two years now and . . ." He shook his head.

"Do you think I'm crazy?"

"Crazy ain't always bad."

"Breaking the law is bad. I'm sure of it. That's why we have jails."

"Don't worry. I don't plan on telling anyone what you're doing."

"I know you won't." She looked at him levelly, and realized for the first time she was seeing him not as Jazmyn's impetuous friend but as a man with some sense in his head. "I've never been a bad influence on my own daughter before. And now look at me."

Dakota was silent for a minute. Though his blue eyes never left her, he seemed to be gazing elsewhere, perhaps into some font of unlikely wisdom. His blond hair lay scattered on his forehead and his small pectoral muscles made saucer shapes under his white T-shirt.

Past life? Sally queried herself. *Need I ask?* She wondered if young Dakota had ever heard of James Dean.

"I had a dog once," he said.

"Okay . . ."

"I got him when I was four. A mutt. He was the best dog that's ever lived."

"I'm listening."

"Our house caught on fire when I was eleven years old. One of those big, inferno kind of fires like you see in the movies. I ended up in the backyard, and the rest of the family ran out the front. Half of the walls in between us collapsed, and I could see straight through what used to be our living room. My old man was in the front yard, waving his arm and shouting at me to back up, back up, just back the hell up and stay safe. It was like looking through a burning tunnel."

Sally saw it in her mind. Her imagination had never been

known for its multiple dimensions, being rather flat and shapeless. But the pictures assembled themselves before her inner eye with remarkable clarity, their textures so rich that she could almost feel the heat of the flames as they licked from the eaves of Dakota's boyhood home. She stood beside him at the mouth of that blazing corridor, staring through the smoke at his family.

"What happened next'll stay with me if I live to be a hundred," Dakota said.

Beside him, Crespin looked on, rapt, though he probably grasped very little of the tale.

"The dog," Sally said.

"Yeah. The dog. He'd run out of the house with the others, and there he was, right beside Dad, barking his shaggy ass off at the fire like it was his mortal enemy. And the damn dog saw me."

And Sally saw the dog, a brown, bunched mass of sinew, ears cocked high, hackles as erect as wires down its back, yellow teeth bared to the conflagration.

"The dog loved me, I guess. Couldn't stand to be away from me. Don't get me wrong, he liked everyone, but he had something special with me. I was the leader of our pack of two."

Sally empathized. Among her own pack, she was the alpha female.

"I think he was trying to save me," Dakota went on. "He thought I was in trouble, that I was inside the fire and burning, so he came running. Shot into that tunnel like a little brown missile, ears laid back against his head, eyes half closed against the smoke." Dakota made a study of the floor. When he looked up again, Sally saw the moisture filming his eyes. "He caught fire. That shaggy brown coat of his . . ." He shook his head. "Anyway, he died trying to save me."

Crespin, either comprehending the gist of the story or responding to his new friend's quiet grief, touched Dakota on the elbow.

"Hey, man, I'm cool," Dakota told him. He shoved a smile to his face. "Damn, I'm a softy, ain't I?"

"Thank God for that," Sally said. "We need more softies. There's not many of you left."

"Yeah, whatever. I guess what I'm trying to say is . . ."

"You don't want me to get burned by trying to save someone's life."

"Uh-huh. Something like that."

"Are you comparing me to a dog, Dakota?"

Now his grin was genuine. "Looks that way, huh?"

Sally felt a rush of relief when Dakota's sorrow made a visible retreat. "Enough sob stories for one night, okay? I appreciate your concern, and I'm not just saying that. I really do. But your dog chased after you because of loyalty. What I'm doing is something else. What, exactly, I'm not sure, but my motivation isn't the same as his. I'll let you know when I figure it out. In the meantime, we should all get some sleep."

"I just don't want you charging into a burning house."

"The charge has already begun."

"It's not too late."

Sally saw Juan Doe lying in the dirt beside the road, chased to his death. "When you were in school, did you ever run track?"

"Huh?"

"Track and field. You know, hurdles, shot-puts, pole vaulting—did you compete?"

"Nah, I had other things to do. I've never been a jock. Why?"

"The girls and I have always run, at least until recently,

197

because nowadays it seems like such an effort. At any rate, we ran in elementary school, and we ran in junior high, and then all the way up to when we were seniors. I know it's hard for you to believe, but yes, I was a killer in those skimpy little shorts, and these fleshy thighs you see before you were once positively svelte."

Dakota's grin flared again, and it was a heartbreaker.

"Annie and Tatyana were the sprinters. Dawn could high-jump with the best of them. And me, I was our long-distance queen. But what I'm doing right now, this charge I'm on, it's like a relay race. One runner passes the baton to the next, and away she goes. Well, a Mexican man whose name I'll never know started the race hundreds of miles south of here, and then he died, but before he died I ran into him, and in doing so I accepted his baton. Now it's mine. I've got a death grip on it, and I plan on holding up my end of the deal and running like hell until I can pass it on to somebody else."

Dakota slipped his hand from his pocket and crossed his arms, if somewhat awkwardly, as his left was twice as thick as his right. "So what are you running for? What's at the finish line?"

"Like I said, I'll let you know when I get there."

Dakota seemed to find this answer acceptable, as if its ambiguity appealed to the poet in him, or at least to the renegade. "Then what's the plan?"

"So far? The plan is to play at Jude Yarbuck's honky-tonk two nights from now. The plan is to practice our little fannies off between now and then. The plan is to call Jill to keep the shop for me in the morning, because the plan is also to drive Crespin down to Mexico tomorrow and tell his family that we're bringing them in. But until then, the plan is to sleep, and maybe to dream."

Dakota's expression didn't change. Maybe he'd been expecting Sally to broach the subject of a Mexico run, so that now when she finally tipped her hand, he wasn't surprised. "What can I do to help?"

"You're doing enough already. I'll see you at rehearsal."

After a moment, he gave her a crisp nod. "I'm not going to tell you to be careful, but be careful anyway." Then he touched her arm, as quickly and lightly as a butterfly brushing her skin. The contact was ephemeral, and almost immediately he was heading out the door, but he left something behind, lingering at a point just above her elbow.

Crespin was watching her.

Sally blinked away her reverie and offered him a sagging smile. "See you *mañana*."

"Goodnight." It was one of his newly minted English words. *"Gracias por ayudarme."*

"You're welcome, for whatever you just said." Sally didn't wait to see him to his cot in the garage. She lay in bed for an hour with the fireworks of her new life keeping her awake. In the next forty-eight hours she would cross the nation's border, make arrangements to sneak a dozen illegals into the country, arm them with forged papers, and send them with her ramshackle blessing out into the world. She would become, if she wasn't already, a bootlegger of humans.

A people-legger, she thought. That wasn't very funny.

After that, she'd perform her first paid gig—oh, what a word. She'd parade around in front of strangers and sing rock anthems that everybody knew, along with some Patsy Cline because old Patsy was requisite material for any band playing for the kind of clientele who patronized a joint like the Texanna. Along the way she had to get her hands on enough money to pay the rent so as not to lose the store, and hope that in a past life she'd been a saint because she was going to need some heavy-duty karma to keep the police from tumbling onto her game. And then, if that wasn't enough, she'd like to find a few moments to spend with a certain officer from Immigration, because the last time she'd had a lover the dinosaurs had walked the earth, or at least it felt that way on certain nights. Add to this the fact that—

The phone rang and scared her.

She swung her arm out and nabbed the cordless, guessing it was Dawn with one last cucumber jibe because that's what Dawn had always done, kept them going with her humor and her unsinkable spirit—"Hello?"

"Mom, it's me."

"Jaz?" At once Sally sensed there was trouble. She sat straight up. "Jaz, what's wrong?"

"I just . . . I just got a call from Kelli, one of my friends in school." Jazmyn's voice was threaded tightly, so that no emotion was allowed to slip between the stitches. "Kelli's dad is an EMT. He drives the ambulance . . ."

Sally closed her eyes. The breath had fled her, so that her lungs felt like they were floating. "Honey. Tell me what happened. Who was in the ambulance?"

"Jeffrey Longbranch."

"Oh, God."

"He died, Mom."

"*Jesus.*"

"He had a seizure. In bed. Diabetes, you know. His parents didn't find him until . . ." Her words trailed away, replaced by a hiccup, a sniff, and silence.

Sally opened her eyes. Her room was dark, the window outlined faintly with moonlight.

"Mom?"

"I'm here, baby. Are you okay?"

"Just shaky. I'll be all right."

Long after they'd disconnected, Sally sat there, knees drawn to her chest, afraid to relax. She thought of Jeffrey's mother, and of the gross injustice of childhood disease, and of the great silences that would pervade the Longbranch home.

The tears stormed her like an enemy army.

She fell over on her side and wept without sound. A minute later she realized that she wasn't crying for Jeffrey's mom, but for herself. The world was a tyrant, and just when she thought she was finally standing up to it, the hammer dropped and cracked her heart again.

Her bedroom grew darker as the moon was stolen by the larcenous clouds, and her vision was further obscured by her tears. Yet . . . in a mirage as potent as any she'd ever known, suddenly she saw Jeffrey standing in front of her, eyes gripping her like little vises. He stood tall and peacefully. Never relinquishing her gaze, he held his arm out and gave her the sign she'd seen him deliver at the Ampi, forefinger and pinky extended. This symbol was a message, a code of body language, like the semaphore flags used to send warnings between ships.

Sally lay there and wondered what he was trying to tell her.

Chapter Fifteen

Thursday, according to Anne, was named for Thor, the god of thunder.

As keeper of obscure and arguably useless lore, Anne also felt obligated to inform them that America was rife with such pagan heirlooms, such as Easter, which everyone thought was a Christian holiday but was actually named for Eostre, old Anglo-Saxon goddess of spring and fertility. Eostre once transformed a bird into a magical hare that could lay eggs, hence the Easter bunny. "Which means," Anne concluded as they were warming up their instruments in the garage, "when we celebrate Easter by honoring Christ, we're mixing our mythologies. Attaching Jesus to Easter is like giving the Pope a national holiday during Mardi Gras."

"I'm sure the old Popemeister will be thrilled to hear it," Dawn said.

With an avalanche of drums and guitar, the women of Radio paid homage to their own thunder gods—REO Speedwagon.

After hours of it—one song following another until it became more toil than fun—Sally called it quits. Her throat ached from all the singing. Dawn's fingers were covered in white first-aid tape, and she'd fractured nearly every nail she had. Anne, hands working continuously above the keys, was starting to make comments about carpal tunnel syndrome. The only one who wasn't complaining was Jazmyn, the flaxen-haired, miniskirt-wearing reincarnation of Jimi Hendrix. She was perched atop an amplifier, eyelids painted with blue sparkles, alternating between her two guitars and rendering sizzling performances of every piece of sheet music they put in front of her. They'd purchased the music from All That Jazz, the little store downtown that got most of its business from high school students needing new reeds for their clarinets but was now unwitting supplier to the most unlikely garage band around, also known as Radio, daughters of the Anglo-Saxon gods.

"I can't do anymore," Sally said, sinking down into the beanbag in the corner. She leaned her head back against the wall of the garage. "I've moved beyond the point of feeling silly about what we're doing, so now I'm begging off from pure exhaustion instead of embarrassment."

"It's not even noon yet," Anne reminded her. "We have the whole afternoon. I don't think we can afford to squander our time. Have you seen the crowds they have at the Texanna?"

"Have you?"

"I've been there. Once or twice."

"With or without Barry?"

"With."

"So what you're saying is, it's been a long time."

"So what? Dancing isn't something he and I do anymore. Is that somehow germane to the discussion?"

Sally felt the edge in her friend's words, so she put on the brakes. They were wearing one another thin. Though she felt the childish need to argue, just for the sake of arguing, she forced herself to concentrate on the important

203

stuff. "I need to call someone and ask if a date has been set for the funeral."

No one said anything.

Sally wasn't surprised by the silence. Jeffrey's death had affected them all, each in her own private way. In a town as small as Fresh Waters, you always knew the deceased, or at least you'd heard of them in passing. And Jeffrey was only a boy, and those undersized caskets were diabolical. . . .

"I expect the service to be held on Saturday," Anne finally said. The fight had gone out of her voice. She sat down heavily in a folding metal chair they'd borrowed from Alex's card table. "If he passed away last night, Saturday seems the most logical choice."

There seemed little to say on the subject after that. They'd already spent a good part of the morning discussing it, getting angry and sad by turn, and dabbing away tears. Invariably you thought of your own children when you heard of someone Jeffrey's age dying. Dawn kept getting up from her drums to check on Coy and Caleb. Anne had called twice to talk to Trevor. Sally's eyes returned to Jazmyn, her prayers selfish little thank-yous that her daughter was healthy and whole.

"Besides," Sally said, returning to the former topic, "we have something to take care of this afternoon, so we don't have any choice but to stop for awhile and get out of here."

Dawn absently twirled a drumstick. "Mexico."

"The sooner we leave, the sooner we can be back and rehearse."

"How many of them do you expect to fit in the car?"

"We're not bringing anyone back. We're only making arrangements."

"Getting ourselves arrested is what we'll be doing."

"People drive across the border every day," Sally informed her.

"Yes, and people get their asses thrown in jail every day too."

"You don't have to come."

"Yeah, right. I suppose you'll also be leaving your left arm behind."

Sally was in no mood for further debate. Damn diabetes and damn immigration laws. She counted herself an enemy of both. Her mission, as a matter of futile revenge, was to escort Crespin back to Mexico, where he could reunite with his family and make arrangements for them to come across. Sally would be waiting for them on the other side, along with a purse full of false IDs. And no, she wouldn't be leaving her left arm behind. Or any other part of her anatomy. "We're going to need to use the Chieftain again."

"Lex'll want to know why."

"Make something up."

"Lie to my husband? It'll never work. You know how Pinocchio's nose grew whenever he fibbed? Well, I suffer from the same condition, except with a different body part. When I don't tell the truth, my butt gets bigger. Sucker actually increases exponentially in size with every lie I tell. As you can see, I haven't had an honest day in years."

Sally felt the smile, but it was down deep and never found her face.

"Ah, hell," Dawn sighed. "I guess I'll think of something to tell him. Annie, what about you? Care to split a bottle of tequila when we get there?"

"If I remember correctly," Anne said, "the last time you sampled tequila, we were twenty-one years old, and I found myself camped out all night in Jody Haskell's bathroom in order to make sure you kept your hair out of the toilet."

"Funny, I don't remember that at all." She struck a contemplative pose. "Nope, can't recall a single thing. Are you positive that happened?"

"Jody's mother said that blackouts are a sure sign of alcoholism."

Dawn laughed sharply. "She did say that, didn't she? Man, that woman was steamed. Sal, you mean we're going right now?"

Sally had stood up and was making a pointless effort to pat the wrinkles from her pants and not think about Jeffrey and how he reminded her of a combination of Buddy Holly and a kid from *The Bad News Bears*. "Jaz, you'll have to stay here and watch Coy and Caleb. Do you mind?"

Jazmyn had been plucking out notes in a kind of trance. When she glanced up, she wore the look of a medium shrugging off a visiting spirit. The music did that to her; her guitar was a Ouija board awaiting her next touch. "How come you guys get to have all the fun?"

"The prerogative of old age." Early this morning Sally had bumbled through a heart-to-heart with the girl, trying to explain her reasons but not getting very far. She hoped her daughter would be wise enough not to learn by example. "So will you play babysitter for awhile? We'll try to be back by dark."

"Yeah, sure, whatever." Jazmyn returned her attention to the guitar and its captive voices from the great beyond. "Just please try and not get yourselves nailed by the Mexican police. That would be so uncool."

Sally picked up the fanny pack she'd brought along just for this occasion and strapped it to her waist. "Believe me, being uncool is my biggest fear in this life."

"That and menopause," Dawn said. "Let me go talk to the boys for a sec, then I'll be ready to fly."

"I'll throw some snacks together," Anne added. "Dawn, do you still have that little ice chest?"

"Your idea of snacks," Dawn said as they passed through the door from the garage into the house proper, "is protein bars and spring water. When I say snacks, I'm talking hardcore Twinkies, nachos, soda, and those big-ass cookies wrapped in red foil. . . ."

The old Pontiac Chieftain carried them south through the desert.

Sally rode in the backseat beside her lost-cause-in-the-flesh, Crespin Onofre y Ramos. Up front, Dawn kept turning around and asking Crespin questions about his mother and his politics and his girlfriends, and Anne interpreted as best she could while keeping the big car on the road. Crespin said his mother was a saint and his father worked himself sick. His politics were apparently as scattered and undeveloped as any boy his age. And as for his girlfriends—he fidgeted a little and suddenly grew uncertain—he'd only dated two, the first when he was fourteen and knew of nothing beyond holding hands, and the second a year ago; her father had moved the family to Mexico City, and Crespin had received only one letter from her since.

"What was her name?" Dawn asked.

Crespin understood the question without need for translation. "Joaquina."

"Wow. Good name. How come all the other countries get all the good names?"

Ninety miles separated Fresh Waters from the Mexican border. Sally rode those miles in silence, watching the barrel cactus and bright desert marigolds turn to a blur on the side of the highway. Great escarpments of red clay, carved by millennia of wind and maybe the tides of some prehistoric sea, appeared to her not as the familiar landscaping of her lifetime home, but rather something from another planet, one that up until now had been seen only in artists' renderings and grainy photos sent to earth from robot scouts. That's how removed she felt from her life.

After awhile even Dawn ran out of things that seemed important enough to talk about. Anne turned on the radio but quickly changed the channel away from Alex's classic rock station; the three of them had heard so much of that raucous genre recently from their own instruments that now it seemed excessive from someone else's. She listened to a news channel until Dawn started making barfing noises and demanded a change. They settled on George Strait, who was singing of being a fireman and putting out old flames.

NOGALES, MEXICO 25

They all saw the sign, but no one commented.

Southbound on I-19, Sally could look to her right and see, stenciled against the afternoon sun, the humpbacked shapes of the Sierrita Mountains. Again, it was a sight that should not have captivated her, as those slumbering giants had been a part of her world since she was born. She had hiked them in her college days. She had collected colored stones from the shallow washes between their shoulders. Yet for all the sense they made to her now, the Sierritas might have been the Ural Mountains that she'd read about in *National Geographic*, beyond them the bitter plains of Siberia.

They stopped for gas at Rio Rico. Speaking little. Keeping to themselves. Brushing against one another more often than usual. Transmitting messages of solidarity.

Waiting for the tank to fill, Sally stared at a lone crucifixion thorn on the edge of town. This gaunt, friendless bush had no leaves, only devilishly sharp barbs protruding from its blue-gray branches. In a moment of time-capsule quality, Sally saw Tatyana dive into the razor clutches of a certain, long-gone crucifixion thorn on the edge of the mine shaft. In the newspaper the next morning, the journalist had referred to the plant by its colloquial name, *corona de Cristo,* the crown of Christ.

"Here," Dawn said, offering her a box of white powdered donuts. "Beware of Greeks bearing cholesterol."

"Thanks. I never knew that people-smuggling could be so bad on the diet." She accepted the box—

—and remembered.

"Uh, Sal? Something wrong? You look like that proverbial goose just did the foxtrot over your grave."

"Jeffrey," Sally breathed.

Dawn frowned. "What about him?"

"He gave me a box. A shoebox. As a gift."

"Yeah, I remember. You had it in the truck Sunday, right? What was in it?"

"I . . . I don't know. I forgot all about it. I never opened it. And now he's . . ."

"In a better place, that's where he is. Or so they say in Sunday school."

"Remind me to open it when we get home, okay?"

"On one condition."

Sally looked at her and waited.

"I won't let you forget about opening the mystery box as long as you promise to eat at least a third of these albino, artery-murdering donuts, because I don't want Crespin to see what a hog I can be. You know how I am when trapped in small spaces with sugar."

"Deal."

Dawn made a manlike noise in her throat and pretended to spit on her palm, then offered her hand to Sally.

Sally didn't have the spirit to feign the spitting, but she clasped her friend's hand, squeezed tightly, and as the car got a refueling, so too did Sally's heart.

Anne realized what was wrong with America. It had no villages.

Dusk was upon them. The western sky was the color of rust, as if the dome of the world had begun finally to oxidize and fall to pieces, and soon all the good air would be lost to space. Reinforcing this strange image in Anne's mind was the eastern horizon, where blackness encroached as if from holes in the atmosphere. It made her feel uneasy, so to occupy herself she studied Crespin's village and catalogued each of its components in her mind.

The twilight shadows were long among the little houses. Car without tires served as playgrounds for the village's children, of which there seemed to be dozens, all with brown hair and deep, wonder-filled eyes. The streets were made of packed earth, darkened with patches of dried motor oil. One roof was fashioned entirely of plastic milk crates stuffed with straw and patched with tar. The house beside it was painted a celebratory shade of red. Its proud owner had decorated the plywood windowsills with multi-colored soda cans, fastened by twine around the sashes. Four of the homes, perfectly square and identical in appearance, were built of gray cinderblock and likely the product of an American church group on a week-long mission trip. The village's centerpiece was what appeared to be a grocery and dry-goods store, its sides covered in old gas-station signs and faded posters of Spanish-dubbed versions of Hollywood hits.

Anne noticed that she was the object of placid scrutiny.

People with quiet, peaceful faces stood under the awning

in front of the store and watched. Others peeked from their
windows. A man looked up from his work under a pickup's
hood, met Anne's gaze, and slowly touched the brim of his
straw hat in salutation.

Anne lifted a hand and nudged her fingers in a wave.

Meanwhile Crespin and Sally were conversing, at least as
best as their poor language skills allowed. Sally kept saying,
"Annie? Annie, help me out here," and Anne would duti-
fully regurgitate to Crespin whatever it was that Sally
wanted him to know, but for the most part, her thoughts
were elsewhere.

"*Señora.*"

Anne turned to look into ancient eyes. The face around
those gray eyes was like a hard, sun-shriveled gourd. A lack
of teeth caused the mouth to fold inward. The earlobes
were elongated and baked like leather thongs from a lifetime of exposure. The man wore a fat piece of turquoise
around his neck. In his native tongue he asked, "Ma'am,
would you like to purchase a knife for your kitchen?"

Displayed on his open hands was an unrolled square of
rawhide, to which had been tied a variety of hand-made
knives with handles made of antler and animal bone.

Anne smiled politely. "No, thank you."

"But, ma'am, these knives, they are very sharp, and in
your cooking they would be very useful, very purposeful. I
have made each of them myself."

"No, really, I don't have any need. I'm not much of a
cook." This may have been true—Barry and Trevor could
attest to it if asked—but culinary deficiencies aside, she
simply didn't want to spend time trading with the locals, regardless of what they were selling. She only wanted to go
home and try not to think about the officers from Homeland Security knocking on her door.

"This one, pretty ma'am, is very special, very sharp."
With a dexterity that defied the skeletal appearance of his
hands, he whisked one of the instruments from its tether
and held it before her. The blade, likely ground on a ro-
tating stone the man had powered by foot pedals, was not
as shiny as the ones for sale in a cutlery shop, nor half as
graceful, but it was thick and plainly heavy, ending in a
point as finely honed as a surgeon's scalpel. "The handle I
carved from the leg bone of a mountain lion. The mountain
lion is a lucky totem. This knife, it will help you well."

"Help me well, huh?"

"Annie, tell Crespin he's got to be back in an hour, no
later than that."

Anne relayed this command without looking over, and
with a certain flourish Crespin promised he would be like
the wind, and off he ran.

Anne sighed and said to the knifesmith, "How much?"
Now that she considered it, buying from this man might
put food in his children's mouths, and Anne felt obliged to
help out where she could, even if that meant purchasing
something she'd probably never use. "Twenty U.S. dollars?"

The pale eyes brightened. The wrinkles bunched and
relaxed. "Twenty is too much, ma'am. I would not ask
you—"

"Sold," Anne said, ignoring him and fishing the money
from her pocket. She'd left her handbag in the car, but she
was nothing if not prepared. A woman who carried two
phones, binoculars, and a graphing calculator always had an
extra twenty stashed away for buying knives.

Their transaction complete, the man issued a stream of
thank-yous and bowed repeatedly at the waist. Anne waved
him off, tested the weight of her new knife, and in the dis-

tance saw Crespin disappear into a house with a corrugated metal door.

"America needs villages," she said to no one in particular.

"Used to have 'em," Dawn said, wiping the perspiration from her forehead with her palm. "But we got too big for our britches, and now look at us, afraid to walk the streets at night. Nice dagger, by the way."

"It's not a dagger."

"Could've fooled me."

"He says the handle is made from the bone of a mountain lion."

"I didn't know mountain lions hung out in this neck of the woods."

"I guess they do."

"Either that or that old man lied to you and it's actually made out of cow bone."

"Cow bone isn't very elegant. Let's say we just call it mountain lion."

"Fine by me. I'm too nervous to argue. I don't want to debate, just get the hell out of Dodge. Besides, I make it a point never to contradict a woman who's wielding a cow-bone knife."

Careful to keep the sharp end a safe distance from her body, Anne stepped into the small space between Dawn and Sally, so near that their shoulders touched. The three of them leaned against the car and watched the village. The village stared right back.

"Promise me something, Sally," Anne said.

"I'm not sure if I can do that, but go ahead and ask."

"This is it, this trip down here to get people, it's the first and the last. No more."

"My promises are pretty fragile these days, but I'll give it

213

a shot. Either way, you don't need to worry about it. We'll be okay."

"I'm holding you to that."

The setting sun stroked the blade of the knife, flashing, flashing.

Chapter Sixteen

A hand grabbed Sally in the dark.

Gasping, she sat up, hair in her face, shirt twisted around her like a straitjacket—

"*Salee.*"

Crespin's hand lay on her arm. He looked down at her, his slender face caught somewhere between amusement and concern; he was plainly sorry for having to wake her up, but mischief lit his eyes. "*Salee, debemos ir.*"

Sally, knowing only that she'd fallen asleep on the sofa with a pillow over her head, waited a few seconds before responding. Her heart began to settle. Her grandmother's Victorian-era pendulum clock told her that it was nearly seven. That would be p.m., not a.m., and this was Friday and she'd spent all day not in band practice but instead slaving under her own whip at Sole Mates, working brutally hard so as not to get too caught up in the sudden unreality of her life. But now here was Crespin, living proof of the rabbit hole through which she'd fallen, pointing at Grandma Jasper's clock and saying, "*Salee, debemos ir.*"

The only part of this statement Sally understood was her own name, Salee, spoken in such a way that it sounded exotic. Sally wished everyone pronounced it like that. Maybe that was all it took to stop living a life of quiet desperation:

215

start saying your name so that it harkened of Spain or France or anyplace that put accent marks above their vowels.

"*Casi es tiempo,*" Crespin said.

"It's time, isn't it?"

Crespin nodded.

"We're supposed to be at the Texanna by seven."

Another nod.

"I don't know if I can do this. Do you understand? It's too much. Too big."

Crespin, as if he knew better, grinned and showed his teeth.

Sally sighed. Crespin had smiled in that very way when he'd displayed his fake ID to the cop at the border crossing last night, on the return trip from Mexico. Personally, Sally had almost thrown up right there, a good, nerve-wracked upchuck that she somehow managed to sublimate, at least until she made it home.

"Fine, you win." She swung her legs off the couch. She spotted her boots, the supple leather Ropers that were part of her disguise. More evidence that she hadn't been dreaming. She looked up at Crespin. "You sure about this?"

Crespin just kept on grinning.

The neons of the sprawling roadhouse made a false day of the night.

The Texanna's humble roots as a hay barn were still evident in the shape of the main building, though its walls had been knocked out and moved back to triple the original square footage. The main entrance simulated a pair of big, sliding barn doors. Nearly a hundred pickup trucks were parked outside. Light arrays the size of billboards stood on the roof, proclaiming *TEXANNA DANCEHALL*, followed by *BEER* and *BAR-B-CUE*, and most pertinently *LIVE MUSIC*.

It's enormous, Sally thought. *It'll squash us flat.*

"Dawn," she said aloud, "now would be a good time for a cucumber joke."

Dawn's face was pressed against the van's window, eyes wide, her nyctalopia no match for the spiraling circus lights of the roadhouse. "I don't think I can remember any."

"Remember or die."

"Uh, reason sixty-eight. No matter where you are, you can always get a fresh cucumber."

"Thanks."

"Don't mention it."

Dakota parked the van and bounded out. He and Crespin, playing the parts of dutiful roadies, would spent the next thirty minutes hauling guitars and amps inside and smiling at all the women in cowboy hats, and the women would certainly smile back. The parking lot was full of them. They wore blue jeans designed with only the posterior in mind.

"I'm nobody's cowgirl," Anne said. "This is not my kind of place."

"That's why we're not making you wear a hat," Dawn said. She threw open her door and made a production of stretching so as to say that she was undaunted by all of this, which was a lie that Sally gladly let her get away with.

Eventually Sally had to get out of the van. She joined the others, and wondered if their stomachs were curled up as tightly as hers.

After a minute of realigning their bearings, the four of them trekked across the gravel lot toward the tavern's yawning front doors. Noise and light flooded out, the honky-tonk waters spilling over the dam.

A pair of half-drunk cowhands stepped through the doors, saw Jazmyn, and gave her the look. One of them touched the brim of his hat. Jaz was a marvel in a denim miniskirt, with legs she certainly hadn't inherited from her mother because Tatyana had been nothing but a knob-kneed misfit. Jaz returned the men's admiring smiles with a cool look and a gentle turn of her chin.

Sally wondered where the girl had learned that particular move. Since when had her daughter become such a sea-soned and subtle flirt? Had she been attending some night class without Sally's knowledge?

They reached the entrance and none of that mattered anymore. A linebacker-sized guy stood on either side of the portal, their shirts stitched with the Texanna logo. "Cover charge is five dollars, ma'am," one of them said to her.

Sally didn't even look at him, her eyes trained inside. "I'm with the band."

She walked in.

Backstage.

Anne's careful scaffold of logic was teetering. She lived her life by rote, and now the pounding music in the walls and the stampede of dancing boot heels on the floor threat-ened to shake something important loose inside her. She was about to step out under the spotlights and perform goofy rock songs from her teenage years to a beer-smelling mob of would-be cowboys. She was about to be someone she was not. She was about to take a leap of shaky faith. Most of all she was about to faint.

She sat down on a stage prop that happened to be a saddle slung across a sawhorse.

"Mother, are you going to pass out on me?"

Anne didn't lift her head, just focused on her daughter's boots, the way a seasick traveler will stare at a single point on deck to keep her stomach from rolling. "Tell me why we're doing this again."

Jazmyn sank down in front her. "For Trevor, right? Isn't that what you told me? The thought of you up here doing this is blowing Trev's mind. Too bad he's not old enough to get in. But you know he's at home rooting for you."

"Topophobia."

Jazmyn raised her eyebrows. "You must be feeling at least a little okay if you're throwing around words like that. What's it mean?"

"Topophobia is the fear of performing in front of groups. Otherwise known as stage fright."

"You know, everyone at school thinks I'm weird because I know so many hellacious words like that. I tell them that if they think I'm weird, they should see my mother."

Anne nursed a smile to her lips. "I'll take that as a compliment. And please don't say hellacious. At least not unless you really need to."

"If I need to? Does that go for every word? Like, can I swear if I really need to?"

"Sometimes a woman must get the world's attention any way she can."

"Cool." She was beaming.

A man in a Texanna shirt stuck his head around the corner and said, "Alrighty, ladies. Shine up your spurs and buckle up your belts. You're on in three."

"Come on, Mother." She locked onto Anne's hands and pulled her to her feet. "This is one more way a woman gets the world's attention."

Anne permitted herself to be righted and steadied. "I

don't suppose you'd let me call in sick at this point?"

"Not on your life."

"Obstinate child."

"Like mother, like daughter."

And then, entirely against her will, Anne found herself propelled toward the stage.

At least I can hide behind my drums, Dawn thought, staring through her cymbals at the crowd.

How many were gathered here? A couple hundred? The dance floor was vast, like a basketball court. It was sprinkled in a fine, powdery sawdust. Beyond this expanse, a bar was tended by a pair of hot young guys in black ties and T-shirts. The tables were crowded with middle-aged people in trendy cowboy apparel, but also quite a few college co-eds and the young men who had come here to hook up with them. Sculpted neon signs advertised beer and smokeless tobacco. The four pool tables at the opposite end of the great building seemed miles away, but Dawn knew the sound she was about to make would easily span the distance.

Breathe in, breathe out.

She was not unaccustomed to the stage. In the last few weeks she'd gotten some laughs as an amateur comic. So she knew how to face them, knew how to stand. But this was different. She was comfortable with making people laugh—always had been—but her novice drum skills and her fear of this unfamiliar venue conspired to make her thighs sweat inside her pants.

Here comes Sal. I'm with you, honey!

She watched Sally weave through the speakers and step over the tangled snake-pit of cords. The crowd began to quiet as Sally neared the mike. Dawn was relieved to see that her friend was more or less holding it together. Sally was famous for that. For holding it together. For preventing their boat from sinking. For simply keeping her feet.

She kept them now.

Dawn cracked her knuckles. Arranged around her were her drums, the bass, the snare, the tom-tom—she had learned their names and hopefully a few of their secrets. The lights on the ceiling tracks above the stage were aimed directly at her, hot on her skin. Beyond the glare, more and more faces turned to look. Conversation broke off. People at the bar stopped ordering local microbrews and shots of whiskey, and—sensing a change in the air—craned their necks to see.

Sally stopped before the microphone. Dawn took heart from the sight of her. Sally wore new, pressed jeans and a fringed shirt with lace sleeves that flared at the wrist, like something Joni Mitchell might have sported at a folk festival in '68.

Bounding onto the stage came Jude Yarbuck. His black felt hat bore a band of colored feathers. A huge silver belt buckle was half hidden by the generous slalom of his belly. He nodded at Sally, lifted his arms above his head as if he were casting a blessing on the crowd, and shouted, "What do ya'll say we get this party started?"

Dawn closed her eyes.

". . . so I'll shut my trap now and give you Radio!"

Yarbuck's fading words were Sally's cue. She glanced back at Dawn and then quickly at Anne and Jazmyn. Anne was colorless and Jaz looked like a cocked gun. People were applauding and some were talking, and Sally swore she could feel the wings spreading in her again, giving flight to something inside.

Dawn started them off by banging her sticks together—one-two-three—

—Jazmyn tore into her guitar and Anne's keyboards began to wail.

Sally had no more time to ready herself. She coiled her fingers around the mike and took in all the faces on the floor, and it startled her when her own voice filled the building with the opening verse of a female-filtered version of Grand Funk Railroad's "We're an American Band."

This song choice had been Dawn's inspiration. It was a classic and it was pure rock, and it engendered a rowdy patriotism in those who heard it, reminding them that music from the U.S. of A could out-muscle that British fluff any day, the Beatles be damned. Sally wasn't sure she believed in any of that; her sense of country was diminishing daily, but she sang the tune now as if it were a battle anthem and she was mustering the morale of the troops.

The troops responded.

The crowd threw out a barrage of yells and howls and wolf whistles. The older ones who knew the lyrics sang along, and the younger ones drank and shouted and caught on by the second time the chorus rolled around and Sally told them we're coming to your town, we'll help you party down, we're an American band.

They pushed closer. Others far back at the billiards tables put down their sticks, picked up their beers, and came forward. Something was pulling them, drawing them in.

Sally had expected them to dance. After all, this was a dancehall. But midway through the second number—a sassy cover of the Eagles' "Take It to the Limit"—she realized that instead of a mass of gyrating bodies, she was facing a thousand watching eyes. These were not dancers packed in front of the stage, but an audience.

The way they were looking at her . . . it was more helium for her soul. With no choice but to sing recklessly or be laughed from the room, she shut the door on her famous Sally Sensibilities and leapt from the balcony.

The wings caught and carried her.

Jazmyn, of course, was idolized. At each guitar solo, she pranced forward to the edge of the stage and laid into her strings with a fluid energy that seemed to suck the light from the room and make her the sun in the small universe of the Texanna. Hands reached up and touched her. Young hunks in the front shouted their devotion. Jaz for the most part was oblivious to their adoration, her concentration welded to the guitar and the act of her hands flying up the neck to execute a high-speed riff at the limits of the instrument's range. At times, however, she seemed to come awake and realize they loved her, and her smile became incandescent. Whenever this happened, she played with them, locking eyes with individual men in the mob and winking or blowing careless kisses at them.

Filled with the immensity of it all, Sally laughed.

That laughter was a drink she'd not tasted in years. Like an elixir it rushed down her throat and spread through her bones, cooling and quenching her. For the rest of the night she had nothing but fun, no longer herself but a woman she'd met only briefly in her life, one who was beyond the hard reach of the world, one who drank wine in the morning and probably slept naked more often than not.

After an hour and ten minutes of it, they finished the set with "Sweet Home Alabama," and the place now truly went wild.

Sally, sheathed in sweat and bouncing on the balls of her feet, didn't notice the half-dozen Mexican men trying to get past the security jocks at the door, at least not until she had taken her last bow in front of her rapacious fans and Anne said from beside her, "DATFUG."

The Mexicans were arguing with the bouncers, and now Crespin was among them.

"Come on!" Sally said, jumping off the stage and pointing herself toward the disturbance.

But the crowd wanted to absorb her. They were everywhere. Most in cowboy hats. Lots of studs from the university with bottles in their hands, saying things to her as she shoved her way through them. Everyone wanted to meet her gaze. It was a new and not unpleasant sensation. The middle-aged men called her ma'am. They tipped their hats and smiled hopefully. Sally smiled back. She could no sooner resist responding to their adulation than she could slow the slamming of her pulse. She didn't know if Anne and the others were following her, nor did she turn to see. Her head was still swimming from her enduro performance. Her steps were light, and this was how it felt to be a star, fighting your way through the grasping hands of those who only wanted to touch you for the sake of saying they did.

It's crazy, I'm a nobody.

But the hands didn't believe that. They kept reaching for her hair and shirt and arms because for an hour she'd touched *them*.

For a moment she was unable to part this rambunctious Red Sea, and she came face-to-chest with a guy ten years her junior. He looked down at her with undisguised craving in his eyes. And what eyes they were. Sally had never been the kind to swoon over the latest beefcake of the month, but the intoxicants were in her blood now and this twenty-five-year-old Adonis would take her back to his place if she asked. The sudden surety of it unnerved and elated her. *I could have him*. Fantastically, she felt a hotness spread through her legs, so unexpected that it caused her to pause there and actually—*Holy shit, what am I doing?*—place her palm flat against his chest.

"Hey," he said, barely heard through the din.

Sally parted her lips to say something, God knows what, but her inner struggle stymied the words in her throat. She had to get to the door. She had to unravel whatever knot was currently being tied by the security men. But she was still flying freely and it was hard to give a damn about anything but maintaining that feeling. Let this stranger in the white silk shirt take her hand and lead her away to a place where they could forget they were human for awhile and instead exist only as elemental forces, her fire pierced by his hard earth, her air flooded by his sea.

Only Dawn's hand on her back saved her.

"Keep the line moving, girlie." Dawn pressed her onward.

Sally held the man's stare until the bodies folded between them, and then she was on the move again, still smiling vaguely, letting the hands of people she didn't know make not-so-casual contact as she passed.

I am the wheel in the sky, she thought, and didn't know why.

They reached the big barn doors just in time.

"No cover, no admittance," one of the bouncers was saying, his sasquatch-sized body forming a barrier in front of the Mexicans.

His partner, smaller but bald and scarred and obviously vicious, screwed his fists to his hips and made a wall of himself, challenging anyone to step closer. "All of you get out now, *vamoose*, you got it? You *comprende* that?"

The Mexicans were agitated. Crespin was trying to converse with them but the meat-grinders in the Texanna shirts kept saying, "Exit the building *now*. Right now."

Sally swooped in. "It's okay, it's okay! They're with me." Anne and Dawn and Jazmyn were right behind her, Anne already giving rapid instructions in Spanish for the men to turn around and leave, Jaz catching on quickly and putting her language skills to use. Between the two of them they managed to herd the men through the door and out into the night.

Sally turned to the bouncers. "Dial it down a notch, boys. The women have everything under control."

"You know these dudes, ma'am?"

"Part of the road crew."

A shrug of massive shoulders. "Whatever. Just tell them that nobody else is getting in tonight without paying the cover. And by the way, that was a kick-ass show you just put on."

"Thanks." For a woman who'd never been told she'd done a kick-ass anything, she took the compliment with surprising nonchalance. As if every day she were involved in at least one or two notably kick-ass events.

"Sally, wait up!" Dakota rushed to her side, holding his splinted arm against his chest. "Damn, Sally, that was awesome. Do you hear these people?" With a grin splashed on his face, he spun around and gestured at the horde. "They freaking love you."

It was true: the hoots and shouts still reverberated between the walls.

"Love is a fickle thing," Sally said. Her breath was not coming any easier. These heady altitudes of performance were a boon for the ego but hell on the lungs. What she wanted to do more than anything was dive back into the crush of bodies and let them assimilate her. She wanted to take Dakota's hand—

—so she did so without thinking. Dakota didn't try to pull away, but squeezed her hand in reciprocation, sensing her need. The urge to drag him across the sawdust-covered floor and get lost for hours among the nameless, faceless dancers was so complete that the last sensible part of her was very nearly overrun. Having a hand in hers felt so good.

"You okay?" he asked. He stood so close to her that she felt his air on her face.

Just go with him.

Yes, just go, back into the press of humanity, back into the thrill of being wanted by people she'd never met, back into her moonlight job as a goddess, and bugger the consequences. She smelled the beer and her own sticky perspiration and Dakota's woodsy cologne. She began to sway on her feet . . .

The next thing she knew, she was outside. A breeze cooled the moisture on her forehead.

Dakota, alarmed, had hustled her through the doors. She opened her eyes and saw Crespin and Anne and men from Mexico and a moon over them all that seemed to know they were rushing toward a collective and perhaps calamitous end.

"Can someone please get me some water?" she asked.

While she waited for a drink to cool the flames within, she thought of nothing but the hunger of the crowd and the anchoring feeling of Dakota's hand.

Chapter Seventeen

"Six Mexicans," Dawn said, "a guy with a broken arm, an Asian-American, and an amateur comedian. God, this sounds like the beginning of a really lame joke."

"What about me and Mom?" Jaz said. "Don't forget about us."

"Oh, I could never forget you two. I could sooner forget my period."

Crespin and the Mexicans were talking, Anne right in the middle of them.

"How can they chatter so fast and understand one another?" Dawn asked no one in particular. "Who are they? What are they doing here? Help me out here, Jazzy."

"Well . . . I'm not sure. I'm not catching it all. I think these guys are all related to Crespin. They're from the village you visited. And their women are . . . hiding out there somewhere."

"What? Their women are hiding? You mean in the desert?"

"So they say."

"These fellas are Crespin's relatives? We just invited them yesterday. How'd they get here so fast, unless one of their names is Speedy Gonzales?"

Jazmyn probably shrugged but Dawn wasn't sure. They

were standing beside the van in the crowded Texanna parking lot, and though the mercury-vapor lights cast their blue pallor over the asphalt, the light wasn't strong enough to compensate for the insufficiency of rods in Dawn's retinas. She wished Sally would say something, because without this aural landmark, Dawn had no way of knowing if her friend was still among them.

"Mama?"

"Yeah, hon?"

"We rocked in there. You know it?"

"Yeah."

"I mean, we were fabulous."

"Personally, this part of we was as scared as a cat in a room full of rocking chairs. But yeah, we were pretty fabulous nonetheless. What's happening now? What're they saying?"

"Sounds like trouble."

"Why am I not surprised?"

"Um, let's see . . . they used the money you gave them in the village to buy water and . . . and cheap food. When they got across the border they got a ride from a friend who picked them up at San Miguel. They walked the last few miles, and they avoided the water stations, just like we told them to do."

"We only gave them twenty bucks. They crossed a hundred miles on that?"

"Guess so. They're probably good at making money go a long way."

"And what's this about the women?"

"Two of the men are married and one has a daughter. The men left them somewhere out in the desert. For safety, I guess. Oh, and one of the guys is Crespin's older brother. And he's kinda cute."

"Terrific. All I need in my life is one more cute Hispanic older brother." She raised her voice and said, "Hey, Annie, can we please hurry this up already? Let's get the stuff loaded and make like a banana and split."

Dakota said, "I'm all over it, Dawn. Crespin, grab two of your amigos and let's go pack up the equipment."

"For that matter," Dawn interjected, "grab 'em all. The more the merrier and all that."

Anne provided a translation. The Mexicans, responding gamely to the need for unity and hard work, sounded honored to be asked to contribute, and seconds later they were rushing off after Dakota.

"Six men," Dawn said, "plus three women. That makes nine, at least if I remember math from second grade. I realize that second grade was like an entire Ice Age ago, but six plus three is likely still nine. Are we supposed to cram them into the van like those clowns in the little cars at the circus?"

"Yeah, what are we gonna do with them all?" Jaz asked. "The van's already about to be totally loaded with us and our gear. Nine more bodies just ain't gonna fit."

"Aren't," Anne said, "and you're correct, they won't. Honestly I wasn't expecting so many of them so soon."

"At this rate Mexico ought to be depopulated entirely by Christmas." Dawn extended her hands in front of her until she found the van, then leaned against it, blessing it for its solidity in a world that now made for treacherous footing. "Sal, are you out there somewhere?"

When she received no immediate reply, Dawn's first thought was that Sally was still in the bar, still onstage, still strutting like an X-chromosome Mick Jagger. But then Sally, prompted by a word from Jazmyn, said, "I'm here," in a voice like a land-bound sailor pining for that fabled tall ship and a star to steer her by.

"Are you injured?" Dawn asked.

"Of course not."

"Sick?"

"I don't think so."

"Stoned?"

"Not since college."

Dawn snickered. "Yeah, I remember that party. At least most of it . . ."

"And let that be a lesson to me," Jazmyn said. "The bad experiences of my elders are mistakes I won't have to make, et cetera, et cetera. But seriously, how are we supposed to get all these people out of here? Are they riding on the roof of the van?"

Dawn wished she could get a look at Sally, because the moon was definitely changing phases in that woman's private sky. And Dawn was worried. "Salster, this is where you take charge, be the quarterback, call the play, pick up the maestro's baton, conduct the damn symphony, something. So what's your something?"

"Well. I don't know. Let me think for a moment."

There was a pause that was so maddening that Dawn wanted to shriek. But shrieking, though viscerally satisfying, would do nothing to alleviate the tension. Shrieking would, in fact, only compound it. So she settled for closing her eyes and tapping the tip of her index finger against her forehead, waiting, waiting . . .

"My something is this."

Dawn looked up, though she couldn't see a thing.

"First we get our things loaded," Sally said with careful deliberation. "Then we get the women and let them take our places in the van. We stay here with the men while Dakota drives the women somewhere safe. And don't tell me

231

there is no such place because we don't have a choice and we have to risk it anyway. They unload the equipment and the women. Dakota turns around and comes back and picks up everyone else. The van will be crammed, but without the instruments, we'll all fit. Because again, we have no choice. We *have* to fit."

"There, great, wonderful—see that?—I knew you had it all under control. What the hell was I ever concerned about?"

"Here they come with the stuff," Jaz said.

Dawn opened her useless eyes and felt her way to the rear of the vehicle. "Then what are we waiting for? Come hit the road with Radio." She yanked open the doors and stepped aside. "Give us your tired and weak, and we shall clothe and feed them. Give us your Hispanic music-lovers, and we will rock them. But only after they tote all our shit."

There followed a session of grunts and quick words and efficient teamwork. Dawn could barely see them, but her nose was functioning perfectly and she picked up their hot, hunted scents as they moved around her. The question that she wanted to ask most of all was one better left unspoken, at least for now. But where were all these nine eager, frightened people going to sleep tonight?

Sally, surely, would figure something out. Didn't she always?

"I guess we'll see about that," Dawn muttered.

"*¿Qué dijo?*" Crespin asked as he shoved a drum case into the van.

"Never mind," Dawn sighed. Even if she had possessed a full command of Spanish, she wouldn't have been able to express what was happening to her, and what was happening was this: her nyctalopia was spreading, because she could no longer see into her friend's heart, as if Sally's

232

thoughts and motives were—for the first time—hidden in a private and unbreachable darkness.

An hour later Sally's house was an inn of the lost and road-weary.

Like a way station for the homeless and the disenfranchised, her living room crackled with hope and uncertainty and a shared knowledge of looming peril. The nine newcomers sat on the sofa and on the floor, impeccably polite, smiling tentatively, looking for all the world like expectant children. Their faith, without need of translation, had been placed squarely in Sally's hands.

"Okay, how's everyone doing?" She met each of their gazes individually, so as to reassure them, even though she herself was about as far removed from a state of assurance as a woman could be. "You're name is Eleazar, right?"

Eleazar nodded. He was Crespin's brother, late twenties, with a neatly trimmed mustache and a shape in his hair from where his cap had been before he'd politely removed it upon entering the house.

"And you speak English?"

"Yes. Some. A little."

"Some and a little will have to suffice. We've brought every blanket we can muster. You and your tribe here will have to make do with camping on the floor." Indeed, between Anne, Dawn, and Sally's linen closets, the living room was piled with more blankets, pillows, and toothpaste than a hurricane shelter. Unfortunately, Anne and Dawn had husbands and families, to which they had returned a few minutes ago. Now, at two a.m., Sally was left to handle these pilgrims alone. "Just spread the blankets on the floor, okay? *Mi casa, su casa.*"

Everyone smiled and nodded at this.

With a little more prompting and a lot of body language, Sally got them moving, and soon she had to retreat to give them room. She watched them from the kitchen doorway, wondering how her hot-water heater was ever going to handle this many showers come morning.

She hardly slept that night.

At three-thirty she finally made it to bed, but that was only a place of silence for her, rather than a place of sleep. The Mexicans in her living room were as quiet as parishioners during church service. They expressed a nearly palpable respect for Sally and her home; they knew the value of hospitality, and honored it. When one of the women had taken Sally's hands and thanked her with tears brimming her dark eyes, Sally had seen the depths of true gratitude. In the Mexicans' esteem, the gift Sally was trying to give them had surpassed all others; she'd put *libertad* within their reach.

Tomorrow was the funeral.

Was this what was keeping her from falling asleep? She thought of the unfairness of Jeffrey's death and the guilt of performing carelessly onstage tonight while Jeffrey's mother wept in matchless grief. Over and over Sally relived that hour before the Texanna crowd, the scintillating feelings that coursed through her blood, the way her muscles twitched and the taste of hot sweat on her lips. Again she felt the smile play across her lips. . . .

Exhaustion blew into her like the sandstorm that had enveloped the town.

Mentally and physically depleted from her day of hard-rocking and people-legging, her thinking self evaporated and she slept fully clothed, wearing everything but her boots. Her last thought was of Leigh Surry. If he had phoned her in that instant she would have asked him without hesitation to come over, and then she could have expelled at least a little of this frightening voltage that surged like a new-found energy within her.

She awoke Saturday morning to the smell of . . . what?

"Bread. Homemade bread."

That aroma alone was enough to inspire her. The industry of her guests shamed her into getting up and finding her way to the bathroom. Here she was at dawn still snoozing, and her visitors had likely been up for a solid hour, giving thanks for the new day. The first thing she thought about when she sat up was that her raffle ticket could pay off today, if the statue at the park had the decency to collapse at the appointed hour. But the whole thing seemed so trivial now, and Sally wondered why she once cared about such things.

She found the women in her kitchen and the men—

—a glance from her window revealed them at work in her yard.

"All of this really isn't necessary," she explained to a woman named Beatriz. "Don't get me wrong, this breakfast is really mind-boggling"—she licked cheese from her fingertip—"but I didn't invite you here so that you could give my house a makeover."

Beatriz smiled.

"Right. That's what I'd thought you say." She spent the next twenty minutes using sign language and Crespin's patchwork English to get her point across: when she returned from the funeral, she would bring a camera for photographs.

"Green card," Crespin relayed to his family, eliciting nods of understanding and thanks.

While Crespin explained Sally's forgery plan to the little

congregation of immigrants, Sally herself explored her walk-in closet for suitable funeral attire. Making it a point not to dwell on the subject, she quickly settled on a black pants suit and an expensive but low-key pair of suede T-strap pumps with rounded toes. American women were renowned for the quantity of shoes they kept. Sally, long-time owner of a shoe store, left them all behind.

One entire wall of the oversized closet supported a pigeonhole shelving unit designed to hold no less than sixty pairs. Sally had some of the slots doubled up; she'd found she could actually fit three pairs of sandals and ballet flats in certain holes, though boots of just about any kind had to go it alone. Dawn-Marie had long ago worn out her last shoe joke, and this monument to the footwear gods was not the topic of awed conversation anymore.

And those women in my living room are lucky to own even a single pair.

She felt more guilty at that moment than she ever had. The next time she wanted to buy something new that she didn't need, she promised herself she'd use the money to buy somebody sneakers or socks.

On her way out the door, she picked up the orange box Jeffrey had given her.

Having decided it appropriate to open the box at the funeral, she stood with it under her arm and waited for her ride. Around her, the neighborhood slowly began its Saturday morning routine. Soon cars would be washed and skateboards ridden, and the normalcy of it all was numbing. Sally wanted the stage back. She wanted the sweat and the sound.

The Mexican men had found her yard tools and were busy pruning and trimming. They seemed to be experienced gardeners, and in the hour that they'd been working, they'd done more for Sally's yard and sagging birch trees than she'd managed in the last two years.

Leigh's word returned to her: *Hózh'q*. He'd pronounced it like hoe-shik.

She realized there was something very *hózh'q* about the way they behaved, a simple gladness for life expressed through their work and in their words. Every time one of them met her gaze, he smiled or nodded or in some small way acknowledged what she was doing for them.

She turned around to see a stranger watching her.

His truck was gray and nondescript, creeping down the center of the street in front of her house. The pickup's windows were open, and an elbow rampant with black hairs protruded from the driver's side. From that elbow Sally's eyes traveled to the man's face. His neck and fleshy cheeks were razor-burned. His dull brown hair was combed back from his forehead, though it failed to provide sufficient coverage for the bald patch on his crown. He drove with one hand slumped over the top of the steering wheel. He was not at all looking where he was going, but staring with lusterless eyes at Sally and the men at work on her lawn.

An earlier version of Sally Jasper would have looked away, uncomfortable beneath this stranger's ill-mannered glare. But standing in the driveway today in these ninety-dollar shoes was Sally A.D., or Sally As Diva, and this guy with the meaty jowls had no power over her.

He cruised by, slowly, watching the Mexicans, watching . . .

On the truck's rear window was a decal depicting Old Glory crossed by a snake.

Oh, hell.

The truck rolled on, finally turning a corner and vanishing.

Sally bit her lip and thought too many things at once. So

much for the indomitable Sally A.D., unless that stood for Sally All Distraught.

"Something not good?" Crespin asked, appearing beside her with hedge clippers in hand.

"Yeah." Sally exhaled and blew a curl from her face. "Something not good at all."

". . . and so we commit Jeffrey's body to Your hands, Lord, where he will be given peace and laughter and the peerless joy that is heaven. Amen."

Dawn said amen not softly, but with force. "Amen." She almost shouted it, drawing looks from those assembled around her, but screw them because Jeff would have yelled it had he been here and not soaring through the ether, diabetes-free.

"Mr. And Mrs. Longbranch want to thank you all for coming here to the graveside, and they'd like to invite you immediately to their home for a few hours of fellowship and fond remembering. May God go with you all."

Dawn felt the tension slacken as the mourners began slowly to disperse. Personally she was frozen, standing ten feet from where the casket was suspended above a hole that wasn't really a hole because the clever funeral gents had covered it with green fabric so as not to remind everyone where Jeffrey's body was going. She hated funerals more than she hated anything, more than she hated abortion, more than she hated hecklers at her comedy show. No wisecracks bubbled to the surface of her brain to save her. She was forced to stand there, lanky knees locked, staring at that sculpted cherrywood box, as sleek as a torpedo, imaging Coy or Caleb in there, dead before their time.

"Can we go now?" Anne said from beside her. "I'd rather not linger, if that's all right."

Dawn wetted her lips with her tongue and finally hoisted her eyes from the casket. The sky was bright. These people in their black wool suits would soon be sweating. "Unless one of you two has a hard-on for those little sandwiches they're serving at the Longbranch house, I'd just as soon skip that particular get-together."

"You'll get no argument from me," Anne assured her. "Sally?"

"Hmmm?"

"Do you want to speak with Jeffrey's parents?"

Sally remained motionless, in the exact spot she'd been standing for the last half-hour. Unlike Dawn, she wasn't staring at the coffin and its polished handles, but instead at the slightly dented shoebox she clutched in her arms. After a moment she shook her head. "No, I'm fine. But I can't leave quite yet."

Dawn thought she knew why. "So go ahead and open it already."

Sally didn't move.

"Come on, Sal, the boy didn't give you that damn box so you could keep it taped closed for the rest of your life. You should have opened it days ago. Maybe it was something that could spoil, like his mother's banana nut bread or something."

"No. It's too light. Feels empty."

A minute later they were the only ones still lingering at the casket. Jeffrey's mother had been the last to depart, physically supported by her husband and brother. Dawn had made it a point not to watch her, for fear that the bottomless depth of the woman's sorrow would be more than anyone could bear to see without turning to stone.

"Who is that standing over there?" Anne asked.

Dawn followed her gaze. She saw a burly man at the

edge of the cemetery, hands thrust into his pockets. Her first thought was that the goon Sally had spotted in the pickup this morning was coming to make trouble, but then she realized—

"Jude Yarbuck," she said. "What the hell's he doing here?"

"Waiting for us, by the looks of it."

"Terrific. I'm sure he's here to play Godfather and make us an offer we can't refuse. Probably wants us back at the Texanna tonight. And now that I think about it, that sounds like just the kind of thing I could use right now. Let's go see what he wants."

"Wait." Sally began peeling the tape from the box. "Just wait, okay?"

"On pins and needles, sister. Pins and needles."

Sally took her time with the box. This was nothing noteworthy. Sally was the kind who always opened her Christmas gifts frustratingly slowly, mindful of savoring the moment, as if it might be the last present she ever received. Dawn, on the other hand, tore into any wrapped parcel just as she'd done as a kid, too anxious to see what was inside to worry about injuring innocent bystanders with her flying fingernails.

After removing each strip of tape, Sally folded them and handed them to Anne, who was her usual stoic, straight-backed, maddening self and acted like she was the axis that had to keep sturdy lest the earth spin out of control.

"You're some kind of damn Vulcan, you know that?" Dawn said to her.

Anne just looked at her with those half-moon eyes.

"Yeah, right back at you." Dawn crossed her arms, looked over her shoulder at where Yarbuck waited in his cowboy-cut blue blazer, and then returned her attention to the box as Sally finally, at last, lifted the lid.

Chapter Eighteen

"... so for one show tomorrow," Yarbuck was saying, "I'm paying a thousand bucks."

Sally let Dawn handle the negotiations. She was too intent upon the open box in her hands and the unshakable feeling that she was now attended by three ghosts. One of these was Tatyana, of course; for sixteen years she'd been the benign spirit guide over Sally's shoulder. But now there was Juan Doe, talking in Spanish about freedom, and most recently Jeffrey Longbranch, and this thing he'd given her.

"Whoa now, partner," Dawn said, screwing up her face as if she hadn't heard him correctly. "You said only five or six songs. And that's worth a thousand clams?"

Yarbuck rolled a toothpick from one side of his mouth to the other. "It's like this, ma'am. You ladies stomped 'em dead in there last night. I know a hit when I see one. Maybe you ain't the greatest musicians to come down the pike, except maybe for the kid, who's the damndest chord-picker I've ever seen, by the way. But what the hell? People love you. So tomorrow afternoon I'd like to squeeze your act in between a couple of others at the annual Coors Light Country Music Fest."

"In Tempe," Dawn said, probably for lack of anything else to say.

"In Tempe, as sure as my mama makes moonshine."

"Isn't that a little out of our league?"

"Not from what I saw last night."

"We don't know many country-western songs."

"Don't matter. Give them folks some of that Lynyrd Skynyrd like you did last night, and they won't let you leave the stage."

"How can you get us in the show on such short notice?"

"The Texanna is one of the sponsors. Besides, I've been buds with the fella who runs the event for years now. Trust me when I say he's gonna trip on himself to get you up on the stage."

"Sure, whatever. This is worth that much money to you?"

"Call it an investment."

"Who else is going to be there?"

"What do you mean?"

"I mean the other bands. Anybody I know?"

"Mostly smaller acts, artists that only recently got their Nashville record deals and are just now starting to make a name for themselves. But we do have what you might call a name-brand act headlining the show." He smiled, devilry coloring his cheeks.

"I'm afraid to ask. Who is it?"

"The Dixie Chicks."

Dawn's eyebrows leapt on her head. "Like hell."

"True story, ma'am. Tickets sold out a month ago. It's gonna be a packed house."

Anne put a hand to her forehead as if experiencing a sudden fever.

Dawn was visibly reeling. "What do you mean packed?"

"Sun Devil Stadium seats seventy-three thousand."

Dawn went completely still. Then, after staring at

Yarbuck for several seconds, she cast her head back and laughed, a shrill, obnoxious guffaw that went on and on and violated the cemetery's code of silence. The men from the funeral parlor who were attending Jeffrey's grave were clearly irritated by the intrusion. But Dawn just kept laughing and shaking her head.

Yarbuck swiveled his gaze to Anne. "I'm being serious here."

"We know you are, Mr. Yarbuck. It's just that we aren't quite ready to—"

"Are you *shitting* me?" Dawn interjected, stepping in front of Anne and getting in Yarbuck's face. "You think we're actually going to go out in front of that many people and get our asses booed off stage by seventy thousand country music freaks? These people have paid good money to see this show, Jude my friend, and they don't want to waste it on a joke act like Radio."

Yarbuck held out his hands in defense. "I've seen you. I've heard you. You've got charisma"—he pronounced it like ker-izma—"and you're as good as half them folks with record deals."

"But we have no experience. You can't expect us to go out there in front of that many screaming maniacs and look even halfway like we know what we're doing." Dawn's voice kept rising with every sentence. "I don't even think I could *breathe* in front of a crowd that size. Wait, it's not a crowd, it's a goddamn *nation*. There are entire *cities* that don't have populations that big, and now that I consider it, if you assume for one second that—"

"We're not a joke act," Sally said.

Everyone looked at her.

She gestured with the lid of the shoebox. "We may be a lot of things, but we're for real, maybe for the first time in our lives, we're for real. And we're definitely not afraid. Pigtails are antennas for bravery."

Dawn closed her eyes and lowered her head.

Sally looked at Jude. "We accept your offer. But you'll have to provide us with a trailer to help haul our gear. And it better have a lot of room, because we have an ever-growing road crew."

Jude nodded. "It shall be done."

"Fine. Call me tonight and fill us in on the details. Right now we're late for an appointment."

"By all means." He stepped aside and made a sweeping motion with his arm. "You ladies won't regret this, I promise you. Gonna be one hell of a party."

He said something else as they walked away, but Sally heard nothing but the voices of her friends, replayed from five minutes before when she'd peeled back the tape and opened Jeffrey's box.

I don't get it, Dawn said when she saw it. *Damn box is empty. Is this a trick?*

Wait, it's not empty, Anne realized. *Look at the lid.*

Wow. What is it?

A drawing of some kind. Looks like—

"A map," Sally said, just as she had said earlier.

And a map it was. Though the box was indeed quite vacant, the underside of the lid was a wild display of reds and greens and delicate black lines. Jeffrey had taken colored pencils and vividly rendered what appeared to be a topographical map, complete with mesas and washes and escarpments. His talent as a cartographer was surpassed only by his penchant for detail; elevations were marked in fifty-foot intervals and contour lines scaled with mathematic precision.

Sally's eye was drawn again to the jewel.

Jeffrey had drawn the shape of a tiny blue gemstone near the center of the map. Beside this symbol he'd printed two words: *HIDDEN SCHATZ*.

In light of everything that was happening around her—the funeral, the Mexicans hiding in her house, Yarbuck's invitation to share the stage with one of the biggest acts in America—Jeffrey's map should not have seemed particularly surreal. Yet its cryptic nature enticed her. The map's purpose, though undefined, harkened of adventure.

"So," Dawn said as they reached her car. "Does anyone really believe that by this time tomorrow we're going to be opening for the Dixie Chicks? Jesus, somebody kick me in the shin so I can wake up from this psychedelic dream."

"It is a little intimidating," Anne admitted.

"A little? If I get any more intimidated, I'm going to curl up and die. I mean, us and the Dixie Chicks? Get real, Lucille." She laughed again, unable to conceive of it. "We better practice our fannies off between now and then." She climbed in behind the wheel. "What's Lex going to say? What's my mother going to say when I call her? They'll be too stunned to talk, probably. And now that I think about it, I kind of like the idea of them not being able to talk. I should stun them more often." She started the car, while in the backseat Anne was already on the phone with Barry, relaying the news of tomorrow's impossible concert.

Sally got in beside her and said, "Hidden Schatz."

"What? Oh, right. The box. Strange stuff, huh? What do you think it means?"

"I'm not sure. But I think it has something to do with Farrington Schatz."

"Huh?"

"Farrington Schatz. Pioneer, rattlesnake hunter, prospector, Indian killer—"

"Yeah, I know my local history, but what on earth has Schatz got to do with Jeffrey Longbranch? And what's so special about that spot on the map?"

"I don't know. But I think we need to find out."

"Great. Between you and Jude Yarbuck, I'm headed to Ulcer City, for sure."

They drove to Sally's and found Isadore Presper waiting.

He stood on the sidewalk with steel in his hand.

They all saw him at once. Sally recognized him from the picture in Leigh's file—*Oh no, not yet, I'm not ready*—and something like an insect crept across her flesh and teased the fine hairs on her neck. Dawn stopped the car in the street. Quietly she said, "Somebody please tell me that's not who I think it is."

His pants and suit coat were an unremarkable gray, but his shoes defined him. Even from twenty feet away, Sally could see his cap-toe oxfords, gallant yet pragmatic. Though a man could get away with wearing wing-tips or monk straps with less formal attire, cap-toes were reserved for suits with serious business afoot.

Size thirteen, at least. Jesus.

"Sal, what do we do?" Dawn asked. "Should I keep going, drive on by?"

Presper held a long metal club, bright aluminum, with buckle clasps at either end.

"Sally, please don't vapor lock on me now, okay?"

Standing in Sally's yard, hands fixed to her hips, Jazmyn faced Presper and was saying something that Sally couldn't hear. Plainly there was fire in Jazmyn's words. Dakota was at her side. Three of the Mexican men stood behind them. They looked seconds away from bolting.

"You want me to just run over him?" Dawn offered.

"No," Sally finally said. "Pull up to the curb."

"Whatever you say. I hope you know what we're doing."

"Don't count on it." Sally opened the passenger's door even before the car fully stopped. She still held the lid of Jeffrey's box, the bright colors of the map flashing up at her, as if trying to tell her something. She slammed the door and approached.

". . . but it doesn't matter at all," Jaz was saying, "because it's none of your business." She cocked her head indignantly. "Now if you don't mind, sir, my friends and I here are going back in the house, and in case you were wondering, no, you're not invited."

Dakota put his hand on her arm. "Hey, it's cool. Ease up. You made your point."

"No, Dak, it isn't cool." New color crept into her cheeks. "If this racist bully doesn't get out of my face—"

"Jazmyn." Sally silenced her with a word. All heads turned toward her as she approached.

Now what?

Holding the box lid like a shield in front of her, Sally spent a moment collecting herself, recalling the lustful feeling of the crowd calling her name. In front of those strangers last night she had been capable of anything, a superheroine who gained strange powers under the stagelights of this needful planet, and fear had lost all purchase in her heart. All it left behind was pure *libertad*.

She surprised herself and looked away from her daughter to meet the gaze of the man in the cap-toe shoes. "Isadore Presper, isn't it?"

The first thing he did was raise a surprised eyebrow, and then, like thunder chasing after the faster lightning, he smiled and said, "Indeed. And you, ma'am, are someone I recently saw performing a rather spirited rendition of 'Jumpin' Jack Flash.' "

"It's a gas, gas, gas," she replied. "My name is Sally Jasper."

Presper nodded. "The pleasure is mine. I assume this is your home?"

"Actually it belongs mostly to the bank."

"Then that would make this vigorous young woman your daughter."

Sally spent the next few seconds appraising him. His slacks fit him well and broke perfectly against the leather of his shoes. But the staidness of his attire ended there, as his coat was slung over his arm and his French cuffs had been rolled blithely up his forearms, exposing skin tanned from a lifetime under the Arizona sun. He wore no tie, and in the brown hollow of his throat lay a piece of stone the color of gunmetal. As Anne and Dawn-Marie stepped up on either side of her, Sally motioned toward the object that Presper held nonchalantly at his side. "Are you in the neighborhood trying to sell something?"

"Selling something? Oh, you mean this?" He hefted the bright metal tube and smiled disarmingly. "A bad habit, I'm afraid. I spend so much of my time trekking about the hills that I don't feel proper without a walking stick. Or at least a handy approximation. It's a chart case. I'm not here to offer any deals on the latest Amway products."

"Then why *are* you here?"

"Honestly?" Smiling faintly, he looked out across the homes lined up along Sally's street. Set into his lean and wind-carved face, his brown eyes gave nothing away, only a glimmer that was either amusement or anger. "I am a man who knows only truth, Ms. Jasper. I hunt for it in the rocks and I read it in the strata of those who lived here long ago.

And as a man of truth, I am perforce a man of law. I came here this afternoon after receiving word that the law I so dearly love might be in need of assistance."

"I have no idea what you're talking about."

"Haven't you?"

Sally sighed. "Mr. Presper, my friends and I just returned from the funeral of a fourteen-year-old boy. Needless to say, we're not in the mood for anything but a quiet house. But as it turns out, what we have to do instead is go in there and make a racket with guitars and drums because it looks like tomorrow is going to be a big day for us. Maybe the biggest. So if you have some kind of problem with my daughter and her friends, then I kindly ask you to put them off until Monday, when hopefully the world will be sane again."

"Her friends, you say?"

"That's right."

"I see."

"Jaz, Dakota, get Crespin and the others inside."

"This is a hazardous part of the country we live in, Ms. Jasper."

"Is it? I didn't notice. Unless you're talking about the sandstorms, and then I agree. I'm still picking that crap out of my hair."

"The law is constantly being tested, pushed, challenged."

"And you're a—what? A cop?"

"Not at all. But it has been said that a nation's laws are only as strong as those they govern. It's up to us to be strong. One does not have to be a police officer to act on behalf of the law."

"Sorry, but I fail to see how standing on the sidewalk in front of my house in any way acts on behalf of the law, unless you're here to keep the neighbor's terrier from pooping in my yard. Now if you'll excuse us . . ."

"I couldn't help but notice that currently you have quite a lot of visitors."

Before Sally could reply, Dawn moved. Sally lifted a hand to try and restrain her, but by then it was too late. Dawn took a step toward Presper and said, "And I couldn't help but notice your nose, sir, because it's smack-dab in the middle of someone else's business."

Presper never let the gleam leave his eyes. He looked at Dawn as if waiting for more.

"Dawn, come on."

"There's no reason for you to be here," she told him. "Nobody's done anything wrong."

"And I've accused no one of anything."

Sally had reached her limit. The graveside service and the presence of Jeffrey's spirit in the shoebox lid was her quota of grief for the day. "Dawn. Shut up and leave the man alone."

"But, Sal, this wannabe vigilante is standing twenty feet from your front door and threatening your guests."

"He hasn't threatened anybody. Now let's go."

"But . . ." She scowled at Sally, then looked back at Presper. "You should be nice to strangers, you know. Mean people suck."

Presper seemed unfazed. " 'Laws unsupported by force soon fall into contempt.' Charles de Gaulle, 1934."

Dawn leaned toward him and said, " 'To really free your body, you gotta free your mind.' Jon Bon Jovi, 1988."

She spun on her heel and tromped toward the house.

Sally kept her eyes on Presper. He seemed content to return her stare. Meanwhile Anne was herding Jaz and Dakota and the rest of them up the walk, the tone of her voice brooking no rebuttal. As soon as the others were all inside and no doubt peering through the blinds, Sally said, "A week ago I wouldn't have been having this conversation with you. Frankly the whole thought of confrontation would have scared the shit out of me."

Presper appeared pleased to be sharing this moment with her. Though he was likely aware of the eyes watching them through the curtains, his posture assumed a new intimacy. His voice was less direct though no less engaging. "I assure you that the last thing I want is a confrontation, especially with a fellow citizen of Pima County, especially with a woman, especially with a *beautiful* woman." The compliment left his lips so easily that Sally almost didn't notice it. "But I have obligations. I have responsibilities as an American, and also as a man. There are gaps out there, Ms. Jasper. Gaps in society, gaps in the legal system, gaps in the wall. I have taken it upon myself to fill one of those gaps, to stand in the breech and defend it against all comers."

Sally wasn't sure how she was supposed to respond to this rhetoric. She only wanted to go inside and turn up the amps and forget who she was. When she was in front of the crowd, she didn't have to stand for anything or represent any cause. She had only to fly.

"I too am hoping to avoid confrontation," Presper said. "As a matter of fact, I'd like it very much if we could be friends."

Sally let her eyes play over the aluminum chart tube that supported Presper's weight like a cane. She couldn't help but think that he would have turned that object into a weapon had any of the Mexicans given him a reason. She looked back at his face and said, "I've done nothing wrong. As it turns out, what I'm doing these days feels more right than anything I've mustered up in years. If you want to call me your friend, then stop by my shop sometime and talk about the weather. That's how friends start out. By sitting around a shoe store talking about rain." She gave him a curt nod. "Have a nice life, Mr. Presper." She walked away.

Marching toward her front door, she concentrated on listening to the sounds of his footfalls, but she heard nothing. Apparently he wasn't moving. She felt his eyes stinging the back of her neck, a scorpion stare whose venom coursed through her and let her know that nothing had been settled, that the subject wasn't finished, that he was still blocking the breech that Sally and her refugees were about to enter.

The door pulled open just as she arrived and an agitated Dawn was there to sweep her inside. "You should have let me run over him."

"I know."

Chapter Nineteen

By ten o'clock that night, Sally had memorized the lyrics of Reba McIntire's "Fancy" and was sending them into the mike with such passion that Dakota had to dial down the volume on the speakers to keep Dawn's neighbors from calling the cops. Though the other immigrants were huddled around Sally's TV or listening to the Hispanic station on her upstairs radio, Crespin was here in Dawn's garage, manning his post beside Dakota, ready to adjust the electronic output as necessary. He was cobbling his English together with such proficiency that he had little trouble being understood when he explained to Dawn that maybe she shouldn't be quite so loud on her drum roll in the second verse.

"Everybody's a critic," Dawn said, rolling her eyes. But then she shot him a smile, and they both laughed.

Anne observed them and felt a surge of guilt.

For the last three hours she'd been pushing herself through pages of sheet music, trying to master some rather complex passages, her back aching from having been bent over the keyboard for so long. Her curse was her brain. It never shut up. Sometimes she felt as if Dawn could go for entire days without thinking anything in particular, as if she'd set her mind on cruise control and just coasted along,

253

making people chuckle and chasing her kids around the house. But Anne had never enjoyed such a luxury. She was a thinker. Not to mention a worrier. Even while her fingers moved across the keys and Sally sang of a low-rent girl turning into a fancy, high-rent woman, Anne thought of Jeffrey's family, and how good cheer such as that on Dawn's and Crespin's faces would be an extinct animal in the Longbranch house for months, and perhaps even years.

But her guilt didn't end there.

She felt guilty for breaking the law. She felt guilty for paying more attention to her doctoral research than to her son. And don't even mention her husband. But most of all—and this was the part that really confounded her—she felt guilty for not stepping up beside Sally this afternoon on the sidewalk and telling Isadore Presper just where he could go and what he could do with himself when he got there. The more she thought about her inactivity, the more she disliked herself. Had she forgotten what it was like when they were young? Had she forgotten the fearless pledge of their youth? Had she forgotten the soulstrings?

It was then that Anne Kobayashi-Greene truly realized she was an adult. Sure, it was one thing to be thirty-six years old and have nearly two decades of grown-up life behind you. But to sit on a hard stool in the middle of a sonic thunderstorm and come to the conclusion that you were no longer a girl . . . it struck her like a blow to the chest, because something irretrievable had been lost.

Or had it?

The next time Sally called for a break, Anne voiced the first thought that touched her lips.

"Hematite."

Sally, breathing shallowly, looked back at her. "Huh?"

What am I doing? Anne asked herself. She couldn't fully

answer that question. But fighting the sense of loss that now filled her lungs, she said, "Hematite is an ore of iron that occurs in rhombohedral crystals. It's also called red ochre."

"You'd think by now," Sally said, still dazed from the song, "that I'd have gotten used to this Trivial Pursuit stuff that comes out of your mouth."

"He was wearing hematite."

"What are you talking about?"

"Isadore Presper. The stone around his neck was hematite. It begins as a deep red color, but when polished it takes on a dark metallic sheen."

No one said anything. The mention of Presper's name was like a curse, and Anne wouldn't have been surprised to see Crespin making the sign of the evil eye. "This is how it is," Anne said. "Is everyone listening?"

Apparently they were. Dawn folded her sticks in her lap. Jazmyn cupped her guitar pick in her palm.

"We haven't seen the last of him," Anne said. "I'm quite certain that even now he's marshalling his resources against us, even tonight, even at this moment. He'll attempt to ferret out the identities of Eleazar and Beatriz and the rest of them, and somehow he'll force our hand. We'll either have to present their paperwork to Immigration and Customs Enforcement and concoct a watertight story to explain their presence among us, or we'll have to move them immediately."

"I don't have their documents yet," Sally reminded her.

"Then you better hurry the process along. This man will not wait, Sally. I wouldn't be surprised if he and his hoodlums showed up on your doorstep as soon as tomorrow."

"You're probably right, Annie. You usually are. But we can't worry about that now. We have the concert. We have seventy-three thousand people to think about. We have television crews and music critics. We have the Dixie Chicks, for God's sake."

"Then we're going to have to take care of it all at once, the concert and the Mexicans."

"That's asking a lot."

"Yes, it is. *Lot* is exactly what's required. I know you have a lot. I've witnessed it."

"I guess we'll see, won't we?"

They stared at each other, and Anne pushed telepathically across the garage. *I'm sorry for failing to back your play this afternoon. Next time I'll live up to the soulstrings.*

"Hey," Dawn said from behind her drums. "What the hell's hematite got to do with the price of goat milk in Katmandu?"

Anne waved it away. "Nothing. Or at least almost nothing. Mystics believe that hematite has protective powers. Certain warriors in history rubbed their bodies with a hematite stone before battle, believing it made them invincible."

"Terrific. The last thing I want to hear is that old Isadore Pecker is wearing a magic rock that makes him immortal."

They played until the midnight hour.

"Sal?"

"Still here, Dawny."

"When people use the phrase, 'one hell of a day,' I think they're talking about days like tomorrow."

"We'll be okay."

"Promise?"

"No."

"Lie to me, then."

"Okay. We'll be fine. Our show will go off without a

hitch, and we'll get the Mexicans safely on their way, the police none the wiser."

"Girlfriend"—she touched Sally's cheek—"as a kindred spirit and a lead vocal you are my first and only choice, but as a liar you really suck."

Sally slept that night and dreamed that her houseguests were kidnapped one at a time by assailants who wore American flags for masks, but she awoke the next morning to the soothing smells of fresh coffee and frying corn tortillas.

"Miz Sally?"

"Yes, Beatriz?" she said in the direction of her closed bedroom door.

"Sunday today, Miz Sally. We pray. You pray with us?"

Sally lay there for a moment, staring at the ceiling and wondering what Leigh was doing at this hour—and what he was wearing—then she smiled lazily and stretched her way out of the covers. "Praying sounds like just what I need on a day like this, Beatriz. In fact, the more prayers, the better. I'll be right down."

Jude Yarbuck's driver showed up with a horse trailer.

The big diesel-engine pickup idled at the curb. Hitched to its bed was a customized livestock trailer designed to transport up to four horses in a fully enclosed, climate-controlled environment, a luxury rodeo machine if Dawn had ever seen one. Painted with scenes of stampeding mustangs and the wild-faced cowboys who chased them, the trailer looked as out of place on Dawn's somnolent Sunday morning street as a porn star scoping out a nunnery.

That reminded her of a joke, but she didn't think anyone was in the mood.

Under Crespin's direction, the Mexican men loaded the trailer. By now Dawn knew all their names. Her favorite was a shy little man named Javier. With a mustache like black drapery and laughing eyes, Javier reminded her of a diminutive Groucho Marx. Though he spoke only pidgin English, Javier always snorted in delight whenever Dawn made a wisecrack about the expanding geometry of her own butt or the general stupidity of men. He was a good audience, and for this Dawn adored him.

He also had a strong back. He had hoisted an amplifier only slightly smaller than a baby grand piano and was lugging it toward the trailer. And whistling. Over the last two days, Radio had acquired additional equipment, wrangled up by Dakota from guys he knew around town. Most important was an array of monitors so the women could hear themselves above the thunderstorm of the crowd, and a complex mixer board that Dakota and Crespin were learning to use. To Dawn, the mixer board and all of its dials, buttons, and levers looked like a control panel from the U.S.S. *Enterprise*.

Javier added his burden to the trailer and then stopped abruptly when something snared his attention. Dawn watched him as he crouched near one of the trailer's rear wheels.

She walked up to him, looked down. "What's the matter?"

Javier glanced up, pointed at the tire, and rattled off a paragraph of inexplicable Spanish.

"You don't say." She turned a complete circle, hunting around until she found the nearest translator. "Yo, Kobayashi. Come here and play United Nations interpreter for a second."

After ensuring that her keyboards were properly packaged and stored, Anne came over and listened to Javier repeat his soliloquy.

"Well?" Dawn prodded.

"He says he used to work in a tire factory. It was owned by an American company. He worked fourteen-hour days for the equivalent of a hundred U.S. dollars a week."

"No kidding? How much is that per hour?"

"Mmmm . . . about seventy cents."

"Seventy cents? You think there'd have been a revolution by now. If there is one, I'm joining up for sure."

Javier spoke again, this time indicating the tire itself.

"He's telling us how necessary the tire's tread is to safety. It's the most important part, where all matters on the highway are determined. He says each groove of the tread is like a line on a battlefield where the victor and the loser are decided. Where the rubber meets the road."

"Old Javier here took his job way too seriously."

"He was proud of it."

"That's the sad part. People at least get paid minimum wage in this pigheaded country of ours, and we still complain about the work." She extended her hand to Javier, and then helped him to his feet. "Tell him that I'd drive on his tires any day."

"I'm not sure he'll know what that means. For that matter, I'm not sure that *I* know what that means."

"Just tell him."

Anne relayed Dawn's message.

Javier's response was unexpected. He kissed his fingers, touched them to his forehead, and bowed slightly at the waist.

"What the hell was that about?" Dawn asked after he was gone.

"I could not begin to guess."

"Here's a better question. What the hell's that thing in your backpack?"

"Hmmm?" Anne wore her tidy leather backpack, the one in which she toted her laptop and research texts to class. Now the pack was filled with pages of sheet music, bottled water, and her blue Ropers. Slid into a mesh side pouch was a long knife with its blade wrapped in a washcloth. "Oh. That's the knife I bought from the old man in Crespin's village."

"The cow-bone knife."

"Mountain lion."

"Since when did you decide to carry it around with you?"

"Maybe it's a good luck charm."

"You don't believe in luck."

"Then maybe it's for self-defense. I certainly believe in that."

"Who are you defending against?"

"Only time will tell."

The men filed into the trailer, followed by Jazmyn and a distant-eyed Sally. Crespin waved broadly at Dawn and Anne. "*Señoras,* we ride!"

Sally hoped that the drive into Tempe would bring her peace, yet it did not.

The very air was like kindling, crackling with the promise of fire, portending of a conflagration that might burn down the day. A disaster of inferno proportions was just waiting to happen. The four of them would seem so very small on that stage, surrounding by those teeming thousands. She doubted if their sound would even carry past the first dozen rows. They would be booed. Crushed under the raw tonnage of humiliation. Like the hapless victims of some sick reality TV show where people were mortified for the enjoyment of others.

Then they'd return home to find government agents waiting for them. People-legging was a federal crime. Sally had looked it up.

"You know what I miss the most?" Dakota said. He was sitting beside her on one of the deeply cushioned benches at the front of the trailer.

"I'm sorry?"

Dakota lifted his injured arm. "I miss being on my bike."

"Haven't you learned your lesson about motorcycles?"

"No, never." He grinned and looked half his age. "I still think they're cool."

"Well, maybe they are." In her mind she saw him astride his black and chrome street bike, unkempt blond hair like a banner behind his head. "You didn't look half bad riding it, if you want to know the truth."

Color came to his cheeks and he took a sudden interest in an errant thread on his jeans.

Sally had never seen him look more endearing. "Would you believe me if I told you that this old woman has never been on a motorcycle before?"

He didn't look at her, just kept picking at his pants. "Everybody should ride one at least once, just because they won't be able to get over the wind. The wind against your body is the best part. It's hard to describe. But it makes you feel like you're flying, you know what I'm saying? And on some days nothing else matters but flying. The sensation is just—"

"*Hózh'q,*" Sally said. "The sensation is *hózh'q.*"

"Come again?"

"Nothing. It doesn't matter. But I know what you mean. Being on the bike is being free, at least for awhile. And recently I've been thinking a lot about freedom and what it really means. Now here's a word of advice for you."

"Sure."

"Whenever I refer to myself as an old woman, always contradict me."

He grinned, and maybe a few days ago Sally wouldn't have found that look on his face so fetching, but now her body was tuned to a new and unreasonable frequency. She wanted to be eighteen years old and the sweetheart of this quicksilver boy.

She said, "Maybe we can go for a ride one of these days."

"Hey, as soon as the doc gets this thing off my arm, you got a date."

"Wait a minute." Something just occurred to her. "Today is Sunday, isn't it?"

"Yeah. Why?"

"Nothing." She had just realized that the statue hadn't fallen yet. Her time slot didn't hit the money, and no kewpie doll for her. As if she cared anymore.

Before she expected it and long before she was ready, the driver's voice came over the trailer's intercom and said that Sun Devil Stadium was five minutes away.

Already? She knitted her fingers together. *Is it too late to turn down Jude's offer?*

"Okay, soldiers!" Dawn announced in her best drill-sergeant rumble. "Drop your cocks and grab your socks!"

Sally wondered if she should take a moment to induce vomiting, just to get the inevitable out of the way.

The first thing Anne saw upon stepping from the trailer was a towering digital sign.

TONIGHT!

The lights flashed and changed.

COUNTRY MUSIC FEST!

Another flash.

SOLD OUT!

"Sold out," she said to herself, as the Mexicans hurried around her to unload the gear. The implication of sold out made its way into her bones. When she'd told Barry about the concert, he'd done the worst possible thing: he laughed. But after his laughter had faded, he'd done the best possible thing: he hugged her.

Then he'd phoned a colleague at the university and the proper strings were forthwith pulled. He and Dawn's hubby, Alex, were driving down later this afternoon, assured of a place in the box seats. Though the two men were so dissimilar that they almost seemed to represent different species—Barry was excessively educated and spent his free time analyzing the spectra of distant galaxies, while Lex watched *Junkyard Wars* and lived for monster-truck rallies—their fates were entwined due to the soulstrings that stitched their wives together. Anne would have enjoyed being a fly perched on the dashboard of Barry's car as he and Alex pretended to have common ground and tried not to bore each other to the point of exhaustion.

Trevor had howled to come along. But he was going to have to be satisfied with listening to the concert on KSPI, the station that called itself the Raging Bull of Boot-Stompin', and never mind the fact that his friends were razzing him for tuning his radio to a country channel; his mom was playing live in front of thousands and that, his friends would agree, was very, very *tight*.

An hour passed.

In that hour Anne realized that she had indeed stepped through the looking-glass, and here on the other side was a world made of energy and motion. Most of the sensations came piecemeal, a dizzying montage of color and sound: roadies running with pieces of gear, men with headsets, women in mystically tight jeans, sound tests, tunnels under the stadium, news crews, security studs with *EVENT STAFF* printed on their bulging shirts, clicking cameras, echoes from above as the seats began to fill—

"Omigod," Dawn said, grabbing Anne's arm. "Look. Over there being interviewed. Is that Hal Ketchum?"

"I'm afraid I'm not very current on my country-music stars."

"God, that man is even more dishy in real life than on the tube. Do you imagine he'd think I was a total shameless groupie if I went over and threw myself at his feet?"

"He might raise an eyebrow, yes."

Dawn closed her eyes and put a hand on her head. "I can't believe we're actually here, Annie-cakes. If I somehow make it through this day, which is in serious doubt, then can you please tell me all about what happened so I know it wasn't a dream?"

"Why don't we go out to the trailer and change clothes? Perhaps the act of putting on your new black bra will settle your nerves."

"You're right. Gotta get my Buddha back, even if that means changing underwear. Shit, he's coming this way." Dawn stiffened, and Anne couldn't help but do the same, even though she felt ridiculous standing erect beside her friend, with Dawn clutching her hand so tightly that their elbows shook. In a moment he was walking by, the dishy man with the silvery hair—what was his name again?—and Anne glanced obliquely at Dawn—

—Dawn was grinning like a simpleton, wearing a full-on blush.

Anne decided that her friend must be in good graces

with heaven, because the man looked right at her as he passed, his retinue trailing behind him.

Dawn swallowed. "Howdy."

The man smiled graciously. "Hello."

And then he was gone.

Dawn collapsed. "Save me, Annie, my knees are Jell-O."

"Come on then." She shouldered Dawn down the tunnel. "You haven't changed since junior high, you know that? You had that same look on your face when you claimed that Bryan Adams looked at you while he was singing."

"He did, dammit. Don't you remember the concert? He looked right at me during the second chorus of 'Heaven.' We made eye contact. Made soul contact."

"And your heart was never the same again."

"You got that right. I wonder how Bryan's heart is doing?"

"I'm sure he's been barely holding it together since that night. Now can you walk by yourself or are you going to pull my arm out of its socket?"

Thunder shook the hall.

Frozen, Dawn said, "That wasn't thunder."

"I know."

"People."

"Yes."

"A mucho, mondo, mega-lot of people."

"The trailer, Dawn. The black bra. Can you make it or not?"

"I don't know. I'll try. But if I pass out, call Hal to give me mouth-to-mouth."

"Well, for Hal's sake, let's try to get you to the trailer under your own power."

They made their way up the long concrete ramp that led

outside to the lot where all the buses and semi-trucks were parked. High overhead, a helicopter from the local NBC affiliate was shooting footage of the concert-goers who were gathering in multiple queues near the stadium entrance. The lines were already half a block long.

"He may have to give us both mouth-to-mouth," Anne said.

Mutual support got them to the trailer.

Sally stood with her back against the cement wall and her boots firmly on the floor.

This is what Juan Doe was looking for, she thought.

The women occupied an inclined corridor that led from the dressing rooms up to the stadium and onto the stage. Great, tidal sounds came from the tunnel's terminus.

Juan Doe was running toward this. He died in search of it.

Chirping voices came from the radios and headsets of men in the tunnel. Roadies hurried back and forth.

It lives at the end of this passageway.

Out on the stage, Crespin and Eleazar and the others were positioning speakers, adjusting mikes, making ready. Somewhere Dakota was ensconced in the sound booth with technicians who were paid to make music into something dramatic, and to make it loud.

Freedom.

"Okay, Radio," said a man with a walkie-talkie and a *FULL ACCESS* badge around his neck. "You've been cleared for takeoff."

Sally pushed herself away from the wall. Dawn stepped up beside her, her hair moussed into a fury of wild delight. Her boots made her almost six feet tall. Anne and Jazmyn were right behind them.

"Remember your monitors," the man instructed them.

"You will not be able to hear yourselves play unless you have a monitor nearby. Do not forget this."

A pair of bodybuilders in black T-shirts took up places on either side, massive and handsome guardians on this long walk toward *libertad.*

"Are you ready?"

Sally felt warm hands inside her, releasing the fetters, unfurling the wings.

"This is it," Dawn whispered. "Where the rubber meets the road."

As one, they began to move.

Chapter Twenty

Sound cracks the sky.

The noise is the beginning and the end. It is the air Sally breathes. It is the wind that stirs her hair. It comes not from the mountain of black speakers looming on either side of the stage, but from human throats. Tens of thousands. Not cheering. Just screaming. Seeing their faces is like staring into the sky on nights the stars cannot be counted. But hearing them . . . it steals the breath from Sally's lungs.

Drums.

First the drums. A rumble. A beat so much louder than in a garage or a honky-tonk that it paralyzes Sally with its size. Surely sound cannot have so much pressure, such weight. Yet it does, and it grows. Dawn-Marie drives the foot which drives the pedal which drives the mallet into the drum. This in turn drives blood through the crowd, like a gigantic beating heart.

Guitar.

Jazmyn alone is neither breathless nor stunned. She radiates. Her shoulders are bare and her hair woven with silver tinsel. In her arms is the source of the crowd's building frenzy, and she smiles as her hand dances up the instrument's neck.

Keyboard.

Anne's face is drained of color, but her fingers move, likely through sheer force of will. She plays the opening bar of Dolly Parton's "Jolene," and the notes must be known to these thousands because their hands rise and their mouths open to follow the words.

Sally feels these words rising in her. The words. The words are keys. All she must do is send them out across the arena and the locks will fall away. And as she takes a single step forward and parts her lips, she realizes that locks account for too much separation in this world. She is about to chase this thought to what feels like a revelation, but then the moment comes. And she sings.

The best part of all is that seventy thousand voices sing with her. . . .

Chapter Twenty-one

The desert at night had a music of its own.

With the setting of the sun, the birds and jackrabbits had fled. The nocturnal creatures that crept out of holes and caves had their own sounds—wolf cries and the fluttering of heavy owl wings. Cicadas spoke in tongues, their messages unintelligible. The highway, too, added to the nighttime chorus, a blacktop percussion instrument against which tires droned on for miles.

The wheels of the trailer hummed without ceasing.

The darkness of the outside world went unbroken within, as the trailer's interior lights had been dimmed. The gentle sigh of the air-conditioner joined the monotone of the rolling highway, but other than this, all was hushed, despite the fact that twelve pairs of eyes were wide open, twelve faces waiting silently in the dark.

"That's my girls!" Jude Yarbuck had hollered, hours ago. "I'll be dipped in snuff and spit out sideways if that show wasn't a crowd-pleaser!" He'd hoisted Jazmyn into the air as if she were weightless, and spun her around.

Jaz had laughed like an heiress and kissed him on the cheek.

Twelve faces, half of which belonged to the men from Mexico. The wonder of what they had seen was written on their faces in a language that peeled back their years, so that they seemed like children. This fabled nation was in many ways not so grand as they had dreamed, but tonight their faith had been renewed.

"We're coming to your town!" the men had sung from their positions backstage, mimicking the words as Radio delivered them to the audience. "We'll help you party down! We're an American band!"

That song had been the band's finale, and its lyrics were among the first English sentences the men learned and understood.

"We're coming to your town," Eleazar had said to Javier after the show, just for practice.

"We'll help you party down," Javier had replied.

Together they'd said, "We're an American band."

Two more faces, huddled close: when fragments of moonlight alighted on Crespin, he seemed to be watching Jazmyn with a mixture of awe and trepidation. The two of them sat on a fold-away cot at the back of the trailer. Jaz had kicked her boots off, and her bare legs barely touched Crespin's knees. She was nearly hoarse from shouting her glee after the concert. When a group of adolescent girls had tracked her down and asked for an autograph, she had nearly split in half with delight. It still showed in her eyes.

"Your name is Jazmyn?" the reporter from the *Arizona Republic* had asked. "Very interesting name. Could you spell that, please? How long have you been playing guitar, Jazmyn?"

One of the faces was Dakota's, though half hidden in the shadows, he might have been anyone at all. Only the cast on his arm, glimpsed occasionally in the gloom, marked him for who he was. The cast had been signed by all three Dixie Chicks, and now Dakota held it against his chest as if it were the holy relic of a saint.

"Hey, kid," one of the techs in the sound booth had said. "Those broads may be just a cover band, but they're one of the best I've seen. Got a helluva way with the crowd."

Dakota had grinned. "Yeah, they're cool, ain't they?"

"They got pluck, I'll give 'em that."

Of the three faces remaining, only one of them was smiling.

It wasn't Dawn. She bit her lower lip and didn't let go. Never before had she known such a terror and such a thrill. The alchemy of the two emotions had made her sick. Puking in front of your friends was bad enough, but when you lost your lunch in public it was a first-class foe paw, as she liked to say. Except foe paw wasn't funny now. Nothing was funny. Nothing was funny because for once in her humdrum existence everything had been so real. The colors were brighter, the sounds more true to the ear. She'd only felt such full-force emotion twice in her life, just twice, once when the doctor said that Tatyana was dead, and once when Coy and Caleb were placed in her arms for the first time. That half-hour on the stage was like that, as stark and vivid as dying and being born.

"Dawn-Marie Johnson," Yarbuck had said, "this is my friend Stanley Ashford. He's a music promoter and the producer of this here shindig. Stan, Dawn-Marie."

"Truly a pleasure, Mrs. Johnson. I must admit that you impressed me out there tonight, and I've seen enough in twenty years of the business not to be easily impressed."

Anne looked as if she hadn't smiled for days. Though she knew nearly nothing of Japanese culture and even less of her ancestors' mysticism, she retreated into a posture of penitent silence and folded her hands complacently in her lap. Her face bore no expression, and she caused her eyelids almost to close, trying to appear as isolated and in control as Asians were purported to be. She hoped her façade was more convincing than it felt. Inside she was in shambles. She attributed this emotional ferment to the fact that, for nearly thirty minutes, she had forgotten who she was. She was no longer Anne the class valedictorian, whose socks were always spotless white and whose deodorant always lasted twenty-four hours. The woman who'd been wearing her skin had been capable of killing for food and making love to anonymous men she met on a train.

"This is Jason Booker coming to you live from Sun Devil Stadium. As you can see behind me, the excitement of tonight's big event has yet to die down, as several hundred eager fans are still lingering, most hoping to get a glimpse of any one of the concert's star performers. Standing here with me now is one of those performers. Anne Ko . . . Kobayashi, you're with the band Radio, is that correct?"

"Yes. I play . . . I play the electronic keyboard."

"How did it feel being onstage at a concert of this scale?"

"Well . . . it's . . . I'm sorry . . . this is my first interview. I would have to say that the experience made me feel rather contumacious."

Sitting alone near a window, Sally smiled without knowing why.

Contumacious. Only Anne would say something like that in an interview. Sally wasn't even sure what it meant, but she was glad that Anne had sufficiently stumped young Mr. Booker from Action 9 News.

With the touch of a button, Sally reclined the seat and spent a few moments stretching her arms above her head. Still the grin lingered. The second she got home, after her guests were settled in for the night, she was calling Leigh Surry without thought of the consequences. Without thought of anything at all. She would drive out to his place and meet his dog Francine, and maybe the shop would get opened tomorrow morning and maybe it wouldn't. All she could think about was expelling the heat within her. All she could think about was his hands. . . .

She'd been home not quite an hour when the man with the badge showed up at her door.

Jude Yarbuck's driver had dropped Anne off and then swung around to deposit Jaz and Dawn. At Sally's, the men had adeptly unloaded the equipment. They were met inside by Beatriz, Ana, and Lilia, who were waiting up with glasses of iced tea and almond cookies. Sally noted briefly that her house had never felt more homey nor smelled so good. But then this thought, too, fluttered from her mind and she soared upstairs and stripped down en route to the shower.

She came back down just in time to hear the doorbell.

It's Leigh, she thought. *He's outside with flowers. And for the first time in my adult life, I'm not wearing any underwear.*

She glided to the door—

The first thing she saw was an open wallet.

"Sally Jasper, I assume? I'm Manny Delano with U.S. Customs and Border Protection. I realize it's late, but could I have a few minutes of your time?"

Sally wondered why she wasn't surprised. Or afraid.

"Ms. Jasper?" Delano lowered his wallet. He wore a Border Patrol uniform and a black felt cowboy hat. He was one of those men who paid little attention to his skin; his cheeks were flaky and in need of serious exfoliation, and the drooping patches under his eyes could have used a good cucumber cream. "I'm sorry to bother you so late, but I'm here to follow up on a tip."

"A tip." Sally didn't know what else to say. Behind her

was a living room full of illegals. And in front of her . . . she peered into the darkness over Delano's shoulder and saw two vehicles at the curb. One of them was an SUV with Border Patrol markings, and the other was an open-topped Jeep with four shadowy figures inside. She could see by the cherry of his cigarette that the man in the passenger's seat was smoking. She looked back at Delano. "I suppose this red-hot tip came from a man named Isadore Presper."

"The source is hardly relevant. The fact of the matter is—"

"Do you have a warrant?"

"Nope. Can't say I have. To be frank with you, I've been off-duty since six. But I ran into some friends of mine and they had interesting things to say about you. Like maybe you've got a passel of aliens doing housework for you."

Sally gathered a breath, then slowly released it. "That's right, Officer Delano, my forty-room mansion here also requires the skills of a butler and a full-time laundress, not to mention the little orphan girl I pay a dollar a day to shine the family silver. Now go patrol someone else's borders. Yesterday I might not have been so rude, but today I saw a million faces, and I rocked them all."

She closed the door before he could speak.

She stood there and imagined touching Leigh's face.

Ten seconds later, Beatriz screamed.

The sound was jagged with fear, a broken-glass cry that shattered Sally's thoughts.

The living room.

Sally ran that way without hesitating, rounding the corner in time to see a face withdrawing from the big window behind the TV. Eleazar had leapt to his feet and was pointing at the darkness beyond the glass, speaking rapidly. Beatriz and Ana were holding each other.

"What?" Sally demanded. "What was it? Who was it?"

She crossed the room amidst a frenzy of Spanish she couldn't understand and peered through the window into the night. All she saw were the bushes in front of her house, streetlamps at the curb, and mounds of shadow. "Wait a minute. . . ."

What was that? Something was moving. . . .

"Kill the lights," she said. She looked over her shoulder. "Crespin, can you get the lights so I can see through this . . ." She realized Crespin wasn't there.

Where is he?

Now that she thought about it, she didn't recall seeing him get out of the trailer with the others. Which meant that he must have disembarked at Dawn's house. With Jazmyn.

Jaz and Crespin?

Sally had no time to consider this latest wrinkle in her life because the doorbell chimed, followed by a harsh knock and a voice saying, "Ms. Jasper, maybe we should talk about this a little bit more."

"Go away, Officer!" She turned her attention back to the shapes outside—and they were moving now, no doubt about it, two men splitting up and taking opposite paths around her house.

"DATFUG," she whispered.

"Ms. Jasper!" He banged again at the door.

Beatriz was borderline panicked, holding hands with the other two women and talking ceaselessly. Javier jogged to the far side of the room and cupped his hands around his eyes as he stared through the glass. Eleazar was addressing Sally, and though she didn't comprehend his words she felt the rising tide of his fear.

When she most needed her soul sisters, she was alone.

"Shit. Okay. Upstairs. Eleazar, I need you to get everyone upstairs. Can you do that?" She pointed at the stairs, then at the ceiling. "How the hell do you say up? Uh, *arriba*." Then she remembered the most important Spanish word she could have used at that moment, and it meant go. "*¡Vaya!*" She shoved Eleazar in the direction of the stairs, and from the kitchen came sounds of someone trying to get in the back door. "*¡Vaya, vaya, vaya!*"

The Mexicans bolted. Frightened and uncertain, they hustled into a clumsy line and helped one another up the stairs.

Now what?

The police. Call the police. Sally ran to the phone—and along the way she had a crazy thought, crazy because when she thought of the police, the first thing that came to her music-laden mind was Sting and his band The Police, singing "Every Breath You Take."

I'll be watching you. A face appeared in the window again.

Isadore Presper met her eyes.

Sally grabbed the phone.

Presper held up a hand. In that gesture he said, *Wait.*

Sally kept her grip on the phone, fingers poised above the buttons, but didn't touch them.

Presper displayed an envelope, bright red even in the dim light, like a Valentine's card.

Sally didn't breathe, so as to hear anyone trying to break in.

Presper placed the envelope so that its edge rested on the windowsill.

Sally never took her eyes from his.

He made a placating gesture and backed away until he was out of sight.

Sally waited. But no one smashed a window. No one threw a shoulder into her door.

Eleazar padded down the stairs and said in a harsh whisper, "Men remain?"

After a long moment Sally said, "No. No men remain. But keep everybody upstairs for awhile, okay?" After returning the phone to its base, she went to the door, listened, heard nothing. Her pulse stroked the veins in her wrists. Perhaps a few days ago her body would have hoisted the white flag. Her fearful heart would have beaten too hard against her ribs. She would've collapsed onto the couch on the verge of hyperventilation. But stronger energies than these had passed through her marrow in recent hours. It was hard to get worked up about the danger of shocking yourself on a household appliance after you'd been struck by lightning.

She opened the door and went out into the night.

The air was stagnant, the day's heat still lingering. Sally's neighborhood looked like any other such idyllic street in America. Soft silhouettes moved behind glowing windows. Three houses down, boys played basketball in the semi-darkness of their driveway. The taillights of Presper's Jeep winked out of sight.

This is a hazardous part of the country we live in, he had warned her yesterday.

"Obviously he hasn't heard about the pigtails," Sally said as she set off through the yard.

The envelope balanced on the sash like a love letter left by an admirer too timid to knock. Sally sidled between the bushes and plucked this spurious billet-doux from its resting place and went back under the porch light to tear it open.

She saw the crowd again, and the vision stopped her in

mid-stride. She'd never beheld so many faces in one place at one time. Their collective voice was like the speech of gods. It belittled even as it uplifted. It made Sally feel so very small, while concurrently making her a giant. Out on the stage her song had been magnified to dimensions so great that she'd felt capable of calling down rain or changing the spin of the planet with a word. The response she received from the multitudes was no less immense, equally complete in its ability to make her temporarily immortal.

She realized her eyes were closed.

When she opened them, she was surprised to see her feet still firmly on the porch. Surely there was enough residual power in her wings to lift her skyward on a whim. And if such euphoria as this was the reason people got hooked on drugs, then Sally would never again say a bad word about junkies.

The envelope was still in her hands.

So Presper was playing games with her. Even before Sally examined the contents of the bright scarlet parcel, she sensed that she was being taunted, toyed with, goaded. Isadore Presper was a grown man, but apparently also a child, inclined toward such immature tomfoolery as scaring people through windows and leaving threatening letters in his wake. Writing him off as a bigoted bully, Sally sliced open the envelope with her fingernail and let its contents spill onto her hand.

On her palm lay a single guitar pick, painted with the unmistakable blue, red, and white lines of the British flag.

Sally forgot everything else and stared.

Jazmyn.

This was one of Jaz's picks. Somehow Presper had acquired it.

Sally was wrong about him. Presper was no mere thug, but a threat. The unspoken message sent in this guitar pick was not idle intimidation, but a warning. He would go to grave lengths to do his part as a patriot. He would strike at his enemy's heart.

This is a hazardous part of the country we live in.

Sally raced inside for the phone.

Chapter Twenty-two

Dawn belched.

Standing in the hallway outside the bedroom, wearing sweatpants and one of Lex's Harley-Davidson T-shirts, she stared at the silent telephone in her hand and wondered if Sally was going crazy.

"Try to saw some logs, Sal," Dawn said to the inert phone. Only seconds ago she'd pressed the end button after wishing Sally sweet dreams. But she was sure that Sally wouldn't sleep tonight, even after Dawn had tromped through the house down to Jazmyn's room and peeked in on her, just to ensure that Presper's lackeys hadn't stolen her away in the night. Enough light from the hall had fallen into Jaz's room to permit Dawn's night-blind eyes to confirm that her daughter was indeed present and accounted for.

And she wasn't alone.

Crespin lay snug on Jazmyn's floor in one of the camouflaged sleeping bags that Alex took up to the hunting lodge twice a year. Upon finding the kid lying there, Dawn had two thoughts on the subject. One, why the hell would a sleeping bag need to be camouflage-colored in the first place? So you could sleep in the woods without the bears seeing you? No, the bears would see you anyway, and smell you, and eat you and your silly green bag whole.

Two, since when had Crespin been granted sleep-over rights?

Dawn clucked her tongue. A second later she realized she sounded like an old woman, so she smiled to herself, went to the front door to recheck the deadbolt, and tried to fight a rising premonition of dread.

He's coming for us.

Presper was after the Mexicans, and he wouldn't stop until he'd rousted them from Sally's house and gotten the conspirators thrown in the hoosegow. Lex would have a conniption if he had to come bail his wacky wife out of lock-up. She could hear him in there snoring right now. He was twenty pounds heavier than the day Dawn said "I do." He had a little less hair, but his humor was just as robust as it had ever been, if maybe a little bit raunchier, and he still enjoyed reading the boys to sleep. Dawn adored the oaf, and he wasn't half bad between the sheets. So she didn't fancy the idea of calling him for help while wearing an orange jumpsuit with *PIMA COUNTY* printed on the back.

She walked softly through her house, guided by the frequent night-lights placed at strategic corners for her convenience. She inspected the windows, thinking of the night she'd given up her virginity in exchange for a hickey on her neck so big that even her most godawful turtleneck couldn't cover it up. Tommy Vohmeyer had been as lanky and awkward as Dawn herself, which had made the union somewhat stick-figurish for both of them. And it had barely lasted five minutes. Scale of one to ten?

"One to ten?" Dawn said to herself. "Maybe a two-point-four. Five being average. One being intercourse with a cadaver." She went to the door that led from the kitchen to the garage. The lock had never worked well. In a town the size of Fresh Waters, in-home burglaries were kind of like Tommy Vohmeyer's sexual performances: they rarely showed up on radar.

Tatyana, on the other hand, had made it for the first time with a quarterback named Derek Falkers, who everyone in the girls' locker room assumed had to be a good lay. Just look at him. The boy was built. Derek gave Tatyana his class ring, took her to two proms, said he wanted to marry her after college, knocked her up when she was nineteen, and then fled like a draft dodger when she told him the news.

No one ever heard from him again, not even nine months later when she died.

The phone rang and scared Dawn into dropping it.

"Shit. What now?" She picked up the phone, expecting Sally, but it was Anne who said, "You're still awake."

"No, I'm sound asleep and having a nightmare about people calling me up when I'm trying to dream about Denzel Washington. Do you know what time it is?"

"Vaguely. Do you want to see something incredibly peculiar?"

"Annie, it's two in the morning. Are you aware of how many times in our lives I've spoken to you on the phone? Roughly about nineteen thousand and six. How many times at two a.m.? Certainly hundreds. But unlike you, my body is no longer full of vim and vigor, whatever the hell vim might be. And guess what? Your freaky friend Sally Jasper just called me and started ranting about Presper making threats on Jazmyn."

"I know. She called me too. I assume that all is well?"

"Other than the fact that I'm standing here in my PJs instead of curled up in bed? Yeah, everything's peachy. Do you think she's flaking out?"

"Not at all. I advised her to call the police. She said she couldn't—"

"Because she has illegal company."

"Correct."

"Should we go over there?"

"I offered, but she said no. She seems to think that Presper and his minions won't be back again tonight, and I have to concur. But first thing tomorrow morning she intends to finish up this plan to outfit them with false paperwork and move them on to greener pastures."

"I second the motion. So what's this incredibly peculiar thing you're talking about?"

"You'll have to go to your computer."

"What? At this hour?"

"There's an Internet site I want you to see."

"Honey, you know how I feel about dot-coms and technology in general. To me, 'www' stands for Woman With Web-phobia."

"Just get online, Dawn. I'll wait."

"Of course you will." Tossing out a sigh, Dawn went into the cramped little room the computer shared with the washer and dryer. While she waited for her archaic machine to boot up, she said, "You want to know the cold hard truth, Annie?"

"The colder the better."

"This Presper guy scares the pants off me."

"If it's any comfort, I'm just as pantsless as you are."

"Are you? You sound like your usual irritatingly calm self to me. The man's got his own pet Border Patrol officer. If they come back in the morning with a warrant, we're doomed."

"We are not doomed."

"We'll see. Remember the Magic 8 Ball we used to have

when we were kids? If I had one of those suckers now, I'd shake it and get an answer about how tomorrow is going to turn out. Didn't Sally say that Presper's group was based in Maxon? Barry spends a lot of time over there. What does he know about them?"

"I haven't asked. I don't want to worry him. Are you on-line yet?"

"Getting there. What did Trev say when you got home tonight?"

"Honestly I haven't seen him like that since he was little." Dawn could hear the smile on her friend's face. "I've never known what it was like to have my son's stamp of approval. I didn't realize it could mean so much."

"So your kid thinks you're cool. Nothin' better than that. And Barry?"

"Stunned, like everyone else."

"Did you two get it on tonight?"

"What do you think?"

"So he was stunned but not turned on. Too bad." The computer screen showed the current homepage of the Johnson family computer, that being the Nickelodeon Web site. "Okay, I'm up and running. What am I looking for?"

"Go to the CNN site. What about you and Alex?"

"Sex? I had a headache. Or I had to wash my hair, I can't remember which excuse I used. Actually I'm bouncing off the walls and can't concentrate enough for anything more demanding than a hand job. So Lexy didn't get lucky tonight. But me, I feel like I could devour the world."

"Me too."

"You know I can't stand CNN. The news sucks. Always has. What am I doing here?"

"Along the right side of the page, about midway down, there's a section labeled 'Offbeat.' Do you see it?"

"Uh . . . let me scroll down and . . ." Dawn withdrew her hand from the mouse when she saw the text printed in the little box. "Son of a bitcheroo. You gotta be kidding me."

LATE-BLOOMING LADY ROCKERS

Anne said, "Word travels fast, does it not?"

But Dawn was already clicking the link and—with a hand on her forehead in disbelief—reading a story about four Arizona women who performed a brief opening act at a major concert in Tempe and stood out from the other performers due to their gender, their age, and their spirited delivery. The article said, *In a culture where instant pop stars are manufactured by the producers of such programs as* American Idol, *and reality shows transform everyday people into household names, the unlikely quartet called Radio should have no trouble climbing to the top.*

"No way." Dawn shook her head. "They're writing about us."

"So it would seem."

With public appetite for artificially created entertainers being what it is, the four women of Radio will likely find themselves beset upon by eager agents and music-biz execs. But they're also going to need some songwriters. All of the numbers they performed Sunday evening were covers of classics, the crowd favorite being an up-tempo rendition of Jimmy Buffett's "Let's Get Drunk and Screw." Though the thought of this ensemble might induce laughter—the lead singer is a 36-year-old single mom who owns a shoe store—their music is pure and their verve unfeigned.

"Our verve is unfeigned, Annie."

"So they say."

"Look at that picture! Holy shit, that's *me*."

"They caught you in the midst of a cymbal crash."

"I'm on CNN!"

286

"Trevor was also pretty excited."

"Pretty excited? Annie, we're goddamn *famous*."

"Hardly."

"Hardly nothing!" Dawn still could not believe what she was seeing. "How many people visit this site? Tens of thousands. Maybe hundreds of thousands. *Millions*. And there I am. Right there. I don't know what people mean when they say that something is the cat's meow, but this is it, sure is, the cat's mother-effing meow. . . ."

"I'll come by tomorrow. Sally may need help with the paperwork Dakota's contact is supplying. Are you going in to work in the morning?"

"I can't get over this. I gotta get the word out." She shot up from her chair and tried to think who to call first. Her mother? Her hairdresser? "You know what's next, don't you, Annie-cakes?" She broke into song: "We'll keep gettin' richer and we'll get our picture on the cover of the *Rolling Stone*."

Anne laughed. "Maybe so. I'll see you *mañana*."

"You bet. Tallyho!" She shut off the phone and bent over the computer, reading the article a second time and letting the thought of it wash down her throat like vintage wine. "And everyone will say, 'I knew her when.' " She giggled and ran down the hall. "Lex! Jazzy!" she shouted. "You snooze and you lose, 'cause yours truly's in the news!"

She got them all up, the whole house, Coy and Caleb and Crespin included, and dragged them into the little utility room, and when she saw the link to *E-MAIL THIS STORY TO A FRIEND* she stayed up for another hour typing in addresses and sending it to everyone she knew, and to many people she didn't.

When she finally made it to bed, she found a note on her

pillow. She opened it to see familiar handwriting: *Sleeping beside you is your number one fan.*

Startled by a sudden onrush of tears, she woke him up and told him she no longer had a headache or had to wash her hair, and he seemed happy to hear it.

Monday morning, an avalanche struck Sole Mates.

The sun burned orange above the chaparral and scrub brush, a harbinger of summer. It seemed no kind of weather for the makings of an avalanche, not to mention the fact that there wasn't a decent mountain around for a hundred miles, but the onslaught that crashed through Sally's door at half past ten made her think of landslides: hold on or you'll be swept away.

It all started with the stuck-ups.

The Ramsey twins—Bobbie and Rae Lynn—were nineteen years old, dark-eyed, leggy, former co-captains of everything in high school, spoiled senseless, and current darlings of U of A, having just ended a successful freshman year. They'd been seniors at Fresh Waters High when Jazmyn was in the ninth grade. They had never spoken a single word to her. Jaz had not shed any tears over this.

"Morning!" Bobbie Ramsey said, bebopping into Sally's store with her sister. "Oh, Rae, look at these boots! I absolutely would die to have them."

Sally let the twins ooh and ahh all they wanted, offering no help at all, too busy thinking about Presper and the cops and just what might be taking Dakota so long with those papers. He was supposed to be here any minute now, unmarked parcel in his one good arm, fresh from the forger's studio.

"Excuse me, ma'am. Hello?" It was Rae Lynn, pointing daintily at a pair of silk pumps with pleated fronts and covered heels. "Are these truly on sale for half price?"

"Truly they are."

Bobbie extracted a microscopic phone from her bag. "Rae, we have to tell the girls."

By *the girls* Bobbie Ramsey apparently meant a good portion of her sorority sisters from Alpha Chi Omega. In an hour and a half, six more of them had descended upon the store. They spent their parents' money with practice aplomb. Yes, Sally had that in a five, no, we don't take American Express but your daddy's Visa will do just fine, yes, we have plenty more in the back, no, the jewels on that pair of burnout-velvet Mary Janes aren't real diamonds, you silly sheltered girl.

Maybe it was because Sally had decided to prop open the door in order to get a little fresh air, as all the concentrated perfume and body spray was making her gag. Or maybe passersby saw all the activity in the shop and thought they were missing out. Or maybe word was spreading about Radio's killer performance the day before, and everyone wanted a piece of the Sally Jasper action.

Whatever the reason, the customers rolled in, and the avalanche was on.

Sally went from being preoccupied to being immersed. She jumped from one needy person to the next, measuring feet, making recommendations, watching them test-walk their new footwear, jogging back to the stockroom, searching through boxes for a different size, and—best of all—working the cash register.

Comments came. Folks had heard about the concert. The morning deejays over at the station in Maxon had been talking and joking about Radio since the sun came up. A few shoppers who stopped in had attended the show. After signing a credit card receipt, one such customer then handed the pen back to Sally and asked for her autograph in return.

"My what?" Sally said.

Her first autograph was rendered with a shaky hand. After she was finished, she examined the letters, as if she'd never written her name before and was unfamiliar with the completed product.

By three in the afternoon she'd sold a third of her stock. She hadn't had a run like this since the day after Thanksgiving last year. Jazmyn had stopped by to bring her lunch from the Cheshire Grin. Crespin was with her. They came through the door holding hands.

Normally Sally would have been taken aback by this. Seeing your kid making bodily contact with a member of the opposite sex was something you never got used to. But between the giddy look on Crespin's face and the general furor of the day, Sally saw no reason to give the subject any unwarranted thought. In fact, God bless them both. May Jaz and Crespin love each other madly and never die.

Twenty minutes later, Jude Yarbuck walked through the open door.

Sally left a customer pondering over a pair of weskit pumps with satin tuxedo collars, and caught Yarbuck off guard by throwing her arms around his neck.

"Whoa, little lady." He chuckled and hugged her back. "That's a welcome I'll take any day of the week."

"I owe you everything," Sally said after they parted.

"Everything's a lot to owe."

"You need new boots, they're on the house."

"Wouldn't dream of a freebie. You think you got any-thing in my size around here?"

"Hmmm. What are those? Twelves?"

"Damn, woman, you got an eye on you."

"I have the size in stock, but not the style. Are those snakeskin?"

"Ostrich, actually. But it don't matter none. I didn't come here to shop. Do you have a minute?"

Sally looked over her shoulder. "Well, an hour ago I would have said no, but I think the rush is finally dying down. Why, what's up?"

"I want to be your manager."

Sally let that roll down the pipes of her brain.

"Here's why," Yarbuck said.

"I'm listening."

"I got a call over lunch from Stan Ashford. Remember him from yesterday? He promoted the show. Seems as if he got a call from a woman by the name of Roxy Williams. As it turns out, Ms. Williams is an associate producer for Nancy Holiday."

Apparently the pipes were clogged, because none of this was making any sense. "I don't understand a word you're saying. Sorry, but I'm a little stoned right now. Figuratively speaking, anyway."

"Don't watch a lot of TV, huh? Can't say I blame you. But what I'm talking about is *The Nancy Holiday Show*. It only airs here in the Southwest, 'cause old Nancy hasn't gotten up the steam to go national yet, but she's got herself a right loyal following. She's sort of like Oprah on a regional scale."

"I still don't get it."

"I think you do."

"This Oprah on a regional scale wants us?"

"Wednesday morning. Live." He grinned and hooked his thick thumbs in his belt.

The pipes eventually unjammed. Sally pursed her lips and considered. She had too much to do. Dakota had just called and was on his way. Presper and his sharks were circling. And she wanted to make time to follow Jeffrey's hand-drawn map to see where it led.

"Miss?" It was the customer with the weskit pumps. "Miss, do you think these match this belt okay? Or should I go with the black?"

"And you can set this up?" Sally asked Yarbuck. "You can take care of every little detail, the paperwork, the equipment, everything, so that all I have to do is sing?"

"Darlin', I'm the genie in your bottle. All you gotta do is pop the cork."

"How much is this popping going to cost?"

"Fifteen percent of whatever I can wrangle out of Nancy Holiday's people."

"Then do us all a favor and wrangle their asses off."

Yarbuck smiled. "I call that a deal." He held out his hand. Sally shook.

"Miss?"

"I better go. I feel like I need to say thank you again . . ."

"Thank me by practicing. You ladies have to be a showstopper."

"We'll see."

"I'll be in touch." He tipped his hat and left Sally to her customers and her doubts and her flashbacks of flight. The sense of soaring abided, the feeling that she was above all of this and might at any moment stretch out her wings and leave it all behind.

Then Dakota came in with a package tucked covertly under his arm, and she was grounded again, pulled back down to the trenches, where her battle for *libertad* was being joined.

She finally turned around the *CLOSED* sign at ten past

six. Around her, the shop was chaotic with the rubble of aftermath. Though the landslide had ceased, its debris remained.

Dakota patrolled with a black trash bag, trying to clear a path.

"I appreciate the help," Sally said. She was tired and thirsty, and her hair—ye gods!

"Not a problem."

"I'm talking about the package. You're really putting your neck out."

"What can I say? I sort of like the risk. Never been too fond of the cops anyway. Besides, it was you who asked me to help."

"What do you mean?"

"I'm a sucker for a pretty face." He said it without looking up from his work.

"And I'd be a sucker to fall for such flattery." She went about gathering boxes and trying to restore a measure of order where currently existed only entropy. But she was smiling.

"So what happens next?" he asked.

"We keep our fingers crossed and hope we can get our visitors outfitted and on their way tonight. Anne's at my place right now, overseeing the operation. Everyone's busy making bags of food and clothes. We spent two hundred dollars today at the thrift store, making sure everyone has adequate socks."

"You know something?"

"Hmmm?"

"I've never known anyone like you. Heck, I've never even *heard* of anyone like you."

"I'm not so special."

"Doesn't look that way from where I stand."

Sally glanced over at him, and they shared a look. "You're a charmer, I'll give you that. But how are your digging skills?"

He raised his eyebrows. "My what?"

A thought had just occurred to her, and she chased after it, because she was running purely on instinct these days and that's the kind of thing instinct-chasing people did. Or so she assumed. "I have in my possession what may or may not be a treasure map. Somewhere out in the desert, X marks the spot."

"Sounds cool."

"Tomorrow night then? After the Mexicans are safely on their way and the shop is closed?"

"Won't you be rehearsing? You're on live TV the next day."

"I'll wing it."

Dakota grinned. "I'll bring my shovel."

A knock on the glass door caused them both to turn around.

Leigh Surry stood there, with Border Patrolman Manny Delano beside him.

Chapter Twenty-three

"Dakota. Get the package. Go out the back."

"You sure?"

"I'll take care of them. Just go." Sally started walking toward the door, heaving a smile onto her face."

"Go where?"

"Find Anne. She'll know what to do."

Dakota left off his work and walked casually toward the rear of the store, natural actor that he was. "Be careful, okay?"

"Way past careful now, stud, but thanks for caring." She twisted her key in the lock and pulled open the door, causing the chime to sound. To Leigh she said, "Hey, you."

Though Officer Delano was scanning the store's interior, Leigh only had eyes for Sally. "You won't believe the rumor I heard."

Sally increased pressure on the door so as to support her shaky legs. "Rumor?"

"Yep. And it revolves entirely around you."

Sally wanted to bite down on her teeth but couldn't risk giving up her protective smile. "You know me, always the center of the gossip storm."

"May we come in?"

"Only if you don't mind walking into a place that the

president is about to declare a national disaster zone."

Leigh and Delano strolled in. Leigh stopped in front of Sally, apparently uninterested in the rest of the shop, but Delano prowled.

Sally forced herself not to look away from Leigh. "So what did you hear?"

"I heard, dear Ms. Sally Jasper, that you and your co-horts . . . how should I put this?" He scratched his chin. "That you were bigger than the Beatles yesterday."

A rush of relief washed over her. She barely prevented herself from sighing. "We weren't all that big. Don't believe everything you hear."

"No, really. It went as well as everyone says? You were that good?"

Sally lifted her hand and pointed to her palm. "See this?"

"Yeah."

"This is where I had the crowd, all seventy thousand of them."

"Sweet."

"Sweeter than you know."

Leigh passed a hand through his rowdy hair. "Sally, you are a woman full of surprises. And I'm not a guy so easily surprised. And this leads me to two very important reasons for this visit."

Great, here it comes.

"The second reason is personal. I suppose I'm going to ask you to dinner."

"You suppose?"

"Yes. I suppose. But not quite yet. Personal stuff in a minute. First I need to talk to you about an event that took place at your house on Saturday night."

"Where?"

"Your house."

"No, I mean dinner. Where do you *suppose* you'll be taking me?"

"I haven't thought that far ahead. Somewhere where we won't be mobbed by rabid fans wanting your John Hancock."

"Yeah, that can be so annoying during dinner."

"Seriously, Saturday night. What happened at your house?"

"Hasn't your sidekick here already filled you in?"

Delano heard the word *sidekick* and scowled at her from across the room.

"He told me his version. I want yours."

"I don't have a version, Leigh. I have the truth. *My* truth, which I'm learning is the most imperative truth there is. And my truth is this. Saturday night Delano shows up with his racist friends, and while he's interrogating me at the front door, they're creeping around the flowerbeds and playing Peeping Tom in my windows. And now that I consider it, I think I'm going to file a complaint." She fired a look at Delano. "I was being harassed. I have the footprints in my petunias to prove it."

Delano looked at Leigh, and Sally easily read the message on his face: Are you going to believe this crazy broad?

"Maybe dinner isn't such a good idea," Sally said.

"The hell it isn't." Leigh exhaled. "Look. Manny here has a rotten job. He spends all day patrolling the line. These aren't hardened criminals he's arresting. These are malnourished mothers and skinny kids who've never done anything wrong in their lives. You think it's easy to tell a pregnant woman to turn around and go back where she came from because we don't want her?"

Sally lowered her eyes.

"Be that as it may, it doesn't give Manny the right to go overboard." He trained his gaze on Delano, and the young officer made a sudden inspection of the floor. "Here's the deal. There will be no need to file a complaint, and there will be no need to tromp through innocent flowerbeds. Does everyone in the room agree to that?"

Sally nodded. She assumed Delano did as well, though she didn't check. She was simply happy to be getting off the hook so easily.

"But, Sally, I *am* obligated to ask you."

Only now did she look up. "Ask me what?"

He seemed embarrassed to have to say it. "Are you at the present time harboring nondocumented residents of a foreign country?"

"I'm not even sure what that means."

"Sally, please."

"Okay, sorry, sorry." She fluttered her hand in the air to dispel the notion. "No. I'm not. All the residents of a foreign country that I'm harboring are quite sufficiently documented."

Leigh bit his lip, then said, "You refuse to take this seriously, don't you?"

"You expect a woman to be serious on an empty stomach?"

Delano took that as his cue. He made for the door. "Thanks for coming along, Agent Surry. Sorry it was a wild goose chase. I'll keep you informed."

"I'd appreciate it."

Delano didn't say a word to Sally. The door chimed, and he was gone.

"He's the kind of guy the Border Patrol is hiring these days?" Sally asked.

"He's young."

"Unlike us."

"That's right."

"You should have seen me up there, Leigh. It was incredible."

"I won't miss it next time."

"Maybe there won't be a next time."

He took a step closer. "You'd be willing to give it up so soon?"

"No. Actually, I think I'd rather die."

"You die on me, I'm never going to forgive you."

Sally held her arms at her sides and looked up at him. The feeling that infused her was a less potent version of what she had known on the stage. Less potent, but no less desired.

He touched her hair. "Why do I get the feeling I need to hold on for dear life?"

"Word of advice?"

"Sure."

"Always go with your feelings."

His hand traveled from her hair to her shoulder. "Looks like you sold a lot of shoes today."

"Are you saying the place is a mess?"

"Popularity must be good for business."

"Thank God something is. Leigh?"

"Yes?"

"What we're doing now is called idle talk."

"Sorry. I'm an idle talker from way back."

"I have no time for idleness anymore."

He edged closer still, so that only inches separated his forehead from hers. "My apologies. I forgot I was standing here in front of a superstar in the making. Promise me you won't forget the little people."

"I'll do my best." She said it so softly that her lips hardly moved. She lifted a quarter-inch on her toes.

"In the meantime, I'll take you up on that suggestion to hold on for dear—"

299

A siren blared to life.

The sudden blast caused them both to start. They looked toward the door, his hands on her arms, her next breath abated.

The sharp wail turned into a disconcerting warble, resounding down the street and making odd echoes off the buildings. At first Sally thought it was the police. Her plot had been discovered, and they were coming for her. No, the sound wasn't right. Was the city testing a new fire alarm or storm-warning system?

And then she knew.

"Farrington Schatz has fallen."

"Who?"

Sally grabbed his hand. "Come on!"

She dragged him out the door at a run.

She made him drive because she hadn't sat behind the wheel since Juan Doe died.

"So you bet on when this statue was going to collapse?"

"It wasn't a bet. It was a raffle. For a good cause."

"Did you win?"

"Nope. Not even close."

"Then why are we in such a hurry?"

"Just pull in over there. See all those people?"

"If you didn't win, then what difference does it make?"

"I'm a woman in need of a distraction."

"Frankly, I was kind of hoping to provide that."

"Then you can provide one in the form of dinner. But after that I have to hook up with the band and decide what number we're going to play for Nancy Holiday."

"Who? The talk-show host?"

"I'll fill you in on the details over wine. You do drink wine, don't you?" She opened the door and sprang out of

the car, hardly giving Leigh time to shut off the engine before she rushed over to the site of Farrington's fall. Leigh
hurried to catch up.

". . . which makes the official time approximately six-
thirty-three," Mark Cheevey was saying.

"Approximately," someone else reiterated. "For all we
know, he coulda dropped at four minutes before that, which
would change the winner."

"Yeah, that's right."

"I looked at my watch the moment I heard the klaxon,"
Cheevey explained with notable impatience. "The time was
thirty-three minutes after six."

"But the clock on the First Baptist read six-twenty-nine.
I was looking at it when all the racket started. And the First
Baptist is a lot closer to the park here than your house is,
Mark."

Sally sidled through the little knot of people, not bothering to see if Leigh was trailing her, just wanting to get a
look at how the mighty had fallen.

"My watch is the official time," Cheevey said.

"Whatever."

Sally stepped up to the tumbled statue. The foundation had broken in half. Long sticks of rebar jutted from
the concrete base like cracked bones. As a result,
Farrington's feet were now higher than his head, which
had left an indention in the earth upon impact. The monument's upraised arm was tangled in the wires that had
activated the air-horn. Sally didn't know what she'd been
expecting to see, but it was all rather ignominious now
that it was over.

Showing its disdain for the whole affair, one of the park's
omnipresent pigeons took that moment to settle on the
statue's shoulder.

"So who won?" Sally asked, causing everyone to shut up and look at her.

Then they looked at Cheevey.

Cheevey shuffled his papers and couldn't meet anyone's gaze directly. He cleared his throat and said, "No one."

Sally arched her brow. "Excuse me?"

Cheevey wet his lips, stood firm. "No one bought the winning time slot, I'm afraid, that being the time period between six-thirty and seven o'clock. An unfortunate occurrence."

"However," Becky Doolin inserted, "if the dumb thing really fell at six-twenty-nine—"

"It didn't," Cheevey said.

"—then my sister Rhonda is the winner. Because that was her slot. And I think she should just win anyway, even if your watch is the official time, Mark, because that's better than having nobody win at all. By the way, Sally, I keep hearing about how great you ladies were in Tempe last night. Congrats."

"Thanks. We did all right."

"All right nothing," said the young guy who worked down at the Texaco. Sally couldn't remember his name. He pushed his Stetson a little higher on his head, smiled and showed two rows of lopsided teeth. "I ain't seen many shows better'n yours. Tell you God's truth, ma'am, I don't know which one of you is hotter, you or your daughter. If you don't my sayin' so."

Sally did not blush. Days ago there would have been no doubt. But now . . .

The pigeon fluttered its wings as if feigning flight.

"At any rate," Cheevey said, "since technically we have no winner—"

"Sally," Becky said, holding out her hand, "I envy you."

Ellie from the library crossed the ring of people and touched Sally's arm. "I heard it all on the radio. I wish that I had half of your spunk." Ellie was frail and pale and seldom ventured beyond the library walls. "What you're doing is something I can only imagine. Thank you."

"You're not needing a backup singer, are you?" Becky asked.

The man in the Stetson said over their heads, "What do I gotta do to get a backstage pass to your next gig?"

Sally looked around and found herself surrounded.

"Rhonda's not bad, either," Becky said. "What I mean is, she can carry a tune. Maybe we could come audition sometime?"

Ellie nudged her glasses up her nose. "Would you consider speaking at this month's meeting of the Library Boosters?"

"All the fellas down at the station are talkin' about you," the Stetson man assured her. " 'Course, not all of it's repeatable, at least not around lady folk. . . ."

Leigh leaned over her shoulder and whispered, "I've always wondered what it was like to date Madonna."

Sally gently elbowed him in the ribs.

"So it's settled then," Mark Cheevey said over their heads, trying to draw their attention back to what he thought was important. "At least until the city council deems otherwise, there is no winner in the Farrington Schatz raffle."

If he were expecting a reaction, he was met only with disappointment. The thunder of Farrington's demise had been accidentally stolen, its thief busy shaking hands and saying thank you and ignoring Leigh's muttered sarcasm. Riding an impulse, Sally stepped up onto the statue's truncated base, making her a head taller than anyone around her.

They fell quiet.

"I, uh . . . I want to thank all of you for your support and encouragement. You're really fantastic, all of you. But it's been a long day. I'm hungry. And that hunky guy right there"—she pointed at him, and everyone looked—"has promised to buy me dinner. And no unattached woman in Christendom is going to turn down an offer like that. So I have to go. But I want you to spread the word that Radio will be doing our thing on live TV in two days. Make sure everyone tunes in to *The Nancy Holiday Show*. We'll try not to embarrass the town too badly."

With that, she allowed Leigh to help her down. After a few more parting words with her well-wishers, she left the statue. At the same time, the pigeon twitched its head and took flight.

As they neared the car, Leigh said, "Other than stirring up a pot of gossip about our dinner date, did we accomplish anything here?"

"No." She watched the bird until it had left them all behind. "But I know what song we're singing Wednesday morning."

As he walked away, Trevor turned and hollered, "You're the best, Mom!"

His friends pivoted like clumsy soldiers, four boys in various shades of gray clothing, their piercings numerous and proudly displayed. The grungiest of them saluted, and the others followed suit. "You got that right, Trev," one of them said. "Keep kickin' it, Mrs. Greene!"

"I'll do my best," Anne promised them.

Laughing, pushing one another as boys have pushed for ages, they ambled off down the sidewalk, talking about how Trevor's mom was going to be bigger than Nine Inch Nails.

Anne assumed that being bigger than Nine Inch Nails was good, though she had never heard of the band—if indeed a band is what it was. For all she knew, it could have just as easily been a popular brand of black fingernail dye that all these little Goth soldiers were using.

"To each his own," she said, and went straight toward the bathtub in hopes of submerging herself for the better part of the next hour. Usually her Mondays were spent behind heaps of books; her doctoral research comprised a large wedge of her life's pie graph. But today, needless to say, had been different. She'd spent the afternoon with her son, and later with her son and his friends. She'd made them noodles for lunch and taught them how to use chopsticks, the only facet of her father's culture she'd ever bothered to explore. The boys had enjoyed their own fumbling efforts, and more noodles had ended up on the kitchen floor than in their bellies. Anne drove them all to Dairy Queen for dessert.

"Thanks, Dawn, for losing that bet."

Though she uttered these words to an empty bathroom, she vowed to repeat them to Dawn first thing in the morning. Because the music was magic. The music had made her cool in the eyes of her son. There were nights when she'd lie awake wishing she could give everything she possessed and everything she would *ever* possess just to have Trevor look at her the way he'd looked at her today. And because of a lost wager, she had finally done it. She'd gotten to that place where he sequestered himself. Like Jim Morrison said, she broke on through to the other side.

She adjusted the water and then roamed the house, lighting every candle she could find.

Along the way she inserted an Itzhak Perlman disc into the stereo. Odd, how her musical tastes had evolved while

Dawn's had remained essentially inert. Anne enjoyed the intricacies of modern opera, while Dawn would be a Def Leppard disciple until the day they pried her cold dead fingers from her worn cassette of *Pyromania*. Granted, Anne still got nostalgic whenever she heard one of the tunes from their past—to this day she carried a secret torch for Richard Marx—but while she wasn't looking, she'd grown up, and now here she was preparing a bath instead of cruising the streets looking for boys Trevor's age with whom to flirt and share a stolen beer.

She came to the candles on the mantel and stopped as if she'd been shot.

The picture stood there in its simple sablewood frame, just as it always had. But looking at it tonight, really seeing it, froze her where she stood.

The lighter slipped from her fingers, hit the floor. She put her hand over her mouth.

The picture was six inches long and four inches tall. The background consisted mostly of bleachers and a concession stand and the big steel bell the cheerleaders rang when the Sidewinders scored a touchdown. Except this wasn't football. This was track and field. Specifically, it was the annual Fresh Waters Elementary School Track Meet, to which every town in the county bused its fifth- and sixth-graders to compete in scaled-down versions of classic athletic events.

"Fifty-yard dash," Anne said to herself, unable to look away.

That had been her forte: sprinting. Dawn's long legs had served her well in the hurdles, and Sally's endurance made her a natural in cross-country, but Anne had been the sprinter. She loved the feel of the starting blocks under the balls of her feet. But the starting blocks hadn't come along

306

until junior high. Before that, she'd been only one more girl with her foot behind the chalk stripe, staring at the finish line so far away it seemed to be a mile. She remembered the feeling of that one afternoon, the way the wind had seemed to push from behind her, the way the ribbon stretched across her chest when she touched it, half a step in front of the nearest chaser.

She reached out and touched the picture.

Four girls were depicted there. They wore sloppy smiles and had their arms slung across one another's shoulders. They were garbed in matching tank tops bearing the Sidewinder mascot. Anne recalled that the tops were generally too big, exposing the occasional embarrassing white of training bras. The girls in the photo were all a little on the skinny side, and grinning. Their smiles—that's what touched Anne's heart. Their smiles were pure. Not smiles for the sake of the camera, but smiles for the sake of life.

Dawn was on the left, the tallest of the four. She'd bent her head to the side so that it was resting on Anne's. Anne wore her hair in pigtails. Her smile was so big that it made her eyes squint up even more than usual. Next to her was Sally with freckles on her nose, her mouth open in mid-laugh. And finally, there on the end, a girl with the brightest yellow hair. . . .

"Tatyana."

Tatyana was the kind of blonde to make a choir boy trade his rosary for a box of chocolates to give to her. The dimple on her chin could lay them low, whoever *them* might be at the time, and though Anne had seen that face in that snapshot more often than she could count, it seemed brighter this evening, more real, as if this impossibly beautiful girl were about to speak.

Anne listened.

The only sounds she heard were the gentle music from the stereo and the running of the bathtub water.

The front door swung open.

Anne gasped and turned, expecting that child and that blond hair—

Jazmyn said, "Mother! Guess what?"

Anne closed her eyes.

"Mother? Hey, what's wrong?"

"Nothing." Anne braced herself and forced her eyelids up.

It was Jazmyn, and not some benign doppelgänger from the past.

"Guess what?" Jaz held something behind her back. Crespin stood beside her, the grin on his face an indication that he was privy to the secret.

"I have no idea," Anne admitted, still sensing an odd vibe emanating from the picture in the sablewood frame. "I hope it's not an invitation from the White House for Radio to perform in front of visiting diplomats, because quite frankly I can only take fame in small doses."

"Mom's decided on the song we're doing for Nancy Holiday."

"She has, eh? Then please end the suspense so I can start practicing."

Jazmyn whipped the sheet music in front of her face. "So what do you think?"

Anne looked at the title, then at her daughter, who was peering around the upraised pages with revelry in her eyes. Anne nodded. "I suppose it's only fitting."

"Mom thought so, too."

Crespin gave Anne a thumbs-up and shouted, "Viva la rock and roll!"

Chapter Twenty-four

Dawn saw Tuesday like this:

Alex's alarm . . . what time was it? Crack of dawn. Or "My crack," as Dawn liked to say. "My hubby's alarm goes off at my crack." Then breakfast. Out of sausage. No toast. So pancakes for everyone. Including, apparently, Crespin. "Are we gonna need to build a guest room?" Jaz just grinned. Probably spent the night making out. Couldn't blame her. Crespin was the last of the sweet guys, and a cutie. Of course they didn't call it making out these days. Kids called it *muggin' down*. So Jaz was muggin' down with a boy who, by tonight, would be on his way to a new life, with a new ID. Sure to break the poor girl's heart. But no time to worry about that now. Got Alex on his way to work. Welcomed the babysitter. Kissed the boys. Off to the Cheshire Grin. Waited tables for the lunch rush but begged off again for the afternoon. Boss rolled his eyes but said, "Hell yeah, you can leave. You're the best thing this town's got going for it these days." Met the girls at the high school band room, as Jaz had gotten permission to rehearse there. "Hey, Sal. Who's minding Sole Mates?" Apparently it was Dominique, who'd finally gotten a date with the gorgeous Swede from the lumberyard. Good for her. Luck seemed to be in the air. Then came agony. "If anyone cares, the percussion part for this number is, to put it in PG-13 terms, a bitch." But evidently she was being ignored. Dakota helped as much as he could. Sally seemed spaced out. But darling Jazmyn had the worst of it. The guitar solo was a bitch times two. Anne called it Byzantine. Nobody bothered to ask what that meant. Three hours later the session ended. Time to get the Mexicans on the move, under the cover of dusk. Sally said, "Thanks, everyone, for the hard work."

Dawn scoffed. "That ain't working. That's the way you do it. You play the guitar on the MTV."

Dakota brought out the false driver's licenses, and they drove to Sally's to pass them out.

"I love the smell of diesel fumes in the evening," Dawn said.

Sally heard this quip and forced a smile to her lips, just in case Dawn was watching. They stood at the Fresh Waters bus station—it shared a building with Yardarm's Travel Agency—the sky darkening, the town settling in for another sleepy pre-summer night. The bus idled noisily at the curb. The placard above the front window read *LOS ANGELES*. It would seek L.A. via Needles, California, where half of the Mexicans would be met by eager relatives.

"Anne." Sally gestured toward the gaping bus door. "Tell them they've got to get on."

Dawn sang out, "All aboard the Orient Express! Last one on the bus is a three-legged dog! Hey, Annie, how do you say 'three-legged dog' in Spanish?"

Anne ignored her and gave a few final instructions to Javier and the others. Of the remaining immigrants, Eleazar and Beatriz had arranged to meet friends up in Denver. Their northbound bus departed in an hour. Crespin was staying one last night, ostensibly to assist with the equipment during tomorrow's TV performance, but more likely because Jazmyn was a tricky girl and was no doubt trying to conceive of some plan that would let him stay.

Sally wished he could. He was a dear boy. And Jaz had a crush on him only slighter smaller than the crush he had on her. But he couldn't remain in town without putting them all in jeopardy. Sally had already given her daughter the lecture. Maybe when Crespin got settled somewhere. Maybe after his identity'd been accepted. Maybe, maybe—too many maybes for a girl of sixteen.

Javier said, "Thank you." He'd stopped in front of her, Ana at his side. He put down his new nylon duffel bag, shifted his ersatz ID from his right hand to his left, and offered her a handshake. "Thank you."

Sally hated herself for wanting to cry. No time for softies now. She shook his hand, and then Ana was throwing herself around Sally in a hug, and Sally squeezed her back.

Damn tears were unavoidable.

It got no easier after that. Sally had come to know these peaceful souls in the last few days. So what if she could hardly speak a lick of their language? Words weren't always necessary. They were simply human beings sharing a kitchen and good food.

The bus pulled away.

Everyone watched it go. Eleazar held Beatriz. Jazmyn had her arm through Crespin's, her head on his shoulder. Anne stood with her hand over her mouth. Sally gripped the card they'd given her, their signatures and best wishes filling up nearly every white space. One of them had drawn a skillful picture of the American flag.

They waited for the Denver bus, cried all over again, and when Eleazar and Beatriz were on their way, the five of them walked down the sidewalk together, staying close for

311

mutual support. Anne would drive them home. Tomorrow they had to be on the road by five a.m., as they were going live shortly after nine. Sleep, then, was the most pressing order of business.

Sally had no intention of sleeping.

"That's okay," she told them when they reached the car. "I'll walk."

"Sal, you live halfway across town," Dawn reminded her.

"I'll manage."

"Manage to get a blister is what you'll do."

"I'm a big girl. I'll see you in the morning."

"G'night, Mom!" Jaz called.

"Sweet dreams, honey."

"I'm not popping your blister!" Dawn called out as they drove away.

And then Sally was on the move. Alone in the night. The desert air warm on her skin.

She knew that if she put herself to bed, she'd only end up staring at the ceiling. Leigh had phoned twice today from his office. He couldn't make the drive over from Tucson, as his work was starting to pile up, but he promised to make up for it by taking her out tomorrow night, unless her stardom prohibited her from being seen with ordinary Joes. She had readily accepted his offer of dinner, stardom be damned. But it wasn't the thought of Leigh that disturbed her. Her restlessness was due to one part worry and one part anticipation. She was afraid that the forged documents would be discovered and traced back to her. But she was simultaneously fearless, the expectation of tomorrow's performance granting her the intoxication for which she had come to yearn. Already the presentiment of it lightened her step.

So this was no night for sleep, but for an adventure. Like exhuming buried treasure.

She reached the base of the wooden stairs that led to the small apartment above the garage. Nearby, Dakota's motor-cycle was covered by a tarpaulin, awaiting the mending of his bones. His parents owned the garage and the big house to which it was connected. Sally hoped they wouldn't choose this moment to glance outside, lest they see her pad-ding softly up to their son's door and wonder just what the hell she was doing.

Sally wondered the same thing herself.

Dakota opened the door. He was shirtless, wearing only blue jeans, no shoes.

"Surprise," Sally said.

"Hey."

"Is this a bad time?"

"Uh . . . no, not at all. I was just watching TV."

"Anything good?"

"Is it ever?"

Sally made it a point to keep her eyes on his face and not roam his half-clad body—God, what a mood she was in! "I thought maybe we could go follow that map I was telling you about."

"Oh, right. Sure thing."

"If you'd rather do it another time . . ."

"You joking me? You offer to let me in on something like this, there's no way I'm turning you down. When I was a kid I used to dig holes in the backyard and pretend I was looking for dinosaur bones. Hold on and I'll get dressed. Come in if you want."

Sally stepped inside, looked around, while Dakota talked from what must have been the bathroom. He rattled on about tomorrow's gig. He said the whole town of Fresh Waters had heard the news and would be tuning in. Nancy Holiday would probably have her best ratings ever.

"Yep," Sally agreed, "it'll be just as big as Elvis on Ed Sullivan."

"Who's Ed Sullivan?"

"Forget it."

Dakota emerged wearing a black T-shirt that was a size too small, the left sleeve slit wide to accommodate his cast, and a pair of cowboy boots he'd probably inherited from his father.

Size ten, though they look a little roomy on him.

"Okay," he said, "let's do this quest. That's a good word, don't you think? Quest."

"It's a good word," she agreed. "Let's do it."

It wasn't until they were downstairs that Sally remembered she had no car.

Dakota scratched his youthful face, where there were only whispers of a five-o'clock shadow; he was young and his stubble took its time. "So, uh, how far is the place marked on your map?"

"I'm not sure. I'd guess at least halfway between here and Maxon."

"So walking is out of the question."

"Way out of the question. We'll hoof it to my house, but you'll have to drive. I don't see eye to eye with cars these days."

"How about with bikes? Do you see eye to eye with them?"

"I'm sorry?"

A grin hooked the corner of Dakota's mouth. "You could drive the motorcycle. It's not a car. You should be fine."

"Why do I get the feeling you're serious?"

"Because I am."

"I've never driven a motorcycle in my life."

"I'll teach you."

"I'm a terrible student. Ask anyone who went to school with me."

Dakota laughed. "No, really, it'll be cool. We don't want to walk all the way to your house, and I don't think asking my folks to borrow their car is such a great idea. So our only option is for you to get on the bike, because I sure can't work the brake, much less steer the thing."

"And where will you be?"

"I'll ride behind you. We'll go slow. I'll teach you along the way."

"That's crazy."

He laughed again. "And Radio isn't?"

Sally had to concede the point. "You know that a week ago I never would have considered doing this."

"A lot can happen in a week."

"No one knows that with more certainty than me."

"So is that a yes?"

Sally didn't have to consider it. In that moment, she wanted nothing else. "I don't have to wear a helmet, do I?"

"It's a lot safer if you do."

"Safe, dear boy, is not always something I want to be."

Together they pulled the tarp from the bike.

The bike's single headlight bored a tunnel in the night.

They had stopped at Sally's for a flashlight and the map. Now Sally sat astride the rumbling motorcycle and cruised the black highway miles from town. Though she rarely topped fifty miles an hour, the wind played with her hair and the big machine vibrated in her thighs and up the staircase of her spine. She held her arms out straight, gripping the handlebars, her right wrist flexing and giving the bike a little more gas. Her left foot worked the odd clutch arrangement, pushing up or down as she was instructed. She felt him behind her. She sat in the V of his legs. His hands touched lightly at her waist.

In a past life, Sally thought, *I was a biker chick.*

They'd started off slowly. Dakota had twice barely kept them from falling over. Shifting gears wasn't easy. But Sally stubbornly refused to lose the battle. And now, miles later, the payoff: flight. Orville and Wilbur had struggled for this same result, this same unequaled feeling.

Though for awhile Dakota had spoken directions in her ear and Sally had shouted back at him, the last few miles had been filled with only the sound of the engine and the soothing rush of the wind. Sally dared to crank out a bit more speed. Dakota edged a little closer. Or did he? Sally felt his right hand resting on her waist and his cast touching her on the other side. If she leaned back any at all, she'd feel his chest against her.

So don't lean back.

Blame it on the sweet liquor of the wind, but Sally ignored the voice and pushed back just enough to make contact. Half a minute passed, and then Dakota responded by coming forward so that his chin rested against her head, his lips an inch from her ear.

Sally wondered what Dawn would say if she could see them now. Plenty, for sure.

They'd studied Jeffrey's map before departing. Dakota thought he recognized two of the prominent features drawn there. One of them, he believed, was Hangman Mesa, a small hill so named because it was capped by a rock formation that vaguely resembled a gallows. And one of Jeffrey's elegant blue lines likely represented a dried-up creek that had once trickled its waters through the desert's alluvial soil.

Finding it at night was the trick.

They drove down a two-lane blacktop, passing only a few cars, content with each other's company and the sound of the pavement beneath the tires. The stars were infinite. Only the desert had stars like this. When Dakota nudged her, Sally found that she was staring at the vast expanse overhead instead of at the road.

She guided the bike back into the right-hand lane.

"Do you know what this is?" she hollered over the engine and the wind.

"No, what?"

"*Hózh'q!*" She gunned the engine up to sixty-five.

Five minutes later, Dakota tapped her on the arm and pointed. Sally saw the roadside reflectors that marked a point where the highway was intersected by a dirt track. She slowed down, working her way through the gears, and eased into the turn. The bike's tires crunched the fine silicates that comprised this narrow path. "Last time I was out this way," Dakota said in her ear, "I was on a field trip with my earth-science class. Back in my junior year. So it's been at least three years."

"What's out here?" Sally kept her speed at under ten miles an hour so that she could be heard over the din, but more importantly so that she wouldn't drive into something unexpected. Now that they'd left the beaten path, anything could happen.

"Basically it's a whole lot of nothing in these parts. I think the Boy Scouts come out here to camp sometimes and practice their orienteering skills."

"How far away is Maxon?"

"Only about three miles. If it was a normal town you'd be able to see it from here, but since they don't use street lights, the place is hidden at night."

"Just the way the astronomers like it. Where's this Hangman Mesa?"

"If I remember right, it's a few hundred yards down this road."

"And the dry creek bed is on the other side?"

"I guess so. Why did he give you this map, anyway?"

"I've been wondering that myself."

"Do you want the bad news?"

"I wasn't aware that there was any bad news."

"We forgot the shovel."

Sally smiled to herself. She'd been expecting something worse. Something bad. "Yeah, I guess we did. Kind of hard to bring a shovel along on a motorcycle."

Soon she reduced the bike's speed and rolled slowly to a stop. Dakota extended his legs to support them, as Sally's weren't quite tall enough to keep the bike from tipping.

"I think this is it," he said.

Sally killed the engine.

For seconds there was nothing but the distant churn of insects and the occasionally tick of the engine.

"What now?" Dakota asked.

"We find the spot. Mark it. Come back tomorrow after we're finished with Nancy Holiday, and this time we're not forgetting our tools. Is that shape I'm seeing right there Hangman Mesa?" The starlight was bright enough to reveal the dim outline of a hill rising from the desert floor.

"I guess there's only one way to find out."

Sally dismounted. Dakota engaged the kickstand. From the leather saddlebag connected to the seat, Sally extracted the flashlight and the cardboard lid that was the map. "So what do you say? Up for another field trip? It'll be just like science class."

"I don't think I believe that."

"Neither do I."

They headed for the mesa and its gallows crown.

"There's something I've been meaning to ask," Dakota said.

They had made their way around the far side of the embankment and now stood in the cracked clay of what once had been a natural watershed. By panning the flashlight back and forth along the ground, they were able to pick up the impression of the scar which the departing water had left behind. If they were reading the map correctly, the creek bed would eventually abut another rock face, this one a quarter-mile away. Halfway between those two points, Jeffrey had written *HIDDEN SCHATZ*.

"Shouldn't be much farther now," Sally guessed. She kept them moving.

"Scorpions come out at night, you know."

"That's why I brought you along, scorpion-slayer."

"I can't even see them, so I sure can't slay 'em. Anyway, I have a question."

"Uh-oh, sounds like trouble to me."

"What happened that day?"

"I'm afraid you're going to have to be a little more specific."

"That day when you were kids. You and Dawn and Anne. The day at the mine."

"Oh. That day."

"People still talk about it, every now and then."

"So you already know the story."

"But not a first-hand version."

"It was over twenty years ago, Dak. I was twelve. Memory no longer serves."

Evidently he was going to let her get away with this lie, at least for now. They kept walking. Sally smelled the dust they kicked up, each step breaking little bits of clay and clumped sand. Every now and then her light revealed a cluster of cacti or some other brand of stalwart flora, but for the most part their jaunt was rather like trekking across the barren face of an asteroid.

"Here, look at the map." Sally stood close to him and they both studied the drawing. "Jeffrey's drawn a tree here, a tree without leaves. Do you think he's talking about that tree right there?" She fired the light at an emaciated Joshua tree twenty feet away.

"Could be. Move the light to the left a little. If there's a big rock—"

"There it is." Sally hustled over, stopped at the rock, turned toward the tree. She was getting caught up in Jeffrey's game, the excitement of finding these landmarks making her a little giddy. "On the map there are six dashed lines. I'm betting that means six feet."

"Or six paces."

"Right. We'll try paces." She took six strides, then looked down. In the meek puddle of light, that small circle of ground looked no different than any other. Yet still, Sally felt the tingle of childlike anticipation. "I think this could be it. I could be standing right on top of it." She dug experimentally with her heel, raking up a tiny furrow of dirt.

"Too bad we forgot the shovel," Dakota said. "I hate just marking the spot then leaving it for tomorrow."

"What? You don't like the idea of digging with your hands?"

"I'm not afraid of getting dirty, if that's what you mean. But Jeff might have buried this thing deep, whatever it is, which means we're going to need some tools."

"Are you telling me you're not simply enjoying my company?"

"Yep, you got it. I'm bored to tears. Truth is, I'm worse than bored. In fact, I'm having a really shitty time hanging out with you." His face changed suddenly, and he looked at her uncertainly. "Sorry."

"For what?"

"It just slipped out."

"What? 'Shitty' just slipped out? Do I strike you as a woman who is so easily offended? Nothing offends me these days. Shitty happens."

In the backsplash of light, she saw him shift his feet and nod. "Yeah, I guess it does."

"I'm not the same woman I was that day Jeffrey gave me the shoebox."

"I noticed."

"I'm no longer concerned about petty things. I don't get out of bed thinking about what I'm going to do at work that day. Do you know how liberating that is? I haven't read the newspaper. I haven't watched a single sitcom. Jesus, it's like I finally woke up and stopped sleeping through my life."

Dakota didn't seem to know what to say.

"All those things were tying me down. They were bolting me to the ground. Do you understand? I am no longer bolted." She walked over and stopped only a foot away. She pointed the light up at her own face, forcing him to look at her. "What do you see here? Hmmm? Look close. Tell me what you see."

"Well . . ."

"Come on now." She inched even closer. "It's not that hard. Stop jittering around and look at me."

He held still and stared at her.

"So?" she prompted.

"You're beautiful."

Sally raised an eyebrow. "Not what I was expecting, but a good answer." She found his hand and interlaced her fingers with his. Her pulse started to pick up the pace, but she ignored it and said, "When the bolts let loose, so does everything else. I know that doesn't make any sense to you, but it's a lot like the feeling of being on that motorcycle. Except imagine being on it every minute of your life. What could be cooler than that?"

Dakota, hypnotized, said nothing.

"I have no age," Sally said. "No age, no job, no label, and damn sure no country. All that I am is a—"

"A woman."

Sally smiled faintly. "That's right. You're catching on." She could feel his heartbeat in his hand—or was that hers? It didn't matter. For days she'd been heaping coals into the furnace of her body, and now the fire licked toward the surface, wanting air. She hadn't sought Dakota out tonight with any motive other than recruiting a digging partner. Or had she? By now everything was too blurred together to separate truth from the little fictions she told herself. Not that it mattered, not with his hand in hers, not with the scent of him so close.

"Sally, I . . . I'm not sure what we're doing here."

"Seems pretty matter-of-fact to me." She pushed herself toward him so that their bodies touched. She lowered the flashlight. Now they were only two more forms in the dark. Maybe if she took a step back and considered what she was wanting so badly, she'd realize that she was seventeen years older than this man-boy, that outdoors was no place for this kind of activity, and that the poor kid was probably scared stiff.

Well, *something* had made him that way.

Sally giggled on the inside. On the outside, she touched her lips with her tongue. "Dak?"

Faintly: "Yeah?"

"Girls just wanna have fun." She stood on her toes and kissed him.

For a moment he didn't respond. . . .

The moment passed.

He put his good arm around her neck and crushed his mouth against hers. Sally dropped the flashlight and with both hands grabbed the front of his jeans, sliding her fingers into the warmth behind his button-fly. Without thinking she let her tongue explore his mouth, tasting him, loving the hardness of his jaw against her face.

She tugged a button free and sank her hand between his legs.

Dakota made a sound and bunched her hair in his fist.

Sally kept kissing him, not wanting to break contact, afraid that by decoupling she'd somehow break the spell. But then again, she no longer feared anything.

She pulled back.

Dakota stood there, startled, breathing in and out.

Sally bundled her shirt in her hands and pulled it over her head. She let it fall to the ground, feeling the night against her skin. Her eyes had adjusted just enough so that she could see his face. He watched her. And as he watched, Sally reached behind her, and then her bra joined her shirt.

Dakota bit his bottom lip between his teeth.

Dimly, far back in her mind, behind the heat of these flames that were about to consume her with their need, she recalled a woman who would have been mortified by the thought of standing in front of this young man with her boobs on full display. Though she wasn't disproportioned in any way, she'd never had a body like Anne's. And she was thirty-six, so things didn't hang quite like they used to. But this inhibition was the last of its kind, and then it too was burned away by the fire. "Are you waiting for a written invitation?" she asked.

Dakota came to her and swept her to the ground.

On her back, Sally battled his shirt, finally got it free of the cast, all the while kissing him and closing her eyes when his tongue traveled the curve of her neck. It had been too long. Dakota pawed at her pants, but he was forced to support himself on one arm and his other wasn't doing much good. Sally assisted him, stripping and kissing him at the same time—

What underwear am I wearing?

She glanced down and was relieved to see that they were frilly and black. God forbid she'd be caught in anything that might be considered . . . well, old.

Then she wiggled out of her panties and stopped thinking altogether. Dakota's mouth had found her breasts. Sally lay on the ground, the earth still warm from the day's heat, her eyes filled up with the stars. The forgotten flashlight threw a lopsided beam across them.

Dakota moved farther down her body. Down, down . . .

Sally stiffened, bit back a sound.

The stars began to blur, and Sally's eyes closed of their own accord. She gave herself up to the little discharges that began to ignite within her, feeling it build, straining the muscles in her back as if she could pull that implosion toward her, hurrying its arrival.

Dakota stopped too soon.

Sally groaned and pulled him into a roll, ending up on top of him where his stupid broken arm wouldn't have to do any work, and he seemed stunned by the move but Sally gave him no time to react. She was straddling him like she'd done with his bike. Her knees were pressed into the soil. Sweat dappled her neck. She positioned herself, poised above him.

When she lowered herself, slowly, they cried out as one.

Chapter Twenty-five

They lay entangled on the desert floor, feeling each other breathe.

Sally rested on his chest, loving the way it felt when the air cooled the sweat on her back.

Dakota smoothed the damp hair from her face. "Tell me what happened."

"Just now? I thought it was obvious."

He smiled. "I mean back then. You and the others. I want to know what you saw, and what you did."

Sally was quiet for a time. She just wanted to remain in this drowsy state, smelling their mingled scents. But the images had already been summoned. The story was there for the telling. If relating the events of that day would permit her to linger in this embrace awhile longer, then she would gladly go on for hours. "It all started at the track meet. It rained later that day. But at first there was only sun. Lots of it. And four goofy girls. . . ."

"Say cheese!"

"Limburger!" the girls chant as one.

The snapshot freezes them in time. For less than a second, the four of them, all smiles and baggy shorts, do not age or change in any way. But then the flash fades, the earth resumes its rotation, and Dawn's father lowers the camera. "You gals were spectacular today," he exclaims. "Absolutely speck-tack-u-loor! I never in my life saw anyone move as fast as you four. Now wait right here and I'll go bring the car around." He jogs off toward the parking lot. "Speck-speck-speck-tack-u-loor!"

"Dawn," Anne says, shaking her head. "Your dad is really bizarre."

"Yeah, he's got a fifth-degree black belt in weird-fu. You guys just wanna walk home instead? I can tell him that we'll walk, if you don't feel like riding. Sal?"

Sally looks up from the red ribbon she's been examining. Printed on the ribbon in gold lettering is *2nd PLACE FRESH WATERS ELEMENTARY TRACK MEET*. Her abundant curls hang in her face, forcing her to brush them away. For a moment she wonders why the others are always asking her what she wants. Why does it always have to be her decision? "Walking's cool with me."

"Great." Dawn reaches down to scratch at a scab on her knee, even though her father keeps telling her not to pick at it. When she straightens and falls into step beside her friends, Sally is reminded again of how tall she is—taller even than most of the boys in their class. Dawn says, "Hey, do you think our folks'll let us have a sleep-over? We could camp out in my backyard. as long as we have plenty of flashlights, you know, because . . . well, just because."

"Sounds good," Anne decides. Then she stops, causing Sally to bump into her. She looks back the way they've come. Sally follows her gaze.

"Hey, slowpoke," Anne says. "You coming or what?"

Tatyana smiles.

She has removed her shoes, as well as her socks, and now comes running at them barefoot, shoes tied together by their strings. Her blond hair is everywhere, having been freed from its braid upon the conclusion of the meet. She has the cutest dimple of anyone that Sally has ever seen. On Sally's tenth birthday, she'd blown out all the candles and wished to wake up the next morning with a dimple like that.

"You gonna walk all the way home with no shoes?" Dawn asks.

Tatyana looks down at her bare feet, then shrugs. "Sometimes toes just have to be free."

This answer seems to satisfy everyone. It's just one of those things that Tatyana says that make sense, even if no one is really sure what it means.

They meet Dawn's dad on the edge of the parking lot, and he gives them the okay to walk home as long as they promise not to go by Edna Tuttle's house and torment her dog. Last week the sheriff stopped by and had a talk with them about taunting the old poodle through the fence.

All four of them cross their hearts: they'll go straight to Dawn's and nowhere else.

A block later they're talking about boys.

Dawn hates them. Tatyana adores them. Anne tolerates them. Sally . . . Sally doesn't know what to think of them, or why she should even want to think about them at all. Yet she *does* think about them. At least every now and then. Of course the boys in sixth grade don't count. Those boys are dumb. The cute ones and smart ones are all in junior high. Yesterday Travis Burton offered to give Tatyana a ride home on his new bicycle. And he's an eighth-grader.

"So why didn't you say yes?" Dawn wonders. "Seems like you'd want to get a ride, if you're so absolutely, positively in love with him."

"I'm not absolutely anything," Tatyana says.

"Then why do you talk to him all the time?"

" 'Cause I like to see him blush."

Dawn snorts. "That's why my mom says you're a tease."

"A what?"

"Sal, don't you think a girl's a tease if she just talks to boys to make them blush?"

But Sally doesn't want any part of it. "I think you two both just need to shut up."

"Shut don't go up," Dawn says, "but prices do, so take my advice and shut up too."

Anne makes a dismissive gesture. "Please, Dawn-Marie, that might've been funny the first thousand times you said it, but it's not anymore. You're like a broken record."

"Record!" Tatyana declares. She prances ahead of them and turns a ballerina circle on her toes. "Have any of you heard the new Rick Springfield record? My cousin bought it last weekend. Rick is soooooo cute."

"Hey, check it out." Anne points toward the sky. "Looks like rain."

They all look up. "Are you sure?" Dawn asks. "How can you tell?"

"Because those are stratocumulus clouds," Anne explains. "They're moving in fast. Probably rain in an hour or so."

If Anne predicts it, then the others take it as gospel.

"You ever seen Scorp City after a good rain?" Dawn asks no one in particular. "The water ends up like a big dirty pool down in the pit, and tadpoles swim all over the place."

Tatyana wrinkles her nose. "Tadpoles are baby frogs, right?"

"Yep. You can catch 'em and put 'em in a jar."

"Then what?"

Dawn shrugs. "I dunno. Take 'em home and grow yourself some pet frogs, I guess."

"For real?"

"For real."

"I want some." She looks at Sally. "You think it'd be to-tally breaking our promise to Dawny's dad if we went out there before we go home?"

"Out where?" Sally is already suspicious. Her own father has repeatedly warned her about the dangers of playing near certain places around town, such as the old flour mill, Coulter's junkyard, and the dead silver mine that everyone calls Scorpion City. He doesn't have much to worry about, because the flour mill is boring, the junkyard is home to two of the meanest dogs in the county, and the mine is where all the older kids go to kiss and do whatever else they do, things that Sally only partially understands. "I'm hungry. Let's just go to Dawn's and see what's in the fridge."

"But, Sally." Tatyana hangs her tied-together shoes around her neck and latches on to Sally's hands. "I can grow my own frogs in a jar."

"Why would you want to do that?"

"Because I've never done it before."

"You've never lit your hair on fire either."

Tatyana laughs. It is the best sound in the world.

Sally pulls and pushes against Tatyana's hands so that their palms make little clapping sounds. "You know we shouldn't."

"Shouldn't never did anything," Tatyana retorts. "At least not anything fun."

Sally keeps rocking back and forth in their miniature tug-of-war. "We can't stay long."

"Deal."

"We leave as soon as you have a tadpole."

"Deal."

"Even if it's only *one* tadpole."

"Deal, deal, deal. Now let's go. We don't want to be late getting home and make anyone worry."

They set off toward the edge of town and the mine with its dented *DANGER* sign.

The clouds gather, darken, and choke out the sun.

The first thing they see is the chain.

The links are thick and discolored by rust, stretching across a gap in the metal fence. Along the fence, weeds have grown in thick patches. They look like weeds that something might be hiding in, so the girls investigate along their way to the gap in the fence. But they find no mama rabbits with babies, and thankfully no snakes.

"There's no sign," Dawn observes, stopping before the chain.

Anne stands on her right. "What do you mean?"

Sally stands on her left. "She means one that says 'keep out.' "

Behind them, Tatyana has dropped to the ground and is pulling on her shoes. "I think there used to be a sign, but somebody stole it."

"Well, if there's no sign," Dawn reasons, "then they can't get mad at us for being here." She lifts one leg over the chain, then the other.

Sally and the rest choose to duck under instead.

Beyond the chain is a dirt lot crisscrossed with countless tire tracks. Here indeed is a sign, reading *DANGER*, knocked down and lying in the dirt. Cigarette butts seem everywhere, and broken beer bottles and smashed cans. Further on stand half a dozen buildings without windows.

"What are those places?" Dawn asks.

"Mine offices," Anne explains. "At least they used to be.

And probably tool sheds and rooms where they kept all their mining stuff."

Tatyana is wearing her socks on her hands like strange mittens. "Do you know what they do inside those buildings now?"

"Who?" Dawn picks up a rock and hurls it at one of the structures. "You mean the miners?"

"No, silly, there are no more miners. I mean the older kids. Like Jodi Ramsey and her boyfriend from the football team. Do you know what they do in there?"

"No, what?"

"They do things naked."

"What things?"

"Things, Dawny, dirty things."

"That's gross."

"Jodi doesn't think so."

Sally freezes. "Stop."

Without question the other three don't move.

Sally points. "Do you see that?"

The girls turn and look as one.

The dirt lot gives way to rough pavement, on which the buildings have been erected. Most of the space between those buildings is choked with trash and overgrown crucifixion thorns that have grown up through fissures in the stone. But in one of the clearings, out of sight of the main road, is a car. Sally can barely see its back end.

Dawn whispers: "Nobody's supposed to drive around out here."

Anne follows suit, lowering her voice: "That's why they put up the chain."

Tatyana: "Maybe the car was here before the chain. It looks pretty old."

Sally says nothing, but lets her eyes travel the car.

Though she can see little more than the trunk, she gets a good enough look at the back tires to tell that they're not flat. Any car sitting out here for long would've been bashed up by the teenagers. The tires would not have air.

A drop of rain strikes her cheek.

She walks toward the car.

"Sal, what are you doing?" Dawn leaps at her and snags her by the arm. "Maybe rattlesnakes have made a nest in that thing. Even worse, maybe Jodi Ramsey and her boy-friend have been in there naked."

"I want to check it out."

"What for?"

Sally considers telling her about the tires, but then de-cides against it. She can't explain what makes her want to investigate. It just feels like something that needs to be done. "It'll just take a minute. Nothing can happen in a minute."

Rain falls.

It comes down a little heavier than a sprinkle, enough to make the girls look up and feel it splatter their faces.

Sally puts her hands on her hips. "Are you guys with me or not?"

There is no need for her to ask.

They approach the car side by side. Not speaking. Keeping their steps light. Brushing the hair from their faces when the water begins to drip from their bangs. As they near, more features of the car become apparent. Its tail-lights are like narrowed eyes, with a frowning brow of a trunk. Though it has only two doors, it is a huge whale of a car. Part of the tires are painted white. And on the bumper is a long sticker that Anne carefully reads aloud. " 'Don't tell my folks I'm a truck driver. They think I'm a piano player in a whorehouse.' "

Anne exchanges glances with Sally, then looks back at the car.

"What's that mean?" Dawn wants to know.

Nobody answers.

Sally begins to make her way around the car. She wants to get a look inside—

No. The windows have been darkened. They're almost black. And with no sun to assist her, the only way that Sally is going to see into the car is either by putting her face against the glass or opening a door.

She comes to the passenger's door. Rain patters against the car's roof.

"You guys wanna hear a funny joke?" Dawn asks.

Anne glowers at her.

"Sorry."

Sally opens the door gently, just a few inches. The smell is bad. Like cigarettes and sweat and something distinctly adultlike that Sally can't name. The upholstery is faded. A plastic likeness of Jesus hangs from the rearview mirror.

Sally sees the backseat and gasps.

Tatyana shoves her aside and looks. "DATFUG."

Dawn and Anne jostle closer to see. For seconds they can only stare.

"Holy shit," Dawn says. "Holy shit."

A woman lies tied and gagged, staring at them with desperate eyes.

Dawn sinks her fingers into Sally's arm. "Who is she?"

The woman makes a small noise. Something has been shoved into her mouth. She is about the age of Sally's mother, but not as pretty. Her wrists and ankles are bound with gray tape. She wears a skirt and matching top. Her body shakes.

"Sally?" Tatyana looks from the woman to her friend,

then back again. "Sal, what do we do? Please, please, what do we do?"

Sally doesn't know and she wishes with all her heart that no one would ask. She doesn't know who this woman is or who tied her up. And was that person coming back? If Sally and the others stayed here too long, would they also end up like this?

"She's been kidnapped," Dawn realized. "Sally, somebody kidnapped her."

Finally Sally tells herself that she has no choice. They've got to get out of here fast, before whoever did this returns. Because that person—whoever they are—must be bad. A bad man, a killer or freak or maybe something worse.

The woman makes another noise, louder this time, and jerks against her bonds.

"Okay," Sally says. And then it all comes out in a rush: "Anne, we gotta get the cops, so go, just run, run back, stop at the first house you see." She grabs Anne's hand. "Do it, okay? Run your ass off, got it?"

Anne nods. Her face is drained of color.

"Get going then." Sally kisses her quickly on the forehead, Anne takes a few uncertain steps backward, and then turns and runs, natural sprinter that she is.

Sally looks back at the woman. "Dawn, keep watch. Tatyana and I are gonna get her loose."

"Keep watch? Keep watch for what?"

"Anything." Sally slips into the backseat, and without question Tatyana follows.

"Anything like what?" Dawn's voice is strained. "You mean the bogeyman who did this to her? Is that your anything? Why do I get all the scary-ass jobs?" Dawn runs a few steps to the end of the building, looks around the corner, then she races to the other side and does the same. "I see two things, Sally, and their names are jack and shit. Can I stop watching now?"

The rain falls harder.

Inside the car, Sally hovers over the woman's body, wishing she knew what to do. The blood is the worst. There's so much of it. The woman has a deep gouge in her arm; blood paints her shoulder and seeps into the crack of the seat. *Come on, Annie, run.* Though she is afraid of getting any closer, Sally forces herself to move. "She's really bleeding. Give me your socks."

Tatyana has been wearing her long white tube socks over her hands, for no reason other than she is Tatyana and given to such behavior. She slides them off.

Sally ties them together. Then, squeamishly, she begins to wrap them around the woman's injured arm. She squints as she works, as if by not seeing as much of the situation she can make it less real. "Can you get the tape off her feet?"

"I don't know, it's tight."

"Use your teeth."

Tatyana obeys. She sinks down, wiggles herself into position, and screws her face into the small spot at the woman's ankles.

With the wound wrapped up, Sally pinches a corner of the fabric that's been stuffed into the woman's mouth. The woman is crying now, and making noises that Sally doesn't want to hear. From between the woman's teeth, Sally extracts a wad of moist fabric.

It's her underwear. She had her panties stuffed in her mouth.

Sally almost retches. Her stomach clenches and she braces herself on the seat to try not to upchuck.

Tatyana tears through the tape and begins yanking it free.

"Hurry," the woman implores, spittle flecking her lips. "Hurry, please, he's coming back."

Sally doesn't know who *he* is, but the thought of him returning scares her more than she can remember ever being scared.

"What do I do now?" Tatyana asks.

"Her hands." Both girls attack the tape restraints, and the second the woman's hands are loose, Sally grabs them and tugs. "Come on, lady, you're free."

The three of them scramble from the car.

Dawn screams.

Sally looks through the rain to see Dawn running away from the edge of the great crater that is the mine's central pit. Her elbows beat at her sides like bony wings. The first-place ribbon she won in the high jump flutters against her tank top. "There's a man down there! Run! Goddammit, run!"

Sally shoves the woman in the back. "Go!"

The woman tries to run away. But she's wearing only one shoe. And fear is choking her, so that each indrawn breath squeaks noisily down her throat. Sally has never seen a grown-up so scared. She didn't think they were able to be so scared. She wishes she could wave a magic wand and make this tripping, crying woman young again. Escaping seems to be a lot easier when you're a kid.

Dawn rushes by them. "Let's go!"

Sally and Tatyana break into an all-out sprint.

A man steps out from around a building and grabs Sally by the wrist.

She's snapped off her feet. She doesn't even have time to make a sound before she hits the ground. Pain sizzles up her tailbone and burns all the way up her spine. When the sudden darkness clears from her eyes, she sees the man has let her go and is chasing Tatyana.

The man wears faded overalls with mysterious black stains down the legs. The toes of one of his boots has been repaired with the same kind of tape he's used on his hostage. He wears no shirt under his overalls. The backs of his shoulders and the base of his neck are carpeted with curly black hair.

"Tatyana!" Sally shouts.

Tatyana cuts to the left just before the man's hand finds her hair. He's not fast enough to match her sudden change of direction. When he speaks, his voice makes Sally feel as clogged up with fear as the woman from the car. "Come give me some love, little bitch!"

Sally pushes herself to her feet. It feels like someone has struck her in the back with a hammer. She sways . . .

Dawn stops fifty yards away, turns, looks back.

Tatyana races blindly between two of the shacks.

The man follows. And quickly closes the distance. In a moment he will have her.

Without knowing what she will do when she arrives, Sally goes after them.

Rain splatters her face. Rainy days make her curls frizzy and hard to control. Her mother always sighs when she's dragging the brush through Sally's hair, whispering about the knots and wondering when her daughter will start taking better care of herself. As she enters the little alley between the buildings, Sally decides she'll probably never see her mother again, and this brings the first sting of tears to her eyes.

The man reaches out—

Tatyana dives between the crucifixion thorns.

Four of the hideous, blue-gray trees have grown up through the broken stone like monsters rising up from the grave. They tower ten feet tall. Their bladed limbs are like a barrier of swords.

Tatyana has crawled into the base of the clustered trees, avoiding most—but not all—of the razory branches. A few feet behind her, the man pulls up just short of impaling himself.

Sally, without knowing why, runs right at him.

"Come out of there, hot pants!"

Tatyana pulls herself deeper. She yelps when she lances herself on one of the barbs.

The man bends over and leers at her. "Come on out and let's have us some—"

Sally slams into his back.

The force of impact hurls him forward into the knives. The sharp clutches of the crucifixion thorns embrace him fully, and he squeals as he's impaled a dozen times.

Tatyana shoots out from beneath the bushes. Side by side, she and Sally run.

The man thrashes, burying the spears deeper in his arms and face.

Sally and Tatyana reach Dawn, and the three of them turn on more speed than they ever did at any track meet on any day.

The man breaks free, squirting blood, making sounds that aren't quite human.

But these sounds are dwarfed by the truck. The engine roars as the big flatbed fishtails around the corner, tires squalling. It stops hard.

Sally sees Anne sitting in the middle of the seat. The doors fly open.

The Harmon brothers fly out.

The younger of them is an offensive lineman for the Sidewinders and the older is an amateur saddle-bronc rider with a temper that often lands him in jail after yet another tavern brawl. "You kids all right?" he asks, already running toward the mine.

Sally can only nod.

The Harmons fire themselves like warheads at the bleeding man.

Sally isn't sure what happens next. Anne gets out and the girls come together. They put their arms around one another's shoulders, forming a kind of football huddle. Minutes pass. Sirens draw near.

Sally looks at Tatyana across the circle. "I thought I lost you."

"You won't ever lose me." She winks, wiping the blood from her forehead. "You couldn't get that lucky."

The four of them stand there holding on, and the rain falls.

Chapter Twenty-six

Anne wondered why they called it the Green Room.

The walls were actually khaki. All four displayed oversized photos of Nancy Holiday in action. Chatting with the coach of the Arizona Cardinals. Interviewing movie stars. Feeding small children in some unnamed African state. The rest of the not-green Green Room consisted of a buffet table the size of a river barge, multiple floral arrangements, and a variety of mirrors for last-minute makeup checks.

Anne sat in an overstuffed chair that smelled like the perfume of Bia Singh. Author of a bestseller on the topic of women's psychology, Ms. Singh was currently out on the set, chatting it up with Nancy Holiday, probably relating the same anecdotes about her childhood in Delhi that she'd told to Anne while waiting here in the Green Room. She'd given Anne a copy of her book. Anne had just finished the first chapter. She found its premise to be as insipid as its author's writing style.

Anne looked over at Dawn, who was sprawled on one of the sofas, arm draped over her eyes. Anne closed the book. "Dawny? You're not snoozing over there, are you? Because I find it unfair that my stomach is in knots while you're in blissful repose."

"My repose ain't so blissful. Does that make you feel better?"

"No."

"Maybe this will. Reason number ninety-one. With cucumbers, you don't have to fake it so as not to bruise their egos."

Only Jazmyn laughed.

Anne wished she could tap into her daughter's insouciance, maybe siphon a bit of it into her own veins. Jaz and Crespin shared a small couch built for two—Anne refused to call it a love seat because it was her own daughter who was sitting in it with a boy—and neither of them seemed fazed by the imminent performance. Trevor and Barry and practically everyone else in Fresh Waters was tuning in. Viewers as far away as the Oklahoma panhandle would soon know the name of Radio. They might have seemed laughable a week ago, but now they were for real.

And what was up with Sally? She sat backwards on a wooden chair, arms resting on the back of the seat, a long-stemmed wine glass in hand. Only an inch of red liquid remained in the glass. The look on Sally's face was one that Anne didn't know. But a new confidence lived in her heart, evident in the set of her shoulders and the diamond glint in her eye.

What's happened to you, Sal? Anne wondered. *And when will your wings grow so big that you have no choice but to leave us all behind?*

A beep on the intercom was followed by a voice: "Radio, please report to stage four. Radio to stage four."

Anne rose to her feet. Under her breath she whispered, "Time to forget who I am for awhile."

Dawn sat up. "You say something, Annie?"

"That's not my name," Anne said on her way to the

door. "At least not for the next half-hour."

"Who are you then?"

"Woman," Anne replied. "Hear me roar."

When they finally started, when Nancy Holiday finished her introductions, when the stage manager gave the sign, when the lights dimmed, when the crowed quieted, when the single yellow pool of light appeared around her . . . only then did Sally do what she'd been waiting for.

She raised her hand and gave them the sign that Jeffrey had taught her.

Her thumb pinned her two middle fingers, leaving the two others pointing out in a gesture that she couldn't define but couldn't deny. On that cue, Jazmyn fell into her guitar work, loud and more garish than ever before, with Anne chasing after her on a bullet train of keyboard melodies.

Sally kept her arm uplifted as she sang the first few words of "Freebird."

No other song could suffice. No other song could so fully express who she was, and what she desired. She may have been standing here in these strapless red shoes with the two-inch spiked heels, but that was only an illusion. She was soaring. The bolts had come free again, and now her pinions stroked the air.

The cameras followed her as she roamed the stage.

Nothing had changed since she'd left Dakota last night. Making love to him had been but one more pattern in the beating of her wings. This was another. Even pulling on her clothes had felt different this morning, no longer a ritual but a sensual act. Along with her scarlet shoes she wore black suede pants and a white scoop-neck top with enough scoop to make things interesting. Respectable women didn't show cleavage, but free birds didn't care.

During Jazmyn's elaborate guitar solo, Sally danced. There was no form to her movements, only a whirling dervish of twists and leaps and other spontaneous flourishes. Images cascaded through her mind as she moved. A fallen statue. A flying pigeon. Dakota's body half seen in the flashlight glow. A guitar pick painted like England's flag. Tatyana with socks on her hands. A silver locket on its chain, spinning, spinning . . .

When it was over, the studio audience stood up.

On their feet, they cheered and waved their hands. Of the 300 people gathered there, ninety percent were women, and they must have felt a gut connection with Sally and the others because their reaction seemed to surprise even Nancy Holiday herself. They could sense the thermal current of *libertad,* and they envied and applauded it.

Too soon it was over.

Gravity pulled at her. The earth wanted her to return, to stop this immature flying business and get back to a practical life and take off those insensible shoes. Nancy Holiday sprang from her seat and spoke words that caused the crowd to yell even louder. Nancy's smile outdid the spotlights. She took Jazmyn by the wrist and hoisted her arm into the air. Jaz gave a whoop of victory. Cameras changed position and the red strobes blinked on, signaling a commercial break. Technicians scampered across the set. Interns swooped in with bottled water. Nancy went to Anne and the two of them talked like pals from way back. And through it all Sally breathed in and breathed out and wondered how she'd ever live the same again, if she had to give up these altitudes and return to her below-the-radar existence. She asked herself if she'd rather be dead.

At the moment she didn't have an answer.

★ ★ ★ ★ ★

"Don't spend it all in one place," Yarbuck said.

Sally accepted the envelope but didn't bother to open it. "Never can tell. I'm feeling frivolous lately. Maybe I'll just drive up to Vegas."

"Maybe you should. But not to gamble. We should get you booked."

"In a casino?" She smirked. "I don't think we're quite ready for such a venue yet."

"Pardon my French, Sally, but that's a wheelbarrow full of bullshit, and you know it."

She patted him on the arm with the envelope. "We'll see. You set up the shows, and we'll play it by ear."

"You got yourself a deal. What about the rest of the day? You need lunch?"

Sally considered it. She hadn't eaten since that bagel in Nancy Holiday's Green Room, and that was ages ago and she'd flown to the moon and back since then. It was now two in the afternoon. They'd spent the last several hours chatting it up with various folks from the TV studio, getting a tour of the station, signing the occasional autograph, and taking loads of pictures with Ms. Holiday and her staff. "I think the girls and I are going shopping. We don't get to Phoenix very often. We need to spend a little of our earnings in the mall. I'm sure we'll get something to eat along the way. But thanks for the offer."

"No, thank *you*. Can't rightly tell you how much of a difference you've made in my life these last few days. Sorta exciting, if you want the truth. My wife thinks I'm crazier than a pet coon, but I know a handful of aces when I see one."

Sally smiled. "I'll talk to you later, Jude."

"You bet your pretty little bottom you will." He seemed about to give his usual parting gesture—his fingers were already reaching toward the brim of his hat—but then he stopped, fixing her with a hopeful gaze. "What if I need to call you tonight? Will you be home?"

"That depends. Why are you calling?"

"What if I really could get something set up. In Vegas, I mean."

"Jude, we're a cover band, remember? Nobody's going to pay to see us on the Strip."

"Pardon me, but I think you're dead wrong. In fact, I get the feeling you've hit a nerve that this here country's been in dire need of getting hit. There's too many fake entertainers out there. You ladies are singing other folks' music, but you're singing it real. But you let me worry about that for now. Can I reach you at home?"

"Only if it's late. First thing I'm doing when I get back to Fresh Waters is climbing on a motorcycle and driving out to find a buried treasure. Then, if the planets align and I get really lucky, I might be receiving a certain gentleman caller who's promised me dinner. He's already phoned and raved about the show. I guess he sent out a mass E-mail and asked every Border Patrol office in the region to tune in. Nancy can thank me later for the spike in her ratings."

Yarbuck smiled. "I'll just call Anne if I have any news. You sound like you might have a busy evening in front of you."

"And to think that I used to be in bed every night by eleven."

By the time she swung her leg over Dakota's bike, dusk was purpling the sky.

They said little as they prepared to go. A new element existed between them, a cool enjoyment of occasional contact fused with a heat that simmered just below the surface of their skin. They rode the miles in silence, her body curved against his, the western sky a fading canvas of lavender brush strokes. For the first time in days, Sally entertained no thoughts at all. She'd gotten the Mexicans safely from her home. She hadn't been arrested for her part in a crime that she didn't really consider a crime at all. She had explained to Jazmyn, *It's never wrong to give someone a chance.*

She saw the reflectors like eyes in the dark.

By now she was comfortable enough with the motorcycle's operation that she could ease the machine to a stop without Dakota's guidance. They dismounted. Dakota wore a canvas rucksack containing the necessities, including a collapsible camp shovel, Sally's purse, flashlights, a bottle of wine, and two Styrofoam cups. Sally had purchased the California blush for sixteen dollars at Dale's Liquor & Smoke. And there was the scene of another of her recent crimes: contributing to the delinquency of a minor.

Dakota handed her a flashlight. Sally didn't turn it on, preferring to walk by twilight until it gave way fully to night. She smelled the motorcycle's hot engine and Dakota's cheap cologne. She realized she was still wearing her stage shoes. The heels were tall and narrow and not made at all for this terrain. She slipped them off.

The red earth warm under her bare feet, she set off into the desert, Dakota at her side.

Anne stood naked in the steam.

The full-length mirror was fogged. She wiped enough away to see herself. Behind her, the shower ran hot and loud. Her body was still wet. She dripped onto the floor, something she never did, because she hated soggy bathroom rugs as much as she loathed stains in the sink and toothpaste tubes not properly rolled as they emptied. But the water ran down her calves and tickled her neck, and she didn't care. She was too intent upon her inspection of the woman reflected in front of her.

That woman's hair was blond.

The dye had been as good as advertised. What started out as pale highlights had evolved into a more radical change. For the last two hours she'd been working at it, following the directions on the back of the box, and behold: a platinum goddess. Her hair, freshly blow-dried, was a long shimmering cascade of gold.

What next?

Logic was as carved into Anne's being as the faces rendered in the stone of Mt. Rushmore. Reason was an immutable part of who she was. Ergo, she could only think of one plausible action that a woman with newly blond hair could take.

She put on a red dress.

A year ago she'd bought it while in Belize with Barry for an astronomers' convention. It was a cocktail dress with spaghetti straps and more exposed skin than Anne usually found comfortable. But tonight was different. The slinky fabric caressed her. She strutted before the mirror, not entirely familiar with the person she saw staring back, but taking an immediate liking to her. She spent twenty minutes with makeup, and followed this with another parade before the mirror. When at last she deemed herself more than mortal man deserved, she left the bathroom.

Trevor saw her. His face changed. "Mother?"

"And a whole lot more," Anne replied. She spun a circle for him there in the hall, arms outstretched, sun-colored hair fanning around her.

"Mother, you're"—he blinked—"I mean if you weren't my mom, you'd be really hot."

"But since I am your mom, I'm merely stunning. Is that what you're saying?"

"Yeah. Sure. Where are you going?"

She brushed past him, but only after kissing him on the cheek. "Do you think your father will share your opinion of how stunning I am?"

Trevor shook his head. "No. He'll think you're really hot."

"Perfect." She headed for the door.

Trevor ran after her. "What a minute!"

"Nope. Waiting is a thing of the past. I'm now a person concerned only with the present tense."

"But I think a flying saucer abducted my mom and replaced her with an alien replicant."

"That, my son, is not so far from the truth."

She left him standing there and went to surprise her husband in Maxon.

The flashlight beam found the gallows.

From there it was only a brief walk to the dry creek, and then to the boulder, and then—revealed in a pool of yellow light—the rough groove Sally had cut into the ground with her heel.

Dakota removed the rucksack and withdrew the shovel. "You sure this is the place?"

Those were the first words either of them had spoken since they left the bike. The sound of a human voice fell strangely on Sally's ear, seeming out of place in this dark expanse. By now the sky was limitless, the stars as numerous as sands on a celestial shore. The sense of flight had not abandoned her, so that she felt as if those stars were streaming past her. "Someone should name a comet after me," she said.

"Huh?"

"This is the spot." She walked over to it, dropped her shoes, stared down at the little furrow she'd made the night before. "Jeffrey was very precise in his drawing. The distance between here and that boulder is dead on the money. I'm sure of it."

"So . . . you want me to go ahead and start?" He hefted the shovel.

"No. I'll dig. You just hold the light and make wisecracks about my poor shoveling abilities." She traded him the flashlight for the shovel.

"The army calls it an entrenching tool," he informed her.

"You stole this shovel from the army?"

"It's my dad's. He's in the National Guard."

"Hey."

"What?"

"Let's not tell him you loaned his entrenching tool to a barefoot madwoman with delusions of stardom and fantasies of buried gold."

"My lips are sealed."

Sally grinned. "Well, hopefully they won't be sealed all night."

She drove the shovel into the ground.

Dawn watched the popcorn bag begin to swell in the microwave. Every light in her house was on, and the place was in its usual state of pandemonium. The kids were in the living room, hooting over a video game. The TV in the bedroom was blaring, just in case Radio's morning performance was mentioned on the late-night news. Alex was in the hallway with the vacuum cleaner, taking care of the first bowl of popcorn that Dawn had attempted to deliver to the boys. Tatyana used to say that Dawn's middle name was

350

Grace. And that stunt in the hall was proof that some things never changed.

"And some things do," Dawn said, thinking of the look in Sally's eyes.

The popcorn made fireworks noises. Dawn looked at the timer. Thirty seconds to go.

She left the corn to its countdown, guessing she'd probably end up with a burned batch, as their microwave was older than Coy and Caleb combined and was not to be trusted. But she was worried. Worried because Jazmyn was supposed to be back by now. Worried because Jaz had promised the boys that she and Crespin would play Ping-Pong with them when they returned. Worried because in many ways her daughter was still a child, but as far as promises went, she was all grown up. She never made one she didn't keep.

Dawn checked the answering machine. Between the vacuum and two blaring televisions, the phone could have rung unheard.

Zero messages.

"She's celebrating," Dawn said to herself. "Sure can't blame the girl."

Jazmyn had received a call upon their return from Phoenix. The man's name was Riley. He was the manager for an L.A.-based band called Weasel Fist. Dawn had never heard of them. Jaz sure had.

"Mama, they want me to join!" she shouted after hanging up, her face aglow.

"Who wants you to join what?"

"Weasel Fist! Their guitarist left the band a month ago. They want to *interview* me."

"Do I know Weasel Fist? I don't think I do."

"Are you joking me? They've only released one album so

far but it sold, like, a zillion copies. They're on MTV every day. The lead singer is from Taos, and he saw the show this morning. I can't believe they called!" She gave an inarticulate cry of joy and jumped up and down like someone half her age. "Crespin! Guess what!" She bolted upstairs, shouting all the way.

That was three hours ago. She and Crespin had shot out of the driveway, the big Buick leaving black scars on the pavement. She wanted to tell everyone the news.

"They're young," Dawn said, tapping a finger against the answering machine. "They just lost track of—"

No. Better safe than sorry. Dawn would send Alex to find them. Odds were strong that they were at a friend's house, having a hell of a good time, dreaming about being a member of a world-famous band whose album had sold a zillion copies. Or maybe they were out necking. Smooching. Getting frisky in the old convertible. And if that were the case, then Dawn knew exactly where they'd be.

She pulled Alex's vacuum plug from the wall and asked him to drive to Scorp City.

Eight inches into the desert floor, Sally's shovel struck something solid.

She looked at Dakota, though she could barely see him in the flashlight's feeble glow. "Is this cool or what?"

"Damn straight."

Her pulse quickening in her wrists, Sally set to work feverishly, stabbing the shovel blade into the ground and tossing out clumps of moist sand without care for where they fell. "Bring the light closer."

Dakota did as instructed. He dropped to his knees and aimed the beam directly at the hole. "What is it? Can you see it yet? Uncover that corner there. Is it a box of some kind?"

"Easy, big guy. I'm not exactly . . ." Her breath came harder. ". . . the most experienced gal when it comes to entrenching tools."

Half a minute later she'd excavated a moat around the object, leaving only half of it still buried. It was metal and dented and wrapped in strips of duct tape. For a second Sally was struck by the image of a bleeding woman lying in the back of a car, her hands and feet bound in makeshift manacles just like this; ever since then, she hadn't been able to use duct tape without remembering that afternoon in the rain.

Don't tell my folks I'm a truck driver . . .

"Sally? You okay?"

She closed her eyes, opened them, and all there was to see was a hole like a mouth with a metal container wedged down its throat. "I'm more than okay, Dak. I'm having the time of my life." She set the shovel aside and got down to business with her hands.

When she finally started wiggling it, the object came free with relative ease. Sally yanked it clear with a soft grunt. Dakota never let the light leave it. A damp smell wafted up from the hole.

"What is it?" Dakota asked. "Jesus, Sally, open the thing already, I'm going nuts here."

"It's a tackle box."

"You mean for fishing?"

Sally set it on the ground. "I need my purse. We've got to get this tape off."

Dakota groped around in the dark, found the rucksack, and dragged it over. Sally extracted her purse and fished around inside among her checkbook, phone, loose change, and the condoms she'd brought along without even a trace of the self-consciousness that days ago would have made her blush. Eventually she located her metal nail file. Bending over the box, she shoved the file under the tape, positioned it, and then raked it free, ripping through the tape. She repeated this process twice more, and then only the container's simple metal latch stood in her way.

"If this thing is filled with hundred-dollar bills," Dakota said, "I'm warning you now that I plan on screaming my head off in joy."

"It's not money. Jeffrey's family wasn't rich. Whatever he buried out here has nothing to do with gold doubloons. He knew what was important, and what would fade away."

"Sally?"

"Yeah?"

"Open the damn box."

Sally drew the banged-up container to her knees. Her feet were folded under her, so that she knelt before it like a penitent before an altar. Dakota scooted closer. Sally could hear him breathing. He held the light between them, pointing it directly at the box.

Sally unfastened the latch. She put her hands on the sides and lifted the lid.

Her phone rang.

Neither she nor Dakota moved. They might not have even heard it, though the phone was only inches away and the sound was alone in the otherwise silent desert. They were too intent upon the three items in the box.

Sally reached inside and lifted out a note wrapped in cellophane.

"Give me more light." She unfolded the paper, and Dakota angled the flashlight so that it made a smooth yellow circle on the page. The edges of the paper were rough, pulled as they were from the spirals of a school notebook. The wide-ruled lines were printed with Jeffrey's careful penmanship.

Miss Sally,

I am sitting in Mr. Kovarovic's American history class. It doesn't suck as bad as most kids think it does. Today we are talking about Farrington Schatz. I guess he is some kind of hero and outlaw at the same time. Mr. K. says that "Schatz" is the German word for "treasure." Farrington changed his name to Schatz when he came to the Wild West. Anyway, I think Schatz is a good word for the shoes you gave me. So I am putting some of my own Schatz in a box for you. And I think that all Schatz is supposed to be dug up by someone who has followed a map to find it. I hope you like this adventure, Miss Sally.

Your friend,
Jeff

The phone rang.

Still Sally paid no attention to it. That's what voice-mail was for, to take a message when you were busy unearthing the riches of a dead boy's heart.

"Schatz means treasure," she said. "I'll be damned." She put the letter aside and took out the next object.

A baseball.

The ball was scuffed and stained green along an inch of the seam, evidence that it had skidded through the outfield grass. The white leather covering was marked with two distinct autographs. The first was Jeffrey's own. The second belonged to—

"Barry Bonds," Dakota said. He whistled through his teeth. "If this is authentic, Sally, then it's a gem. Bonds is one of the greatest hitters of all time, and maybe the greatest player of the modern era. He plays for the—"

"I know who he is," Sally said. "But what's more important to me is that Jeffrey also signed the ball. Like he's telling me that one of these days he's going to be just as good as his idol."

The phone stopped ringing. Ten seconds later, it started again.

Dakota snatched up her purse, inside of which the phone chimed rhythmically. "Just answer it, will ya?"

The last thing in the box was a pair of shoes.

They were Jeffrey's old cleats. Torn at the seams and crusted with dirt, they were the ones he'd worn for baseball before Sally had given him new ones. The imitation leather had cracked like plastic. The laces were frayed and stained a permanent infield brown.

"Size seven," Sally whispered.

Looking at the shoes made her smile, though she didn't know why. She held them the way she might have held the winged sandals of Hermes.

The light moved as Dakota put down the purse, delved inside, and pulled out the ringing phone. Holding the flashlight between his cast and his body, he pressed the button to take the call and thrust the phone at Sally.

In somewhat of a daze she accepted it, her eyes still on the shoes.

"Sally, are you there?"

The fear in Dawn's voice snapped Sally back from her dream state. In an instant she was alert, the shoes a forgotten weight at the end of her arm. "Dawn, what's wrong?"

"He's got him, Sally, Jesus Christ, he grabbed him . . ."

"Who? Dawn, slow down. What are you talking about?"

"Crespin. He was out with Jaz and the bastard got him."

"Dawny, please, I don't understand what you're—"

"Crespin's gone, Sally. Isadore Presper took him."

Chapter Twenty-seven

The desert turned suddenly cold.

Sally cupped the phone in both hands, as if by cradling it so carefully she could hold together the pieces of the disintegrating night.

"They went to celebrate," Dawn said, "after the call from that band in L.A., and I'm sorry, I'm sorry, I know I'm the worst of us when it comes to being her mother. . . ."

"Stop." The word came from Sally's mouth of its own volition. But once it was there, it seemed to make sense. She tried to follow it with something stunning, a plan that would make everything right again, though no one could blame her if she was fresh out of heroics. "Is Jazmyn safe?"

"She's with Alex at the hospital. But she's fine. She got cut on the rocks when she went after her car keys. She said something about the men throwing her keys into the mine pit after they grabbed Crespin. On the way back up, she slipped and gashed herself bad enough to need stitches. Alex is with her and she's getting sewn up as we speak. She's crying. She's upset. But she'll be all right after they patch up her knee."

Sally absorbed this with an equanimity that surprised her. Her baby had been hurt. Though Presper's men hadn't injured her directly, she was bleeding and scared. Sublimating her rising anger, Sally said, "Jaz is with Alex, so she's okay. That's the first important thing. The second important thing is that you are not the worst anything when it comes to being a mother."

"Sally, forget I said it, we've gotta help him."

"And we will. At least we'll try. But first you have to—"

"All right, I know, I'm not a horrible mother, Tatyana would think I'm doing a bang-up job and all that bullshit, now can we please do something?"

Sally looked around, as if searching the darkness for a solution. But all she could see was Dakota's worried face and the pool of light that fell on the open tackle box. "Have you called the police?"

Dawn snorted. "You must be joking, right, because I'm sure you haven't forgotten the fact that Crespin is carrying around a fake ID that we gave him. If the cops get him in their hands, we go to jail, and please spare me that crap about you taking the blame by yourself because you know the captain doesn't go down alone with our ship. The crew of the S.S. *Radio* sinks or swims together, always have. Next plan, please."

"You realize you're saying that we'll have to go get him ourselves?"

"We know where they're taking him. You said yourself they're based in Maxon. I'm betting the assholes took him to their headquarters or hideout or wherever they go to sharpen their swords. Sally, they're going to beat him up bad. Maybe even worse."

"So we're going to Maxon?"

"If you say we are."

And there it was again. This asking. This waiting for Sally's word. Briefly she wondered what gods had decided that she should wield such power. Most of the time she couldn't even keep herself on an even keel, much less be responsible for the fate of her friends. Even that day after the track meet, when Dawn asked if the others wanted to walk home instead of getting a ride, everyone deferred to Sally. Had she not given her approval, they wouldn't have ended up at the mine, and that woman in the car might have been killed. Everything, then, hinged upon what Sally said next, and she felt the gravity of it in her bones. "We have to go."

Dawn exhaled a shaky breath. "I thought you'd say that. Anne's already there."

"What?"

"She went to surprise Barry. I think she was buying a bottle of wine along the way."

"Call her. Tell her what's going on."

"Will do. Now come and get me and let's get there before something awful happens."

"I can't come and get you."

"What the hell are you talking about? Of course you can."

"Right now I'm only about a mile and a half away from Maxon. If I come back, that means a hike to the motorcycle, a drive to your house, then a thirty-minute race down the highway to Maxon. I can make it a lot faster if I just go from here."

"Hiking to a motorcycle? Where are you?"

"Digging up Jeffrey's treasure in the middle of the desert. It doesn't matter. But if Alex is with Jazmyn then we're going to need someone else to drive you. So be ready when Dakota shows up to get you." She watched his face as she spoke. "I'm sending him back right now. He'll drive into town and get you, and by that time you'll have called the girl across the street to come and watch the boys. Meet me at Barry's observatory."

"I thought you said you were in the middle of the desert. How are you going to get to the observatory?"

Sally looked down at Jeffrey's shoes. "I'm going to fly."

Sally wore size nine. Jeffrey's were sevens. Sally had never understood why men's and women's sizes were segregated, but she knew the conversion well enough. A men's size six would be a better fit, but a seven was manageable.

She slid the shoes onto her feet.

"Can I ask you a question?" Dakota said as he hurriedly donned the rucksack, which now also contained Sally's purse and the autographed baseball.

"Only if it's a quick one."

"What do you expect us to do when we find Presper? Those guys are dangerous."

"Jude Yarbuck would tell you not to worry about the horse, just load the wagon."

"What's that supposed to mean?"

Sally tugged the laces, which were stiffened with dirt. When they pulled taut through the metal eyelets, little puffs of dust breathed from the shoe. "It means get your ass moving and we'll cross that bridge when we come to it. Now go. Dawn will give you the keys to her car when you get there because it's way too dark for her to see. Drive to Maxon as fast as you can without getting pulled over by the highway patrol. Don't stop along the way, and tell no one where you're going. By the time you two reach the observatory, hopefully Anne and I will know where the Partisans are holding Crespin. And Barry will be there to help out, unless of course he has a coronary when we tell him we've been buying forged documents and smuggling Mexicans across the border." She looked up at him. "Now why are you still here?"

He picked up one of the flashlights. "You'll be okay? Charging across the desert in the middle of the night doesn't sound like the safest thing to be doing."

"Pigtails are antennas for bravery."

By his face it was evident that Dakota had no idea what she was talking about, but it was also evident that he wasn't about to ask. He held still for one more moment, then swooped down and kissed her on the mouth.

Sally kissed him back.

He shot back up, nodded once, and headed off into the darkness. The sound of his boots striking the ground soon faded, and Sally was alone.

She licked the taste of him from her lips. Stood up. Pointed the light at her feet.

The cleats had once been white. They were now the color of the cabinets in Sally's kitchen after a few months of not cleaning them. Fingerprints around the handles turned the white wood into something neither gray nor brown. It was a used shade. In the case of cabinets, used wasn't the hue you wanted to show the neighbors. But for a boy's shoes, shoes that had stomped puddles, kicked soccer balls, outrun bullies, and beat out throws to home plate, used was the color of choice.

She shifted her feet, getting the feel.

"This isn't real," she said to the night.

The men who dragged illegal immigrants behind the bumpers of moving trucks had not just abducted her daughter's boyfriend. The men who chased Juan Doe to his death, the men who caused Sally to kill him—they were phantasms, and if Sally ran all the way to Maxon she would find she'd dreamed it all.

This is a hazardous part of the country we live in.

That was no phantasm. She saw his face again, just as it

had appeared in her living-room window. His gaze had a cruel yet languid cast, as if he were privy to the world's woes but unaffected by them. He hadn't leered at Sally through the glass, but cavalierly appraised her, like someone about to ask another man's date to dance. The very tranquility of his demeanor should have been enough to keep Sally standing still. One phone call to Leigh Surry would be sufficient. Crespin would be saved from whatever bloody fate Presper intended to visit upon his young body. Yes, Sally might face criminal charges for supplying the boy with his driver's license, but that was sometimes the price you paid for waving the flag of *libertad*. She could live with the consequences.

She considered calling out to Dakota, to get the phone from her purse and make a call, but the wings fluttered and distracted her.

Flight was still hers to command. What had been born onstage continued to grow, to find strength, to test the air. She had rediscovered it on Dakota's motorcycle, and she could feel it now, a current to carry her across the sand.

The flashlight thrust a lance of light into the darkness. The hard nubs on the soles of the cleats pressed into the ground.

Sally ran.

And running, she remembered.

She had advanced only a few hundred yards, arms chugging up and down, respiration still more or less even, when she saw the track meet. Because there was nothing else to look at—only the stars were to be seen, and she had to trust she wasn't about to run into a rock and shatter a knee—her mind rearranged the scenery. She saw the girls as they used to be. Dawn was the jumper, her long legs propelling her over hurdles and across sand pits. She looked at Sally and furtively flipped her off. She laughed as she offered the gesture, having just mastered it and now delighted by Sally's reaction. Dawn always learned all the new cuss words first, and shared them with aggressive generosity.

Sally wondered how long it would take to cramp up.

She hadn't run in eons. In fact, the lack of running was probably accountable for the general decline of the adult body. As kids, running was how you got from here to there. You zigged to school, you zagged back home. Grown-ups for some reason saw no reason to zigzag through the house or across the lawn. Sally promised herself she'd run occasionally without justification, if she made it through this night in one piece.

Anne ran the short races. Her long hair bound behind her in a ponytail, her angled eyes narrowed so as to be almost closed, she blasted through the fifty-yard dash as if she had invented it. In that race she had no equal. In the seventy-five-yard version, however, she was duly challenged by that Navajo girl from the visiting town of San Manuel, and also by her own soul-sister, the blond comet—

"Tatyana," Sally said in between breaths.

When other kids won races, they threw their hands into the air or jumped into the arms of coaches or parents. After Tatyana crossed the ribbon in the seventy-five-yard dash, she quickly stopped, turned, and bowed crisply at the waist.

When she rose up from her bow, she was looking at Sally. She winked.

Sally picked up speed.

Jeffrey's shoes may have been a bit too big, but their plastic spikes found solid purchase in the earth. Sweat formed along Sally's neckline and on the small of her back. The flashlight was useless. She couldn't keep it aimed in front of her and work her arms properly at the same time. Trying to do so threw off her rhythm. So she settled for turning it off and holding it like a baton. That reminded her again of relay races, and how she'd told Leigh that she was taking the baton from Juan Doe and finishing the race.

If her body would let her.

Her lungs caught fire somewhere around the half-mile mark. There had been a time when she could have jogged the one-point-five miles to Maxon without this smoldering in her chest. After all, she'd once been a long-distancer, finishing third in the state's amateur 10K, so this small measure of ground should have been undemanding. But she rarely exercised anymore. Hence these flames when she breathed.

To make matters worse, if there were a rock or crevice in her path, she'd end up either face-down or crippled, depending on the trajectory of her fall. Starlight alone was not enough to light the way. But now that they were beating, the wings were reluctant to slow down. So she gave herself up to the visions of that day at the track meet, and imagined she was chasing after the pack in the last leg of a race she was favored to win.

The fire grew. The sweat formed pellets and rolled down her cheeks.

What made it easy was the girls. The track itself formed an oval around the football field, where the Fresh Waters Sidewinders engaged in their Friday-night battles. Lined up along the edge of the field, mere feet from the track's inside lane, were Sally's personal cheerleaders. Anne, Dawn, and Tatyana shouted and waved their arms, their high-pitched voices carrying easily to Sally's ear.

She ran through the dark and heard her name squealed again and again. Jumbled together with her name were *Go!*

and *Come on!* and then the best thing of all happened. The girls began to run with her.

They ran on the grass, separated from the track by a low cement curb. Sally was in third place coming around the final bend. She was also halfway to Maxon. Now right beside her, seen on her periphery, three screaming girls matched her strides, shouting her name.

She asked her legs for more speed, and was surprised when they delivered.

The air cooled the sweat on her face, and this prompted her to run even faster, creating her own wind that smeared the droplets down the neckline of her shirt and brought a welcome chill to her chest. The cadence of her feet beating the ground and her arms working against her sides was a feeling that could not be duplicated by any other activity. The muscles in her legs were complaining, and a stitch was beginning to form in her side, but the wings kept stroking, the girls kept hollering, and Sally kept running.

The ground was not level at times. Sally felt the slight shifts, the little depressions in the soil, the scattered stones. But these changes in topography were not dramatic enough to give her pause.

She pulled into second place.

The finish line was ahead of her. She could see it, even if she couldn't see the shrouded town of Maxon. There were no streetlamps in Maxon, nor any porch lights that weren't by city ordinance night-vision red. But she sensed she was close. Now if she could only catch the runner in front of her, if she could only make her move in the last few yards . . .

She tripped.

The rock caught her toe. She spiraled her arms for balance, and the flashlight flew off into the gloom. Her hands touched the ground, but only briefly, as she rode out her momentum and righted herself, coming back up to speed.

The misstep had cost her. Her opponent had pulled several feet away.

"Suck it up, Sal!" Tatyana yelled.

The voice was so near that Sally almost turned her head to look. But instead she squeezed her fists, burdened no longer with the flashlight, and called upon the last of her reserves. Breathing hoarsely through her mouth, lungs blazing, she flew across the desert until she saw the vague and ghostly silhouette of Maxon's outlying buildings. The houses looked like cut-outs of black construction paper.

The girls called out to her. They ran beside her, screeching for her to go faster, faster, and Sally bit back the pain and forced herself into a final sprint.

She caught the runner in front of her just as she reached the first of Maxon's unlit streets.

Her friends shouted in victory, and then faded from sight.

Sally slowed down and was alone, panting so hard it hurt. Trying to catch her breath, she looked around for Anne and Dawn and Tatyana, but the track meet had evaporated like a mirage and all there was to see was a neighborhood of darksome houses and infrequent headlights sweeping about in the night.

She bent over and put her hands on her knees, gasping.

Sweat dripped from her hair. Her body heaved. She waited for Dawn to put a hand on her back and say, "Salster, you ran that race like somebody shoved a bottle rocket up your butt." But there was only the sound of her own ragged breathing and the distant barking of an unhappy dog.

She straightened. New aches flashed through her legs.

She used her shirtsleeve to dab the moisture from her face. She wanted to stand there until the air passed more calmly into her labored lungs, but she didn't have time. Crespin needed help.

She looked around.

The town was like science fiction. The conspicuous absence of the usual tall-necked lights along the streets gave Sally the impression that the entire place had been evacuated and left for dead, probably due to a radiation spill or other, more freakish catastrophe. Under a few carports and porch awnings, red eyes glared, like warnings to those who might be left behind. The windows in the houses were veiled with heavy drapes, so that only narrow lines of tantalizing light could be seen. Sally had never realized how well-lit most towns were at night until now, and having to depend on her own eyes to discern the deceptive shape of the buildings was unnerving. At any moment, she expected a man in a suit to step out from behind a tree and begin a monologue that would end by informing her that she'd just crossed over into the Twilight Zone.

She wondered how she'd ever see the street signs and find her way to Anne.

At last her breath settled. The excitement of the run still coursed through her, the euphoria of having again achieved liftoff. The sad and amazing thing of it was that she'd waited so long to experience it. Thirty-six years of kicking at *terra firma* was worse on the soul than anyone imagined until they left the ground. The feeling was worth risking it all. This was why Icarus flew too close to the sun.

Sally went to the nearest house to ask for directions to the observatory.

She knew she looked frightful. Hair sweaty. White shirt now gray with dust. Hand-me-down shoes on her feet.

"As if I honestly give a shit anymore."

She intended to walk, but halfway there she could stand it no longer, and ran full speed to the door.

Chapter Twenty-eight

Anne sat in the car with a bottle between her legs.

Her red dress was hiked up around her thighs, permitting the fat bottle of California red to rest in the V of her crotch, like a wino behind the wheel. But the car wasn't moving. It occupied a parking place outside the Maxon Array, the big concrete building itself as dark as the sky which it was intended to observe. No one was inside. Barry and his night-owl colleagues, according to the message on his voice-mail, had driven over to Kitt Peak to meet a visiting astrophysicist. By now they were inextricably engaged in a debate over whether the spectral red shifts observed in quasars were cosmological or gravitational in nature.

Anne hoisted the bottle by the neck, took a deep swallow.

Why had she bothered? Rekindling a romance took more than a matchbook of good intentions. You had to have fuel on hand to sustain the damn thing. You had to have something worth burning.

"And now, Anne dear," she said, "you are on your way to becoming a statistic."

She followed this pronouncement with another pull on the bottle.

Until very recently, she had assumed that holding up her

end of the marriage bargain was the logical course to follow. Staying together just seemed to make sense. Now she believed otherwise. Too often people pledged themselves to one another only to find their dreams hindered by that pledge, or their spirits boxed up, or their passions watered down. Anne wanted to be married to someone who could set her free.

"Here's to late-blooming lady rockers." She tipped the bottle back—

A fist pounded against the window by her head.

Anne started, swore, almost dropped the wine.

The door yanked open. A voice said, "God, you dyed yourself yellow. Please tell me you're not drunk."

"Sally?" The world came back into sharp relief. "What's wrong? What are you doing here? Look at you, you're a mess. What happened?"

"Didn't Dawn call you?"

"Fifteen minutes ago I threw my phones in the trash. Both of them. Why? What's the matter? No, wait." She held up a hand. "I can tell by the look on your face. Deep-ass trouble for us girls."

"The deepest." Sally ran to the passenger's side and got in the car.

"Isadick Presper," Dawn said, "has now officially pissed me off."

Dakota said nothing. He kept his good hand high on the wheel and drove.

"I mean, the nerve of that bastard. They pull into the lot at Scorp City, slug Crespin in the stomach, and kidnap him, for Chrissakes."

Dakota looked over at her, then returned his attention to the road.

"Right in front of my daughter!"

Finally Dakota spoke up, though his words were so soft that Dawn almost didn't hear him over the sound of the tires against the road. "I don't know what you want me to say."

"Say that sucks."

"That sucks. It really does. But guys like those . . . they get away with it."

"Like hell they do."

"Always have. Same way in school. If there's a kid the teachers don't really like, and somebody beats him up . . ." Dakota shrugged. "Nobody ever gets in trouble for what happened, at least not in any real trouble."

"This is different."

"No, it's not."

"This is adults, Dak. This is grown-ups in the grown-up world. Men cannot go around abducting people and expect nothing more than a slap on the hand."

"They can't? Crespin's here illegally. He doesn't have a lot of rights. If he goes to the cops, the main thing he'll have to worry about is not getting deported before he can press charges against the Partisans. Hell, I don't even think he *can* press charges. Maybe you have to be an American to do that. Maybe you have to be an American to do a lot of things."

"Haven't you heard? All men are created equal."

"Oh, yeah? Then why don't we say the Bill of Rights applies to everyone and not just Americans? If we really believe that all people are equal, then why do we let so many of Crespin's friends down there live in poverty like that?"

"Uncle Sam can't feed everybody in the world."

"Why not? We have the money. And equal means equal. Everyone has the same rights, the same chance to eat and have a house that's not made out of cardboard."

"So you're saying our country is a nation of hypocrites?"

"Maybe."

"And you're saying the Constitution is toilet paper?"

"Parts of it, I guess."

"You know what, Dak, my boy?"

"What?"

"If I were fifteen years younger, I'd be on you like margarine on corn-on-the-cob."

Dakota smiled, his embarrassment barely registering in the inadequate glow of the dashboard lights.

"But seriously," Dawn said, "we're in some kind of bad doo-doo here."

"Tell me about it."

"I don't know what we're supposed to do. You're right when you say we can't really go to the cops. We'd end up getting ourselves thrown in the slammer. But what about Sally's friend from Immigration? That Surry guy. He seems reasonable enough. Why don't we call him?"

Dakota had no answer.

"How much farther?"

"About five miles."

"Are there stars out tonight?"

"Lots."

Dawn was quiet for a moment. Then: "This town we're going to . . ."

"Maxon."

"Yeah." She hated looking out the window because there was nothing to see but a field of perfect blackness. A void all around her. Riding in a car at night was the closest thing she knew to being truly blind. "It's called a dark-sky community. By law there are no lights."

Dakota drummed his fingers nervously on the wheel,

then stopped when he realized what he was doing. "You going to be okay?"

"Ask me that again at sunrise. If I make it that long."

"What does that mean?"

Dawn didn't say, because she wasn't sure. The only thing she knew was that—at this moment—daybreak had never felt more far away.

Sally stopped pacing the observatory steps when Dawn's car pulled up.

Anne beat her to the passenger's door, and even as it swung open Dawn was saying, "She's okay, Jaz is fine, only a few stitches, I just talked to Lex three minutes ago."

"She saw the men who took Crespin?" Anne asked, a flinty hardness in her voice.

"Annie? What the hell happened to your hair?"

"Forget it. Did she see the men or not?"

"She was standing right there. They took him right in front of her."

"Can she identify them?"

"I didn't ask."

"Did they have any distinctive features?"

"I didn't ask that either. Sorry, Detective Columbo, but I'm a rock star, not a cop."

Sally put a hand on Dawn's arm. "It's okay. We can talk to Jaz about that later. As long as she's safe, then the next thing we have to worry about is getting Crespin out of there."

"Out of where? Do you know where they've taken him?"

"Maybe." Actually, Sally had a fairly good guess, as she'd spent the ten minutes since her arrival here making a few calls on Anne's satellite phone—after digging that phone from the curbside waste can in which Anne had deposited it. "Let's talk over here, under the light."

"Sounds good to me," Dawn said, permitting Anne to usher her up the sidewalk to the observatory.

Sally jogged around the car. Dakota unrolled his window.

"Hey, stud," she said.

"Hey. Looks like you survived the run."

"Survived and then some."

"So what do you want me to do now?"

"Be a prince and wait here for a minute while the gals and I have a confab."

"No problem."

She rewarded him with a smile, then ran to the great stone building, where the others were waiting under a light the same color as those used in a photographer's darkroom. Engraved into the stone of the observatory wall was the legend *ASTRA NON SUNT ULTRA MANUM.*

Dawn leaned in close to read the letters under the crimson light. "What does this say? What language is this?"

Anne hardly glanced at it. " 'The stars are not beyond our grasp.' It's Latin."

"Latin, huh? How do you say, 'The only good language is a dead language'?"

Sally reached out and took their hands. "Listen up."

They looked at her, silent and attentive.

"This is what we know. Isadore Presper lives on a ranch about twenty miles out of town. He also owns an active metalworking facility here in Maxon. He conducts metallography work for Arizona State, and his workshop or laboratory or whatever the hell he uses is located in that same metalworks. Most of that info was in the file that Leigh gave me, but the stuff about the metalworks building I just learned from one of Barry's cronies at the college.

375

Now, I can't be sure, but I'm betting that the Partisans meet on one of Presper's properties. I say we drive to a convenience store, ask for the address of the metalworks, and go check it out."

She waited for a response, but neither of her friends seemed to know what to say.

"The longer we stand here," she reminded them, "the less chance we have of getting Crespin out of there in time. So what about it? Anne?"

Indecision passed over Anne's face. But just when it looked as if her sensible self would win out, she seemed in that instant to leave it behind. She nodded. "Whatever you say."

Sally gave her hand a squeeze. She turned to Dawn. "Well?"

Dawn shook her head. "Truthfully? I don't know if we can do this."

"We have to try."

"Do we? I've been thinking about that ever since Dak and I left my driveway. Maybe just trying isn't enough. Not this time. Maybe we could have pulled this off if things were different. If we had all of us."

"I don't know what you're talking about."

"Yes, you do. Things used to be different. We had our fourth wheel. We could roll."

"We can still roll."

"Can we?" Dawn curled her lip, and in that simple gesture her inborn optimism fell in tatters, replaced by something that expressed itself in a bitter sneer. "She's not here anymore, Sally. People always say about a dead friend, 'Oh, it feels as if she's right here with us.' But guess what? It doesn't feel that way. It feels like a great big empty hole in my life. I swear to God if it weren't for Jaz and the twins I wouldn't be able to breathe, because one-fourth of me is gone, and it's hard to take a breath when you've only got seventy-five percent of your lungs."

Sally felt the tears encroach. She wanted to refute Dawn's words, but could not.

"You want to know who could have gone in there and saved Crespin? Huh? Do you want to know?" Dawn tugged her hand free and furiously worked the zipper on the little fanny pack she sometimes wore in lieu of a purse. Her fingers tripped over the contents, but then she found the manly wallet she used and flipped it open, revealing a photograph that caused Sally to lose the fight: the first tear slid down her cheek.

"Please put that away," Sally said.

"These women." Dawn held the wallet higher, so that the picture was clearly visible in the red light. "These women, these girls, they could go in there to Presper's hideout and kick his ass. Do either of you doubt that they could?"

Anne closed her eyes.

"Well?"

Sally stared at the picture. Four young women stood side by side. They wore formal dresses made of taffeta, sequins, and lace. Their hair had been permed and perfectly arranged, falling in delicate ringlets down their necks. They were adorned with their mothers' jewelry and the corsages their dates had bought for them. Their arms were tan and their smiles exquisite.

"Senior prom," Dawn said needlessly. "Do you see the power there?"

Sally wet her lips. "I do."

"Do you see all the years, all the energy, all the victories, all the broken hearts, slumber parties, pep rallies, whispered secrets . . . all the connections?"

"The soulstrings," Anne said, opening her eyes.

"Yeah. The soulstrings. Do you see the bond here, wrapped around these chicks like . . . like *goddamn skin?* Can you feel it?"

Sally didn't want to move her eyes from those four perfect faces. "I feel it."

"But not as much as you used to, huh?"

"No. Not as much."

"Why not? I'll tell you why." She snapped the wallet closed, causing Sally to blink at the gunshot sound. "Because the skin's come undone, that's why. Part of our body got chopped off. And without that part, maybe we'll go in there to confront Presper and end up on the receiving end of a whole lot of hurt. Personally I like our chances with your dreamboat Leigh Surry and a whole platoon of Border Patrolmen. I say get on the horn and dial C for cavalry."

Sally absorbed all of this without rebuttal. Dawn was right. They were less than they used to be, and with that subtraction had gone much of their will to stand up for themselves. But now there was something new between them. Wasn't there?

"Believe me, Dawn," she said, letting the words come out unconsidered, "I know that she's gone. No one feels her absence more acutely than I. You're right when you say that all of that good stuff we used to have between us isn't so strong anymore, not with one of us missing. But you know what? I've got something else now. Something I didn't have back then. Something I didn't even have last week. I found this thing because you lost a bet with Jaz. And for this I owe you everything."

Dawn opened her mouth to speak—

"Hush," Sally told her. "There's no need to argue be-

378

cause I'm either going with the two of you or I'm going alone. Anne, what's the Latin word for freedom?"

"Uh, *libertatis*, I think."

"Good word. *Libertatis* and *hózh'q*. The first two words in my new private language. You know, I used to see you two just like I saw the moon. It's not really the moon we're looking at, right? It's the moon of the past. Isn't that what you said, Annie?"

"Yes."

"I'd look at us like that, not as we are today but how we were back then. I guess I was so fond of those times that they blocked my vision of the present, like an eclipse or something. I'm not sure what the me of the past would've done in a situation like this. I'm not who I was back then. But right now, tonight, I'm the me that's going to find the location of that metalworks and save a man's life."

Dawn looked down. She held the folded wallet in both hands, as if to keep it shut.

"I'm going now," Sally said. "I'm getting in the car and having that handsome chauffeur drive me someplace I can ask for directions. Come or stay. It's your life." She headed for the car.

"I didn't lose the bet," Dawn said.

Sally stopped, turned. "What?"

"The wager with Jaz. You said I lost. Well, you should know that's not exactly true."

"Meaning what?"

"I never intended to win. The plan all along was to fail. I wanted us to have a band. I thought it'd be fun."

Sally rolled that through the conduits of her mind. "Can you see my face?"

"You know I can't."

"Good. So you can't see me smiling." She gave herself

up to the feeling, letting the smile seep like groundwater down to her roots. She backhanded the tear from her chin. "I'm glad you're a sneak and you lost on purpose. I guess I owe you for that, more than you know. And I'm also glad you've decided to stick around and keep breathing, despite the fact that all three of us are a little short on lung power. But right now, I'd really feel a lot better if you both got in the car, because you know there's no way I'm going to do this without you."

She got in, shut the door.

Seconds later, two doors slammed behind her.

"Stubborn bitch, isn't she?" Dawn said.

"The stubbornest," Anne agreed.

Sally smiled to herself and sent them both a mental thank-you.

Behind the wheel, Dakota was trying his best to look unafraid.

"Do you know your way around this town?" Sally asked him.

"I've only been a few times. We used to come as a class to visit the observatory."

"So in other words, you're as lost as we are. Think you can find Main Street or whatever it's called around here?"

"Eventually."

"Good. We need to ask someone where to find Presper's metalworks. Everyone be on the lookout for a convenience store. Now let's go, preferably as fast as we can."

Dawn spoke up from the backseat. "Hey, as long as we're going to go through with this ill-fated enterprise, there's something I've always wanted to say."

No one invited her to say it, whatever it might be.

"Fine. I'll say it anyway. Dakota?" She cleared her throat. "Put the pedal to the metal."

Dakota was, at heart, still very much a boy, and didn't hesitate to oblige. He dropped the car into gear and crushed the accelerator to the floor.

The kid behind the counter had a lazy eye.

Sally made it a point not to follow the damn thing as it strayed off course and pointed at the potato-chip rack beside her. The name on his plastic tag said *STEVIO*.

"There's supposedly a metalworking facility here in town. Do you know of it?"

Stevio stroked the sparse hairs on his chin that approximated a goatee. "You must mean the old gym."

"Pardon?"

"Part of the old school. Back in the day, you know, Maxon had a high school. But that was, like, you know, forty years ago or something. Most of the schools in the county have consolidated. School auditorium and stuff got torn down before I was born. But the gym's still there."

"And now it's a metalworks? Is that what you're telling me?"

"Somebody bought it is all I know. Now it's a lab or something where they study mines or history or rocks and crap like that."

"How do I find it?"

Stevio gave her directions.

"Thanks. Have a nice night." She made for the door.

"Hey, aren't you famous or something?"

Sally stopped, looked back. "Or something." She stepped out into the night.

Back in the car, she relayed the route to Dakota, then listened to Dawn conclude a phone conversation with her husband. In the space of two minutes, Dawn said *Don't worry* no less than seven times. Sally counted.

"Jaz is sewn up and doing fine," Dawn said after hanging up. "Mad as a hornet with a bruised stinger, but fine."

"And Alex?"

"Endlessly patient, praise the Lord."

"Anne, weren't you wearing a dress the last time I looked?"

Anne poked the backpack beside her. "I thought Barry and I might stay at the observatory tonight. Watching the stars, you know. I brought a change of clothes. But romance wasn't reborn."

"I'm sorry."

"Don't be. Let's just get moving, okay?"

The old gymnasium stood on the edge of the city. Dakota pulled up half a block away and shut off the engine. When he doused the headlights, darkness enveloped them.

"God, I hate this town," Dawn said.

"Are we certain this is the place?" Anne asked.

Sally stared at the line that delineated the roof, a black shape that was a few shades darker than the sky. Like the rest of Maxon, these grounds were bereft of the security lamps that serviced normal cities. All she could see was a formless hulk broken by a few narrow yellow lines that she knew to be windows covered with heavy shades.

Anne said, "Anything could be out there and we wouldn't even know it. Every member of the Partisans could be standing less than a hundred yards away, and we couldn't see them until it was too late."

"We'll be okay," Sally said, and was surprised to hear the sincerity in her own voice. "Our eyes will adjust in a few minutes. There's plenty of starlight. You'll be able to see."

"Speak for yourself, sister," Dawn growled.

"Dawny, this is no time to be belligerent."

"Sue me."

They sat without speaking, eyes never leaving the building they could barely see.

When she knew they could wait no longer, Sally said, "Dak?"

"Yeah?"

"You're our backup."

"I am?"

"We're going to go in there now. If you don't see us again within twenty minutes, come get us."

"Come get you how?"

"I don't know." Her voice had taken on a dreamy quality. "Drive the car through the wall, I suppose. You're an inventive fellow. You'll think of something."

Dakota put his hand back on the wheel and grabbed it hard. "Shit."

Sally opened her door. "All ashore who's going ashore."

Both back doors opened. Anne and Dawn got out. Anne wore her backpack. Dawn worked her way around the back of the car, then found Anne's elbow and held on.

Sally surveyed the metalworks again. Already her vision had altered and the structure had taken on new dimensions. It now had length and height, and both measurements were considerable. A chain-link fence encircled the property. The gate was rolled back, permitting access to a presumed entryway that remained obscured in shadow.

"You know what this moment is?" Dawn asked.

"No," Sally said. "What is it?"

"Where the rubber meets the road."

Finding not a single ounce of comfort in this statement, Sally led them to the gate.

Chapter Twenty-nine

Inside: voices.

Dawn heard them, even if Sally and Anne did not. She attributed her keen sense of hearing to her nyctalopia; when one sense failed, they claimed that others expanded to pick up the slack. She knew that Sally had heard nothing, because the woman never slowed her advance, just kept on truckin'. Anne followed her, and since Dawn's fingers were hooked into the back pocket of Anne's jeans, then Dawn had little choice but to—

"Tug," she whispered, and did just that.

Anne stopped abruptly.

"Someone's in there," Dawn said, keeping her voice as low as she could.

She couldn't see Anne's reaction. Hell, she couldn't see anything at all, save a few random yellow ribbons wavering in the ocean-dark depths. She assumed these infrequent stripes of color marked where light leaked from windows. "Tell Sally to wait up."

Anne's voice came out of the darkness: "She's already gone. Come on."

Anne took off again, dragging Dawn behind her like a pet on a leash.

Dawn tried to count her steps, if only as a way to make

sense of the world. Simultaneously she forced herself not to think about all the things that could go wrong in the next few minutes. Someone could end up hurt. Or maimed or broken or worse. Though old Sal seemed to be oozing confidence these days, Dawn could hardly muster up a decent bravado. She'd always nurtured in her heart a beloved cowardice, which is why it always felt so good to practice even mediocre bravery. With one exception, the whole Radio thing was more gutsy than anything else she'd ever done.

The exception being that day at the mine.

Something changed. Dawn found herself against a smooth stone wall. The wall was dry and cold, having already released its heat to the empty desert air. She felt and smelled her friends on either side of her. Judging by their proximity and the general feeling of enclosure, Dawn guessed they'd worked their way to the building's entrance, which was likely set into a deep recess in the wall.

She located Sally, grabbed her, and said into her ear: "There's people talking in there."

Sally held still and listened.

"They're not right behind the door," Dawn clarified. "Actually I can't hear 'em so well anymore. They must be moving around. And can't you hear that grating noise? What is that? Sounds like a big piece of metal being dragged across the floor."

Dawn couldn't place the sound. She was thankful for the diversion, however, because it distracted her from the tossing sea that was her stomach. She wanted to be sick.

Sally's voice in her ear: "I'm opening the door."

Dawn almost said, *Don't.* She wanted to make a wisecrack about leaving. *Let's just make like a shepherd and get the flock out of here, eh Sal?* But she kept her mouth shut.

The next noise she heard was the door.

The portal wasn't locked, but came open without resistance. Dawn expected welcome light to spill from the opening, but nothing changed. She listened as the heavy door drew back on what sounded like a pneumatic arm. The space beyond the door, whatever it might have held, was just as dark as the space outside.

Now it was Anne's voice, an inch from her face: "A hallway. Runs straight ahead. About twenty feet in or so, there's an intersection. Passages to the left and right."

"That's it?"

Anne didn't reply. She started walking.

Dawn resisted the urge to scream. Her friends had gone off the deep end, and they were taking her down with them. They had every right to do so, of course, according to an unspoken pact the four of them had made long ago. Keeping her fingers tucked into Anne's pocket, she got moving again. She found it absurd that she was trying to walk on her toes. Did people actually tiptoe when sneaking up on someone in real life? She supposed they did.

She brushed the door as she passed it. She let the fingers of her free hand graze the wood, as if to confirm her plight. *Let's make like pantyhose and run.*

They stopped just inside the door.

Anne dropped to a crouch, so Dawn had little choice but to follow suit. The three of them formed a mini huddle. Sally said, "We need to find where they're holding him. I'll check the left hall. Anne, you have the right. Dawn, stay put."

"Wait a second." Though Dawn's voice never rose above a whisper, her words were spiked with urgency. "Doesn't anyone have a plan around here? Or are we just going to run around like heads with our chickens cut off?"

"We're going to surprise them," Sally said. "Catch them

off guard. Hopefully find Crespin."

"Then what? Demand that they let him go? You think they'll just agree to let us walk away?"

"These men aren't psychopaths, Dawn. They're just doing what they think is right for their country. For the most part, I imagine that most of them are honest, hard-working blue-collar Joes. Stop making mountains—"

"Out of molehills, yeah, I know. Fine. Go. But don't leave me here for long or I'll start singing 'America the Beautiful' as loudly as I can. And you've heard my singing voice."

Sally touched her on the shoulder, and then left her there. Anne also slipped away into the darkness, and before she could say another word, Dawn was alone.

"Terrific," she muttered.

She lowered herself from her crouch the rest of the way to the floor. She drew her knees against her chest, then touched the floor. She traced the lines around the tile squares. The hallway smelled of pine-scented cleaning agents, but also of engine oil and what might have been the tang of hot metal. She turned her head, hoping for a glimmer, but there was nothing.

She imagined the hallway to be lined with glass cases filled with artifacts from Navajo history and certain rock specimens removed from local quarries. Hadn't Sally said that Presper collected archaeological relics? So those glass-walled cabinets were stocked with crude arrowheads and musty potsherds. Pretty tame stuff. Completely harmless.

"See there?" she said to herself. "Nothing to worry about. Guy's just a good ol' boy who digs up peace pipes and occasionally beats up an illegal alien or two. No reason to get my panties in a wad."

She waited two minutes, and no one returned.

Deep in the building, the grating noise came again. Deeper still, a man laughed. The sound carried through the dark corridors, and then dissipated, like smoke on the wind.

Dawn rocked back and forth, back and forth, blind eyes open wide.

Anne took the passage on the right.

Enough light emanated from the end of the hall that she had little trouble finding her way. On either side of her, the walls were covered in panoramic paintings of Southwestern vistas. The building may have once been a school gymnasium, but it had now apparently been completely transformed into a museum of sorts. Pedestals were placed every five feet or so, each bearing a remnant of a past age. In the dark it was hard to make out any particulars, but Anne noticed an army revolver and what might have been some Indian beadwork. She had little respect for the U.S. military of that era. In 1863 men like Kit Carson and Farrington Shatz rounded up over 8,000 natives and packed them off to die of starvation on an infertile reservation in New Mexico.

Get over it, Kobayashi, she told herself, using Dawn's voice because it sounded like something Dawn would say. *Eyes to the front of the classroom.*

She kept moving. A pair of doors stood at the end of the hall. A considerable pool of light lay on the floor, the result of an inch-high gap between the tiles and the bottom of the doors.

She heard the sound.

Something was moving, or sliding, or being pulled. And there were also voices.

Anne slowed, but never stopped completely. At any moment the doors would spill open and whoever was in there would emerge, and they would see her, and they would raise the proverbial hue and cry. And what would Anne do to stop them?

Well?

She knew the answer to that question was nothing. She had no options but to scream and run. Here she was, on her way to taking a doctoral degree, and all that really mattered after all that schooling and all those student loans was the ability to scream and run. When was the last time she'd been this apprehensive? No, scratch that. Apprehensive wasn't quite the proper word.

The proper word was *afraid.*

She reached the end of the hall. As silently as she could, she sank down to one knee and put her eye to the slit between the doors. She stared with one eye as if through a strange telescope. It took her a few seconds to make sense of what she saw.

When she realized what was going on in there, she recoiled.

Instinct nearly got the best of her, and she almost yelled in outrage. Her sudden fury surprised her, and for the moment it overtook fear as the motive force in her heart. She thought a dozen invectives at once—*Those bastards!*—but managed to maintain her silence as she slid the backpack from her shoulder. Though she'd thrown her phones away before cracking open the wine bottle at the observatory, Sally had rescued them and shoved one into a pouch on the front of the pack. Anne worked the phone with her neatly manicured fingers, typing out a quick text message and for once in her life not giving a rat's ass about the spelling. She pushed the button to send the digital note, returned the phone to her bag—

She saw the knife, and her hand stalled.

It was the knife she'd bought in Mexico, the one with the beautiful bone handle that was sold as mountain lion but suspected as being cow. She'd slipped it into the webbing on the side of the backpack, and there it had remained.

This knife, it will help you well.

Thus had spoken the old man in the village. When Anne had purchased it, she'd have never guessed that its ultimate use would not be as a kitchen utensil, but as a weapon.

Slipping the knife free, she got the feel of it in her hand, then returned her eye to the spy hole between the doors and waited for her friends.

Sally took the passage on the left.

She became very aware of her shoes. Every movement caused the plastic cleats on her soles to make noises that sounded like cannon fire there in the otherwise quiet hallway. Far behind her, she heard some kind of metallic sliding, but that was Anne's problem now. Her own end of the passage was silent. Fifty feet in front of her stood what appeared to be an office door. She couldn't be sure, but she thought the oversized maps on the corridor walls represented geological stuff—local landforms, tectonic activity, mineralogy—all the kind of thing that bored her in high school and continued to bore her today. The only interest she'd ever had in rock was the kind that went with roll.

She moved swiftly. The door was ajar. She glanced inside.

The room beyond was a spacious office. A brass lamp on one of the two desks provided sufficient light to see everything. The floor was carpeted and the walls were covered in certificates and charts and geothermal imagery. A wrought-iron image of Kokopelli, flute-playing fertility god, stood like a strange sentinel in the corner. Another door exited the office on the far side.

Snick-snick-snick.

Sally hadn't heard this sound earlier because it had been masked by her own footfalls. But now her eyes were drawn to the corner of the largest desk. She'd seen such knick-knacks before: a metal apparatus consisting of five steel spheres connected to hinged arms. When set into motion, the two outer spheres swung back and forth, colliding with the balls between them in an alternating rhythm and using their own force to perpetuate their cycle. Eventually momentum would decrease and the spheres would come to rest.

The fact that the little machine was still moving meant—what?

That I'm not alone, Sally thought. Yet the idea only minimally disturbed her.

She advanced deeper into the office, heading toward the door on the far side. Perhaps they were holding Crespin in one of these rooms. She hoped to find him tied up in a closet somewhere. Her fear was that they'd already taken him into the desert. Once there, they would either let him loose and then run him down like a pack of dogs, or simply execute him and give his body as an offering to the sand. She wanted to understand how nationalism could spur men to such acts. She wanted to ask them why.

Snick-snick-snick.

She came to the door, listened, and heard the faint yet unmistakable sound of keystrokes.

Crespin was not here. Unless the typist was sitting next to a bound and gagged captive, which seemed unlikely, then Crespin was being held elsewhere, if indeed he was still on the premises.

Sally was torn. One part of her said step around the

corner, shock the hell out of whoever was at the keyboard, demand answers, threaten to call the cops. The other part counseled retreat. The wings had carried her to a point beyond the reach of her fear. These men were not some lunatic cult that would murder her for trespassing, but saw themselves as honest Americans trying to keep their country clean of infection. So she was no longer afraid of reprisal. The best move, then, would be the one that fortune favored: the bold. She took a step toward the door—

Her phone vibrated at her waist.

Actually it was Anne's phone, the bulky satellite model that she'd salvaged from the trash. Sally glanced down at the unit's tiny screen and saw the indicator for an incoming text message. Thankful that the lush carpeting muffled her steps, she drew away from the door and checked the sender's ID. It was Anne.

The message read, *CRESPN IN CHANS 2 MEN COME NOW!!!*

Sally didn't hesitate. She retraced her steps. Anne had found Crespin. The balls on the desk told her yet again, *snick-snick,* but she paid them no heed as she passed. She supposed that *Crespn in chans* meant that he was chained up, shackled like some kind of animal, which was an injustice so grave that Sally bit down on her teeth in anger. Crespin was kind and clever and—like most Mexicans—put family and home before wages and work, and to treat him like a beast was a contradiction so dreadful that Sally vowed this night would not end until she made someone pay.

"No need to hurry away on my account."

The voice came from behind her. Sally spun around, ready for anything.

Isadore Presper lounged in the doorway.

"Hello, shithead," Sally said. It came out of her mouth of its own accord.

In response to this, Presper did something mildly amazing. He laughed. After a moment he said, "And the last time I spoke to you, Ms. Jasper, I thought we agreed to be friends."

"You kidnapped someone tonight."

Presper indicated one of the leather chairs. "Please, sit. I think we're both in a rather singular predicament here. Let's see if we can't talk our way out of it."

Sally knew she had to leave. Anne needed her. And Dawn had to be warned. But how could Sally make contact with them without revealing them to Presper? She cursed herself for letting him catch her in his office, as if she were some kind of neophyte and bumbling burglar, but at the same time, hadn't she expected and even subliminally looked forward to this encounter?

"You've surprised me by coming here," he admitted, "meeting me on my own ground, so to speak. Surprise me again by taking a seat."

She couldn't stay. She had to do something. Yet doing something meant exposing her friends. Could she somehow send a text message to Anne without being noticed?

With no other choice, she sat down.

"Excellent," Presper said. He seemed honestly pleased with her company. He took a chair and rested his elbows on the desk, like someone eager to reminisce with an old friend.

Sally felt the moments slipping away.

Snick-snick-snick.

Dawn didn't know what the hell to do.

How long had it been? Five minutes? Ten? Felt like an

hour. Felt like time to move the flabby old ass and see what was up.

"Come on, you guys."

Another minute passed.

Dawn put a hand in front of her face, waved it. Nothing. Nada. How was she supposed to find her way around this creepy dump without an escort? Sally's total lack of a plan was now fully qualified to be labeled the Dumbest Idea in the History of Womankind. Someone had grabbed Anne. Another someone had grabbed Sally. Otherwise they would've been back by now, right? So they had to be saved. Yeah, right.

"Dakota."

Okay, there it was, a sensible course of action. Just go outside, walk back to the car in the middle of the goddamn dark, and talk to Dak.

"Did I mention that this whole thing sucks?"

She crawled to the doors and pushed one of them open. The only way she could sense the difference between inside the building and out was because the air felt different on her face. Visually, nothing changed.

Wait. What about the phone?

Both Sally and Anne had a phone with them. And by design they'd set their ring tones to a silent setting. So maybe the wisest thing to do was place a call, on the off chance that the bad guys hadn't already seized their phones and smashed them to bits.

First Dawn got herself fully outside. She felt concrete under her hands, and a few inches away she found a patch of grass. If she stood up and started batting her arms around her head, would Dakota see her and come to her rescue? Or were the shadows so thick that even someone with healthy rods in their peepers wouldn't be able to separate them?

There was only one way to find out. But first, the phone.

She put the phone as close to her eyes as she could, then keyed the power. The meager light from the damn thing amounted to little more than a dim green square, hazy around the edges. Any information that might have appeared inside that square remained illegible. Luckily Dawn had Anne's various numbers programmed into her speed-dialer.

She put it to her ear and waited.

"Any day now, Annie."

It rang and rang without result.

"Pick up the phone, Anne." Eventually she snapped it shut. "Dammit."

If Anne wasn't answering, there were only two explanations: one, she didn't want to answer, and two, she couldn't answer. So either she was choosing to ignore the phone, or she was in trouble.

A light appeared briefly in the dark, an elongated white shape in the void.

"Dak, is that you?"

The light moved again, this time shining directly in her face. She squinted and put her arms in front of her as a kind of shield. "Dakota, lower the flashlight, you're killing me here."

Heavy footsteps approached.

Why wasn't he saying anything? Dawn began to back away, hands still shielding her, a serpent of fear coiling up her spine.

"Dakota?"

The light was like a spear, pinning her to the darkness. An unseen form drew closer.

"Dakota?"

Chapter Thirty

Anne kept her eye to the door and seethed.

The room she spied upon had likely once enclosed the gymnasium's basketball court, being a vast chamber with a high ceiling, supported by bare steel crossbeams. The entire expanse was filled with tables of advanced metallography equipment and arcane scientific supplies. Since learning of Presper and his trade, Anne had done her homework, and she tried to match the pieces of her research to the varied apparatus that formed a maze of machinery in the room. The biggest units were the industrial-sized cleaning tanks. There were also great vats of what she guessed to be compression powders, and multiple rows of polishing suspensions. The worktables were cluttered with cut-off wheels, sanders, soda cans, chisels, pizza boxes, and mounting compounds.

Parked in the center of the floor was a dune-buggy.

Anne had seen that vehicle before, or at least one very similar to it. Ten days ago in the sand, when Juan Doe lay dying only a few feet behind her, she'd gazed upon this same dust-clogged, road-weary vehicle. Isadore Presper had been sitting in the passenger seat.

Crespin was walking toward the front tire.

He wore no shirt. Instead, he wore welts and cuts. The

dark skin of his back was marred with red sores and narrow rivulets of blood. His hair was messy and matted to his scalp. His lips were puffy and bleeding. He grimaced with every step, as if pain were forking through his body as he moved. Worst of all, a heavy chain, long turned brown with grease and dirt, was connected to his right ankle. From there it ran twenty feet to the leg of a cleaning tank.

Crespin fell to his knees beside one of the buggy's front tires—which Anne now noticed was flat. Tools pitched from his arms and rang sharply against the bare concrete floor.

"Careful with those things!" yelled a man in coveralls who sat and watched. "You break something, we're taking it out of your paycheck."

The man's friend laughed.

There were two of them. The one in coveralls was the older of the pair. His gnarled workman's hands held a can of beer. His companion was probably no more than twenty years old, with a blond goatee and an NRA T-shirt. He cradled a long pipe wrench in his lap.

Anne's phone vibrated.

Though reluctant to move for fear she might be overheard, she didn't want to miss a return message; there had to be some reason why Sally hadn't already answered her summons. Anne had yet to return the backpack to her shoulders, so it was simply a matter of grabbing the phone with the hand that wasn't already filled with a finely honed hunting knife.

The caller ID read *JOHNSON ALEX AND DAWN*.

Not a text message, but an actual call. Anne couldn't risk it. Her voice might carry to the men in the room beyond, and gone would be that much-lauded element of surprise. Besides, Anne already knew why Dawn was calling and exactly what she'd say. *Where in the sam-hill are you at, Annie-cakes? It's darker than a well-digger's ass in here. Come get me.*

Anne looked back at Crespin.

He was putting his lean body into the act of breaking free the lug nuts from the dune-buggy's wheel. They had pummeled him badly. Despair was etched on his face.

Anne tightened her grip on the knife until her fingers were white.

"After you fix it," the man in the coveralls said, "you're gonna take a ride in it."

"One hell of a ride," the younger man chimed. To his friend he said, "You think maybe we could stop and get some chicken on the way out? I ain't eaten since damn near noon."

Anne came to a conclusion then. She was about to do this alone.

Alone was something she had never done. Always she'd had the others with her, at least for all the important stuff. She had given birth with Sally and Dawn in the room with her. She'd walked across the stage to accept her master's degree with them clapping their hands in the crowd. She'd had the cysts removed from her ovaries while they were within earshot. And those few times when they separated— like when she, Barry, and Trevor had driven up to Pike's Peak for vacation two years ago—the vistas were not as beautiful without the filters of her friends to make them real.

So was she truly about to do this by herself?

She could turn around. Go back. Find Sally. Regroup.

Crespin's hands slipped on the tire iron and rapped painfully on the floor. He made a slight sound, winced, and squeezed his eyes shut.

One of the men grunted.

Anne was never outnumbered. Not when she was standing between the others. She remembered the picture on her mantel, the four of them with their arms around one another, forming a kind of Great Wall of Girlhood that could repel all invaders and weather any storm. But she was outnumbered now.

Without them I will fail, she thought, and then opened the door to see if it were true.

The men looked up.

Anne held the knife behind her back.

Presper laced his fingers in front of him. "You're a dynamic woman, Sally Jasper."

Sally wondered how to play this. She needed to get out of here, find her friends, make Crespin safe, and keep them all from getting stung in the process. But how to extricate herself from this man's steel-trap stare?

"I saw your performance this morning on one of the cable channels. I believe I'm sitting in the presence of a soon-to-be superstar. Have you received any offers yet from record producers? That's all the craze these days, slapping bands together and promoting them to fame and fortune. It's all about marketing, really, don't you think?"

"I'm not here to talk about that."

"I know. You've come for the boy. And for that I thank you."

"Thank me?"

"Yes, for providing me with such an unforeseen diversion." He leaned back in his chair and crossed his arms over his chest. He was dressed much as he'd been the last time Sally had see him, although now his French cuffs were clasped at his wrists with links made of some rich red stone.

"I assist the peacekeepers of this country, Sally. The men and women of the Border Patrol are stretched too thin. National security is the new rallying point. They permit me to lend my efforts to that esteemed cause."

"They permit you? I don't believe that at all. What you're doing is illegal."

"Is it? This country is like no other in the fact that it was founded on the concept of the frontier. Almost by definition, the frontier must outdistance the legal system. Settlers come first, carrying along their own fledgling and ragtag democracy, then the marshals and judges and jails show up later. The frontier still exists today. It's out there in the sand, beyond the reach of our magistrates. And until the judiciary system is able to provide the proper guardianship, it's up to the settlers to do what we can."

"And you're one of those settlers."

"In a manner of speaking, yes. I'm assisting in the capture of wanted men. It's my privilege as a responsible citizen to do so."

"Capturing is one thing. But you're also beating the poor people to death."

"Now, Sally, I've never murdered anyone."

Sally felt the ire turning in her. She wanted nothing more than to lean across the desk and slap this arrogant monster. The last of her fear dried up in the high Fahrenheit of her anger. "Maybe you never dealt the death blow, maybe you never pulled the trigger, but you're well aware of the fact that Mexican men and women have died because of you. You've tortured them and left them in the desert to rot."

Presper leaned forward again, nothing but a maddening sincerity in his eyes. "Do you realize that in a matter of years, Spanish will be the primary language in almost half of the United States?"

"So what? Is that supposed to affect the quality of my life?"

"This country is being diluted."

"Yeah, I'm sure the Navajos would agree with you a hundred percent. Why? Because the Navajo tongue is no longer the primary language spoken by the tribe. The primary language is English. But white people moved in, and times changed. And now Mexicans are moving in. And times are changing."

"This is different."

"Sure it is." Sally was in no mood to debate. This man's ideology was so much a part of his identity that she might as well be trying to convince him to change his name. He believed that his actions were safeguarding his fellow Americans. Others like him donned white hoods and burned crosses in people's yards. He was the same breed of animal, to be pitied but not taken seriously. "I came here to get Crespin Onofre y Ramos, who is only half your age but twice the man. You can either give him to me, or I'm taking him."

She stood up.

Presper studied her. The look on his face was that of a teacher trying to comprehend the actions of a recalcitrant student. In the soft light of the desk lamp, the piece of hematite at his throat was as black as a chunk of coal.

Snick-snick—

Sally reached down and stopped the stupid clapping balls. "Where is he?" Even as she stood there, she was trying to send telepathy to the others: *I'm coming! Don't do anything drastic without me.*

"Help me understand why you're assisting aliens across the border."

"You're fighting against them. Someone's got to fight *for* them."

To her surprise, Presper acceded the point. "Fair enough. You and I competing for the well-being of these parasites does sound somewhat interesting. Actually, I find the idea intriguing."

"Actually, go to hell."

Presper rose to his feet, stripping Sally of her momentary height advantage. Now she was forced to look up at him. "I suppose it's only fair that I permit you to have the boy. After all, you did me such a favor, and I've never been one to ignore a rightful debt."

Sally tried to guess where he was going with this, but her mind was cluttered with thoughts of Anne and Dawn and Jazmyn and so much more, and this additional riddle was one too many to consider. "What are you talking about?"

"I'm talking about that runner you assassinated on the highway."

Sally leaned forward to steady herself against the desk.

"You hit him so hard that, by the time I arrived, there was nothing to see but an overturned truck with a radiator bearing the impression of a man's body."

Sally saw Juan Doe as he lay mangled on the shoulder of the road. She remembered thinking that the globs of blood on his mustache reminded her of red jellybeans.

"You killed him graveyard dead, Sally. And for this I owe you."

A wave of nausea rippled through Sally's stomach. She wanted so very much to sit down, but she wouldn't allow herself the luxury. All along she'd assumed that Presper and his gang were too far away to witness any details of the accident. All along she'd been wrong.

"So I suppose it's only sportsmanlike to do you a service in return. Then we can begin our game with an even score."

"Our game? Can't you see?" Sally's voice was not as firm

as she would have liked. "I don't want to play any game with you. I don't want to spend my life rescuing one immigrant for every one that you destroy." She took a stabilizing breath. "If you want me to feel miserable for running into that man, then I'm sorry to disappoint you, but you're too late. I've been seeing him in my dreams ever since it happened. Now . . . maybe I'd be more willing to discuss this calmly with you if you hadn't made that childish threat with my daughter's guitar pick. But as things stand, I think that after tonight I will never speak to you again. Where's Crespin?"

Presper rolled his tongue around inside his cheek. "I apologize for that. The stunt at your window, I mean. It was purely theatrics, I assure you. You know I would never even consider harming any innocent American, much less a teenage girl."

"Goddammit, just tell me what you've done with—"

Someone screamed.

The sound silenced them both. They turned their heads, tracking the direction of the noise. Though distorted by the walls of the building, the cry was distinctly that of a woman.

Presper looked at her sharply. "You didn't come alone, I see."

Sally spun around and ran down the hall.

"Dakota? Say something, please."

The flashlight never left her face. Its candle-power was so intense that Dawn's vision became a nova of alternating white and black pulses. She could already feel the headache encroaching, and that was bad.

And she knew, even worse, that this was not Dakota.

"Hey, I'm just lost—okay?—and I'm not very good at night, you know what I'm saying? Shit, I can't see a thing.

You know how bad my night vision is? My night vision is so bad that I have to turn on the light to see if it's dark. Funny, huh? What I'm trying to say is, I didn't mean to trespass, it's just that I got sort of turned around, I mean my friend and I, we got turned around, lost is what I'm talking about. My friend, see, he's right over there in the car. Hey, Dakota! Dak, we have a little problem here!"

"Shut up."

Dawn began to shake. The trembling started in her knees. "Listen, mister, whoever you are . . .'"

The light fell away. Rapid colors flew in front of her eyes.

Where, where, *where* was Dakota? Dawn blinked and tried to think of something heroic to do, something Sallyesque, but she was just a housewife and barmaid and drummer, and not exceptionally gifted at any of those pursuits, and matters didn't get any better when she noticed his gun.

The flashlight, now pointed at the ground, offered sufficient illumination to empower her piss-poor eyesight, and what she saw was a man in uniform with a hat on his head and a gold badge on his breast and a holster on his belt.

"Are you a cop?"

"Come on, lady. Let's you and me go inside and make some introductions."

"Thanks anyway, but I'll pass. Maybe next time."

She saw his shape move toward her, the flashlight swirling at his feet.

She took a step backward. "Really, we don't need to go inside—do we?—we can just go on over to my friend in the car, have our talk over there. Okay? How does that sound?"

His hand enclosed her wrist. She never saw it coming, only felt his fingers lock tightly around her arm.

Then Dawn did something she hadn't done in over twenty years: she screamed in terror.

Anne got only a few feet into the room before the men stood up.

Her stratagem was simple. Move fast. Talk quickly. Keep them off balance.

Stab only if necessary.

She slipped the bare knife blade into her back pocket, thinking that she'd be lucky not to slice open her jeans and lacerate her ass. Though reluctant to let go of the smooth bone handle, she released the weapon so that the men would assume she was unarmed—an assumption that would cost them dearly if they assaulted her.

Her voice rang out: "Good evening, gentlemen." She knew that *gentlemen* was no fitting appellation for these two; *scumbags* was more apropos. "I was wondering if I could have a moment of your time."

The men looked first at each other and then at her.

Anne kept her eyes stitched to them, pointedly not giving Crespin even a glance. In her peripheral vision she saw that he'd stopped working altogether and was gaping at her, his back against the deflated tire.

"I'm sorry if I interrupted your work," she went on, "but this will only take a minute."

Clearly they were flummoxed. The sudden appearance of this not-bad-looking blonde with Asian eyes, right in the middle of another monotonous night of bullying abductees, was obviously an aberration for which they were unprepared.

Anne became aware of the room in a kind of subconscious way. The ceiling was crisscrossed with girders and ringed with dirty windows far too high to see through.

Which meant that she couldn't see Dakota or signal him for help. Empty sockets in the cinder-block walls were evidence that rows of bleachers had once been anchored there.

The man in coveralls said, "Lady?"

Anne held his gaze and advanced.

"Lady, what are you doing here?"

"I've come for him." She jerked her thumb in Crespin's direction and tried to sound nonchalant, as if she had every right to sashay in here and relieve them of their sport. "Do be a dear and give me a hand, will you?"

She couldn't believe her own bluster. Her blood was streaming through her veins and she had to fight to keep her breath under control, but her steps kept coming. And most impossible of all was the fact that she was alone. If she had done anything noteworthy over the last two weeks it wasn't her keyboard solo on live TV or the phone interview she'd given on National Public Radio this afternoon. It was walking into this den of cutthroats unflanked by her guardian angels.

"Uh, I don't think you should be here." He didn't seem to know what to do with his hands. They made vague swirling motions in front of him. "Did somebody let you in?"

"Never mind then," Anne said, veering suddenly toward Crespin. "I'll just do it myself."

The younger one blurted, "Jesus, Paul, she's settin' him loose!"

"I see that, goddammit." He pinched the bridge of his nose, apparently reached some sort of decision, then came toward her. "Look, lady, I don't mean to be rude or nothing, but nobody told us a thing about you coming and taking him away."

As Anne knelt before Crespin, she met his eyes for an instant.

She'd expected fear. Instead she saw only relief. Blood had congealed on his lips.

She wished she had the *élan* to wink at him, but it was all she could do to keep her hands from shaking as she set them on the chain. She kept her back turned away from the man called Paul, so that he couldn't see the bit of mountain-lion bone jutting up from her pocket.

"Hey, you deaf or something?" Paul said loudly, closing in on her fast, his lackey at his heels. "I'm talking to you. You get away from him, you hear?"

"Yes, I roger that, Paul. Sorry, but I have to ignore you." Thank God the chain wasn't fastened with a padlock. A thick steel hook imprinted with the phrase *DROP FORGED* had been inserted through one of the links, forming a loop around Crespin's ankle. The chain was even heavier than it looked. Trying to keep one eye on Paul and the other on the task at hand, Anne tugged hard—and the hook came free.

Anne shot to her feet. Standing beside Crespin, she faced the two men, who had stopped no more than five feet away. The younger one still held a pipe wrench.

"You shouldn't have done that," Paul said.

"You may be right," Anne concurred.

Paul kept his eyes on her even as he turned his head and spit a tight wad of saliva and tobacco juice onto the floor.

"Paul, what're we gonna do with her?"

"Tie her up, I guess. Then tell the boss."

Anne had expected no less. She felt the heat of Crespin's arm against her and knew that she was not going to be tied up, not tonight, not by these Cro-Magnons with prejudice like tumors in their brains. She indicated the wide scrolling garage door. "We're going outside now. It would be best if you didn't try to inhibit us." She looked at Crespin. *"Vamos, amigo."*

Paul came toward her. "You ain't going nowhere."

Anne and Crespin began to move.

Paul took a step and cut them off. "I said"—he pointed for his friend to block the door—"that you two ain't leaving, not until I talk to the boss and find out what the hell's going down here and what I'm supposed to do about it."

Anne, having completely forgotten who she was, kept going, clutching Crespin's arm.

Paul's face reddened. "Lady, I don't want to have to hurt—"

His words were overrun with the sound of a woman's scream.

It came from outside.

Dawn.

All at once Anne's tenuous plan collapsed. Paul was right in front of her and Dawn was *in extremis* and the punk with the pipe wrench was moving in.

With a growl, Paul lunged at her.

Anne reached for the knife.

But it was gone.

Chapter Thirty-one

Jeffrey's shoes propelled her.

Sally ran down the hall to the intersection. In front of her—the direction that Anne had gone—light spilled from an open door. Anne was not there.

Presper came at a jog behind her.

Sally veered right, toward the front of the building, where she'd left Dawn huddled in the darkness.

No Dawn.

Sally struck both hands against the door's push-bar and burst out into the night, cleats clattering against the concrete.

Presper chased her, faster now.

Sally didn't slow down, couldn't slow down, but ran on with abandon, knowing only that Dawn was in trouble. Her double vision returned, so that she was seeing another place and responding to another of Dawn's cries. For a moment the two realities converged—*There's a man down there! Run! Goddammit, run!*—and Sally stalled.

Presper caught up, stopped beside her, looked around. "I see no one."

They'd left Dakota parked at the curb. Normally Sally wouldn't have been able to see inside the car, but the driver's door was open and the dome light was on. Dakota was gone.

"What's going on?" Sally said, more to herself than to Presper. She hated the fact that he was standing right here next to her. She hated not knowing what happened to Dakota. She hated assorted other things, and quickly decided that hate was clogging too many of her thoughts.

"There." Presper pointed.

Dim human forms disappeared around the far corner of the building.

Sally took off.

The intended treasure of Jeffery's buried *Schatz* had been the autographed baseball, an item of monetary worth, something to be kept in a glass case on your bookshelf. But the shoes were the true plunder. They were a size too large and rubbed hotly against Sally's heels with every stride, but they got her around the metalworks in seconds.

She saw the gun and stopped just short of colliding with the man who held it.

A big garage-style door had begun to ratchet upwards, filling the night with an angry din and causing a plane of light to grow at Sally's feet. Dawn faced the opening door, and so did Dakota, and behind them was a man with a pistol at their backs.

"Manny Delano," Sally said.

The Border Patrolman jerked around at the unexpected sound of her voice.

Caught up in her own wingspan, Sally attacked.

Anne reached for the knife, but Crespin had already grabbed it.

He swung it in a short arc. The blade whipped in front of Paul's hand.

At first Anne thought that Crespin had missed, that he was attempting only to drive the man back. But a moment later a red line appeared on Paul's palm, perfectly straight from his little finger to his thumb. Bright blood ran from the wound.

He howled and recoiled.

Anne's mind went offline for the first time in her life. She didn't take time to consider her actions or give respect to her fear. She picked up the fallen tire iron and swung the shit out of it.

The kid got his pipe wrench up and blocked the oncoming blow. The harsh sound of metal-on-metal rang out. He staggered backwards, clutching the wrench in both hands.

Anne's arm buzzed painfully with the force of vibration.

Completely nonplussed, the kid looked at the older man for direction.

Blood seeped between Paul's clenched fingers. He cupped his fist in his other hand, and his eyes were vicious. "For Chrissakes, kill the bitch!"

The kid moved as if to engage in battle, but the sight of both the knife and the tire iron discouraged him. Anne took advantage of his vacillation, and pressed her advantage. In breathless Spanish she said, "Move to the door, fast, but don't take your eyes off them."

Crespin gave a brisk nod, and then Anne advanced, walking sideways and not feeling foolish at all for holding a tire iron like a club and readying herself to use it. This was a primitive version of herself, a person she didn't know, but nevertheless one she was damn glad to become.

Paul shouted, "Get your punk ass moving and do something!" He shoved the kid in the back and then snatched a phone from a workbench and used it like a two-way radio. "Boss, the shit's really hittin' the fan in here. Copy that?"

411

The pipe wrench whistled through the air.

Crespin ducked. His natural agility saved him, but it left him out of position for a riposte.

Anne saw the opening and went for it. Making a feral noise in the back of her throat, she brought the tire iron down as hard as she could on the kid's forearm.

There came a noise like a pencil being snapped in half.

The kid opened his mouth but no sound emerged. The wrench dropped from his limp grasp.

Anne kept moving, and Crespin followed.

Now the kid found the air to yell. By the shrill agony of that cry, Anne assumed his arm was broken.

Holding his bloody fist near his chest and muttering epithets, Paul stepped over the kid and picked up the fallen weapon. "Useless, that's what you are. Goddamn useless." He set his stare on Anne and gave the wrench a wicked test swing. "You want to dance, sister? Then let's you and me get it on."

Anne had no intention of fighting him. She'd spotted the control box that activated the scrolling door and advanced on it as rapidly as she could while maintaining her defensive stance.

Even before she got there, the door began to rise. Someone on the other side had activated it.

The first thing she saw as the door rolled upwards was a pair of navy blue Ropers.

Dawn. Thank God.

She also recognized Dakota's worn footwear, but there was a third set, black workboots with a bright sheen, that snuffed her small candle of hope.

From beyond the door she heard a familiar voice say, "Manny Delano," and hope returned.

Paul rushed her, the wrench flashing silver in the air.

412

★ ★ ★ ★ ★

Dawn saw it all as one sees the scenery from a moving train.

That's how the images appeared to her in the insufficient light, blurs of color bearing only intermittent shapes that made sense. Dakota had been rousted from the car by this same guy who now had his gun on Dawn. There wasn't any time to consider this, however, because Sally had appeared from that same place that Juan Doe had lurked before materializing on the highway—nowhere. The cop or immigration officer or whatever the hell he was started to turn around, but then one of the blurs happened. Did Sally go for the gun? And who was that behind her?

At the same time, the door had reached a height of about six feet, and there was Anne, her hair dyed that crazy blond. There were other people in the room with her, and they were all moving.

It was too much. Dawn yearned to pass out and let it happen without her.

No such luck.

Her instinct was to go to the light. Maybe if she lowered her head and charged into the room with Anne, she could get her bearings and lend her efforts to the team instead of just standing here with her dick in the dirt. That's what the men called it. Standing there with your dick in the dirt. It was a male phrase only slightly less poetic than balls to the wall. And that's where Dawn found herself, balls to the wall.

Screw the light. Dawn tackled the cop.

Sally got her hands around the pistol just as it went off.

The shot was louder than she anticipated. Having never fired a gun nor been in the vicinity when one was dis-

413

charged, she wasn't prepared for the obtrusiveness of the sound, nor for the brightness of the muzzle flash and the shudder of recoil in her wrist.

The bullet punched into the ground at Delano's feet.

It was hard even to contemplate the existence of a gun in her world, and now she found herself fighting for control of one.

Hands clasped her upper arms.

Presper. He was ordering everyone to stop.

Delano was too strong. He tore the gun away with a grunt.

And then Dawn slammed into him. The two of them went down, Dawn on top, Delano hitting face-first.

Sally's only thought was of the gun. She tore free of Presper's hold much like she had torn free from earth's gravity while performing before the crowds—it was the same untouchable feeling—and dropped to her knees, pinning Delano's hands to the ground. He fought wildly, swearing, Dawn writhing atop him and striking his face and chest. Presper kept shouting. Sally took the pistol by the hot barrel and ripped it from Delano's fingers.

When she rose to her feet, slick with sweat, her only desire was just to keep on rising, up and up into the clear night. But instead she pointed the gun at Presper.

He held up his hands, palms out. "Wait."

Sally began to pull the trigger.

Anne braced herself for another blow. Twice already Paul had brought the thick wrench down with increasing force, and though Anne had managed to parry both times, her arms were singing with pain and she knew the next assault would blast the tire iron from her grip.

But Paul changed tack in mid-swing.

"Crespin!" Anne warned.

Too late. The wrench turned the knife aside and hurtled into Crespin's jaw.

Crespin dropped as if his legs had turned to putty.

For the small second that Paul's attention was on Crespin, Anne wanted to take the opportunity to turn and run. Her friends were only a few feet away, and together the three of them would surely stand a better chance. But the other Anne, the base and hungry one, still controlled too much of her. She threw the tire iron at Paul.

He batted it away with the wrench. It flew end-over-end and landed with a clatter on a table of metal specimen bowls, knocking them in all directions.

But her throw had only been a diversion. It had bought her a fraction of time, just long enough for her to pounce on the bone-handled knife. This knife, she knew, it would help her well, or so she'd been told, and she gave it a perfunctory swing and was not surprised when Paul took the bait and launched his most brutal salvo yet.

Forced to wield his truncheon in only one hand, Paul couldn't achieve the control he might have otherwise mustered. He swung the wrench at Anne in a sweeping curve, as if he were intent on decapitating her.

It happened quickly. Anne stepped into the attack and then under it. She brought the knife up. The tip of the blade entered Paul's arm at the bend in his elbow. It went half an inch deep. Paul bellowed in pain and reflexively pulled his arm back. This caused the knife to split the skin all the way to his wrist, resulting in a trench of blood.

He screamed.

Anne watched him stumble across the room. He tripped over the chain and went down, both arms folded tightly against his chest.

She tasted a drop of moisture on her lips. She touched it, and her finger came away red. Paul had flung droplets of blood across her face when he flailed backwards. Now he was trying to get to his feet and shouting, "I need an ambulance! Somebody call 911, goddammit, I'm bleeding to death!"

Anne turned away and ran to the melee at the garage door, knife still in hand.

"I said wait."

Sally had already applied pressure to the trigger. She knew nothing about guns, only that this was some kind of automatic and not a revolver. She wondered how much force she could put on the trigger before the gun went off.

"Officer Delano," Presper said. "Unhand that woman immediately."

On the ground, Dawn and Delano became aware of the situation and slowly released each other. Dawn had pulled out a clump of hair and left fingernail divots in his cheek. Delano had backhanded her across the teeth, and her lips had split.

Dawn shoved him. "Get the hell off me, asshole!"

Delano rolled away, and both of them stood up.

Inside the building, a man yelled, "Boss, I need an ambulance here, okay?"

Anne latched onto Dawn, both of them breathing audibly. "God, you're bleeding. Are you okay?"

"Philadelphia, Annie-cakes. I'd rather be there." She spit out a glob of blood.

Sally barely heard them. She had reached a state where murder no longer seemed anathema. She'd been let loose from the mores of the world, and the only things that mattered were lift and altitude and perhaps the occasional sonic boom.

"Do you want to talk about this?" Presper asked, his voice still mostly composed. "Or would you simply like to get down to this nasty business of killing?"

She heard both Dawn and Anne respiring heavily, working to catch their breath.

"Sally?" Presper made a placating gesture. "We have to end this. End it here tonight. One way or the other."

She realized then that Dakota was nowhere to be seen. Apparently he'd run away during the struggle. Smart lad.

"Hey, boss? I'm calling the paramedics!"

"You're calling no one!" Presper returned.

"But I'm bleeding real bad!"

Sally said to Presper, "You can't call anyone, because you can't afford to. Am I right? The police will start asking questions about your operation here, about what you do to people like Crespin, about how this sack of shit Delano here isn't exactly abiding by Border Patrol regulations." She kept the gun trained on him, aiming precisely at the nugget of hematite at his throat, the one that was supposedly a talisman which rendered him invincible. "That about sum it up?"

After a moment, Presper nodded like a chess player acknowledging mate. "Indeed."

The moon caught her eye.

She saw it bright and white over Presper's head. She knew that the only people who'd ever seen the real moon were the men who had walked on it. To everyone else it was the moon of one-point-three seconds ago. Earthlings had to make do with a moon that was just a vision of the past. She and Anne and Dawn were the same way, seeing a second-hand version of themselves, of the girls they used to be.

Until now, that sense of something lost had made Sally incurably sad. But tonight . . .

She raised the gun to the moon and fired.

Everyone started as the first shot echoed through the night. But Sally kept pulling the trigger, one shot after the next in a rapid and deafening succession. Cartridges ejected from the port on the side of the pistol and the stink of cordite filled the air, and Sally kept squeezing, gunning down the moon and what it stood for.

Presper ducked and covered his ears as the bullets passed only feet over his head.

Sally's hand bucked with every shot, but she kept it on target and jerked the trigger.

Anne pulled Dawn close. Dawn rested her head on Anne's. They closed their eyes to ride out Sally's storm.

After a dozen shots, the slide locked open on the empty gun. Smoke snaked from its core.

Presper slowly stood up.

Dawn and Anne opened their eyes.

For several seconds, the night was as silent as the vacuum of space. Sally kept her eyes on the shot-up moon, a fresh calmness permeating her veins. She lowered her hand and let the gun fall to the dirt.

The crickets and cicadas began buzzing again.

Then, from blocks away, a new sound: sirens.

The smile Presper put on his face looked forced. For the first time since Sally had initially encountered him, he appeared ill-at-ease in his cap-toe oxfords. "You've successfully drawn the attention of the local constabulary. Match point to you, it seems."

A car barreled at high speed through the gate.

Everyone turned.

Dawn's car slammed to a stop a few feet away from

them, throwing rocks before its tires. The door flew open
and Dakota leaned out. He hadn't run, as Sally had
thought, but had gone for the car. "Cops are coming! We
gotta get Crespin out of here *now!*"

Anne pulled Dawn back into the building. "Help me,
he's hurt."

While they got Crespin to his feet and ushered him to
the car, Sally looked back at the moon.

Isadore Presper, misjudging the direction of her gaze,
gave her a small salute.

Sally didn't notice, because he was too far below her to
see. Presper and the car and the metalworks—they were
rapidly getting smaller, the landscape turning into a quilt of
colored squares and the oxygen thinning out. The sky was a
map leading every direction at once.

Sally would fly them all.

Epilogue

Tatyana stands barefoot in the culvert and watches the water swirl around her toes.

Her toenails are painted. Last night, when she should've been doing her math homework, she'd borrowed her mom's brightest, reddest polish and spent half an hour with the tiny brush. Now it seems as if ten sparkling rubies are lying under the water.

"Hey, blondie! You coming or what?"

Tatyana looks up. The others are standing in the street, waiting for her. Annie has a bookbag over her shoulder. Dawn is trying to make a farting noise with her underarm. And Sally, she's giving that come on motion with her hand, and since Sally is usually right about things, Tatyana steps out of the culvert and joins her friends. For the first few steps, her feet leave wet prints on the street.

"Don't lose your shoes this time, okay?" Sally says. Tatyana has been holding her shoes in her hands, but now Sally takes them, ties the strings together, and hangs them around Tatyana's neck. "That's for safekeeping. Last time you took them off in Mr. Aker's field and we never found them. Your mom'll kill us if it happens again."

Tatyana nods. "Okay. But sometimes things makes better sense without shoes."

"Whatever. Let's go."

The four of them set out, side by side, walking down the center of the street. Fresh Waters is a town small enough that you can get away with being in the street, even though your parents say you shouldn't. As they walk, Dawn talks about the new boy, Tommy Whats-his-face, and Anne says he's kinda cute and Sally agrees. Tatyana just likes listening to them talk. Maybe one of these days she'll tell them that very thing: "Hey, guys, I just like being around you when you're saying something." But that sounds like a stupid thing to say, so maybe she'll just keep her mouth shut.

"Does anyone know where he lives?" Dawn asks.

"I think his family moved into the place where that old banker guy used to live," Anne says. "You know what I'm talking about? The house on Orchid Street?"

Tatyana knows the house that Annie is talking about. But sometimes Annie loses her. She's so smart, and just knows things. Tatyana probably wouldn't have gotten many decent grades at all if it weren't for Annie helping her out, showing her how to set up a story problem in math, sometimes even doing the homework for her. Tatyana promises that one of these days she's going to make it up to Annie, give her something in return. But what?

"He sits two rows in front of me," Dawn says. "So I can't really see his face most of the time, but I get a real good view of his neck. Can necks be cute? I think necks can be cute."

Tatyana laughs. No one else does. But that's how it goes. Tatyana loves Dawny because that girl cracks her up. Tatyana sometimes feels foolish for laughing so often. None of the other girls just snicker like that for no reason. But she can't help it. Everything just seems so funny most of the time, especially grown-ups, because they waste their days on the dumbest, funniest stuff. Dawny makes fun of adults, and Tatyana giggles every time. If she had paid Dawny a penny every time she'd asked her to tell a joke, then Dawny would have enough money to buy new clothes and her mom wouldn't have to get stuff from the Salvation Army. Or the Starvation Army, as Dawny likes to say. Tatyana would make Dawny rich if she could.

"Okay, we're here," Sally says, slapping her palm against the corner street sign.

Tatyana isn't very fond of this place. Here at the corner of Richmond and Second, everybody has to go her own way. Annie's house is right there, just three doors down. Tatyana lives in the opposite direction at the end of the street. Dawny has to go up two more blocks. Sal must cut through a couple of backyards to get to her place over on Fifth. They have stood on this corner a thousand times and will likely stand on it a thousand more.

"So we're going to the arcade tomorrow, right?" Sally asks.

Dawn fakes a yawn. "It's Saturday tomorrow. I'm sleeping till noon."

"I'm knocking on your window and waking you up," Sally warns her.

"Hey, nobody's allowed to knock on my window but Tommy the new kid. Got it?"

"Tommy the new kid doesn't even know your name."

"Are you kidding? That boy's been dreaming about me ever since he turned around and caught me staring at his neck."

Tatyana smiles.

Sally looks at her. "Arcade okay with you tomorrow?"

Tatyana wants to tell Sal that she's silly. Doesn't she know that anything is okay? If Sal said she needed a partner to go fight ten ax murderers in the middle of a toxic waste dump, Tatyana would be raising her hand. She doesn't know much about fighting ax murderers or how to stay alive in a toxic waste dump, but who cares? Dawny once showed them a trick with a calculator. Enter the numbers 1134, then turn it upside down and make a naughty word. Well, even if Sal were going into that awful place on the upside-down calculator, Tatyana would go with her, because that's just the way it is.

"I'll be there," she says. "Always."

And that is her last wish for the day. To be with Sally always.

"I'm outta here," Dawn says. "Talk to you old women later."

"Me too." Anne waves. "Bye for now."

Sally spends a moment tying her shoe—she wears a new pair of tennis shoes with air-filled soles—then stands up and says, "See ya, sunshine."

Tatyana grins. "Yes, you will."

Sally turns and heads off through someone's yard.

Tatyana stands for a moment on the corner, watching the three of them leave.

Then she laughs, and runs for home.

The Oakland Arena was packed.

Ninety thousand rock fans clogged the stadium. Night had fallen, and huge lights panned the crowd, like spoons stirring frenzy in a cauldron. TV screens the size of billboards counted down the final seconds: 47, 46, 45 . . . In the midst of the furor, six rows back from the stage, three women wearing matching T-shirts linked arms so as not to be separated in the surge.

Sally shouted, "Who is No Doubt, anyway? I never heard of them."

"Get with the program," Dawn told her. "This band is huge."

Sally glanced around at the madness. "Yeah, I kind of got that impression."

Anne leaned in. "Personally, my money's on the opening act."

"Amen, sister!" Dawn yelled. Her shirt, like the others, read *WEASEL FIST—NORTH AMERICAN SUMMER TOUR.*

29, 28 . . .

Sally suspected that she'd never lose her love for this. Waiting for Jaz to come onstage was something akin to euphoria. It was like a little miracle bomb going off in her chest. "We're going to have to get her a tutor, you know."

"Tutor schmuter," Dawn said. "Our baby's gonna be a graduate of the school of rock and roll! This time next year we'll be living in mansions with Chippendale dancers waiting on our every need."

Anne frowned. "Let's not entirely abandon the girl's education. A platinum record would be a wonderful thing to have hanging on the wall, but so too would a diploma."

"Platinum?" Dawn beamed. "Do you think their new album will go platinum?"

"Their producer seems to think so."

"Well, holy shit to that!"

17, 16 . . .

Sally smiled to herself. It was hard to stop that these days—smiling—what with Jazmyn's success and Leigh Surry's roses. Weasel Fist had played six concerts to promote their upcoming album, with twenty more on the schedule between now and September. The three senior members of Radio had gladly disbanded so that their daughter could take this first step toward a dream that still didn't seem quite real, even though it had already begun. Radio had performed only one more time after their appearance with Nancy Holiday, and then Jaz had joined Weasel Fist, and the gears of destiny rolled on. And every day for the last week, the floral van had pulled up outside Sole Mates with a delivery for the store's owner. Sally had been seeing Leigh since June—Dawn still liked to call it *going steady*—and this was August, which meant two months had passed without the wreck that Sally had expected. Her ability to maintain a relationship for that long without a hiccup was perhaps a sign that she might indeed avoid the spinster card in the old tarot deck of life.

The crowd started chanting on 10.

Crespin had called this morning to wish Jaz good luck, just as he always did on the day of a show. He was working at the Texanna as Jude Yarbuck's aide-de-camp, tending bar, booking bands, and learning to manage the office computer system. He had applied for and received a worker's visa, using his own credentials and not those of a forged ID. Sally was almost sad to see him cut up the false driver's license she'd procured for him; she had a soft spot for the outlaw in her, and now the last evidence of her desperado days was in the trash. The occasional card from Beatriz, penned in slowly improving English, was simultaneously a reminder of how close she'd come to losing it all, and proof that it had been worth it.

Dawn and Anne were yelling, ". . . five . . . four . . . three . . ."

Jets of smoke poured across the stage. The lights danced.

Sally didn't join in the chant, but let the sound of it lift her up.

". . . two . . . one . . ."

Jazmyn stepped from the smoke, guitar wailing.

The crowd erupted.

Sally flew.

425

About the Author

Erin O'Rourke can be described in many ways: novelist, teacher, game-player, star-gazer, picture-framer, dancer, and counter of chickens long before they hatch. Erin lives in the American Southwest, in the company of cookbooks, fantasy role-playing games, the poetry of Edna St. Vincent Millay, and a dog named Nadine.

A fascination with both shoes and rock-'n'-roll led to the creation of *Fugitive Shoes*, though Erin can neither play the guitar nor walk with any grace in three-inch heels.

Visit the official website at www.erinorourke.com.